# RALEIGH'S VIRGINIA 1587

Islands and mainland are shown as they were, not as they are now

Tribes indicated in capital letters

Chesapeake Bay

N · E · S · W

Chowan River

WEAPEMEOC

CHOANOKE

Choanoke

MORATUC

Moratico River

SECOTAN

Secotan

The City of Raleigh

Roanoke Island

Dasemonkepeuc
ROANOKE

Port Ferdinando

Hatarask

Croatoan

CROATAN

0  5  10  15  20
Scale in miles

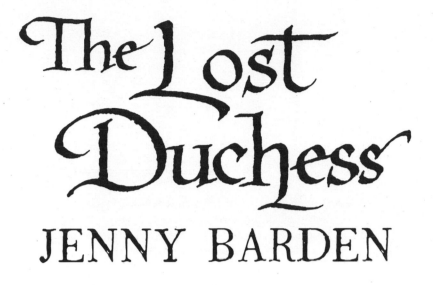

# The Lost Duchess

## JENNY BARDEN

EBURY
PRESS

1 3 5 7 9 10 8 6 4 2

First published in 2013 by Ebury Press, an imprint of Ebury Publishing
A Random House Group Company

The Random House Group Limited Reg. No. 954009

Addresses for companies within the Random House Group can be found at:
www.randomhouse.co.uk

A CIP catalogue record for this book is
available from the British Library

The Random House Group Limited supports The Forest Stewardship
Council® (FSC®), the leading international forest-certification organisation.
Our books carrying the FSC label are printed on FSC®-certified paper.
FSC is the only forest-certification scheme supported by the leading
environmental organisations, including Greenpeace.
Our paper procurement policy can be found at:
www.randomhouse.co.uk/environment

Printed and bound by CPI Group (UK) Ltd, Croydon, CR0 4YY

Hardback ISBN 9780091949235
Trade Paperback ISBN 9780091949679

To buy books by your favourite authors and register for offers visit:
www.randomhouse.co.uk

For my mother,
with love and immense gratitude

'...Who so desireth to know what will be hereafter, let him think of what is past, for the world hath ever been in a circular revolution; whatsoever is now, was heretofore; and things past or present, are no other than such as shall be again: *Redit orbis in orbem*...'

—*Sir Walter Raleigh, in The Works of Sir Walter Raleigh, Vol 1 (prefixed by Thomas Birch, 1751)*

# 1

## *Possession*

'...After thanks given to God for our safe arrival thither, we manned our boats, and went to view the land next adjoining, and to take possession of the same, in the right of the Queen's most excellent Majesty...Which being performed...we viewed the land about us, being...very sandy and low towards the water-side, but so full of grapes, as the very beating and surge of the sea overflowed them, of which we found such plenty, as well there as in all place else, both on the sand, and on the green soil on the hills, as in the plains, as well on every little shrub, as also climbing towards the tops of the high cedars, that I think in all the world the like abundance is not to be found...'

*—From Arthur Barlowe's account to Sir Walter Raleigh of the discovery of Virginia in 1584, first published by Richard Hakluyt the younger in* The Principal Navigations *1589*

## Richmond Palace, England
*August 1586*

'Come with me.'

Emme Fifield started, looked the length of the gallery, and noticed a few courtiers too far away to be heard speaking. She glanced behind her and saw only tapestries and a side table draped with a rich Persian carpet. Then the low voice urged her again.

'In here.'

A door opened at her side, one of the small access doors leading to a spiral staircase that connected the areas of the palace open to visitors with those that were the preserve of the Queen's ladies-in-waiting. The door was usually locked.

A man stood in the shadows. He beckoned to her and she noticed his rings and the lace of his cuff before she made out his face in the darkness: arched brows and a long chin with a smile to match the gleam of devilment in his age-hollowed eyes.

'Lord Hertford!' She bit back his name, looking round again but seeing no one else. 'What are you...?'

'Come!'

He reached out, grasped her arm, and drew her to him. The door closed behind them and the light dimmed to an orange glow from the few candles mounted on the curved turret walls. He spoke over his shoulder as he wound his way up the staircase.

'I have news for the prettiest maid at court, news for your dainty ear alone, if you will allow me to whisper it close.'

He bent to her and grinned again, running a finger under her chin while her feet teetered on the wedge-shaped steps. He was incorrigible, yet so far above her in rank that she could not gainsay him. Giving her a wink and a look that ran from her eyes to her bosom he turned and ascended with an exaggerated display of tip-toeing upward.

She watched the backs of his short legs, slightly bowed and clad in fancy stockings, and wondered how he had come to be in the sequestered heart of Richmond Palace. The Earl had been in disgrace since infamously seducing a virgin of the blood royal and twice getting Lady Catherine Grey with child after a marriage declared a sham. She was surprised he had the temerity to venture anywhere out of bounds. Though the Earl had been released after a spell in the Tower, and Lady Grey had died long ago, he was only occasionally seen at court, and surely he should never have been in the private dressing room of Her Majesty's ladies-in-waiting, the room that he now entered.

Emme's foremost duty was to protect the Queen, and Lord Hertford's presence almost directly above the royal bed-chamber breached the measures in place to ensure Her Majesty's safety, therefore she should challenge him. Yet she could not believe that waggish Lord Hertford was any real threat; he was part of the Queen's larger family, her stepmother's nephew, one of the foremost noblemen of the land. He would have been England's last duke if his father, the Duke of Somerset, Lord Protector during the short reign of Good King Harry's son, had not lost power and his head before King Edward's early death. She was loath to risk offending a gentleman of Lord Hertford's lineage, and his avuncular manner with her made her even more diffident.

'If you will forgive me,' she began hesitantly. 'But . . .'

'Forgive you? Of course I forgive you, Mistress Emmelyne.' With a flourish he took her hand, kissed and patted it, then smiled at her wickedly. 'What have you done?'

She drew her hand away.

'. . . What are you doing here?'

'Ah!' He produced a key from a pocket in his brocaded red and gold Venetian breeches. 'I have friends,' he said, tapping his nose and cocking his head, 'as do you, my dear,' and with his hand over his heart plainly meant she should consider him her friend as well. With brazen assurance he proceeded to use the key to lock the doors to the room, and met her look of astonishment with another breezy quip. 'I have news, and let no one interrupt the telling. I know you will want to hear it,' he added, and left the prospect dangling while he sat on a stool by the dressing table and calmly crossed his legs.

She watched him pocket the key again. As far as she knew, the only gentleman of rank to have been given such a thing was Sir Walter Raleigh in his capacity as Captain of the Gentlemen Pensioners, charged with protecting the Queen's ladies. How had Lord Hertford got that key? She held back the question, since asking would plainly be fruitless, and she was curious about his news even if reluctant to show it. Busying herself with tidying the muddled pots of unguents and pastes on the dressing table, she tried to appear unconcerned.

'Well, what is this news that is so secret you must capture me before revealing it?'

'Sir Francis Drake comes here tomorrow!'

'I knew it already.' She cut across him and turned her back, picked up a farthingale petticoat frame, and shook it hard enough to make the whalebone hoops rattle. That news had been the gossip of the court for days.

'Did you know that he has brought back all of the men sent by Sir Walter to protect his claim to Virginia, every last one?'

'No...' Her voice tailed off in thinking about what that meant: England's first outpost in the New World and now it had been abandoned. She was sorry to hear it.

'Sir Walter will not be pleased,' the Earl said, unstoppering a pot of ceruse and dabbing at it idly. Smearing a gob on his cheek, he began to rub in the lead white with a circular motion of his finger, uttering a small, mock-womanish shriek when it became congealed in his beard.

She caught at his wrist as he picked up a hand mirror. A man old enough to be her father should really have grown out of behaving like a naughty boy. She clicked her tongue and handed him a cloth. 'Please wipe your fingers, my lord.'

He pulled a wry expression but did as she asked, then tipped his head on one side to offer her his daubed cheek.

'Do I look regal?'

'Ceruse is not a plaything,' she said firmly, then dipped a cloth in vinegar and set about wiping the goo from his beard.

His face contorted into a grimace. 'The agonies that the Queen must endure to invest her visage with the radiance of light.'

She smiled despite herself.

''Tis true. We maids-of-honour have been told not to look full upon her face lest our eyes be blinded as by looking at the sun.'

He glanced at her. 'Whereas you, sweet maiden, have no need to be painted fairer; your natural complexion is like pure alabaster.'

'Tush!' Aware that his gaze had lowered from her eyes to her bosom, she whipped the cloth over the top of his head.

'Do you have any more news?' she asked, ignoring his gasp of protest. 'Why did Sir Walter's men leave?'

'I gather the land and its native inhabitants were not quite as hospitable as earlier reports suggested. Storms, savages and hunger seem to have been their chief ordeals.'

'Does that mean Sir Walter's efforts were in vain?'

'It would appear so. In rescuing Sir Walter's men from Virginia, Sir Francis has effectively deprived him of the exercise of his patent to settle the region. He has also lost Sir Walter a lot of money, perhaps as much as twenty thousand pounds.'

'A fortune!' Emme exhaled with a little gasp. She drew a large cushion closer, spread her voluminous skirts and sat down.

'What Sir Francis cannot have known,' Lord Hertford continued with satisfied ease, 'is that Sir Walter despatched, first, a supply ship.' He tapped one finger. 'And, second, Sir Richard Grenville.' He tapped another finger. '…Along with a whole fleet, as well as four hundred soldiers and mariners, to re-provision and strengthen the fort in Virginia some months ago. Sir Richard will probably be on his way back now, having found no one to relieve, and doubtless cursing the man who sent him on such an arduous wild goose chase.'

'T'faith!' She clapped her hands and bit her lip to stifle a grin. Sir Walter Raleigh was the darling of the Queen. How would Sir Francis Drake now be received? 'I wonder whether Sir Walter will be here tomorrow…?'

'I doubt it, though I've heard he is already on his way from his estates in Ireland.'

'Her Majesty will welcome Sir Francis warmly, I am sure. She admires him much.'

'Especially when he brings her trophies of conquest, as he will, having trounced the Spaniards soundly from Cartagena to Florida, and sacked Santo Domingo, their pretty jewel of the New World.'

'To think of such places!' Emme looked up at Lord Hertford, imagining things she could only guess at: palm trees and rainbow coral, flying fish and white cities.

He reached across and touched her pearl earring then moved his fingers to caress her ear, though she turned to stop him.

'You like to hear of the world, don't you? To learn who's doing what and why. For a young maiden you have a lively curiosity.'

She lowered her eyes and stroked the cushion, then fiddled with the shaft of a tiny feather she could feel pricking her fingers. 'Sometimes life at court can be dull.'

'Ha!' He slapped his thigh and chucked her under the chin. '*Dull?*'

'I do not mean that disrespectfully,' she put in hastily. 'I am grateful for the privilege of serving Her Majesty.'

'But you would like more liberty; I sense it.' He put his fingers to her lips before she could object. 'You would like...' he gestured vaguely around him, '...your own grand house with yeomen in livery to take your orders, and a deer park in which to go hunting whenever you chose, a private barge with trumpeters, your own carriage and ship...'

'Oh, yes!' She laughed. 'I would like a ship.'

'Would you promise yourself to a man who could give you a ship and so much more?'

'For certain,' she said with a laugh, shaking her head and working free the feather from the cushion. She thought of Sir Walter, who had everything Lord Hertford spoke of, but who would never consider a minor baron's daughter and lavished all his attention on the Queen. 'I would promise myself to a man who could give me all that – if I loved him,' she added wistfully, 'which in sum amounts to nothing because I can never hope for such good fortune.' At that she pursed her lips and blew the feather away from her hand. Then she pushed herself up and walked to the window.

The Earl's teasing had unsettled her. Why was he baiting her with fancies? Did she have a secret admirer who was using him as a go-between? Much as she would like to believe it, she could not;

she had received no tokens, no admiring verses or gifts of court-ship, and few bachelors knew her beyond passing acquaintance, ensconced as she was behind palace walls, at the beck and call of the Queen at all hours day and night.

A sweet fragrance rose from the herb garden beyond the moat, wafting up to the open window on the balmy air of the summer's evening: the smell of roses and marjoram, thyme and lovers' rose-mary. She breathed deeply as she sensed the Earl draw near.

He placed his hand on her shoulder in a comforting way.

'Your father must have high hopes that you will make a noble match.'

His hand moved to the back of her neck and she did not pull away since she was certain in her bones that all he meant was to reassure her.

She let his touch soothe her and bowed her head.

'He desires nothing more for me than that I marry well. He has worked hard to secure my place in Her Majesty's service.'

'It must have helped that you are Lady Fiennes' goddaughter.'

'Perhaps, and we are distantly related; maybe that helped too.'

'You are related to the Greys?'

'Only in ways so remote and complex I can never remember them!' She shrugged her shoulders and stepped away from him, then opened the window wider, letting the night air envelop her. An owl hooted, and something splashed in the river out of sight that made her imagine a heron pouncing on an unsuspecting fish. 'Lady Fiennes was fond of my mother,' she explained, wanting to show that she recognised her obligation. 'She was kind to me after her death, and I'm sure she would have spoken up for me if the Queen had asked her...'

Perhaps Lady Fiennes had felt sorry for her as well – sorry for the little girl left pining for her mother in the rattling manor house, with her father's jealous new wife and that woman's son by an earlier marriage demanding attention like a monstrous cuckoo. The memory of the fading of her father's love still pained her. She would not speak of that to the Earl, or talk of how Lady Fiennes had intervened, sending her to Broughton Castle until she reached early womanhood, then summoning her to court a year ago to be presented as a maid who might make an agreeable helpmeet for the Queen. Her father had been puffed up at the prospect, and had given much to secure it.

'...But I think my father's *douceurs* – the precious gifts with which he sweetened Her Majesty's opinion – will have counted for more than any importuning by Lady Fiennes.'

Emme looked down into the Privy Garden where torches burnt amongst gilded lions, and dragons held gleaming pennants like ribbons of flame. The beasts snarled at every gate. Drawing a deep breath, she caught the marsh smell of the Thames.

'I had supposed, at first, that I might find someone at court who would wed me, but now I doubt I ever will.'

The Earl put his arm around her and gave her a little squeeze.

'Why do you doubt it when the court is daily full of the finest gentlemen in the realm, and your tender beauty is unsurpassed?'

That was nonsense, though it charmed her. She wriggled free and flicked at his chest.

'You must know that I am bound to serve the Queen to my utmost ability for as long as she chooses. I am wed to her as effectively as a nun is to the church. I have come to realise that only the greatest ladies of noble birth may hope for her permission to marry,

9

and even then she expects attendance uninterrupted by childbirth or anything else. I am frequently lectured on the desirability of remaining a virgin my whole life.'

She stopped short of revealing her private belief: that the Queen abhorred the idea of marriage and considered it an evil. She was convinced that the Queen would have preferred all her ladies to stay untouched into dotage like Mistress Blanche Parry.

'No one can defy her,' she went on, lowering her voice and hardly daring to say more, mindful of the Earl's rank and how he had suffered for Lady Catherine. 'Any lady of the Queen's who weds without her consent risks being thrown into the Tower – and her husband too.'

'Oh, you poor sweeting.' The Earl put his arms around her and swayed with her gently, rocking back and forth. 'I know.'

She realised he would be remembering his own incarceration in that place, and poor Lady Catherine Grey who had died without ever gaining her freedom, and she felt some sympathy for him.

He stroked her hair and nuzzled her cheek, and while she knew she should not allow any man to kiss her, he was not exactly doing that, so she did no more than try to wriggle away from him discreetly.

'This palace is no better for you,' he murmured. 'It's a prison, just the same: a gilded cage.'

'I think of it so sometimes; then I tell myself I am a callow fool. I should be unreservedly thankful to live in the comfort I do, and have the honour of being close to the Queen in her service.'

'Be thankful, darling mistress, but remember Her Majesty will not live forever and she does not know everything. You may always marry in secret,' he whispered, 'and then . . .'

'Shush!' She covered his mouth. 'Do not speak in that way. Long live the Queen! I cannot think of aught else. Whenever she is defied, she always finds out. You must have heard that when she discovered Lady Mary Scudamore's marriage she gave her such a beating that she broke the lady's finger.'

'I had been told the story. But I say again, she does not know everything. Does she see us now?' He placed a kiss on her shoulder. 'Does she know of this?' He kissed her just below the collar bone, more a peck than a kiss; he did not touch her lips. Did that mean it was all right? In truth she knew it was not, and she wrenched free of him.

'I must not do anything of which Her Majesty would not approve.'

'Do not fret, my sweet.' He took hold of her again. 'She is below us now and knows nothing at all of what we do in this room. You are safe here.' He wrapped her in his arms and brushed his hand over her breasts sending a sensation shooting through her that seemed deeply shameful.

'No!' She pushed his hand away, feeling her blood rushing to her face. 'Prithee, no,' she whispered between gritted teeth.

She made for the door, and tried the latch, but of course it was locked. Looking back over her shoulder she saw him coming towards her, a solicitous smile lightening his wrinkled face.

She stood straight and spoke firmly.

'Please open the door. We have been here long enough, and Mistress Parry will be looking for me soon.' She did not know whether that was right, all she knew was that the Earl now frightened her.

As he drew nearer she shrank back against the wall. Then he put his hands to the wall-hangings, trapping her between his arms either side, and pushed his body closer until she felt him against her: thighs, chest and groin, and most of all his manhood hard against her crotch.

'Do not worry, my sweet,' he murmured. 'I will give you everything you want, for by my troth I love you and I pledge myself to you, to take you for my wife and share all I have . . .'

'No!' she gasped. 'You cannot mean . . .'

With a kiss he silenced her, driving his tongue into her mouth along with a bitter taste of sack, while his hands dug for her breasts, pushing down under her chemise, and his hardness rubbed against her inducing a vile sense of heat between her legs.

'We will be married . . .' He panted between kisses, forcing her against the wall while his hips ground faster. 'As you have promised, so I promise you.' He dragged up her petticoats and touched the bare skin above her garters. 'I will honour you with titles. You shall be my Duchess . . .' He breathed the words between her breasts as she struggled to break free, but his arms were like banded iron, and when he raised his head his glassy eyes were dark and hooded, the smile gone from them. He did not seem to see her.

'But we cannot marry!' she cried out. 'Not without a priest.'

'We can.' He dragged her away and pushed her onto the cushion where she had earlier sat, pinning her down with his weight. 'Our union can be blessed later. All we need are our promises – I have yours, you have mine – and to be joined as man and wife.'

'Joined. No!' She pleaded in terror, struggling to get from under him.

'Hush! Remember who is below.' He took hold of her neck, forcing back her head until her shoulders hit the floor. Her buttocks and legs were left arched over the cushion giving her no leverage to escape. She tried to push him off, tear at his face, punch his throat – anything to stop him. But he dragged up her rope farthingale and pushed the bands over her arms, smothering her fists and face with her petticoats. Then he pulled up her shift and yanked down her drawers, and she felt the cold air touch her where no other man had seen.

She could only hear him.

'This is what you want; don't deny it, my love.'

He pushed her legs apart with his knees, and grabbed at her skirts to uncover her eyes. 'My sweet,' he murmured, crouching over and kissing her. 'You do not need to fight to show me your purity.'

She tried to bite him, but he leant back quickly, and for a moment, in horror, she saw what he was about to put in her. She shut her eyes tight.

A scream welled in her throat but she clenched her jaw to hold it back; she must not cry out. If they were discovered *in flagrante* the shame would be hers.

She would be ruined.

His fingers pushed into her, and the pain that came next was like being stabbed with a blade in her most sensitive parts. He was tearing her apart. Only let him finish and it would be over.

The pain went on and on, and each time he almost withdrew it grew even sharper. The more she fought, the worse it became. She tried to tear at him with her nails but he bowed his back and thrust into her even harder.

'God's death!' He shuddered, thrashing against her and pumping frenziedly. 'Oh, Lord!'

She must endure it. She was contorted in agony, and her shoulders burnt as they were rubbed against the floor. She turned her head, eyes closed though she wept, and with her ear against the boards she heard sounds from below: the Queen calling in anger and the soft lilt of music.

# 2

# Guarded

'Am I not well guarded today, with no man near me who wears a sword at his side?'

*—Queen Elizabeth I in conversation with Sir Christopher Hatton while out walking in Richmond Park in 1586, on seeing the would-be assassin, Robert Barnewell, and meeting his eye after recognising him from a portrait of the 'six gentlemen', led by Anthony Babington, who had undertaken to murder her in what later became known as the Babington Plot*

'Mistress Emme, please wake; the Queen calls you!'

*The Queen.* Emme's eyes flicked open in panic to see her maid, Biddy, hovering over her.

Her tongue felt swollen and her mouth almost too dry to speak. A wave of pain flared through her from her belly to her private parts. She curled over and hugged herself, feeling the bulk of the rags between her legs that she had tied in place before climbing into bed, remembering that she had been bleeding the night before. But she was conscious of much more than spotting from the place that hurt; in the rags was the hot stickiness that had become familiar to her every month.

'*Thank God,*' she whispered to herself while Biddy told her the time.

'It's five of the morning, mistress.'

Daybreak after the night she had been spoiled, but surely she could not have been got with child; her menses would drown any seed in her womb. She wanted to ask Biddy whether she agreed this must be so, though all she did was look at her maid's simple face, from her starting eyes to her buck teeth just showing above her full lower lip.

Others were moving about the room: ladies of the royal household and servants. Her young companion, Bess Throckmorton, called out to her shrilly.

'Emme, I'll see you outside. Come quickly.'

Biddy held out her gown. 'Her Majesty is going walking in the garden and you must go with her now, she says.' Biddy lowered her eyes. 'You seem to have displeased her, mistress.'

'What has she said...? Oh, no,' Emme gasped, hearing a flurry of running footsteps and the thud of a door below. 'I must get up.'

She dragged the gown over her shoulders and slipped out of the truckle bed, clutching Biddy as she stood, for a moment creased over.

Biddy took hold of her arm. 'Dear mistress, are you sick? You look ghastly pale...'

Emme straightened and pressed her hand. 'My flowers have begun; that's all.'

'Do you need anything for...?'

'No, thank you. I have to go.'

She pushed her bare feet into pattens and secured the gown with a silk rope girdle, twisting her hair into a caul net as she left for the stairs. Biddy followed, panting softly, all the way from the canted tower, across the moat, through the herb beds and into the privy orchard. There, behind shrubs and fruit trees still blued with dawn mist, she saw the Queen walking at a pace that left her escort trailing behind her. Dainty Bess Throckmorton was amongst them, and Lady Frances Howard, the Lord High Admiral's staid sister. The ladies' maids followed with the Queen's chief intelligencer, Sir Francis Walsingham, accompanied by his clerk, in their wake.

Secretary of State Walsingham saw her first.

'I would speak with you, Mistress Fifield.' He inclined his head, fixing her with his dark hooded eyes while a thin smile formed on his long gaunt face.

Could he have found out what had happened to her? Emme stared back at him in dread, aware that Walsingham knew everything; he was the eyes and ears of the Queen. But perhaps all he wanted was to extract more information from her of the kind which had so far kept her in his favour and for which her father had been rewarded in small ways. Walsingham seemed to value her opinion on what was being said at court out of the hearing of the Queen, and to trust her integrity in delivering him the truth. His interest should have been a credit to her, yet, at that moment, she could not have wished him further away. She smiled back at him uneasily.

'Now, my lord Secretary?'

'I will speak with her now.'

The Queen's strident voice sent a tremble down Emme's spine. She looked ahead and saw that the Queen had stopped and was beckoning her closer.

'Come, Mistress Fifield, and do not keep me waiting as you did last night.'

Emme held her skirts and tripped forwards, eyes averted from those she passed, but feeling their looks like darts in her back. She curtseyed low over the damp camomile as Lady Howard and Bess Throckmorton stepped away, leaving her before the Queen alone.

'Your Grace,' she said, rising with her head still bowed.

'Let us talk.' The Queen walked on. 'What were you doing yestereve?'

'I was...' Emme's mind spun, turning with explanations, none of them convincing. She could not tell the truth, not the whole truth. She would not even mention Lord Hertford's name. The Queen must not suspect that there had been any intimacy between them, that she had been defiled and was now no longer a virgin. She could not believe that Lord Hertford would openly admit to having 'married' her, far less to having ravaged her. He would say she had enticed him or had fabricated a fantasy, anything but accept that he was guilty of any wrong. The blame would be hers if their indiscretion became known. She would be vilified, ruined and sent back to her father in disgrace. No one must find out what had happened to her. Yet she felt as if her shame must show like dirt on her face. She could not lie; lying was anathema, against the deepest principles by which she had always led her life, and something about her demeanour would be sure to give her away. Most of all she could not lie to Her Majesty. If she was found out...

'Well?' The Queen quickened her steps making Emme hurry to keep up. Her proud face showed no gentleness when she turned for an answer. Unmade-up and wan, with deep lines either side of her thin-lipped mouth, her face seemed haggard and she looked every one of her near fifty-three years, though Emme was shocked to think it, even having seen her thus before.

'I was abed,' she said, clinging to the truth. 'I was sick.'

'Oh, give me reasons more convincing!' The Queen's voice rose, snapping back. 'Every maid of mine who dallies with a courtier, making eyes when she should be doing my bidding, will tell me later that she has been sick. What sickness was it that kept you from your duty to your Sovereign yet the next day leaves you fit to walk and talk? You shared a bedchamber with Lady Frances Howard last night and she tells me she was not aware of you being ill. I have no doubt about what you were doing, and do not forswear yourself by denying it.'

Emme bowed her head, seeing no choice but to be admonished for a failing not her fault.

'I am sorry I did not attend on you as I should have done.'

'Sorry! Yes, you should be sorry.' The Queen spoke so loudly that Emme had to force herself to keep walking and not edge away, while the humiliation of knowing that everyone following must have heard was like a brand against her shoulders that made them shrink back.

'I will not fail you again, Your Grace, I promise.'

'Pah! Promises...' The Queen waved dismissively. 'Raise your pretty face, Mistress Fifield, and let me see you properly.'

Emme looked at her, but not at her eyes.

'You are very young,' the Queen said in a much quieter tone.

'I am twenty-one years of age,' Emme responded. Not young at all, she thought, though she did not say so.

The Queen gave a soft hollow laugh and turned towards the bright sunshine that was brimming over the palace walls. Then she wiped at her eye, perhaps because of the light, Emme could not tell; she spoke wistfully.

'Young enough to think that the world can turn around a love sonnet, to have no cares beyond the attention of a favoured gentleman, to nurture ambition without limit, and think that death can never touch you. I know what it is to be that young.'

Emme lowered her gaze, humbled by the Queen's candour, both relieved that she had not suspected the truth and saddened that she supposed her carefree.

'But I am a Prince,' the Queen said in a harder voice, 'and as a Prince I had to leave my youth behind. My duty has always been to England, as yours is now to me. We cannot put our own desires first, or rest from the burden placed upon us, or ever lower our guard.'

She looked quickly round, and Emme followed her gaze, breathing in the fragrance of crushed camomile as she watched the ladies who were following some paces behind suddenly stop, while Secretary Walsingham raised his head from a conversation with his clerk. A hush descended on everyone, broken only by a cockerel's crow and the faint tolling of a bell in the distance. Nothing moved until the Queen raised her chin, nodded, then turned and carried on walking. She spoke to Emme in a way no one else would hear.

'I am loved by my subjects but all my life I have known that there are those who will pose as loyal with treason in their hearts, and they can reach me anywhere.'

Emme felt a chill run through her. Did the Queen fear for her own safety now, here in the Privy Garden? She looked about, wondering what the shadows might hide.

'I would lay down my life to protect you,' she said softly.

'I do not ask for your life,' the Queen answered with a wry smile, 'merely that you come to me when I ask for you, and, if I wish to take ease in a few moments' diversion, that you are always ready to keep me company, even if only to sing to me.'

Emme dropped to her knees. 'Always, Your Majesty, I will always do your bidding.'

'Rise, girl, and be of some use rather than mopping up the dew.' The Queen gestured for Emme to get up, and chuckled quietly. 'We have a pirate to receive, and an ambassador to keep in ignorance.' She looked towards her ladies and signalled for them to come nearer.

'Sir Francis Drake arrives this morning after almost a year spent pricking Spain's pride in the New World and avenging us for past treachery. Let us honour him with a fit welcome, and ensure that His Excellency, the Baron de Chateauneuf, has news of our hero's triumphant return which he may report to his Spanish friends, as well as his master, the King of France. But let the Baron not learn too much before I have spoken to Sir Francis alone. Therefore please stay with him, Lady Howard, and ensure that he speaks neither to Sir Francis nor his men. Charm the Baron to distraction, Mistress Throckmorton, and together keep him company in the Presence Chamber while I hear Sir Francis in private. Meanwhile you, Mistress Fifield, may ensure that any gentlemen Sir Francis brings with him are also entertained in the same place, and not left wandering in the Great Hall or Gallery able to converse with all and sundry. But keep them apart, good ladies, I particularly do not wish the French Ambassador to have a chance to question anyone newly returned from Virginia.' She gestured them away then admonished them further as they drew aside.

'Wear your finest gowns, but no colours, and leave your partlet off, Mistress Throckmorton; the day is already warm enough for your throat to be uncovered.'

Emme noticed her friend's fleeting frown as she curtseyed in response, and felt sorry for her, certain that the Baron's attention would be below Bess's throat. She herself would cover up as much as possible in case Lord Hertford was still at court, but if he was, and he saw her, what then? Should she try to avoid him or act as if nothing had occurred between them? Yet it had, and her whole body stiffened at the recollection of what he had done. Head down, she followed the Queen's ladies last, and each step was a suppressed stamp on the thought of that man.

'You are still in favour, I see.'

The voice startled her, and she turned to find Secretary Walsingham picking his way like a lugubrious black stork at her side.

'The Queen has forgiven you for whatever vexed her last night; that is good. Her moods change like the tide, and never more so than now when her life is in greatest danger.'

Emme caught his eye in sudden apprehension. 'Her Majesty hinted as much. Yet surely no one near her would cause her harm?'

The Secretary of State inclined his skull-capped head.

'There is a priest in the Tower as we speak, spilling out the names of those sworn to a new plot to murder her, and though we have apprehended most of the traitors, the ringleader has so far managed to evade capture.'

'Who?' she asked softly, fearing the answer might be a friend.

'Anthony Babington.'

She nodded with a shiver, remembering him as a vain gallant

and a rumoured Catholic, and that she had been introduced to him once. 'I have met Master Babington at court.'

Secretary Walsingham's hooded eyes slid towards her. 'If you spot him here again then inform the guards immediately, though I think it unlikely that he will dare to show his face, and if he does then he will be disguised. You might bear that in mind.'

'I will.'

'Her Majesty is aware of the danger.'

His jaw clenched in a grimace, and she sensed his hatred of anyone who would think of harming the Queen; it clung to him like sweat – a hatred which must have been inflamed because a would-be assassin was still at large, even making it prudent for him to warn her. She watched him turn his head slowly, looking from side to side; then he hunched his shoulders.

'Now what did Lord Hertford say?'

She looked at him in amazement. How did he know she had spoken to Lord Hertford? Someone must have seen her near him, presumably in the gallery. But could they have been spotted leaving together by the tower stairs? Could Secretary Walsingham have guessed where they had gone? He could not possibly know what the Earl had done to her; the door had been locked . . .

'I . . .' She saw him smile thinly as she began. 'I only spoke with Lord Hertford briefly.'

He would not be interested in what had happened to her, she tried to reassure herself while panic surged through her like cold lightning. All Secretary Walsingham ever wanted from her was intelligence concerning the powerful and to know what others were saying about affairs of state. Though Lord Hertford was important, what he had done to her was not, at least not in the greater order.

Her humiliation would be of no concern to Secretary Walsingham. Her worthlessness was absolute. Oh God, she wanted the ground to swallow her up, and to turn her back on the tawdry affairs of the world. She wanted to die. But life would not let her go so easily. She gritted her teeth and stared at a knot of clipped box like a miniature maze. She supposed she must satisfy Walsingham with snippets as she usually did.

'. . . He told me that Sir Francis Drake had taken all the men from the fort in Virginia and that Sir Walter Raleigh would be angry since he had invested a fortune in the venture, most especially since he had sent Sir Richard Grenville with fresh supplies. He thought Sir Walter would soon be arriving from Ireland.'

'That he will,' Secretary Walsingham put in, with his head on one side as if waiting for more.

They were approaching the moat, and Emme took her chance to step ahead and enter the covered bridge first. Their conversation came to a halt as Lady Frances Howard took her arm.

'Hurry, Mistress Emme. We must get ready.' The lady's fingers dug in as Emme glanced back, but Walsingham was already talking again with his clerk. She noticed Biddy waiting ahead and waved her on.

Lady Howard spoke breathlessly. 'I hope you will help me, dear Emme.'

Help in what way? 'I will, if I am able, my lady.' Emme was taken aback, the more so when Lady Howard kept looking over her shoulder and peering into stairwells and doorways. 'Only tell me how.'

'Not yet,' the lady whispered, 'I will tell you in private,' though they were soon far enough removed to have little chance of being overheard.

What concerned her? Emme glanced at the lady askance, loath to be drawn into sharing another's troubles when she had troubles enough of her own, wanting only to sit and try to order her thoughts. Yet Lady Howard had always been good to her, despite a manner usually so reserved that Bess Throckmorton considered her conceited, and Emme would not fail anyone in real need. Her surprise was that the lady might consider confiding in her at all. Lady Frances Howard was almost past the age of marriage, effectively made a spinster by her loyalty to the Queen, and Emme could not imagine her having any problems she might be coy about revealing yet wish to share with someone like herself – someone much younger with far less claim to nobility. Once they had climbed the tower stairs, Lady Howard looked down into the courtyards through every window they passed. She was plainly anxious, and Emme looked through the windows too, wondering whether there could be a connection between the threat to the Queen and this strange behaviour of Lady Howard's, seeing men too far away to identify wandering about in the shadows below, and light slicing in shafts across the pale limestone walls.

But whatever privacy Lady Howard might have hoped for, it was not going to be found in their dressing room for a while. Opening the door, they were confronted by Bess having her sleeves sewn in place while her white silk skirts were pinned in falling pleats over a bell farthingale and her veil was attached to a huge heart-shaped wire frame behind her head. The only parts of her unadorned by an extravagance of white dress were her face, her hands, and her soft milk-white breast. As soon as she saw Emme, her face lit up, though her body was immobilised by all the pinning and tucking.

'Emme, hurry, you haven't much time. You must put on your

best for Sir Francis Drake. I cannot wait to meet him,' she added, with a shy smile at Lady Howard as if she had only just noticed her. Then she whispered to Emme, 'I'll swoon at his feet if he so much as looks at me.'

'You will do no such thing.' Lady Howard eyed her sternly and circuited past her to reach the bedchamber. 'Your attention must be on the French Ambassador as the Queen has commanded. And why should Sir Francis look at *you*?' She surveyed Bess up and down with a dismissive tilt of her chin. 'Come, Mistress Emme.' She beckoned Emme into the next room, giving Bess another shrivelling look. 'I have something *special* that you might consider wearing.'

Emme followed, and Lady Howard unlocked her chest, rattling the key in the lock, and throwing back the lid with a thud. Then she closed the door, and pressed her back against it, an expression of worry on her pinched and tired face.

'Have you seen Lord Hertford?'

Emme drew breath sharply. 'What makes you think . . .'

'Snuff told me,' Lady Howard forestalled her. 'He saw you meet in the gallery.'

'But how . . . ?' Emme grasped for an explanation while the name 'Snuff' flashed through her mind. *Snuff*: Lord Leicester's man and the Queen's favourite jester. She had not even realised he was back at court, but it was typical of him to reappear and not be noticed. He was the kind of character who could be anything – an invisible nonentity or the uproarious centre of attention. Wasn't he meant to be with his master on campaign in the Low Countries? But Snuff often delivered messages back and forth. He must have returned and made himself inconspicuous so as to pick up observations he could take back to Lord Leicester. Did it matter who had seen her? She had been spotted; she had to accept it. Wherever the court was based, the palace walls had eyes and ears. She thought back to the gallery when Lord Hertford had accosted her, remembering it as being empty near the side door where he'd stood. All she had noticed was a side table and tapestries; could Snuff have been behind an arras or underneath the carpet covering the table? Whatever the explanation, there was no point in denying she had met the Earl; Secretary Walsingham also knew she had.

'Lord Hertford greeted me last night,' she said. 'I believe he has come to see the return of Sir Francis Drake.'

Lady Howard sat down, and Emme watched her carefully, wondering how much had been observed, and what exactly Lady Howard had been told. She was clearly struggling to stay contained; her face trembled then set in a mask of despair, only to quiver again before she spoke.

'Did Lord Hertford mention me at all?'

'No,' Emme answered, puzzling over the question while not even wanting to think of it. Lord Hertford and what he had done to her festered like a foul canker in her mind. She would have given everything she possessed to erase all awareness of him. But she could not say that to Lady Howard. She tried to keep her tone light.

'Why should the Earl have spoken of you to me?'

'Oh, Emme,' Lady Howard spluttered, then leant over towards Emme and sobbed against her chest. Emme took the lady in her arms without understanding her distress, only that it was real and she needed comfort.

Lady Howard wailed into Emme's gown. 'He is here and he has sent me no message. He ignores me as if I mean nothing to him. I cannot bear it any longer…' She collapsed into blubbering incomprehension.

Emme hugged her, gently rubbing her back, guessing that the lady must feel some fondness for Lord Hertford, though wanting to scream that he was nothing but a vile rake.

'I see you care for him.'

'Of course I care! This pretence is killing me. Know the truth because I must tell someone.' Lady Howard looked up and grasped Emme by the arms, her hands shaking as her grip tightened. 'He is my husband!'

Emme stared, dumbfounded. Could that possibly be true? She thought of the Earl with herself. Could he have taken his pleasure with her, after gaining her confidence with lies, and moreover betrayed this noble lady, if Lady Howard was indeed his wife?

Lady Howard clung to her beseechingly. 'Believe me. We have pledged our troth before a priest, but no one else knows of it because of the Queen.'

'Why because if her?'

'She will not hear of it. She flew into a rage when I ventured to ask her permission. She says I must have nothing to do with him, that my lord would not care for me…'

'Perhaps she is right,' Emme said with conviction.

'But she does not know him as I do. He is good, kind, generous and most honourable.'

'You cannot know that for certain…' Emme bit her tongue, on the point of revealing her own anguish, but realising that she might well not be believed, and, even if she was, Lady Howard would probably blame her for leading the Earl on. The ignominy would be hers. A woman of lesser standing would always be held responsible for the transgression if a man knew her carnally outside wedlock. She was not fool enough to think that Lady Howard would give her real sympathy. As one of the Queen's most senior ladies, Lady Howard would be most concerned to ensure there was no scandal at Court, and next she would be concerned to preserve her own position and Lord Howard's. She would probably see Emme banished back to the countryside or a nunnery, condemned to isolation for the rest of her life. Emme forced herself to keep silent as Lady Howard went on.

'The Queen disapproves because she cannot bear the idea of anyone close to her finding happiness in marriage. You know what she is like: always railing to us about the woes and dangers of wedlock. She has still not forgiven my lord for his first marriage to Lady Catherine, and because she will not recognise it, his sons remain bastards denied their titles.'

Lady Howard gave a few racked sobs while Emme tried to make sense of what she had said. The Queen's reaction she could understand, since Lord Hertford's sons by Lady Catherine Grey might be in line for the throne if they were recognised as legitimate. The Queen had been furious with him for getting the lady with child, and perhaps she would not now want to see him marrying Lady Frances, further binding together the powerful families of Howard and Seymour. Yet Emme could still barely accept Lord Hertford's deceit. Why had he abused her when he already had a wife?

The lady took a few deep shuddering breaths.

'If the Queen found out he had wed again to me, she might throw him back in the Tower. She must not know. So we behave like strangers. We have not even dared share a bed for fear I might conceive and our secret be revealed. Yet I cannot bear to continue to act this false part, unable to show my love to my lord as a wife should, always separated, always wondering whether his affection is now waning because we have never been able to know one another fully.'

'The marriage has not been consummated?' Emme asked in a state of shock. If it had not been consummated then it was no marriage at all, and what did that make her? She had exchanged promises with Lord Hertford in banter, and then he had forced an act of love-making upon her. Was she now truly his wife?

'No,' Lady Howard said, weeping with her face in her hands. 'We have not dared to take the risk. Oh, but I love him.' She raised her head and looked at Emme, wiping vainly at the tears that streamed down her cheeks. 'I love him so much.'

Emme put her arms across the lady's shoulders and bent her head close to hers. What could she say? That the lady had married a rogue; that she was not wed to him truly and should do her best to forget him? But to justify that she would have to reveal her own ugly secret and hurt the lady even more. She could not do it. She patted Lady Howard's arm, and she hated herself for compounding the lady's delusion.

'I am sure he will seek you out as soon as he has an opportunity, and the Queen's objection may well soften with time. He is already in favour enough to be welcomed back at court.'

'Yes, you are right.' Lady Howard straightened her back and wiped at her eyes. 'We may not have much longer to wait before we can announce our union before the world.' She composed her face and stood up proudly. 'Please forgive me for a moment of weakness and burdening you with a confidence I should have kept to myself.'

'It is no burden, and I shall tell no one; have no fear of that.'

'You are a darling, Mistress Emme.' Lady Howard kissed her then took a step away. 'Now let us prepare, or Sir Francis Drake will be upon us before we are even properly dressed.'

They were soon engulfed in a ferment of activity. Sleeves and kirtles were matched with gowns and bodices, all in the black and white prescribed by the Queen. Maids tightened laces and secured garments with neat stitches; they tugged and pinned, pleated and tucked. Eventually Emme was transformed into a rigid walking ornament. Her waist was crushed so small she knew she would not be able to eat, and the wooden busk at the point where her bodice tapered over her groin meant she would not even be able to sit. Her hair was scraped back until she winced, and her feet were squeezed into tiny slippers. Whitening stiffened her face and kohl inflamed her eyes. She was ready and she was not. In appearance she was finished once a chain girdle and pomander were hung over her hips, and a pendant necklace with a rope of pearls was hooked around her neck. But her mind remained in turmoil, and she left the chambers of the ladies-in-waiting to try and find somewhere quiet before the arrival of the guests. She walked past bustling servants through rooms smelling of new tapestries and freshly scattered herbs. She wandered down winding staircases, and along galleries and passages, until she came to the tower by the watergate and the covered bridge over the moat that led to the old friars' meadows. From here she could walk beside the river in peace. She nodded to the yeomen guards as she stepped outside.

Bright sunshine warmed her and the gentle sounds of the Thames reminded her of a calmer life. She breathed in the languid summer smells of hot grass and marsh. There was a semblance of freedom even if the reality was different: that she was trapped in a role from which she could not escape, bound in duty to the Queen, subject to Her Majesty's commands and the wishes of her father, unable to leave court without permission, and that unlikely unless a husband was found for her of whom the Queen approved, yet now she had been damaged in a way that would make no decent gentleman want her. Perhaps, if Lord Hertford were to insist upon it, and proclaim the matter in public, she would have no choice but to accept she was already tied to him in matrimony. But she doubted he would do that, and she would not recognise it meekly. She pulled at a head of tall grass and ripped the seed into her hand. She would not willingly be Lord Hertford's wife, his duchess or anything else. She loathed him. He had posed as her friend and then foully abused her trust. She wanted nothing more to do with him, and surely, if she avoided him, then he would not really put himself at risk of once more incurring the Queen's wrath by admitting to another clandestine marriage? She could not believe that he ever meant to wed her, only that he had sought to satisfy his lust. If he was going to admit to any marriage then common sense dictated it would be to gracious Lady Howard. She tore the seeds off another grass stalk and threw them towards the river. Her situation had been made worse, but she would have to find a way of coping. Man's life was full of sorrow, but a woman's sorrow was greater; all she could do was endure. She felt another wave of pain and took some comfort in that; at least she would not be carrying Lord Hertford's child. She must ensure that he never got an opportunity to take advantage of her again and make that prospect a possibility.

Looking downstream, she gazed at the Thames as it turned west between wooded banks, thinking of the twists and turns it would take to reach Hampton Court, and then the great city of London with its thousands of people. She saw the russet sails of the wherry boats glowing orange in the sun, and the herons standing sentry around the nearest river ait, just visible amongst the reeds. Mallards paddled by, honking; swallows skimmed over the shining water; and above a skyline broken by a distant church steeple and the hatched stripes of open fields, clouds seemed to hang in a stupor, fat, puffy and white, while her mind span in anguish, conscious of the hurt to her maidenhood afresh. What should she do? What *could* she do?

Then she heard the faint sound of music: sackbuts, shawms and flutes, and, from around a large willow-covered island, a glittering barge slid majestically into view. It was rowed by a score or more oarsmen all dressed in red livery; from poles behind its canopy flew pennants in Tudor green and white, the standard at its stern bore the cross of St George, and amongst the heraldic shields that adorned its gilded upper-works she recognised the white waves on black with two stars of Sir Francis Drake. He was here. She must get back. As she hurried towards the watergate, a fanfare resounded from atop the tower.

Rushing through the long gallery in the Privy Lodgings, she made for the north gate to cross the bridge, and so through Fountain Court to reach the Great Hall where the visitors would be received. But her skirts hindered her steps, and her corsets meant she could barely breathe; she slowed every time she passed a guard, and her dash came to a standstill once she entered the courtyard beyond the moat. There, in the shadow of the fountain, she saw Lord Hertford stoop to refresh himself from one of the fountain's beasts and roses. He straightened, wiped his mouth and looked towards her in a ray of light. She shrank into the nearest doorway as he blinked, his leathery face twisting into a sardonic smile, eyes narrowed, lips pulled back from his yellowing teeth. She opened the door and stepped inside, closing it behind her fast. She glanced at him from a window and saw him sauntering towards the Hall's entrance. If she went that way she would risk encountering him, yet the visitors were approaching; she could hear music and cheering, trumpets and drums. Her only sure hope of reaching the Hall in time lay in dashing across the courtyard and entering behind the Earl. She would not do it.

She reached the Chapel cloister and almost ran to the far end, then turned left into a passage and left again by the Great Court. She looked out towards the Gate House and thought about dashing for freedom, leaving by the Richmond Road and escaping the palace completely. But of course she would be stopped dressed in the finery she was. Instead she hurried down a stone staircase and entered the cellars beneath the Hall, rushed between barrels stacked almost to the vaulted ceiling, her steps too loud, slowing when she saw a kitchen boy and dodging behind a pillar, emerging once the coast was clear and making for a staircase that would take her back up. Then she took the servants' way to the little door which led into the Hall near the dais.

Her hand found the latch and the door opened onto a crowd. She slipped in behind the ladies-in-waiting just at the moment they all bobbed down to curtsey. She followed suit, head bowed, bending almost to kneeling in the hope she would not be noticed. Only slowly did she raise her eyes, heart pounding, trying in vain to calm her breathing, as the herald's words rang out.

'Sir Francis Drake, General of Her Majesty's West Indies Fleet . . .'

She glimpsed the Queen almost directly before her, clothed as *Gloriana* in the colours of the rising sun. Turning her head in the direction of all the other ladies, she saw the stocky man with reddish hair who proudly advanced to kneel before the throne. Behind him were two men, and there her eyes locked. One of them was very tall and clothed like an Englishman in doublet and breeches, but with dark skin and tattooed lines over his chin and cheeks, and feathers in his hair which was shaved around a central crest. The other man had a face more handsome than any she had ever seen, fair and strong and as perfect as an angel's, with clear blue eyes that held her transfixed.

He was looking straight at her.

# 3

# *Virginia*

'...It is the goodliest and most pleasing territory of the world (for the soil is of huge unknown greatness, and very well peopled and towned, though savagely) and the climate so wholesome that we have not had one sick since we touched land here. To conclude, if Virginia had but horses and kine in some reasonable proportion, I dare assure myself, being inhabited with English, no realm in Christendom were comparable to it...'

*—From a letter sent by Master Ralph Lane, at the new Fort in Virginia, to Master Richard Hakluyt the Elder of the Middle Temple, London, 3rd September 1585*

'I have come here before.'

The tall Indian smiled at Emme in a way that made the lines on his cheeks ripple into crescent moons either side of his wide nose. What he had said was incredible, but little else made any impression on her. Her mind was still reeling from the ordeal of the night before and the revelations of the morning: her degradation at the hands of Lord Hertford and her encounter with the Queen and then Lady Howard. Who was this man? He had been introduced to her as 'Manteo', and thus she would address him.

'But how, Master Manteo? When?'

'Two years past. I came here for learning.'

Inclining his feathered head, with his arms still folded across his broad chest, he walked over to a gentleman with sharp cheekbones who was talking excitedly into the hubbub. She was left with the mariner who had first arrested her with his looks. His blue eyes locked onto her, and she felt touched by warmth as if from the sun that had bronzed his skin, but it was fleeting, like a flash of light from behind dark clouds. What was his name? The events since the last sunset seemed to have fuddled her reason. 'Kit' was all she could remember, but she could not call him that.

'Will you tell me more, good sir?'

The handsome mariner regarded her with an expression between bemusement and gravity, and she realised he had features which would always seem youthful, but that, most likely, he was much older than herself, perhaps by as much as ten years; the tiny creases around his eyes betokened it, and the lack of softness around his jaw. His eyes flickered about the Great Hall, and she followed his gaze, skimming over the hammer beam roof painted blue, red and gold, the battle-scene tapestries brightly lit by candelabra, the portraits of kings between the lofty white windows, the richly dressed courtiers and ladies-in-waiting, the visiting mariners and soldier-adventurers, their ruffs poking above gleaming gorgets, and the door leading to the Privy Lodgings through which the Queen and Sir Francis Drake had just left.

Then the mariner looked back at her.

'Manteo came here two years ago, brought back by the first expedition sent by Sir Walter Raleigh to explore the Americas north of Florida, but Sir Walter kept him out of sight at Durham House most of the time. Master Harriot, over there, taught him English.' He gave a nod towards the man with prominent cheekbones.

'That gentleman can speak Indian?' she asked, amazed.

The blue of Master Kit's eyes washed over her, and she caught a trace of the smell of the sea in his clothes. Close to her he seemed as strong as a mast, and his voice had a soft resonance like the boom of a hull sliding through waves.

'He can speak the Algonkian of Manteo's tribe.' He looked across to the Indian as if deciding how much to tell her, and she drank in his face while she could. He was the one person in the whole assembly she felt she really wanted to be with, perhaps he had come from places far away and seemed to carry traces of distant shores within him. She could see the gold of hot sand in his hair, and the turquoise of coral seas in his eyes. Her gaze took in his tanned brow and cheeks, and the paler shaved skin above his upper lip upon which she could discern a prickling of blonde stubble. A single gold earring glittered in the lobe of his left ear, the kind of ring that sailors wore to pay for their burial if drowned at sea and washed up ashore. She thought of his face against the winds of the oceans as he spoke.

'Manteo returned to Virginia with the second expedition sent by Sir Walter to establish a fort there, and now he's come back again with General Lane and his men.'

'You mean those whom Sir Francis has rescued?'

Master Kit raised an eyebrow. 'We did as they begged after a wrecking storm blew up. Would you like to hear more?'

Before she could answer, he had clapped Manteo on the shoulder, and ushered him back towards her. Master Harriot followed together with a crow-footed gentleman with grizzled hair on a head that seemed too big for his gangling body. His fingers were long and graceful and wrapped around a cylindrical leather case of the kind that might be used for carrying papers. He clutched the case to his breast as Master Kit made the introductions.

'Master John White, gentleman limner, artist and mapmaker.' The man with the large grizzled head gave her a short bow.

'...And Master Thomas Harriot, distinguished astronomer, linguist and mathematician.' The younger man with high cheekbones bowed as well.

She curtseyed, but her attention moved back to Master Kit as he invited all three to enlighten her about the new-found land of Virginia.

'It is most goodly,' Master White began.

'Of a vastness beyond comprehension,' Master Harriot continued.

'...Abounding with fruit and animals: deer and conies, fish and fowl...'

'The soil is so fertile that it yields crops with little toil.'

'...Grapes and melons grow freely...'

'...The strawberries there are four times bigger than here in England...'

'Great cedars grace the hills fairer than any in Lebanon.'

'...The people are gentle so long as treated fairly...'

She soon lost track of who was speaking, watching Master Kit while they painted pictures in words of promise, and she saw their enchantment as a paradise in her mind.

'Virginia can be likened to a second Eden: a clean, pure land free of vice and corruption.'

She turned to Master White whose words had startled her, sensing a shiver of affinity running like quicksilver down her spine. A *second Eden*. A land where life could begin anew. What would she give to go there? Her mouth opened just as a puzzling question occurred to her.

'But why did you leave this country if it is so fine?'

Master White shuffled uneasily, and she felt his tension, supposing he must have come expecting to speak to the Queen and would be apprehensive because of that.

'A settlement cannot be sustained without farmers and builders, women and children. Our New World colony needs workers and families to have hope of continuance.'

*Women.* The word rang through her thoughts; they wanted women. Would they be going back, and would Master Kit be going too? She turned to the Indian, who had barely spoken, wondering whether he thought of his homeland as any less of a delight.

'Master Manteo,' she began, trying to fix on his dark eyes and not his savage markings. 'How would you describe your country?'

The Indian scratched his chin. 'It smells sweeter than this.'

Master Kit laughed loudly, and the cheerfulness flashing from him made her smile briefly as well. She wanted to ask more, but Lady Howard interrupted, bidding them proceed to the Presence Chamber since the Queen wished to greet them.

'You as well,' she murmured to Emme under her breath. 'Her Majesty has tired of hearing General Lane's grievances.'

They swept past Bess Throckmorton, with the French Ambassador leaning over her as if a close scrutiny of her bosom might yield the secrets of English policy, then moved outside and crossed the moat to the Privy Lodgings. In the gallery before the Presence Chamber, Lady Howard spoke to Emme again.

'Intervene if there's any dissention and keep the talk light. Her Majesty must not be pressured now, not when there's another plot on her life and her cousin, Mary of Scots, is implicated with some of the traitors still at large.'

There was no time to respond. The yeomen guard swung open the doors to reveal a shovel-jawed gentleman on his knees who rose, bowed and kept his eyes on the Queen as he walked backwards in leaving.

'Ralph Lane,' Kit said, low voiced at her side. 'Erstwhile commander of the fort in Virginia.'

Emme's eyes were drawn past the ornamentation that had become familiar: the glitter of badges showing portcullises and roses set high around the walls, the gilding on the ceiling chequered azure and white, the plate on polished tables brightly lit by scores of candles, and the light streaming through high bay windows, softened by carpets and hangings of silk. She saw the Queen sitting in state in hues of rose and gold, with a few of her ladies on cushions nearby, and some gentlemen standing beside her, amongst them Secretary Walsingham and Sir Francis Drake. The sea captain's stance was confident, legs astride, and he looked resplendent in damask doublet and Venetian breeches, with a wide goffered ruff and jewelled pendant around his neck. A black-skinned youth appeared to be holding his hat, and the room was filled with a pungent aroma from the roll of smoking leaves that the Captain held in his hand. To Emme's surprise, the Queen appeared not to mind as he puffed on these leaves, thickening the haze in the chamber. He boomed out a greeting while Emme and her companions paid obeisance.

'Master Kit Doonan, Your Majesty, as brave a mariner as sailed the seas, and with him are these gentlemen you have met before:

Manteo of Croatoan, and Masters Harriot and White, pioneer explorers of North America.'

The Queen beckoned Manteo towards her, and spoke when he knelt.

'Manteo, loyal Virginian, we are pleased to welcome you here again. It seems your countrymen have proved not quite the peaceable allies we had hoped for. General Lane tells me they have been troublesome.'

Manteo stood proud. 'The Croatans rejoice in the amity of Your Majesty, great and honoured chief over the water. Our land is yours. The Secotans await the discipline that will teach them to show the same respect.'

'We have found only gentle hospitality amongst the Croatans and the Indians further north,' Master Harriot interjected quickly. 'They have received us like lords, offering gifts and homage. The land is fertile and their disposition beneficent.' He glanced at Master White who began fumbling with his folio case.

'The flora and fauna are bounteous in the wider region,' White said hesitantly. 'If I may show Your Majesty some drawings and limnings: just a sample of the many which I will work up from my sketches, those that were not lost when we left.' He shot Sir Francis a pained look, at which the Captain exhaled a stream of smoke.

The Queen motioned for Master White to move over to the table.

'Please show what you have. I am intrigued to know more, particularly about any findings that suggest this new land may harbour riches.'

White pulled out some papers and spread them out.

'Of the beasts, we found deer beyond number and bears with magnificent pelts; crabs and pearl oysters; turkey hens and stock doves. As you can see, there are fish of many kinds, good and wholesome to eat. This is called a dorado and its scales shimmer like rainbows, while this, exceeding strange, puffs up like a bladder covered in spines.'

Emme gazed in wonder at an exquisite painting of an iridescent fish, its scales bright with blue-smalt and gold leaf, and at another delicately rendered watercolour of a fish as round as a football.

The Queen flicked through the papers. 'But what of the people, Master White, do they live in cities with wealth to rival that found by the Spaniards in Mexico and Peru?'

'They live in townships like these.'

He showed a sketch of what looked like longbarns arranged beside a wide central street; the barns were open-ended and covered in something like reed matting. To Emme they seemed curious but hardly worthy of admiration.

'This is Secotan,' said Master White.

The Queen placed her finger on a part of the drawing showing a circle of carved posts around which Indians were dancing waving sprigs and gourds. 'These are the people who were hostile to General Lane?' She looked up at Manteo.

'Yes,' he answered, folding his arms.

'Their city seems of little substance: a few rounds of cannon fire would flatten it completely. Do you not agree, Sir Francis?'

She turned to Captain Drake who pulled a wry face while White looked aghast.

'Would it be worth expending the shot?' Sir Francis asked jovially and gave Emme a wink.

Master Harriot broke in, eyes flashing, 'I hope that Englishmen would show more civility to native peoples who barely know us and are simple souls in need of guidance.'

'Is there gold to be found here, or mineral wealth of any kind?' The Queen looked from him to White and then Manteo. 'We need to question the advantage of re-manning the Roanoke fort or establishing any other positions in the territory.' She looked back at Captain Drake who blew another stream of smoke in the direction of Master Harriot.

The Captain turned to a model globe and ran the back of his fingers down the east coast of the Americas as far as the Antilles.

'A base from which we could pick off Spanish treasure ships would be useful, the further south the better.'

Harriot coughed, turned his back on Sir Francis, and inclined his head towards the Queen as he placed the drawings neatly together. 'There may be precious metals, though as yet ...'

He was silenced by a disturbance at the doors and the sudden arrival of a gentleman who marched straight in.

'Sir Walter Raleigh,' the herald announced.

The Queen turned and watched as Sir Walter entered, knelt, strode towards her and knelt again. She gave him her hand which he kissed and then motioned for him to rise with a twinkle in her eyes. 'My Walter,' she said softly, and Emme recognised the fond name Her Majesty had for him. 'Come and slake my thirst in a desert of worry.'

Sir Walter replied as gently, 'Always.' Then he wheeled round to face Captain Drake with an expression as hard as flint. 'I would appreciate an explanation in private, Sir Francis.' His eyes narrowed as he took in the papers which Harriot was rolling up. 'And you may report to me next, Master Harriot.' A gesture towards the door made plain where he expected him to go, and Secretary Walsingham spread his arms to motion everyone else away.

The exit was brisk and the doors closed quickly leaving Sir Francis and Sir Walter alone with the Queen. Emme found herself with Secretary Walsingham settling like a raven at her side.

'Find Master Doonan lodgings here, then keep an eye on what he does. Let me know if you pick up anything about Sir Walter's plans for Virginia. The mariner should be easier for you to follow than the Indian.'

With a nod, Secretary Walsingham was gone, and she was left to hurry after the others. She caught up just as stewards led away Manteo, Harriot and White. Master Kit eyed her quizzically and stepped aside at her bidding; only then did she realise that a boy was with him and that Biddy was following as well.

The boy did not intrude; he hung back respectfully behind Biddy while Emme walked with Mariner Kit. She supposed the boy must have been acquired on some exotic voyage because his skin was the colour of cinnamon and his features were like a blackamoor's, except more fine, with a neat pert nose and curling dark lashes to his downturned doe eyes. Another glance back at him prompted Kit to give the boy's name.

'This is Rob, my page. I would like him to stay with me.'

'I'll make sure he has a bed,' she said, deciding that she would not mind the boy since she was pleased enough to have Master Kit at her side, conscious of his lithe, straight-backed stride as they passed through the gallery and the Watching Chamber beyond. A few heads turned as they left, but she acknowledged no one's look, and, once they were over the moat and in Fountain Court, she spoke to the mariner more freely knowing that she had his attention to herself.

'Have you sailed with Sir Francis many times?'

'Yes,' he said, slowing as they neared the fountain, and fixing his blue gaze upon her in a way that made his words seem to slip past formality and reach straight to her soul. 'I have been with him on every voyage since he helped me escape from the Spaniards thirteen years ago.'

'Escape?' She probed softly, aware of a sadness about him lying like darkness behind a veil – she saw it in his eyes as he looked straight back at her.

'I was held hostage by the Spaniards before the battle of San Juan de Ulúa, and taken captive when they reneged and destroyed John Hawkins' fleet. They marched me to the City of Mexico and sold me as a galley slave; then I was sent to the mines in Panama and panned for gold until I was freed by African runaways. I lived as an outlaw with these people, the Cimaroons as they're called, until I heard of English ships nearby, and then I found my brother, who was in Drake's crew, and sailed back to England with Drake and the Spanish treasure he'd seized.'

He turned to drink from the fountain, leaving Emme in awe as the wonder of his story settled over her. It chimed in her mind with legendary tales of Spanish treachery and John Hawkins' defeat, and Drake's famous first victory over the Spaniards in the New World when he had brought back a fortune after raiding a mule train carrying bullion. What must the mariner have been through: imprisoned, enslaved, outcast and then rescued as if brought back from the dead? What had he been through since? She watched him wipe the water from his mouth with the back of his hand, and pictured him in a prison cell, and then in a wilderness, and next on a rolling deck in the thick of a storm. He would have been graceful wherever he was, she decided; he did not need to drink from crystal to look like a gentleman.

'Did you sail with Sir Francis all around the world?'

'I did. I sailed with him to Magellan's Strait, beyond the land of ice and smoke, and into the South Sea where no Englishman had sailed before, as far north as New Albion, and then to the Spice Isles rich in cloves and ginger, from Java to the Guinea Coast and back to England; I've seen the lion in the purple mountains of Sierra Leone, and birds that fly in the sea because the sky is too cold.'

His words both thrilled and unsettled her, swelling her heart then spearing her with longing.

'I would that I could have gone on such a journey.'

The remark was out before she had considered the sense of it. Kit's response was to smile at her as if she could not possibly understand.

'I think you would have wished yourself back home within a month. Two-thirds of the crew died on that voyage.'

She almost protested that she would have gladly endured the hardship or died in the attempt, but she kept that thought to herself.

'Will you sail with Sir Francis again?'

'I might not.' The sounds of splashing filled his pause. 'The next voyage I make will be with Manteo, I have promised him.'

'To Virginia?'

'Yes.'

'Does Virginia hold better prospects for you now? Greater even than finding fortune with Sir Francis Drake?'

He looked away to the arch that led through to the gate; then he turned back to her.

'Fortune is not everything.'

'You are right.' She smiled to show how much she agreed with him, though that soon faded before the gravity in his eyes, and not smiling was easier since she was still bleeding inside and out from the pain of her violation. She ushered him on in silence, with the boy padding behind, while her mind swam, and she mourned inwardly for the affinity she felt with this man, and the certainty that neither he, nor anyone like him, could ever be part of her life, so far removed from her was he in station and experience, and so tarnished was she now that no man of merit would ever want her.

'There were many reasons why I sailed with Drake,' Kit volunteered, carrying on as if their discussion had never stopped, and her heart opened to him at that, because she knew he was trying to be both considerate and forthright with her. He paced steadily at her side as he went on.

'Gratitude and loyalty come into it, and searching too – searching for something,' he added quickly, as if correcting himself.

'What?'

'I . . .'

Their words were uttered together, and with a wistful smile he carried on.

'I now know that my search is at an end. There is no need for me to sail again with Drake, not to the Indies or anywhere else.'

They had reached the Gate House, and it was only natural that she should go inside to speak to the Yeoman Steward and collect the key to the mariner's room; this done, she knew their conversation was close to a conclusion, though she wondered at his last words, and wanted to know more about his travels and why his search was over. She escorted Master Kit to his lodgings overlooking the Great Court, checked there was a pallet for his page, and prepared to say goodbye.

'I suppose you will be meeting Manteo to discuss your return to Virginia?' She put the question as blithely as she could.

'Yes, there'll be meetings, and Sir Walter will want a report, and to speak to me as well since it's his capital that will finance the voyage. I hope he considers me worthy to be included in the enterprise.'

'Oh, he will,' she blurted out, which induced in him another small smile. 'I would like to attend, if I may,' she rushed on impulsively, simply not wanting to end their association and the glimpse of freedom he had given her. 'I am very interested in this new land.'

'You?' He raised a brow and looked at her, and again his eyes locked onto hers, but the laughter that she thought might come did not. He spoke gently.

'Well, John White is determined upon having women amongst his settlers. Perhaps you might be able to tell him whether the women who are needed will be encouraged to join.'

*The women who are needed*: the phrase turned in her thoughts, and she knew that such women did not include her. Suddenly she wished all her finery away: her silk dress and pearls, her wired collar and corset, the farthingale, the busk and the whitening caking her face. She wished she had no maid to give him the impression she was pampered. She wanted him to see that she could be useful too.

He tipped his handsome head on one side then gave her a crisp bow.

'I will ask whether you may come along.'

\*

Emme felt herself falling, plummeting down through a lightless void with nothing that she could catch hold of to slow her descent. Her speed accelerated with each tearing moment, though she reached out with arms and legs, twisting and flailing in desperation, clutching uselessly while air streamed past her, filling her mouth which was open wide to scream. But no sound would come. The drop went on and on. Her muscles locked and her nerves burned. She tried to yell again and again, until, at last, with a cry she woke, thrashing and sweating, twisting in her sheets, conscious of where she was just as she realised that someone was close.

Bess Throckmorton reached over from the bed beside Emme in their chamber at Richmond Palace and took hold of her in the darkness. Emme sighed with relief. She was safe and with people she knew. Her maid, Biddy, Lady Frances Howard and others familiar to her would be not far away. She jerked up on one elbow, rubbed at her eyes and gave a small moan. As her thoughts cleared, she realised nothing had changed. It was no surprise to her that she had dreamt of falling. In truth, she had fallen already even if outwardly she appeared unharmed. Still breathing heavily, she rocked back and forth.

Bess got up quietly, ghost pale in the shuttered dark. She squatted down by Emme's bed and put her arms around her.

'It's all right, Emme,' she whispered. 'There's nothing to worry about. You were only having a bad dream.'

Emme hugged Bess back, then buried her face against her friend's linen shift, inhaling its scent of rose petals and human sweetness, aware of the young woman's body beneath, younger than hers, one untouched. Her tears began to gush helplessly because Bess was so kind yet everything was *not* all right. It would never be all right.

Bess kissed her cheek, murmuring with soft sibilance.

'What is it, Emme? Surely a dream should not upset you so?'

'It's not the dream, Bess, not that. It's . . . No, I can't tell anyone.'

'Telling me might be a help, Emme. A trouble shared is a trouble made less; that's what my nurse always said.'

'Dear Bess.' Emme gave her another squeeze. Bess was a true good friend but she could never begin to confess her shame to her.

Bess whispered softly.

'You called out while you were dreaming.'

'What?' Panic gripped Emme again. 'What did I say?'

Bess made her whispering even quieter, squeezing it into hot damp puffs against Emme's ear.

'You said: "*Joined – No!*" and "*Lord* ..." At least I think that's what it was.' Bess gave a small suppressed giggle. 'Were you blaspheming in your sleep?'

Emme shook her head as her tears flowed. She sniffled and groped for her handkerchief. If Bess meant to cheer her, she had failed.

'So were you naming someone?' Bess whispered again more urgently. 'Did you not want to be joined with *a lord*?'

It was too much. Bess knew her too well. Her friend had guessed at her secret before Emme had any chance to try and better conceal it. She blew her nose and covered her eyes and could not stop the great shuddering sobs that racked her. She fell into her friend's embrace and they held one another tight.

'A lord has ruined me, Bess.'

'No!' Bess gasped. 'Who?'

Emme took a deep breath and murmured in a small voice. 'Lord Hertford.'

'But he's so old!' Bess sounded incredulous.

'Not too old for what he did to me.'

'Oh no...He didn't...' Bess took hold of Emme's hand and gripped it until her nails dug in. 'Not with his...Not as a man should only do with his wife...'

'Yes, that.'

Emme sensed Bess was struggling to imagine what had happened,

51

and she supposed the act was as much beyond her friend's experience as it had been beyond her own until that night, just over two weeks ago, when her innocence had been ripped from her.

'He trapped me here in the palace,' she began to explain in an undertone. 'He locked me in a room and then...'

'Shhh!' Bess shot back into bed and pulled the covers over her head.

The glow of a candle passed over them as Lady Howard surveyed all the beds in the chamber.

Emme slumped down and pressed her face to her pillow.

'Who was talking?' Lady Howard snapped.

'I was, my lady,' Emme spoke up, anxious to shield Bess from any blame. 'I had a nightmare and spoke out in my sleep. I am sorry to have disturbed you.'

Lady Howard clicked her tongue.

'I am sure that everyone here does not wish to know the state of your dreams, Mistress Fifield. I'll thank you to be quiet.'

Emme screwed shut her eyes and said nothing more.

She prayed she had not already said too much.

*

The beat was quick, the music bright and Emme saw the Queen gasp after the next high leap, turning in Sir Christopher Hatton's arms with cheeks flushed livid and a hand that trembled, as she commenced the *cinq pas*. Five steps: one two, one two, and Emme sprang with the other ladies, whirling into the cadence, skirts twirling, pulse pounding, her throat raw with gulping at the smoke-sharp air from the open windows. Loose ribbons and hair blurred with white headdresses as she turned. The music flowed and possessed. The thud of tabor and boards; slippers slapping, hands clapping; the flourishes of lute, flute and viol took over from ears to toes, and Emme was glad to lose herself and forget, even if the sound of laughter jabbed at her soul. But how much more would the Queen endure? She had already been out riding at dawn and she had danced four galliards.

Bess Throckmorton took Emme's hand. 'Be Sir Walter for me,' she whispered, stepping close and guiding Emme's hand to the lip of her busk near the hard point where her bodice tapered. Then, with arched back and half-closed eyes, Bess moved with her in rhythm, preparing for the leap, and Emme helped her when she sprang, using all her strength to lift her friend's light body high, though she could not resist the temptation to tickle her ribs as she set Bess down.

'Saucy, Sir Walter,' Bess giggled, skipping away.

Suddenly Emme felt the music slow, and she noticed Sir Christopher leading the Queen aside. The lute played on alone for a while, petering out as the Queen sat and raised her hand.

'Let us have a song, Mistress Fifield,' the Queen said, fanning herself rapidly and fixing Emme with a piercing stare. 'Something gentle while we rest.'

*A song?* Emme froze. Had she gone too far in helping Bess to play out her fantasy? Had the Queen overheard the mention of her favourite's name?

Emme moved towards her while the others drew away. She tried to quieten her panting and think of a song she could remember in both words and melody, yet her mind was a blank.

'I...I am sure one of the musicians would sing better,' she said, gesturing to one of the lutenists renowned for his pure tenor voice. 'Master Chris Bowen, for instance.'

The Queen tapped her foot. 'I would like to hear from you, Mistress Fifield. Do not keep me waiting.'

Emme looked wildly around the Great Hall which seemed still to be turning after all her spinning around, with the Queen's ladies drifting by agape, and Bess gazing at her with her hand over her mouth, and the sunlight throwing daubs of colour through the stained-glass in the palace windows, while outside, above rooftops and twisted chimneys in a clear late-summer sky, she could see the pale disc of a moon left over from the night.

She did not know where the words came from but, after an awkward pause, they issued from her, trembling a little at first, then becoming more certain as she found the melody and Master Bowen picked it up on his lute:

'With how sad steps, O Moon, thou climb'st the skies! . . .'

Together they made the song swell, exquisite and poignant, a song of loss and unrequited love.

> . . . Sure, if that long-with-love-acquainted eyes
> Can judge of love, thou feel'st a lover's case,
> I read it in thy looks: thy languish'd grace . . .

The words were Sir Philip Sidney's, who was now on campaign in the Low Countries, and, as everyone present knew, the 'Moon' of the sonnet was Her Majesty whom Sir Philip had idolised in verse, and perhaps the song set the Queen wondering whether she would ever see him again. Or perhaps she thought of others far from her who had once touched her heart – there must have been someone, maybe Lord Leicester, also fighting for the Protestant Dutch: the man thought by most to be the one the Queen would one day marry, now with his new wife and the Queen still unwed.

Emme reflected on her own lost virtue, and on Drake and his men who had departed for another strike against Spain. Most of all she thought of Mariner Kit who had enthralled her then left without sending any word. He was gone from her life just like all the fine hot-blooded men she had ever met – fleeting shadows passing through echoing palaces – and she sang out her heart while the Queen covered her eyes.

Then all at once, sharp and loud, the Queen clapped her hands and broke the spell. She sat up straight, eyes glistening as she spoke.

'The sun beckons; let us enjoy it! A diversion on the river would suit very well – no ceremony or fuss. I shall travel like an ordinary citizen and pay one of my gentlemen a visit. Mistress Fifield, you may accompany me; you, too, Mistress Throckmorton. Good Sir Christopher, you shall be my guard.'

Excitement about the prospect shot through Emme like a dart. Who would they see? *One of my gentlemen*, the Queen had said. Emme thought of all the magnificent prodigy houses with gardens along the Thames and river gates: those along the Strand between Whitehall and the Temple, the houses of Leicester, Arundel, Suffolk and Salisbury. Perhaps the Queen meant to call on Robert Cecil, but more likely she planned to catch Sir Walter Raleigh at home in Durham Place.

'You may well see him now,' she whispered to Bess, sliding her arm round her friend's waist as they hurried to the jetty.

'*Him?*' Bess raised her brows with an air of naïve perplexity, though Emme saw through it to the hope in her eyes.

'Your dream dancing partner,' Emme answered with a quiet smile.

'Tush!' Bess looked back to their maids who were following in a gaggle, pulled up the hood of her cloak and trotted after the Queen.

Emme hummed the tune of the galliard Bess had danced to and linked arms with her friend. She wanted to keep the mood light, not brood on her own unhappiness or the Queen's changes in behaviour. Whatever troubled Her Majesty was beyond her power to remedy, and shouldn't she be rejoicing along with everyone else? The sound of peeling bells reminded her of one reason to be glad: Anthony Babington had been apprehended, found in an outhouse north of London with his hair cut short and his skin stained with walnut juice. His threat to the Queen's life was over, and another plot had been thwarted that involved Spain and Mary of Scots.

As the royal household barge drifted gently downstream, bonfires on the river banks sent plumes of smoke into the sky, the peeling of bells rang out, and cheering rose from the winding river's edge wherever people were gathered in the villages they passed: Chiswick, Hammersmith, Putney and Chelsea. Once the barge reached the city, the noise became louder, and when the glory of Westminster Abbey came into view, Westminster Palace and Whitehall, then Emme could make out one phrase repeated over and over: 'God save the Queen!'

The Queen seemed not to notice. She sat, head bowed, deep in conversation with Sir Christopher Hatton.

'She denies it?' Emme overheard her ask him.

'She does,' Sir Christopher said in a low voice. 'But her letter is proof of her complicity. She is guilty,' he added with an edge enough for Emme to hear the word clearly. '*Guilty.*'

The Queen shook her head, and Emme's heart went out to her. They must have been talking about Mary of Scots, who was such a treacherous danger even in captivity. Mary had plotted to kill her, not once but several times, and now she was proven guilty in Anthony Babington's conspiracy. What could the Queen do? If she showed mercy she would never be safe – Spain would never stop scheming to have a Catholic on the throne. But if she had Mary executed then Spain would surely declare war, and could she pronounce the death sentence on a queen of her own blood?

Emme watched the great mansions as they came into view, with their lions rampant guarding elegant river steps, and clipped lawns beyond graceful willows rising to patterned knots of box and yew. She found it hard to believe that in the midst of such tranquil grandeur there were dark forces at work that would see everything destroyed, bring down the Queen and the new Church of England, unleash the terror of persecution afresh, and see free England made a vassal to Spain. But at least the danger had receded for a while. A fresh roar of jubilation rang out and the Queen patted Sir Christopher's hand.

'Babington's wealth will be forfeit. Some good will come of that.'

Then she smiled as the barge slowed, and raised her eyes to a white turret beyond a high crenelated wall and Emme knew they had reached their destination; they had arrived at Durham Place.

Cloaked and hooded, the Queen was ushered up steps, through private apartments and across a rising court to an entrance by a carriageway leading uphill to the Strand. Beyond marble pillars, Emme saw the traffic of London passing by: horses, carts and carriages, and streams of people, some of them bunching together, singing and shouting. The hubbub was overwhelming after the peace of Richmond and the river. The clatter of hooves and iron-rimmed cartwheels echoed over cobbles and around paved courtyards; the hammer of construction, the baying of livestock and the cries of hawkers all added to the din. A sewer stench drifted down from the street, and she saw an effigy tied to a hurdle that bystanders were pelting with rubbish and stones. When Emme followed the Queen up a creaking staircase to an airy gallery a floor above, she was glad to pause by an open window and take a deep breath.

The steward knocked at a double door but the Queen waved him aside.

'No announcement. We shall enter.'

She strode in as the door opened to reveal a group of men around a long table, silhouetted against high windows overlooking the Strand. One of the men stood immediately and approached to greet her: Sir Walter Raleigh, tall and proud, with his dark hair curling around his strong, sensitive face and the hair of his chest just visible beyond the neck-strings of his shirt. He should never have received the Queen in such a state, but she had surprised him, the day was hot and neither of them seemed much to care. With alacrity and grace he knelt before the Queen, kissed her hand and, keeping his almond eyes upon her, gave her a dazzling smile.

'Your Majesty. Your servant is honoured. We were discussing the land named for you in the New World. How fortunate that you are here!'

He is in thrall to her, Emme thought; in his gaze was pure devotion. She glanced at Sir Christopher and saw him flinch and raise his chin. He was jealous, Emme realised. Loyal, charming Sir Christopher, who had kept by the Queen's side, aged with her and never wed, was as envious of Sir Walter as a rival for a maid. They both loved her. Though the Queen had lost the flame of youthful beauty, she had the hearts of these men racing at the slightest sign of favour. Emme watched and felt as insignificant as a speck upon the wall. She saw Mariner Kit amongst those assembled, and his look acknowledged her, yet his expression remained impassive. Why should he pay her any attention? He had obviously forgotten her since their talk at the palace. She clearly meant nothing to him. He bowed to the Queen, and she noticed that his long fair hair was tied back behind his neck, and that his leather jerkin accentuated the width of his shoulders and upper arms. His features were so strikingly well-formed it was hard for her to look away, but she swallowed and concentrated on Master Manteo beside him, because she could feel a hot blush rising over her throat.

The Indian wore a loose russet smock that revealed a chevron of tattoos and the fang of a large animal on a thong over his chest. Raw physicality oozed from him, just as it did from Kit and Sir Walter; the faint smell of male sweat hung like musk in the air. The windows were shut against the noise outside, and Emme had a sense that she had stumbled upon something forbidden, yet the Queen seemed to relax. She took off her cloak, and spoke warmly to those present, from Kit to Manteo, to Masters Harriot and White and the other men with them; she greeted them all one by one. Meanwhile Sir Walter sauntered over to the ladies, took Emme by the hand and welcomed her graciously. Then he stopped before Bess and gave her a flourishing bow. His look was intense as he met her eye, and she basked in his attention, turning herself like a flower to the sunshine of his gaze.

The Queen's back was towards them. Sir Walter did not look away, and when Bess finally moved aside, Emme saw Sir Walter's eyes continue to follow her. That he wanted her was clear, though probably no-else was aware of it. Sir Walter, the Queen's favourite, had a yearning for another – and heaven help both him and Bess if ever that desire was given its head. Emme sensed a charge in the air like the tension before a thunderstorm. She glanced back at Kit but he was looking down at a map. No one was interested in her; she felt as if she was shrinking.

Sir Walter stepped closer to the Queen and lightly placed his hand upon her waist, guiding her to look at the map that Kit spread open over the table.

'Come and share a dream with me,' he murmured.

'Of what?' The Queen tipped her face to his.

'Our Virginia.' He bent in answering until their lips almost touched. 'I dream of another England here.' He gestured to the map and glided around the Queen as he spoke, all his movements drawing her to him and to the map beneath his graceful fingers. 'I see this land settled for all time with English families bringing enlightenment to the gentle natives and acting as a beacon to the World: an England in the wilderness, but a wilderness that is an Eden. Can you see it too?' His eyes shone with passion. 'A Virginia to glorify your name evermore!'

The Queen gave a wry smile and tapped his chest with her fan. 'That is a pretty dream, but alas it would seem that General Lane has woken from it. The natives are not so gentle and the Eden is hellish.'

'Sweet Majesty, difficulties may have arisen here at Roanoke.' He stabbed a finger on an island between the mainland of America and a long ribbon of land around what looked to Emme like a vast estuarine lake. 'But we can learn from that and make a fresh start.' He raised his finger before the Queen could object. 'Thirty leagues to the north in the land of the Chesapeake,' he said as he swept his hand over a large bay unmarked by any name, 'the people are as friendly as children and the region is like a garden.' He gave a nod to Harriot and White. 'As these intrepid men will testify – fruit, animals and fish abound. Our colonists could thrive there. I would like to see English farmers till the soil in this place, and English artisans build houses for English wives and children. I envisage a city founded in godliness, following the best principles of good governance, a city of peace and prosperity in which toil is rewarded and all are treated fairly.'

The Queen smiled and gave a small shake of her head. 'You speak of Utopia; it cannot exist on this Earth.'

'It can,' Sir Walter countered. 'We *can* build such a city with enough ships and provisions and good Englishfolk who share this vision. It might be costly but . . .'

'The cost would be enormous, and have you not already invested a fortune?'

He looked pained for an instant as if checked by a blow. 'I have,' he said quietly with his head bowed and his fingers resting on the map below the English coat of arms, 'for the honour of England and my sovereign.'

The Queen touched his hand gently and looked upon him with such tenderness that Emme felt a pang in the pit of her stomach.

'We will always reward loyalty,' the Queen said softly. 'What traitors lose, faithful champions will gain. So let us suppose you have estates and revenues enough to ease the burden of embarking on this new enterprise, where will you find the colonists of the kind you have described: adventurers ready to farm and lay bricks? Women prepared to risk their lives to make homes in the wild? I doubt that many of General Lane's veterans will be prepared to go back to Virginia again. I hear they have been spreading tales of woe about their experiences.'

'Soldiers make poor settlers, and those who complain about hardship are not the kind we want as citizens. These are the gentlemen upon whom our Virginia will be founded.' He indicated the men around the table with a sweep of his hand. 'I would lead the expedition myself if...'

'No! I forbid it.' The Queen clutched at his shoulder, and Emme could see the force with which her fingers dug into his flesh through his thin muslin shirt. 'Sit,' she commanded.

He did, and turned his head to her hand still gripping his shoulder, then he raised his eyes to her face.

'You will stay,' she said softly. 'If Spain declares war I shall need you here to protect us.'

He laid his hand over hers.

'I will stay, just as the Earth always stays with the Moon. I will never be far from you and I will never fail you.'

She sighed, squeezed his shoulder, closed her eyes for a moment and let go.

'Then who will lead this bold venture.'

'Master White, here, has put forward his name as Governor.' Sir Walter motioned to the limner who inclined his shaggy head. 'He is well acquainted with the region having surveyed it for this chart.' He gestured to the map. 'Master Simon Ferdinando will act as pilot for the next expedition just as he did for the last.' Sir Walter turned to the Indian, Manteo. 'Our good ally, Manteo, will assist us from his island of Croatoan.' He pointed to another island, near Roanoke, along the thin line between the huge lake and the sea. 'Others at this table have already volunteered.' He looked round as Kit stood.

'I offer my skills as a Boatswain who has circumnavigated the globe with Sir Francis Drake.' Kit bowed to the Queen. 'It will be a privilege to serve.'

'And I will join as a settler,' another man said as he rose.

'Aye,' said another, 'I also.'

Emme watched Kit standing there and bit back the urge to shout that she would go too. She yearned to tell them all she was prepared to leave everything and risk her life for the chance to start afresh in the land of promise; she could be as brave as any of them for that. But she did not need to make an idiot of herself to know that the reaction would be derision. She would never be taken seriously if she spoke up like a man, so she held her tongue as the Queen spread her arms.

'I applaud you,' she said, clapping lightly before turning to Sir Walter. 'You may have the rootstock, but you will need more than this to plant a whole colony.'

Emme looked from the half-dozen men standing to those still sitting down, Master Harriot amongst them. Perhaps his skills were too great to risk on another voyage. Who else would go? Where would the families come from that Sir Walter had spoken of? In the silence that followed within the hall, the sound of cheering outside seemed to grow louder.

Sir Walter got to his feet, walked over to one of the windows, opened it and leaned out.

A great roar swelled up from the street. He waved and beckoned for the Queen to stand by him and as she moved closer the noise became a crescendo.

'There,' he said to her. 'There are the people we need: the salt of ·the earth.'

A lump rose in Emme's throat. The venture was so courageous

it made her want to weep, but there was no place in it for her. She stepped back feeling excluded, wanting the shadows to swallow her. Then she flinched from the touch of something against her hand.

She looked round to see Master Kit by her side. His hand enveloped hers, and as he turned to her he smiled.

Without thinking, she pulled away.

At the first opportunity before leaving Durham Place, Emme visited the garderobe and washed her hands. She locked the door, used the close stool of necessity, then poured water into a bowl from the silver ewer provided, worked a block of fine white Castile soap around her hands, and used a bristle brush to scrub at her fingers. She wept as she rubbed without knowing why, perhaps because she'd reacted absurdly to Kit's gentle touch, recoiling from the very man for whom she had some real regard. What would Kit think of her now? He must have felt she wanted nothing to do with him, probably that she was aloof and conceited and considered herself superior without any cause. Then what was she doing? She should have been treasuring the affection implicit in his gesture, not trying to wash it away as hard as she could. But she felt unclean. Kit's contact with her had been a shock; she had not anticipated it at all. He had touched her unexpectedly and she'd connected it with Lord Hertford driving his fingers into her.

O me, not that. She hung her head in mortification and rubbed with the brush until her fingers were raw. She felt as if she would never be clean again. In the bowl was her world: the light from a tiny window in a high stone wall and the shadow of her reflection in a greasy film of dirty suds. Her tears plopped onto the surface one by one. She plunged in her hands and inadvertently splashed her skirts. She felt dizzy, not helped by the heady smell of violets in the confined space together with a lingering odour from the privy drain. She longed to escape. She did not know what to do. She no longer understood her own mind. What did she hope to achieve by scouring her hands?

A sharp rapping on the door made her look up.

'Emme?' Bess called softly. 'Are you in there?'

'Yes,' she answered, more brightly than she felt. 'I'll be out in a moment.'

She wiped her eyes and her hands on a napkin, looked out of the little window and saw the river far below. Then she picked up the bowl and threw the water outside.

# 4

# *Knowledge*

'Knowledge is never too dear.'

—*Favourite maxim of Sir Francis Walsingham, Secretary of State and chief intelligencer to Queen Elizabeth I*

'I did not order that Babington was to be tortured in execution.' The Queen's voice rose to a shout. 'Defiled and butchered!'

'You told my Lord Burghley that hanging was not terrible enough,' Sir Francis Walsingham remarked quietly.

'I said that the populace should see and learn from the just punishment of traitors, not that they should be left fainting and retching. This report says that the man's privities were sliced off before his eyes and his innards were drawn out while he was still alive.'

Bess gasped and put her hand over her mouth. Emme stopped sewing in the act of pulling a stitch tight, conscious that her needle was trembling in her hand. They both leant closer together on their cushions in the corner of the Presence Room. Through the damask of her friend's sleeve, Emme could feel Bess shivering.

The Queen tossed a sheet of paper on the table before Secretary Walsingham and slammed her palm down on top. 'This sickens me.'

'It is done,' he said, clasping his hands within his sleeves. 'The quarters of the first seven traitors are displayed at St Giles and their heads are on London Bridge as an example to all.'

'Make sure the next seven are dead before they are cut open.' The Queen picked up a late September plum from a silver plate and turned to face the magnificent view from Greenwich Palace over the Thames. 'What does my cousin Mary say now?'

Walsingham stood behind her. 'She feigns unconcern and says she will answer to no one but God.'

'Pah!' The Queen brought the plum to her mouth, held it close to her lips, then took it slowly away and proffered it to Walsingham.

He held his palm open. 'She must stand trial,' he said gently. 'The evidence is overwhelming.'

To Emme, watching from the corner, Walsingham looked ink black against the light while the Queen shimmered like a fiery ember capable at any moment of bursting into flame.

'Yours,' said the Queen, letting the plum drop into his hand. She folded his fingers around the fruit and pressed them into the flesh until a glistening drop of juice dripped from his fist to the floor.

When she turned to leave, her mouth was closed tight as a sprung trap.

Emme remained motionless for a moment until she shook herself into action. Then she took Bess by the hand and they left, Walsingham louring like a dark cloud at their backs.

Emme looked round and saw him walking slowly behind, head bowed. She knew he would want to speak with her and inwardly sighed.

'You go on,' she murmured to Bess. 'I shall not be long.'

She drifted casually back and offered the Secretary of State a small curtsey, making as if to pass him.

He nodded and turned to walk with her. They proceeded as far as the library where he ordered the yeoman guard to stand outside, beckoned her in and shut the door.

The room smelt of paper and leather, refreshingly pleasant after the stink of the jakes at Richmond which had become so foul, after weeks of use by the hundreds in the royal household, that a change of palace had been deemed necessary. She was still adjusting to the new surroundings, taking delight in the long halls and galleries overlooking the river, her spirits uplifted by a private fantasy, one that had grown and strengthened in the six days since her visit to Durham Place. But Secretary Walsingham's manifest gloom was a warning to her to hide the new-born eagerness she felt inside. She watched him prop his elbow on a high sideboard, rub his brow and close his eyes. Was he ill? Emme guessed he was suffering from one of the migraines that frequently pained him, especially when there was any tension in his relations with the Queen. She almost felt sorry for him, though wariness curbed her sympathy.

Walsingham winced. 'I was expecting to hear from you weeks ago.'

'I have only recently found out the details of Sir Walter Raleigh's plans for Virginia.'

She moved nearer and looked down at a clock on a table. It bore a single hand like an arrow on a flat horizontal face supported by a dome of gilded brass patterned in strands like fine waves. The arrow seemed frozen, pointing to the space between two Roman numerals, to the moment she had to fill. Beside the clock was a large, open book. It showed a heart-shaped map of the globe in which the New World lay stretched out and curved round near the circumference to the west. She brought her fingertip close to the word '*AMERIC*' then ran it up through the southern continent to '*CANIBALES*' near the top. Were there cannibals in Virginia? Master Harriot had led her to believe that the people there were naturally peaceable, but on the map all she could see were the spikes of mountains and the gaping jaws of river mouths where she supposed Virginia might lie. The place seemed a complete wilderness. She could not even make out any names. The clock ticked loudly as she considered what to say.

Her thoughts went back to Durham Place and everything she had heard there concerning the planned expedition to found a new colony, and she tried to separate that out from the tangle in her thoughts about Mariner Kit, the way he had taken her hand and her reaction. Not that her awkwardness with him mattered now. He had probably forgotten all about her; she had not seen him since. Walsingham would want to know about what the Queen and Sir Walter had said. She drew breath and began.

'Sir Walter is prepared to back another expedition led by Master John White as Governor with the help of assistants who will be charged to found a new city in Sir Walter's name. They mean to establish a permanent settlement of around two hundred men, women and children in a bay north of Roanoke which is known as the Chesapeake. Sir Walter is prepared to offer every settler five hundred acres of farmland in Virginia, and Master White is already enlisting volunteers from the streets of London. They mean to sail in the spring with the Queen's approval.'

She glanced up at Walsingham and saw his eyes flicker towards the clock; then he glanced at a note that he pulled from inside his sleeve. He knows already, she thought. She had not surprised him, and he was impatient to be dealing with something else.

'I would like to go too,' she added, stating the fantasy she had nurtured as if it might actually become real.

His brows shot up and he put the note aside. 'Has Her Majesty encouraged you in this?'

'No,' she said and looked him in the eye. 'I thought I would ask you first. I could send back reports with any ship that returns and give an honest account of all that transpires.'

To her relief he did not laugh or rebuke her, or turn aside and walk away. He returned her gaze.

'You would be prepared to risk your life and leave England, perhaps forever?'

'Yes,' she said softly, 'I would.'

'But why? You have ease of living here, the privilege of serving the Queen and . . . possibly good prospects in marriage. Why would you want to abandon all this?'

'I have seen Master White's pictures and heard Master Harriot's reports, and I would like to go to this Eden on Earth in my life. I want to be part of the brave adventure. Sir Walter's ambition is to build a better England in the New World. He needs women for that; I am prepared to be one of them.'

He shook his head. 'I do not believe you have any idea of the hardship that might be involved – or the danger.'

'I am willing to take my chance. I would like to make a fresh start in the new country. I...' She almost told him that she wanted to escape from Lord Hertford and the shame she felt every time she saw him, to be free to take control of her life and begin again in an untouched land without being at the beck and call of the Queen, a husband or anyone else. But she held back from saying any of that.

'The men who have been to Virginia have inspired me, those who have seen its beauty and are determined on returning. They...'

'The men?' He inclined his head. 'Perhaps one in particular?'

She looked down. She would not tell him about Master Kit. What was there to say? She took a step closer. 'I could be useful to you. I could be your eyes and ears...'

He raised his hand. 'Her Majesty would not allow it.'

'She would if you convinced her of the advantages of my joining the expedition.'

His mouth twisted towards a smile.

'You know you can trust my integrity,' she went on. 'None of the colonists would guess that I might be gathering information for you.'

He leant back and cupped his chin in his hand.

She could tell he was taking her suggestion seriously and that gave her some hope. 'I would do whatever you asked. Anything...'

He cut across her.

'In the ordinary course I would dismiss this proposal out of hand. It would put you at grave risk and there is the issue of your service for the Queen which adds another level of complication. But I have recently become aware of rumours which might make your absence for a while expedient.'

She frowned, wondering what he meant, but the mere fact that he was listening to her was encouraging. Then her spirits plummeted. What had he heard?

'What rumours?'

'Tittle-tattle concerning your virtue and your association with certain gentlemen.'

'Who?' she blurted in alarm. 'Which gentlemen? This cannot be. I have always behaved modestly.' She realised she was gabbling, and made herself slow down. 'I am blameless,' she said.

'I have no doubt.' Walsingham gave a nod. Though she avoided his eyes, she felt him scrutinising her intently. 'As I said, the talk is only rumour and rumours are rarely true.'

She raised her chin.

'I am glad you agree, Master Secretary.'

'They are rarely completely false either.'

Her pulse raced but she did not rise to him.

Walsingham turned away from her and picked up one of the books from a shelf, peering at its embroidered back boards as if they fascinated him.

'Some of the names mentioned have been patently absurd, my own amongst them.'

*His* name? There was a rumour linking her with Secretary Walsingham? She could barely credit it. Why would anyone spread such a falsehood? Who would do so?

She made an effort to sound not particularly concerned. As he said, the idea was preposterous.

'Absurd,' she repeated, and shook her head.

'But others . . .'

His voice tailed off, and a sense of foreboding settled over her.

He turned back and fixed her with a saturnine stare.

'Lord Hertford, for example.'

She felt her colour rising and looked back at him.

'No,' she whispered.

His hooded eyes bored into her.

'Do you deny any improper association with Lord Hertford?'

'Yes, that is ... I have never willingly ... He took ...'

She could not go on. No explanation she could give would help her. Even the truth would find her guilty.

Walsingham put an end to her floundering.

'You need say no more. He has a reputation for such indelicacy and you have been unfortunate to allow yourself to be caught. I think it would be best if you were removed from court for a few months, until the rumours die down.'

'Does the Queen suspect?' She blurted out the question, desperate to know, because she felt she could face up to the idea of prurient gossip behind her back, but not the disapproval of the Queen; that would destroy her.

'No,' Walsingham sighed. 'And I will do my best to ensure the rumours never reach her and, if they do, that they are discredited. So let us consider your suggestion more carefully. Do you know who will be the pilot for the voyage?'

Her mind was in turmoil, still trying to make sense of what had happened. How had the rumours begun? She had told no one but Bess about Lord Hertford; Bess, her best friend.

She had been betrayed.

Secretary Walsingham closed the book with a thud.

'The name of the pilot, Mistress Fifield; do you know it?'

'Master Simon ...' She shook her head as she tried to remember the name that Sir Walter had mentioned. 'I did not meet him, but I heard his name as Simon ...'

'Ferdinando?'

'Yes,' she nodded, sure of it. 'Simon Ferdinando.'

Secretary Walsingham frowned. 'Then your danger will be worse.' He picked up a pair of dividers from a shelf, placed one point on the wood, and twirled the free arm around. 'Ferdinando is Portuguese by blood, born in the Azores, trained in Seville and served the Spanish crown as a navigator until, for reasons best known to himself, he converted to the Protestant faith and developed a hatred for all things Spanish...so he says.' Walsingham held the dividers open and brought a fingertip to one of the points, resting the pad against the spike. 'He is not to be trusted.'

His eyes flicked back to her. 'He served as Sir Walter's pilot on the last expedition and almost wrecked the flagship in a storm. He attempted to pass through the sand banks off Virginia by a route which he knew was treacherous despite being aware of a safe channel not far to the north, one which he himself had discovered. The ship was beached and the provisions carried were largely destroyed. That almost led to the complete failure of the expedition before General Lane and his men even set foot on land.' He closed the dividers with a snap. 'Those who work against England do not always do so directly. There are other methods less obvious than conspiracies to murder the Queen.'

She watched him set the dividers down carefully. 'You think Master Ferdinando is an agent of Spain?'

He inclined his head.

'I could watch him,' she said. 'I could observe him discreetly and report to you.'

'If you stayed close to Ferdinando then perhaps...'

She sensed he was wavering; the prospect of her going was becoming more than a dream, though now her leaving would be clouded by whispers of scandal. Better to go than try to carry on under a veil of opprobrium.

'I could do that,' she said.

'He would save his own skin, I am sure.' Secretary Walsingham kept his eyes on her and cocked his head on one side, holding her with his gaze while the clock ticked on. She knew he was deliberating over her potential usefulness against the possibility of her loss on the voyage, and he would also be weighing up the advantage of getting her away from the court and protecting his own reputation.

He rubbed his chin. 'Ferdinando will not stay in Virginia with the settlers. He will come back to bring news to Sir Walter. Apart from anything else, no harbour has yet been found and tested along the coast of Virginia in which ships of deep draught may safely shelter from the autumn storms. It is conceivable that you could sail with the expedition, see the colony settled in Virginia, and then return with Ferdinando before the winter sets in . . .'

Her heart raced. The voyage might yet include her. 'I would be willing to stay in the New World,' she said hurriedly. 'I would not wish to leave the settlers . . .'

'No.' He shook his head and smiled wryly.

He probably thought she wanted to elope with one of Sir Walter's men. Let him, if that was what it took to get him to allow her to go; let him think she would chase after any man. She bit back a protest.

'The Queen would never agree,' he said. 'She may be persuaded to allow you to go if she is assured of your return within a few months. The prospect of a private report on the venture from one of her own ladies might pique her interest and be enough to tempt her. It would bind her more closely to Sir Walter's project and that might help you. But this could never be made public, of course. The

Queen could not be seen to be directly involved. If it was known that one of her ladies was on the voyage you might well become a target for Spanish attack. Sir Walter's investors would be appalled; they would see your presence as unnecessary and potentially damaging. They would never support a venture in which a lady was put at risk. Suppose you were captured by the Spaniards? The repercussions would be . . .' his hand wavered in the air, 'difficult, to say the least.' He grimaced. 'You might face worse than death: imprisonment and examination before the Inquisition. Once in the New World, you could be captured by hostile natives . . .'

She offered him a small smile.

He passed his hand over his brow. 'If you go, you will have to accept all the dangers alone, and you will have to travel under another name.'

'I would be happy to accept that.'

He gave her a nod. 'I will speak with Her Majesty. In the meantime you might consider a new identity for this venture.'

She would. Names were already streaming like ribbons through her mind.

*

In the bitter cold of a harsh November, Kit Doonan felt his muscles begin to relax after gaining shelter amidst the fug of the Boar's Head Inn near Eastcheap. He looked at the soft saffron cake which Rob was pulling apart over his trencher and dunking into his spiced wine. The boy drank the wine, then pressed the yellow cake crumbs into a ball with his slender brown fingers and neatly used that to wipe the cup inside before popping the ball into his mouth. The wooden trencher was left spotless and the earthenware cup completely clean. Rob smiled up at him and he smiled back. He only raised his head when the man with the loud voice spoke out again.

'Virginia is cursed,' the man bellowed. 'It's an ill-yielding wilderness beset by storms and overrun with savages.' He thumped the table, leaning forwards, jut-jawed, to peer at the folk on the tavern benches who turned round to face him.

'Go to Ireland!' He swept out his hand and lurched. 'If you want land in another country then go and work a plantation in Munster. It's only two days' sail away, not two months across the ocean, if your ship doesn't sink in a hurricane. I'll never go back.'

'That's as well,' Kit said, projecting his voice so that everyone could hear. 'Virginia has no need of men like you.'

The loud-mouth remained on his feet, propped up by his hand on the tabletop. He drank deeply from his cup and pushed himself upright. Kit knew he was mulling over how to respond, with the dull wits of a sot and the belligerence of a soldier; Kit recognised him as one of Lane's men smarting from the failure of the last Roanoke expedition.

The man narrowed his eyes. 'What do you mean by that?'

A sudden movement caused Kit to look to the place in front of the benches where John White had been left unnoticed.

Master White spread his arms. 'Prithee, good sir, if Virginia is not for you then hold your peace. There are some who have served there, such as yourself, who are glad to be back in England; I am pleased for their safe return. But there are others who have begged me to include them in the new venture. It is to those who are interested that I wish to speak.'

'Fools,' the veteran muttered, and took a few steps.

I hope he leaves, Kit thought.

The man spat into the rushes. 'You're all simpletons to listen to a man like this who keeps a blackamoor unchained.' He pointed straight at Kit.

Kit felt Rob stiffen beside him. An ugly murmuring rose from those who had gathered to hear John White speak; they looked over their shoulders from the veteran to Rob, and in their eyes was hostility.

Kit contained the flare of ire that surged through his veins. He stood calmly, held up his right hand and waited for everyone to look at him.

They did. They always did. Since leading his band of outlaws in Panama he had become used to taking control when he saw reason to step forwards. The mystery was why this happened, but people would usually follow him if he wanted them to. Perhaps the scar on his palm had something to do with it: the relic of an accident in a smithy long ago – the 'mark of the Moon', so the Cimaroons had believed. His father had said that he only had to hold up his hand to stop his luck running out. So it seemed. He had cheated death many times, and the confidence that gave was with him still; he could feel it as he stood there. He spoke decisively.

'Virginia needs those who are fair-minded, hard-working and strong of heart.' He scanned the faces before him, men and women, young and old, those lined by toil and those whom life had hardly touched. 'If you have these qualities then I hope you will stay. If not, then there is little point in your remaining to hear more.'

'Are you saying I'm a coward?' The veteran took a step closer. He stopped a few paces away from Kit with his hand on his sword hilt.

'No,' Kit replied. 'But neither are these good folk simpletons.'

The man's lips curled to show the stumps of his lower teeth. 'If you weren't Drake's man I'd ask to see you outside.'

Kit raised his hand again, and the look of shock on the veteran's face when he saw what Kit held was worth the risk he took in revealing the wheel-lock pistol he usually kept at his back tucked into his belt.

'But I am Drake's man, so I bid you good day.'

The pistol had been presented to him by Drake after the sack of Santo Domingo, and it gave Kit even more satisfaction to cock the firing dog and see the veteran flinch at the sound of the click then stumble backward and scurry away.

Kit secured the pistol and sat down, then gave Rob's thin shoulder a squeeze. He yearned to do more, to put his arms round the boy and tell him he was ten times better than the oaf who'd just left. For a moment his hand rested on Rob's shoulder, longer than might be expected of a master comforting his page – too long. Should he tell him? The admission was on the tip of his tongue.

'There is . . .' *something I should tell you.* But he did not. He could not. 'There is more to eat, if you would like it,' he said, and glanced at Rob, conscious that the boy remained tense with hurt.

Rob shook his head.

Kit clasped his hands on the table and listened to John White resume his discourse.

'. . . For pleasantness of situation, the territory of the Chesapeake is not to be excelled . . .'

Kit brought his hands to his brow. He could not do it. Rob was not yet old enough to carry the burden of knowing, far less to maintain a pretence and keep the horror of knowing a secret. How could he begin? *Your mother was beautiful, Ololade was her name: a girl from the Guinea Coast, taken to Panama as a Spanish slave and later freed by runaways – the Cimaroons who freed me. We lived together in the mountains with the outlaws who gave us liberty. She accepted my love and carried my child, a child I never saw, because English ships arrived with my brother; then I sailed back to England and could not take her with me. She told me to go...*

He covered his eyes. The guilt never left him, although, at the time, every step he had taken had seemed part of an inevitable course. When he discovered his brother was with Drake on the ships, there had been no chance to fetch Ololade from the mountains. Even if he had, he could not have brought her to England and expected a black woman to be accepted as his wife. Later he had tried to find her. For years he had searched the Caribbean on every voyage he could make. Then what he finally traced was not her, but their child – his son – and a truth about his mother's fate too terrible to tell him.

He looked at the boy with his thick curling lashes, just like his mother's, and his eyes downturned towards the empty cup he cradled, his skin the colour of honey, glowing over his cheekbones as if lit by a sunset, and his mouth as fine as if tooled by a sculptor and edged by a painter with a brush dipped in milk. He looked for Ololade, and saw her in the boy like a reflection in a pool, floating just under the surface. He wanted to reach out and touch him, put his hand to the boy's chin and feel the shape of his growing bones, ruffle his dark lamb's-wool hair and kiss him firmly on the cheek, then take him by the shoulders and present him to the world: *This is my son in whom I am most pleased, the brightest and best that a father could wish for.* He longed to shout it out: *This is my son,* and he wanted to weep it in an embrace: *My dear son.*

He felt Rob's warmth next to him and put his hand on the table as heavy as a cudgel beside the boy's sensitive fingers. So what could he say? To Rob – Roberto as he had been – Adeolu as his mother had named him. *The woman you thought was your mother is not.* Wouldn't that upset him deeply? The boy had begged to be taken away, thinking that he was being offered a privilege in the chance to see the world in return for serving as a page. Even that soft lie weighed hard. Kit had never told the boy why the kindly people who had raised him had been persuaded to let him go: because they had known Kit from the time he had been one of them and lived wild as a Cimaroon. They remembered him as their leader, the man marked by the Moon, someone they had trusted. The woman had been a *mestizo*, a half blood who was lighter skinned than the Negroes from the Guinea Coast. Rob had never doubted she was his mother. Suppose Rob was told that the good people who had cared for him were not his real parents; then surely he would ask: *So who was my father?* and next: *Why did you leave me?* and then: *Who was my mother?* and: *Where is she now?* Kit rubbed his brow. *What happened to her?* How could he answer that question without leaving the boy distraught? Suppose that he did, how would he and Rob live together then?

He held his head in his hands and became aware, once again, of John White speaking.

'...There can be no greater glory than to bring the savage to civility...'

He looked up at the limner and wondered at those words. 'Civility' was all that he wanted for Rob. That was why he would go to Virginia and do whatever he could to help Governor White's colony. He wanted to find a place for his son where he would not have to labour as a servant or slave, a place where he could build his own future and live as any free man.

He patted Rob on the arm, only the lightest touch. 'Let us get some fresh air.'

Outside, the day was sparkling, but so cold after the inn's warmth that he clenched his teeth to stop them rattling and his breath streamed in a cloud. For an instant, the ale-brush over the doorway cast a shadow like talons over Rob's head, then the boy stepped into the street, and Kit looked along it, seeing fresh carcasses steaming and cuts of meat filmed blue on the shop counters either side. The sound of knives sharpening rang around Eastcheap, the squealing of pigs and the bark of jackdaws; butchers cried out their prices and people shouted and haggled; the smell of offal, shit and woodsmoke hung frozen in the air. In his mouth was the taste of blood, and his feet slipped in muddy pink slush.

He walked to the corner with New Fish Street, and looked down the hill towards London Bridge, its overhanging tall houses crammed above a score of high arches, its piers breaking the water like a row of stone barges; the Thames foamed as it surged beneath. Ships were moored downstream prow to stern all along the north bank. Masts and crane towers bristled over jumbled rooftops. The houses were packed so tightly they seemed piled atop one another, their jetties meeting over dingy alleyways, their twisted chimneys dribbling smoke, while above them the spikes of steeples thrust like needles into the eye of the sky. This was London, wonder of the world, in which people streamed through thoroughfares like ants in a maze of tunnels. Rob stood transfixed but Kit beckoned him on; the boy had seen the bridge before. Kit turned his back and made for Bishop's Gate. Perhaps his years of imprisonment and living wild had made him different from most men, perhaps sailing the high seas had changed him as well, but he could not spend much time in London without longing for open spaces.

They left the city and still the houses sprawled along the rutted Shoreditch road, some half built, only empty timber frames, some no more than cob with chimney holes in sagging roofs. But gradually the outlook broadened until the wind whistled through stark hedgerows across small frost-hardened fields. Striking west along a narrow lane, Kit noticed windmills on the horizon, their vanes half boarded and creaking round, and he felt relaxed enough to respond cheerfully to a man who hailed him from a bare orchard.

'God give you good morrow,' he replied. But when Kit looked more closely he saw the signs of want: a cloak fashioned from sackcloth that afforded scant protection from the cold and wet of flooded, ice-covered fields. A young boy was there too, and it gladdened Kit's heart to see the child offer Rob a whittled stick in return for which Rob took off his cap and gave the boy one of its parrot feathers.

Kit caught the man's eye and stretched his hand towards the blighted fields.

'Would you be interested in a country where you could own land better than this as far as the eye can see?'

'Aye, I'm interested,' the countryman answered, and smiled so hard his eyes were lost in deep creases.

George Howe was his name, a widower and a farmer with nineteen acres of sodden land, and Georgie was his only son. By the end of their conversation, Kit had enlisted Master Howe to the colony. Many more would be needed and there was not much time to find them. Kit took Rob back through Moor Gate and walked with him inside the city walls, into Aldermanbury and down as far as Westcheap. John White would need settlers who were resilient and resourceful, who could make much with little and endure hardship without complaint where better to find them than amongst those who had nothing? He knew about such people; he had been one of them once.

He took Rob towards New Gate where criminals and debtors were kept locked in the towers: ruffians and thieves – and those who didn't deserve to be there.

Along the way he bought food: knotted biscuits, cheese and cold capon pie, all wrapped up in cheesecloth, which he gave Rob to carry. At the prison he offered alms, and passed some of the victuals between the bars of a hatch into the hands of ragged men: about forty desperate, famished wretches who shared a dark room, slept on the bare floor and who pleaded with him to help them.

'Have you any more, master?'

'Please, for pity ...'

'Some for my friend who is sick ...'

'Bless you, kind sir.'

To an able-bodied man who thanked him and asked for nothing else, he promised he would return and pay for his release, if the man was prepared to risk his life and sail with him to the Americas.

The man gripped his hand. 'My name is Jack Tydway. You won't forget me?'

'I won't forget,' Kit said, breathing in the stink of damp and ordure, remembering the cell in the City of Mexico in which he had waited for his execution. The smell brought it all back: the dark, the cold, the hunger and the fear. He had been seventeen years old and he had expected to die, held hostage by the Spaniards before the battle of San Juan de Ulúa, imprisoned after their treachery, and marched to the City of Mexico two hundred miles away over mountains and desert. He had been incarcerated, mocked, starved and beaten; then, instead of being hanged, he had been sold as a slave and toiled until degradation had left him indifferent to life. In all the suffering he had borne and witnessed he was not sure which moment could be singled out as worst, but he had never forgotten the misery of being denied his freedom, waking in darkness, shivering on the floor, and feeling cold walls between himself and the sun. He could offer release from that.

'I'll come back for you,' he murmured. 'I promise.'

Suddenly Jack Tydway was wrenched away, pulled off balance and punched in the stomach. He stumbled and struck back, but men fell on him, raining blows.

A prisoner slammed against the hatch, reaching out between the bars, his hands like claws.

'Take me, not 'im!' He caught at Rob's sleeve. 'Gi'me that, darkie.'

Rob recoiled as the man lunged for the remaining food, but Kit was quicker. He drove his fist onto the man's wrist and slammed his arm onto the hatch sill. With a scream, the man let go.

Rob jumped back clutching the bundle to his chest.

Kit drew the boy aside, leaving Jack Tydway in a brawl that was already petering out, curtailed by famishment and weakness. He gave the gaoler a crown to ensure that Jack Tydway was looked after, with the promise of another if the man was hale when he returned.

Rob followed Kit outside in silence, shoulders hunched, head down. Perhaps the prison had been a shock for him but Kit was glad Rob had seen it. One day he would tell him everything; one day the boy would understand that his father had been locked up in a place far worse, that he was captured as a youth, escaped as a man, and that the experience had shaped him and set him apart. The sound of the door slamming shut sent a shiver down his spine.

He led Rob back into Cheapside, and then across to Christ Church, past the conduit in the marketplace with its broken statues of the Virgin and Child, and its taps wrapped in sackcloth dripping daggers of ice. They passed through the gatehouse of the old Greyfriars' monastery, and Kit saw the way Rob looked about him, taking in the dilapidated cloisters and the vast edifice of the church with its empty niches and broken corbels, and the blanks in its windows where there'd once been coloured glass. What was going through his mind? What did a church mean to Rob who had been brought up believing in demons? He had been baptised, but what did he really think of the places of worship of his new faith, despoiled by reformation, bearing the marks like open scars? Rob looked up at the spire then away towards the sound of children's voices echoing through unseen rooms and empty passages. Did he miss his village friends? He must have felt lonely with no one of his own age to talk to.

After finding the sexton, and offering a donation, Kit was shown around the hospital where five hundred of the city's foundlings and orphans were fed, taught and housed. They walked through a dormitory where boys slept two together in long rows of narrow beds; they saw children at work in classrooms, huddled together on benches, heads bent over hornbooks; and they entered a hall resounding with the clacking of looms at which older boys were being taught how to weave.

'Would you like to start a new life in Virginia?' he asked. 'But consider this before you answer: it will be dangerous and hard and there's a chance you might never come back.'

'I'll go with you,' answered a tall, broad-shouldered lad with a quiff of gingerish hair and a lopsided smile around broken front teeth. 'I'll take the risk.'

'Thomas Humphrey,' said the master in charge, and waved his stick at which the boys instantly fell silent and lowered their eyes. 'Found by Sir Humphrey Gilbert's residence in Limehouse as a babe,' he added in a way that made Kit itch to clap his hand over the man's mouth.

The lad flinched as if slapped then picked at the threads of a tapestry on which he was working.

'I'll come back for him,' Kit said quietly.

Rob tugged at his sleeve and whispered, 'Can't he come with us now?'

Kit shook his head and led Rob away. He wanted to explain that they were guests of Sir Walter at Durham Place and could not presume on his generosity to invite anyone else – and if this lad was taken then where would they stop? Yet stop they would have to, and to prefer some over others would sow the seeds of division. But this was no reasoning for a master to give his page; there was not the time to explain and this was not the place.

'Young Thomas must wait,' he said.

Rob's face fell and, to cheer him up, Kit stopped by an ironmonger's and bought the boy a fine bone-handled knife. He'd need a good blade in the New World where there'd be no means of procuring another. He also bought two ribbons in soft deep blue silk from a pedlar-woman in the street. They'd be for Mistress Fifield, the maiden whose hand he had reached for when he'd last seen her nearly two months ago, though why he had been so forward he could not rightly understand, and her response had been to flinch from him as if he'd given her a fright. He had not meant that; he had been too hasty. Maybe the fervour of the moment had taken hold – hearing the cheering outside Durham Place that day, knowing the voyage to Virginia had won the Queen's approval, that it was almost certain to happen and he would be gone in a few months. Perhaps the prospect of another sailing had triggered some impulse to abandon caution, or maybe he had felt sympathy for the maiden alone in that crowded hall – a woman whom everyone else seemed to have forgotten, though her beauty shone like a beacon. The memory of her filled his mind: her sable hair and dark eyes, and cheeks dimpled by smiling, though he sensed that she no longer smiled as easily as she had done once. He had wanted to plant a kiss on her lovely mouth when she had first smiled at him by the Richmond fountain; then, when her smile had faded, he had wanted to say things to bring it back. But he could not kiss a woman freely just because she attracted him as he had done once. Mistress Fifield was beyond his reach. She might want nothing to do with him. She was one of the Queen's ladies, far above him in station, a lady from whom he would soon be separated by an ocean. So why had he taken her hand? He shouldn't have been so rash; it must have alarmed her and left her confused. When he saw her again he would try to make amends: give her the ribbons as a token against the day when he left, and perhaps, after he was gone, pretty Mistress Fifield would wear them in her hair before the memory of him faded and she forgot him altogether.

Without paying much attention he walked out of the city, down to Fleet Street and along the Strand. He only noticed what was around him when he saw the footmen outside Durham Place with the badge of the royal household on their doublets and cloaks.

He turned to Rob, busy examining his new knife. 'Better put that away; the Queen is here.' He strode up the steps and pushed the ribbons into the pocket on his belt.

At the doors of the hall he handed his pistol to the steward and strode inside while his name was announced. He looked for the Queen, ready to kneel before her; instead he saw Mistress Fifield and stopped in his tracks. His eyes met hers and he could not bring himself to look away. It was as if he'd stumbled upon a deer in a glade, one looking straight back at him, uncertain and wary. He was enthralled by her face, the graceful arch of her brows and her liquid, questioning eyes. He took in the sweet dimples in her cheeks, her fragile, nascent smile, and the sensitivity of her mouth with its slightly protruding upper lip that made her seem both vulnerable and striking. He caught his breath; she was even more beautiful than he remembered.

The voice of the Queen brought him to his senses.

'Mistress Fifield, are you with me?'

He saw the Queen at the far end of the chamber, resplendent in pearl-studded satin and a stiff lace ruff that framed her impassive face.

Mistress Emme turned and hurried towards her. 'Yes, Your Majesty. I am here.'

'Good,' the Queen replied. 'I had begun to fear you were lost in another country.'

A wave of muted laughter followed.

Kit tightened his jaw, and watched Emme curtsey low and bow her head until fine wisps of hair became visible at the nape of her slender neck. He glanced down feeling that he should not have noticed, hooked his thumbs in his belt, and felt the weightless change in shape caused by the ribbons in his pocket.

*

All the way down from the tower on the hill at Greenwich Palace the slope was blanketed white. The Queen and her party had ridden up from the east so the snow was untouched: a soft sparkling coverlet that reflected all the tints of winter light from quartz-pink to gold, while deep blue shadows set off the oaks in lapis filigree and transformed the deer trails to tiny opal-studded chains. The prospect was so inviting Emme wanted to give her mare a kick, gallop down ahead of everyone and be the first to mark the drifts. But she kept the reins tight and sat motionless on her side-saddle. The Queen and Sir Walter Raleigh were together in front, the hawk was still hovering and the other ladies had not caught up.

The Queen smiled as she glanced from Sir Walter to the hawk which suddenly plummeted from the sky. With a whoop she raced ahead, and Sir Walter spurred his stallion until they charged neck and neck, hurtling down the hill to the place where the hawk had caught a crow. Let them enjoy the sport together, Emme would not intrude; only when the other ladies trotted near did she give her mount her head and relish a moment of freedom, flying downhill through the freezing air with snowflakes stinging her cheeks and nose. She opened her mouth to the snow, let it melt on her tongue – this was the taste of release, the kind of sensation that Emme Murimuth would enjoy, the woman she would become if she ever left for Virginia. She would be brave and bold, free of shame or restriction. She was a Murimuth in blood, she could call herself one truly. The family had settled in her village over two hundred years ago; as a Murimuth she would be fearless and sail across the ocean. In a flurry of white she galloped into the panorama that unfolded before her, with the Thames like a silver snake slithering across from the horizon, and the towers of the palace glowing red in the sun. The lawns of the Privy Garden were a patchwork in white silk, while the fields of the Isle of Dogs lay like starched linen in the distance, and the rooftops and city spires bristled like a teasel clogged with fleece.

She was on top of the world, seeing everything open out, before she entered the trees and the prospect closed around her. Then, beyond the edge of the wood, she saw the black crow fluttering its last, and the master falconer with the hawk already feeding from his glove, and the Queen close to Sir Walter patting her gelding's steaming neck. Fine snow swirled around them while they spoke in low voices, and Sir Walter must have said something witty because the Queen tipped back her head and gave a light carefree laugh.

Emme rode behind them to the Inner Court in a clatter of hooves over fresh-brushed cobbles, and she was pleased to receive a summons to the Presence Chamber as she alighted. Perhaps Secretary Walsingham had won the permission she longed for and the Queen was about to announce that she could join the settlers bound for Virginia. Why else would Her Majesty want to see her? And if the Queen had given her assent then her father would not dare object. Her way to the New World would be clear. Emme felt as if the jesses that had held her were loosening at her feet; she might soon be leaving. She peeled off her gloves and cloak and hurried to the royal lodgings, but the expressions that greeted her as she was ushered before the Queen made her sink into a curtsey from which she dropped to her knees and hardly dared look up.

The Queen sat flanked by Sir Walter Raleigh and Secretary Walsingham, and the countenances of all three were as cold as blue ice. Only the glow of Sir Walter's cheeks remained to hint at the ride that he and the Queen had enjoyed. With no more than a slight gesture the Queen bade Emme raise her head, and her gaze had the sting of lye as she searched Emme's face.

A shiver of fear ran like quicksilver down Emme's spine. Had the Queen heard the rumours and now believed she was shamed?

The Queen left her kneeling and continued to regard her with a penetrating stare.

'We have received reports which put us in mind to sanction a fresh endeavour with the object of establishing a permanent colony of our realm in a place to be known as the City of Raleigh.'

Emme's blood raced again; the Queen was speaking of Virginia after all. Emme noticed Sir Walter's mouth twitch towards a smile at the mention of the city's name. His hands rested on his knees, one of which was half covered by the voluptuous folds of the Queen's skirts. The Queen blinked slowly, and she must have moved her head a little because the pearls trembled on the jewelled band that had been placed over her auburn wig.

'The Governor and Assistants of this colony have already been determined, and a hundred of our good subjects are desirous of joining this enterprise, which number is likely to rise as the opportunities become better known, so I am told.'

Emme's eyes widened as she hung on the Queen's words. Was she about to be given her freedom?

'Yes,' she murmured under her breath.

'I see you are familiar with these plans.' The Queen's scrutiny held her transfixed as she waited for the nod which Emme felt bound to give.

'Yes, Your Grace,' she said.

'I would like to know why I should consent to your leaving my service in order to accompany this venture.' The Queen inclined her head. 'Well?'

Emme looked from her to Secretary Walsingham, hoping for

some clue as to how she should respond. Would enthusiasm for leaving the Queen's service be considered a betrayal? Her Majesty was notoriously jealous, and vengeful against those she thought disloyal. If Emme showed that she wanted to join the colonists, would the Queen condemn her as perfidious? Had she already decided to refuse her permission and was this now a test that might lead to her dismissal? Or did Her Majesty want to be sure about the strength of her resolve? What had Walsingham said and how had the Queen replied? If only she knew. But the Secretary of State's demeanour gave nothing away. He sat with his hands clasped solemnly in his lap, and looked straight back at her with his dark-ringed hooded eyes, and not a hint of encouragement on his tight-drawn lips or the set of his lantern jaw.

'I wish only to serve Your Majesty,' she began. 'With your leave, I could sail to the New World and report back faithfully on everything I observe. By this means you could have unique insight into the establishment of the colony and the reality of life for an Englishwoman in Virginia. If you have any special instructions, I could carry them out without anyone knowing that I served you...'

'How would they not know?' The Queen's fingers drummed over the arms of her chair. 'I understand that several of those involved in the venture have already seen you in my retinue.'

Emme shot Secretary Walsingham an anxious glance. He turned to the Queen and spoke softly.

'Master John White has been introduced to Mistress Fifield and the same is true of Mariner Christopher Doonan, one of Drake's men, and the Indian, Manteo. These three have seen her at Richmond Palace and Durham Place, but I think they may be trusted to be discreet. They have already proved their loyalty. They need be told no more than that Mistress Fifield has been tasked by Sir Walter to accompany the colonists and account to him for the prospects of settling families in Virginia. Measures could then be taken to ensure that no connection is made in the general perception between Mistress Fifield and her service to you. If anyone else leaving for Virginia has seen Mistress Fifield in your company they would be unlikely to remember or make the association.'

The Queen waved her hand. 'What measures do you mean?'

'She could assume another identity. I believe she has given the matter some thought.' He turned to Emme and raised his arched brows.

Emme closed her eyes briefly, drawing on her inner fortitude to answer with strength.

'I could travel under my old family name and dress like a good-wife's maid. I would be content to serve one of the families who have volunteered to go.'

Secretary Walsingham gave a nod. 'The Governor's family will have need of a maid. John White's daughter will sail with him and she is expecting her first child; she is married to one of the chosen Assistants.'

The Queen looked hard at Emme. 'This service would be very different from the singing and dancing you have been used to per-forming for me.'

Emme clasped her hands and stood rigid. She must not demur and reveal that she considered her service for the Queen likely to prove far harder than anything expected of her by the colonists. 'I would be content to do it, nonetheless. I would work diligently in this role for Sir Walter's endeavour which has so much inspired me.'

'She could return within six months,' Walsingham interjected.

'Master Ferdinando will sail the flagship back once the settlers are established and Mistress Fifield could leave with him. The report she provides might be of use to you and Sir Walter in determining your future policy regarding colonies in America. To act on knowledge is always better than to act on conjecture, and she could help ensure you have a breadth of information about Virginia.'

Emme did not protest. Any contradiction from her might jeopardise her chance of winning the assent she needed, and the Queen seemed caught on the cusp of reaching a decision – she turned to Sir Walter. Emme noticed the flash of affinity shoot between them as their eyes met; she tried not to think of their legs brushing together under the spread of the Queen's dress. She looked at Sir Walter's white silk netherstocks, barely marked by the ride in the snow, then her eyes travelled to the silver-embroidered canions over his powerful thighs, and the line of silver buttons down his broad-shouldered doublet. He cut a dashing figure, and his clothes must have been worth a fortune, but still she did not consider him as handsome as Mariner Kit, not that Kit would give her a second thought now. She watched Sir Walter lean forwards and heard the promise of the New World in his voice.

'A report from a lady could be useful; I am sure Master Harriot would be pleased to have it, as would others who share our objectives. I envisage that our colony in Virginia will lay the foundations for the establishment of English dominions across the world.' His eyes shone as he looked at the Queen. 'We must garner as much knowledge as we can about the experiences of our first settlers. Any information that Mistress Fifield gathers could be invaluable in encouraging other women to venture after her...'

With a small quick motion, the Queen squeezed Sir Walter's hand while smiling benignly as if to take the sting from her interruption.

'I think we are agreed upon the principle, but why you, Mistress Fifield? What impels you to risk losing everything including your life on this voyage?' She turned back to Sir Walter, and the look she gave him suggested that she understood perfectly well and that she would have taken such a gamble for his sake if she could. But would that make her want to deny Emme the kind of chance she could never have?

The Queen inclined her head to Secretary Walsingham, though he kept silent and looked sombrely back at Emme. What had he said? Had he passed on his suspicion that Emme wished to join the expedition because of one 'particular' man, as he had suggested at their last meeting? Or had he hinted that there might be other, darker, reasons for Emme wishing to join the voyage? How should she answer?

'My desire is only to serve Your Majesty and take part in this historic endeavour which should prove a lasting monument to the glory of your reign and to God.'

'Ha!' The Queen gave a sharp derisive laugh, but she looked pleased, then her face transformed to the same forbidding cast that had greeted Emme on her arrival. 'I do not believe you.'

Emme shivered. Her dissembling had been misjudged and now she would pay the price. She lowered her head.

'I am Your Majesty's humble handmaid.'

'Look at me,' the Queen commanded, and Emme obeyed, taking in the tired blue watery eyes that she rarely ever truly saw.

The Queen held out her hand.

'Kiss my hand. Go on this voyage with my blessing. Return to me at the earliest opportunity and report to me alone on everything you observe. Tell no one what you learn and keep secret your service to me. God be with you.'

Heart thumping, too overwhelmed to speak, Emme rose, curtseyed and kissed the Queen's jewelled fingers.

'When will you leave?' the Queen asked.

What could she say? She did not know. She only knew she was leaving. The Queen had said she could go.

'As soon as possible in the New Year,' Sir Walter answered.

Emme's response to all three was a radiant smile.

# 5

# *Great Waters*

'They that go down to the sea in ships and occupy their business in great waters; these see the works of the Lord, and his wonders in the deep.'

—*Psalm 107, verses 23 and 24, quoted by Richard Hakluyt the younger in his epistle to* A Discourse of Western Planting *of 1584, or 'Certain reasons to induce Her Majesty and the State to take in hand the western voyage and the planting therein', addressed to Sir Francis Walsingham at the request and direction of Walter Raleigh*

## Plymouth, England
### *May 1587*

Kit gripped the iron ring knocker and gave a sharp rap. He stepped back and looked up at the lady carved into the arched doorhead. 'Mistress Fortune', Will called her, and from the abundance of diamond-leaded glass in the windows to the gilded sign hanging over the merchant's shop, there was the evidence that Mistress Fortune had looked after his brother well. This new house in Notte Street was one of the finest in Plymouth, rising to three jettied storeys, close studded and slate tiled, with an oriel window overlooking the street and an entry leading to a courtyard with a warehouse and stables beyond. It was the kind of house he could have lived in if he'd settled down like Will after his first great adventure and the long journey that had taken him to Mexico and imprisonment, slavery and life as a runaway, and a return from Panama in Drake's company with his pockets full of Spanish gold. But the lure of the sea had eaten into him, the searching and the yearning, and in the thirteen years since he'd never stayed long enough on land to put down roots in bricks and mortar. The spirit of what might have been seemed to rush out and pass through him like a puff of aether, leaving him staring at Will's door for most likely the last time. The sound of yapping came from inside, then the rattle of a latch before the door swung open, a spaniel pup twined around his legs, a steward beckoned him in, and Will strode forwards with his arms held wide.

'Kit!'

Kit returned his brother's powerful embrace, then took in the changes in Will's face as they pulled back a little, still gripping one another's arms. His brother's eyes glittered from deep-weathered slits, and Kit saw the lines, bumps and blemishes that made Will's skin seem boot-worn, and the way his cheekbones stood out, and the sharp angles of his long jaw. Had time marked his own face as emphatically? Kit had not seen Will since before he'd left for the Indies, and his image of Will after any long absence always reverted to how he'd looked on their first voyage: thick-haired and bronze-skinned with a broad flashing smile. The smile was still there, the confidence and the strength, but Kit saw other qualities too: pride and fulfilment, and when Will turned at the approach of his wife, Kit recognised the source. Ellyn carried a babe in her arms, and the joy in life shone from her as intensely as on the day he'd first seen her, when they'd rescued her from the Spaniards and Will had asked her to marry him. She, too, had aged; there was delicate silvering in her once-rich brown hair, and her dark eyes, still pretty, bore the marks of happiness in crow's feet wrinkles. The affection with which she looked from Will to her baby sent a pang through Kit's heart, as did the way she crooked her finger for the infant to suck when the babe gave a snuffling cry.

'A third child?' he asked.

'Yes,' Ellyn answered. 'This is Alice, your new niece.'

'Nick and Moll are well?'

'They are as full of mischief as young fox cubs and thankfully now at school.'

Kit bent to kiss Alice, inhaling her sweet baby smell as his lips brushed her cheek. Then he looked back at Will.

'You have a moment to talk?'

'Always, for you; come on in.'

The steward made to close the door but Kit stopped him.

'I have something to fetch from the wagon back there.' Kit jerked a thumb towards the wagon waiting in the street.

'Let's bring it in, whatever it is.'

Will walked out, his steward at his heels, and the waggoner jumped down to open the tailgate. At the sight of the sea chest inside, Will's eyes widened with a smile. 'You are staying?'

'Leaving,' Kit answered, reaching to take hold of one of the great iron rings, deciding to say nothing more until he and Will had some privacy. Together they bore the weight and, grunting and gasping, hauled the chest inside and set it down in the store behind the shop, out of sight of the street window. Kit gave the waggoner a ha'penny and waved the man away, while Will ushered out the servants who had gathered round to watch, and Ellyn left gracefully after giving Kit a kiss.

Kit looked round at an array of cloth of all kinds that represented the business Will had taken over when he had married into the Cooksley family, along with samples of caulked planking showing Will's former craft, and a display of singular artefacts collected over two generations of trading. There were ginger roots and figurines, dried pungent tobacco leaves, the skin of a colossal snake and the carapace of a giant turtle. Hanging on the wall was a parchment map of the Americas and a curve-bladed Barbary scimitar, while on a table covered with an oriental carpet was a silver bowl filled with cinnamon sticks and an old brass astrolabe. Kit's attention settled on the astrolabe. Harriot had devised better ways of navigating with the latest quadrants and his own charts, and he'd instructed Kit carefully along with all the ships' officers in the latest developments in the art. They were well prepared, but that did not mean the voyage would be easy.

'I am sailing for Virginia tomorrow as Boatswain aboard the *Lion*; I may not be coming back.'

Will looked down at Kit's sea chest with its great studded bands.

'I have heard of this. The word has been out for weeks that the next ships for Virginia will be in need of men.'

'That's why we're here – to take on more mariners.'

'You are sailing with Simon Ferdinando?'

'Yes.'

'He has a poor reputation.'

'He is trusted by Sir Walter Raleigh, who has given his backing to the venture. Our mission is to establish a new colony in the Bay of Chesapeake, to be known as the City of Raleigh, under the governorship of John White.'

Will looked straight at Kit with blue eyes that drilled for the truth.

'I thought Ferdinando's ships were set to return to England within the year?'

'Yes, but not with me. I mean to join John White as one of his Planters – that's what the settlers are called. I'll stay in Virginia.'

'That's why you've brought this?' Will touched the chest with his shoe.

'It is.'

Will put his hands on his hips and bent his head, brow furrowed.

'It's late to be setting sail for North America, into May already, and with two months' voyage ahead at least. By the time you've revictualled in the West Indies and sailed north of Florida there may be hurricanes blowing.'

Kit settled to an easier stance, legs astride. 'We've been held up by delays in provisioning and getting everyone aboard.' He shot Will a tight smile. 'Town dwellers don't understand that tide, wind and current will wait for no one.'

'And you've had a stay at the Isle of Wight to pick up men newly released from Colchester gaol, so I've heard.'

Kit tensed. How had Will found that out?

'News travels fast.'

'Amongst seamen it does.' Will raised a brow. 'Do you have confidence in your fellow colonists?'

Kit sucked in air between his teeth and clenched his jaw.

'Freed prisoners can make excellent venturers, so can the dispossessed and homeless and anyone else down on luck. Everyone deserves a chance to start again if they've fallen into difficulties.

Would you deny that charity?'

His eyes burned as he looked at Will, but his brother regarded him calmly.

'Some might call such recruiting desperate.'

'There are good men and women amongst the Planters: decent, sober, hard-working, God-fearing people.'

'Women?'

Kit checked himself before rushing on. As ever with his older brother, he felt that Will was out to constrain him with reason, and he was halfway to resisting before he'd even thought through why. No one else had such a hold over him. But he was a seasoned campaigner, one of the few to have sailed around the world, a leader and hero to some; he could look Will in the eye.

'Yes, there are women amongst the Planters, seventeen to be exact out of just over a hundred in total.'

'Not many to found a city.'

'Enough. We have families and we have children; they are the key. They will ensure the new life that will perpetuate the colony into the future.'

Will rubbed his chin.

'Perhaps a woman is the reason for your . . .'

'No.' Kit cut him short with a denial that sounded too loud. 'No,' he repeated softly. 'That's not the reason. There is no woman.'

He thought of Emme Fifield who was travelling with the White family as Mistress Murimuth and whose true identity Secretary Walsingham had made him swear an oath to keep secret. If there was 'a woman' it would be her, but now he knew her real status it was clear he should forget her, except as a passenger he was bound to protect with his life: one of the Queen's ladies who had to be returned safely back to England. Emme Murimuth would not be staying in Virginia; she would be gone from his life in just a few months.

He sat down on the chest and clasped his hands. Should he tell Will about Rob? He wanted to. He *ought* to. Will was his brother. Someone should know.

'There is…' He bowed his head. How could he start? '…I have a son.'

Will rushed over to him and pummelled his shoulders.

'A son! God in Hell, Kit. Why didn't you say so before?' Will pulled up a stool and clapped his arm around Kit's back. 'I'm an uncle at last! Can I see him? Where is he?'

'Aboard the *Lion*.'

'Well, bring him here! Who's his mother? Have you married without telling anyone, you rogue?'

Will's ebullience washed over him, until his silence led to a quietening and Will spoke more gently.

'Tell me.'

'His name is Rob. His mother was Ololade, the Cimaroon I left when I found you in Panama…You remember I told you about her. She was my woman when I lived as an outlaw. I searched for her for years, then on my last voyage I found out she was dead. She had been murdered by the Spaniards but her son had survived. I brought him back with me. I knew he was mine.'

Will shook his head. 'I am sorry for your loss.'

'Ololade and I were as good as man and wife.'

'I remember you talking about her, though it was a long time ago. Rob must be…'

'Thirteen: old enough to pass for my page without anyone

suspecting that he is really my son.' Kit breathed deeply. 'He does not even know it himself. He looks...'

Will inclined his head, frowning. 'Different, I suppose.'

'Different, yes. His colour is like this.' Kit picked up one of the cinnamon sticks and cradled it in his palm. 'And he is fine boned and slight of build, not at all like me; no one would guess our affinity. He travels by the name of Rob Little.' Kit put back the stick. 'I want to find a place where he can hold his head up high and I can call him my son with pride without anyone singling him out as a blackamoor and a bastard.'

'Virginia.'

He nodded, glad that Will understood.

'But Virginia might not be a haven for either you or your boy. It's a raw, untamed land filled with savages liable to turn hostile. Roanoke was abandoned, wasn't it?'

'It's been reoccupied since. Sir Walter's supply ship reached the island only a few days after we'd left with General Lane and his men – that ship turned straight back on finding no one there. Then Sir Richard Grenville's relief expedition arrived not long afterwards.' He smiled grimly. 'The efforts to help Roanoke seem to have amounted to a series of near misses. Sir Richard was loath to leave his entire company of over three hundred men on the island when what had happened to the previous garrison remained a puzzle and a mystery. He arrived back at Durham House in January to tell Sir Walter all about his shock on finding Roanoke deserted. Sir Richard left fifteen men behind to hold the fort under the command of a seasoned officer by the name of Coffin.'

Will smiled grimly. 'Hardly auspicious – and it's a pity Grenville didn't leave more. Fifteen men will be a poor match against the hundreds of savages in the region.'

'We have allies, and the reports of animosity are probably exaggerated. One of the native leaders, Manteo, travels with us as a friend; a kindlier man you could not imagine. The reports of starvation and attacks have come from General Lane and his soldiers who've been keen to justify their conduct in leaving their post. In any event, we're not heading for Roanoke but for the Bay of Chesapeake about eighty miles further north. The natives there are friendly and the land has more promise.'

'You are sure of this.'

'John White avers it. He is taking his daughter and her husband, and his daughter is heavy with child. Would he do that if he believed the region was dangerous? He has described it as a paradise.'

Will looked down at the chest. 'So you don't need this?'

'No. Everything I need is aboard the *Lion* and the flyboat that carries supplies for us, and that's mostly victuals, tools and seeds. I've no need of treasure.'

'Spoken like a Cimaroon.'

Kit smiled back at him. 'Perhaps, in my heart, that is what I have become.'

'There's gold and silver in that chest?' Will grinned. 'It felt heavy enough.'

'And gems and pearls: the booty from thirteen years of privateering with Drake.' He clasped the heavy key he wore on a thong around his neck and slipped it over his head. He placed the key in Will's hand. 'I'd like you to use what's in the chest to buy a house in Plymouth, one with a garden and a view of the sea.'

Will gave a nod. 'I'll do that for you, Kit.'

'Buy the house and use it. If I don't return in five years then the house will be yours.'

'It'll be yours when you come back.'

Kit shook his head and stood, then Will rose too and clasped him in a great hug.

He hugged Will back as hard as he could.

'Goodbye, Will. Don't expect to see me again.'

*

The boom of the ship's guns sent another shudder through the deck and a shiver down Emme's spine. In the aftermath came a faint peal of bells from the chapel on Plymouth Hoe, though whether in acknowledgement or by coincidence, Emme could not rightly tell; their final leave-taking had been quiet, with only a small crowd of well-wishers to bid them God speed. Even so, Emme waved her kerchief madly, leaning out from the *Lion*'s bulwarks, though they were already too far into the Sound for her to see anyone clearly ashore, and she knew nobody in Plymouth anyway. All she could make out were the huddled houses fading from view behind the cliffs, and the round castle towers, and the green hump of St Nicholas Island receding bit by bit. She waved to no one and everyone: all the people she had ever known, her country and her past, while around her were men, women and children all calling, waving and crying their own farewells. A trumpet blared, gulls mewed and the chanting of men at the capstan gave way to ragged shouts as mariners scrambled up ratlines to unfurl the sails and hauled together to tighten the sheets. Pennants rippled, sails opened out, the wind caught and filled, and the ship blossomed white. Looking up, she felt dizzy, seeing the crow's nest atop the mainmast swaying high above her, and the shadows of men balanced on ropes under the yards, while sunshine streamed behind billowing canvas until the sails were set in majestic petal curves. Gradually the wild whip-cracking of sail-cloth was replaced by the settled creak of cable and timbers, and the slap and swoosh of waves against the bows. The *Lion* settled into an easier rhythm, released at last into open water, and Emme felt a power rising through her from deep within the ship, moving in harmony with wind and sea, a power that awed her.

This was the moment from which there would be no going back. After weeks of buffeting close to the shore they were finally sailing from England for good. The wind picked up, blowing sweet from the land; she braced against the roll and pitch of the ship, and fixed her eyes on the only thing she could look at which was not blinding bright or in constant motion: the flat horizon, empty to the south-west – their destination and her future. She tasted salt on her lips, wiped spray and tears from her cheeks, then turned into the breeze for a last look at England.

The coast was a rolling line of reddish cliffs and steep green coombs scooped out into bay after bay that disappeared into a white-hazed distance. The tiny hermitage on Rame Head seemed to remain no further away, only slide up and down with the heave of the ship. But Emme knew the land was slipping from her just as surely as she was being borne from everything she'd ever known, with just one chest of possessions, roped down on the deck below, and wave upon wave of memories breaking over her to wash up on the dwindling shore, conscious that the traces she had left behind would fade like footprints before the tide. She was leaving her old self behind. Emme Fifield was as good as dead. Emme Murimuth was who she must become. 'Emme Merrymoth' as she had been enlisted: an incongruous name for a person who felt like weeping with a heart as heavy as lead. No one aboard really knew her old self, apart from Master Kit who had only known a part of it. What had she done? She had destroyed her past.

She pictured the manor house at Fifield and the visit she had paid her father to say her last goodbye. He had thought the voyage would bring her back and had been happy to bless her on her way, proud that she journeyed with the special dispensation of the Queen. She had kept from him the ugly rumours circulating about her at court and her resolve to remain in Virginia once she arrived there in the New World. Though her childhood had been blighted by his cold-ness after her mother's death, yet she was sorry to mislead him. He would never see her again.

Fifield had rarely looked more beautiful, with flowers festooning the hedgerows and the orchards thick with blossom; the scent of summer promise was in every bud and shoot. Down the lanes and pathways she saw fleeting episodes from her early years overlaid upon one another as if rising up to hold her back: visions of skipping in the courtyard over honeyed Cotswold stone; rolling the pall-mall ball down the passage by the kitchen; burrowing with a kitten into sweet fresh-mown hay; running through the ford until her petti-coats were soaked; finding secret places in which she would never be discovered – she saw them as if anew – in the long grass behind the fallen-down sty and under the ox cart so long unused that old man's beard grew like a curtain from its sides. Little remained, and what did seemed much smaller, yet the power of her recollections was stronger than ever.

She returned in her thoughts to Broughton Castle where she had stayed as a young maiden in the charge of Lady Fiennes. She remem-bered the scented roses in the knot garden glistening with dew, and the autumn mist rising like smoke from the moat, hearing the bells chiming in the village, and a maid singing 'Sweet Robin' beyond a half-open door. The essence of England was in the memories that span through her mind: dancing around the maypole, watching mummers at Christmas, sharing the wassail bowl on Twelfth Night with laughter ringing around her and spiced cider warming her mouth. Even her visions of London were poignant, despite being shadowed by her shame with Lord Hertford and her betrayal by Bess whom she had considered her friend.

At least she could now understand what had induced the unkindness, and she could try to forgive. It all seemed so much made of little now she was leaving everyone behind. Bess had been upbraided by Lady Howard for making eyes at Sir Walter, and she thought Emme had been the cause by claiming that Sir Walter had left her moonstruck. So Bess had told Lady Howard about Emme's secret and the potential scandal involving Lord Hertford. Lady Howard had then spread worse rumours in an effort to protect the Earl, and Emme had suffered more because of the lady's misplaced jealousy. O, to be breaking free from all that! Emme savoured the cleansing of the wild wind on her face, glad to have escaped the web of intrigue at court. She thought of happier times, picturing the magnificence of St Paul's and the Great Hall at Hampton Court, the royal barge drifting by Whitehall and the Queen galloping through Richmond Park. They were all receding from her, the good and the bad. The swell and suck of the waves confirmed it; there would be no going back.

But she was not alone, and the future that awaited her was as open as the sea, so full of excitement that she felt a tingle to her toes. Her life was starting afresh and everything was changing. The companions who would share her journey were brave and determined, even if they came from a strange mix of backgrounds. She felt Eleanor Dare close by her: the Governor's daughter, now her mistress, who clung to the rail with bilious desperation. Mistress Dare was so far advanced in pregnancy she found it hard to keep balance against the roll of the deck. What courage must it have taken to embark on the voyage in such a state? She was a woman who had to cope with an inconstant husband and a visionary father, yet she was loyal to them both with absolute commitment. Her man, Ananias, had his arm around her, but his eyes were on young Maggie Lawrence, the prettiest of the serving wenches. From the silk-doubleted gentleman who styled himself 'Esquire', to the one-eyed gaolbird who could not speak without vilely cursing, through craftsmen and yeomen, a lawyer and jeweller, labourers and artisans whose names were not yet familiar, they were a mismatched band united in ambition – to begin a new life. It was an ambition she shared.

Many of the colonists looked wan and queasy, were visibly shaking and unsteady on their feet, but everyone was on deck, and Emme could feel the exhilaration all around her, their fears and melancholy tempered by eagerness and hope.

'There goes England,' someone murmured.

Emme heard her mistress sniffle and blow her nose; she glanced round and saw Ananias Dare offer comfort, taking his wife into his arms. At the same time she noticed Kit Doonan on the upper deck, standing by the mizzen mast with Master Ferdinando. Mariner Kit had hardly acknowledged her since the *Lion* had left London docks, but there he was, looking towards her: arms akimbo and legs astride, eyes narrowed against the glare, his hair wind-tousled and his tanned skin glowing. As Boatswain he seemed to control every action of the crew and to have settled into his natural element once the ship set sail. He moved at ease under way with lithe agility, and ordered the men in their duties with unforced authority. Perhaps he would remain in Virginia with the colonists; he had once spoken to her as if he shared that objective. Maybe she would get a chance to know him better, though he had seemed disinterested in her since she had shied away from him at Durham Place. More than likely he'd heard the rumours about her and considered her tainted. He wouldn't wish to take her hand again. She wiped at her hands and drew them down her skirts as if even the thought had dirtied her; then she turned from him in confusion.

It was a momentary upset and her spirits soon rose. The mariners began singing to help with their hauling, and she watched them intently, listening to their bass voices melding together in rough harmony.

Away we go to sea, to sea.
Heigh! Lay a hold, heave ho!

The singing swelled in unison, the bo'sun's whistle sounded, Mariner Kit gave commands at the end of each verse, and the Planters joined in with the chanting. She saw smiles breaking across tear-stained faces and felt a bond of comradeship taking root. They would all be in this adventure in a small space for a long while: nearly two hundred souls, including officers and crew, aboard a three-masted barque of a hundred and twenty tons, with a deck that, at its widest, she could cross in six paces. She hoped they'd help one another with forbearance and goodwill; there'd be no room for dissent.

Fresh orders broke into her thoughts:

'Set course due west.'

'To starboard, beam reach.'

She saw Master Ferdinando address the first mate, and signal to Master Kit who had moved to the second deck.

The whistle sounded again, and then she heard Kit's soft but powerful voice.

'Haul home the lateen. Yare! Sheet home.'

Mariners rushed about. Some took hold of cable and heaved together, others scrambled up the rigging.

The *Lion* was turning, she could feel it. The deck tipped and she reached for the rail. Settlers swayed and staggered while sailors dodged around them. Kit continued to conduct every action of the crew, until Master Ferdinando came down to the main deck and weaved through the passengers towards Governor White. The singing stopped.

Ferdinando's tone was so strident that everyone amidships could hear him.

'Your settlers are an impediment to the sailing of this ship, sir. You must send them below immediately.'

Emme felt the sting of the instruction, and Kit must have picked it up too; she stole a glance at him and saw he was standing motion-less, watching intently.

Ferdinando raised his chin and regarded John White with an air of supercilious indifference. However the Governor might protest, the ship's Master appeared in no mood to listen. He looked down his aquiline nose in a way that made Emme think of King Herod in one of the huge palace tapestries. He was clad in a showy red doublet, all swarthy foreign arrogance with his tight black curls and haughty mien. He squared his shoulders and put his hand on his belt.

'But-t,' John White blustered, 'this will not be for long, I trust?' He pushed his unruly hair back under his hat then held it on with one hand. 'We need fresh air and the chance of a little exercise...'

Ferdinando waved the Governor away. 'You will all remain below for as long as is necessary. I will let you know when you may come up – perhaps tomorrow after day break, for half an hour between watches.'

*Tomorrow... Between watches?* Would she be cooped up for almost a full day in the damp stinking dark with not enough room for everyone to even roll out a blanket? Then would she be sent back after less than an hour in the light?

She spoke up. 'Surely you cannot expect your passengers to remain below for most of the voyage, Master Ferdinando?'

'Mistress Murimuth!' Governor White hissed at her in a way that made plain he considered her intervention inappropriate.

Ferdinando slowly turned to her and raised a sleek eyebrow.

'I expect the passengers not to be a hindrance, madam, and I do not expect to be questioned by maids.'

This was the man whom Secretary Walsingham suspected of being a Spanish agent. She could believe it; he was duplicitous in his manners and clearly unconcerned about the welfare of those he carried aboard. She took an instant dislike to him.

Governor White flapped his free hand about. 'This seems an unreasonable demand, if I may say so, Master Ferdinando. I have not known adventurers confined below on previous expeditions. When I sailed with Generals Grenville and Lane...'

'You sailed with soldiers,' Ferdinando cut him short, 'not an ill-disciplined gaggle of town-dwellers. Now if you do not get your people below without delay then I will have anyone left in my sight put in the pinnace and sent straight back to Plymouth. That includes you, Master White.'

The Governor jumped back, red faced. 'By God, sir! Save your breath. I shall order the Planters out of your way – and speak more with you later.'

He turned to the settlers and raised his voice to a shout. 'The ship's Master requests that we all go down below decks for a while. Please return to your quarters.'

He ushered his daughter to the hatch and Master Kit nimbly sprang to help her: a gallant gesture since Mistress Dare was hampered by her pregnancy, but it fell far short of the remonstration with Ferdinando that Emme was hoping for from Kit. She hung back behind the crowd while the rest of the settlers filed below, a process that took many minutes since not everyone was in the prime of health, and there was at least one other goodwife heavy with child, and some with babes in arms, together with men like Ananias Dare who seemed more interested in fondling the rumps of wenches than in descending with any speed.

Emme kept her eyes on Ferdinando and followed him as soon as he moved, climbing to the forecastle top deck with a view over the bowsprit as it languidly dipped and rose in a continuous rolling cycle. She held tight to the rail.

He turned to her. 'Still here, Mistress Murimuth? Shall I summon Captain Stafford in the pinnace and have him take you ashore? He is over there, do you see?' He pointed to a little two-masted vessel that sailed alongside, even smaller than the flyboat that carried the bulk of their provisions which was also nearby. Both craft seemed barely adequate for an ocean crossing.

She matched his knowing smile. 'No, Master Ferdinando, I have no wish to go back, nor to stay below with the chickens and rats.' She checked the urge to reproach him and smiled more demurely. 'I appreciate your concern for us, but I can see no reason why I and others who are fit and eager to see as much as possible on this voyage should not, at their own risk, be allowed to remain above decks if they wish. We would exercise due caution and obey your instructions.'

'Indeed? I am pleased to hear that you are prepared for obedience; that is a good way to start. Yet you question my judgement and that is irksome.'

He moved closer to her, and her impulse to preserve a distance between them caused her to step back, sliding her hand along the gunwale, until her hips were pressed against the stanchions in the corner. She leant away from him and felt something hard digging into her back, something that made her flinch, until she groped behind her and felt cold metal, then looked across and saw the long barrel of a swivel gun on the bulwark the other side.

He looked amused and moved in front of her. 'You see no reason why you should not be on deck. You do not see the danger?'

He leaned towards her and she arched back against the gun casing, aware of the pivot pressing under her shoulder blades. He was too close – close enough for her to see the black pores on his shaved jaw and the glistening black bristles overhanging his upper lip. Her eyes flicked back towards the waist of the ship and, as if he anticipated where she meant to move, he put his hand on the gunwale to the side, hemming her in. She began to slide the other way and he put his free hand atop the forward rail, trapping her in the corner. She shivered, heart jumping like a firework; this was how Lord Hertford had begun, pinning her between his arms.

She must get away. Keep him back. Scream. Her mouth opened to the streaming air, but this man was in command of the ship: what would he do if she did? He could have her locked in the hold. He must believe her to be no more than a wench, the kind of woman with whom a ship's officer might make sport. She leant further away until only her hold upon the stanchions stopped her toppling into the waves. She would try to make little of his behaviour, though fear for what he might do sent her into a cold sweat.

'I am sure we are all safe with you, Master Ferdinando. The sea would not dare to misbehave.'

'Ah, but she does, frequently. She is always dangerous.'

He moved so close that she felt the hardness of his legs through her dress. She jerked back, trying to keep her face away from his, and the heave of the ship almost knocked her off her feet. Suddenly he bent right over and pulled loose her hands. His weight pushed her further, tipping her over the gunwale with the ridge of the rail under the small of her back. He held her arms by the wrists, and the yaw of the ship sent her plunging down towards the sea while the far side of the forward deck rose up above her. Her muscles locked in terror. Nausea engulfed her. Her whole body recoiled. The next instant he let go of her, and she lurched in horror, diving forwards then away from him. He grabbed her just as she was about to fall over the side.

Chuckling, he pulled her upright and stepped smartly back.

'You should be below where you are safe, Mistress Murimuth.'

She seized hold of the gunwale again, shivering, too shocked to speak. Did he think nearly killing her was a game? She itched to slap the smirk from his face, but even that idea made her queasy. Down on the main deck she noticed Kit by the hatch, looking her way. What had he seen? She leant over and gasped for breath. Glancing round, she saw Master Ferdinando staring at her looking both intrigued and entertained. She began to edge clear of him, leaning well away, and in passing contrived to slip and kick the scoundrel in the shin.

'*Deus!*' He rubbed his leg and scowled at her.

'I apologise, sir, but blame the motion of the sea.' She smiled back prettily. 'She can never be predicted.'

She took care to control her shaking. The thought of slapping him had revolted her, but she could hit him with her shoe without any qualms at all.

*

With a splintering crack like the jaws of Hell snapping bone, the ship crashed down into the trough and Emme's shoulder hit the bulwark. She felt the *Lion* rise up again, borne at a sickening tilt on a wave that seemed to reach mountain height, though she could see nothing of it in the pitch darkness below decks, only feel the jarring and grinding of the timbers around her and the remorseless accelerating motion which her whole body strained to escape. A scream welled up within her while the screams of others tore at her ears, and amidst that she could hear retching from Eleanor Dare beside her. Emme's knee struck something hard, then came the inexorable stomach-lurching pivot and the blind panic of weightlessness as the ship toppled over the crest and she felt herself fall. The hull plummeted down and all that was rolling within it: people, animals, sprung barrels and splintering chests, tackle, armaments and provisions. The keel smacked into another depression, like a deep gorge between towering peaks, and Emme collided with struts and planking. She clung to anything solid she could grope for: skin-burning rope, the iron cleats, rings and hooks to which things were tied that were not being smashed to pieces. She curled into a ball to protect her limbs, tried not to gag on the stink of vomit and closed her sleep-starved eyes.

Would the ship sink and take her with it? They had only been sailing for a few weeks and already death seemed to be clawing for her. Couldn't she have longer? Dear God, give her longer – a chance at least to glimpse the New World she had dreamt of. Tears brimmed under her lids, but she screwed her eyes shut and pushed the heels of her hands against them. She would not weep.

'Lord, have mercy,' Eleanor Dare wailed. 'We're going to die.'

'Take heart, mistress,' Emme murmured. 'The storm will pass.'

They were both clinging blindly to the same pillar. She drew back and a coil of rope swung into her as she bumped her head on a wooden brace. The ship climbed another wave and Mistress Dare retched again.

'I cannot keep hold. I feel faint, as if I'm turning inside out.'

'You're not.'

'My baby . . .'

'Your baby is in the safest place. Here, this might help.' Emme half rose, crouching under the low ceiling-deck, grasped at the rope and passed it around the pillar. She fumbled with the ends until she had the rope tied fast and looped securely below the lady's bulge and over a blanket to ease the friction.

'You can let go now,' she said. 'The rope will hold you.'

The ship slid from another wave top, creaking as if it was tearing apart, gathering speed as it plunged.

'Let us pray,' John White exhorted. 'Thou rulest the raging of the sea: when the waves arise, thou stillest them . . .'

In the blackness voices joined him, fearful and quavering.

Emme slipped away on hands and knees, grasping at angled riders and heaps of lashed-down possessions, edging past huddled passengers, though she couldn't help being thrown against some of them. She searched for steps leading up and found a set eventually below a hatch streaming with water. She unlatched the thing and knocked it open, then fell down with the next plunge and took a cold drenching. As the ship climbed once more she shimmied up, crawled out and slammed the hatch closed behind her.

The sky was light, not the inky night she had expected. The sun was lost behind thick grey cloud, but there was a yellow glow near the horizon enough to give the spuming white caps a sulphurous gleam and make the skin of the great wave ahead shine as if it was alive and sweating. It rose up sheer, carrying the *Lion* like a mite on its back. She lunged for the nearest rail and seized hold of it with hands so painfully cold she could barely grip. Rain stung her face, lashing her hair into her eyes. Salt air scoured her mouth and streamed like sleet into her lungs, scrubbing her throat raw. The ship yawed and she slid sprawling across the deck, tipped one side then the other until she thudded against the stanchions. Clutching tight and looking up she saw men wrestling with halyards and sheets, moving like beetles in their baggy tarred clothes. Two of the sails were in tatters, flapping in shreds from odd angled spars; most were loose furled. Only one, high on the foremast, was open and bulging like a wine skin about to burst. Someone came near her: a man with a wool cap pulled low over his brow, a broad jaw and sculpted mouth that showed flashing teeth as he spoke.

'Please go back below, at least until the storm has eased.'

She recognised Master Kit, and flinched back on impulse when he held out his hand to her. Though she longed to take hold of him, she could not make herself do it. She appealed to him with her eyes.

'We'll be safe?'

'Yes. We'll weather this out. Storms in the Bay of Biscay aren't unusual.'

'How much longer will this last?'

He smiled at her, and she realised he could not possibly know.

'I think we're over the worst,' he said.

'What of the other ships?' She scanned the heaving waters beyond the rail, spotting the little pinnace bobbing nearby like a leaf caught on a mill race, though still intact, the gleam of a sail showing near one of her two masts. But where was the supply boat?

'I can only see the pinnace.'

Kit pointed to larboard. 'Captain Spicer is having trouble.'

She saw the flyboat at last, barely more than a speck in the distance, almost swallowed by the seething waves each time they took the ship down between them. 'Is something wrong?'

Kit grimaced. 'The boat's lost her main-yard.'

A shout cut into the wind, a bellowing thick with Iberian accent.

'Master Bo'sun, get to your station. Whichever wench is with you, send her below this instant.'

She turned to see Master Ferdinando looking down on them from the poop deck. He pointed towards the bow.

'Tighten the top foresail. We'll race before the wind.'

Kit frowned. 'Shouldn't we ride bare poles and wait for Captain Spicer?'

'I'll be the judge of what action to take. We've already lost too much time in waiting. Do it.'

'The expedition will fail without those provisions, Master Ferdinando.'

'You'll obey my order, Bo'sun. Sheet home and make way.'

'Aye, Master.'

Kit turned and blew his whistle, sending the men to the winches to set taut the only sail, a puny harness with which to ride a wild demon.

A wave smashed clean over the gunwale, sluicing down Emme's back. The ship pitched and Emme lost her balance, stumbling over and sliding across the deck, cracking her head on the hatch cover before finishing up below the deadeyes the other side. She pulled herself up unsteadily. The wind froze her to the marrow, shrieking around the rigging and dragging at her clothes. Doubling over, she clutched her sides, then a strong arm encircled her waist, and she sensed Kit's body shielding her from the storm again. She fought the urge to push him away. She tensed, breathing fast.

Kit helped her back towards the hatch.

'Are you all right?'

She nodded, though she felt wretched.

He stooped and opened the cover.

'Go down now and get dry.'

'Yes. Thank you.'

'I'll let you know when the gale is spent.'

'But Captain Spicer...?'

'He'll catch up with us. Don't worry.'

The bellowing of the ship's Master ripped towards them through the wind.

'Why is that doxy still here?'

The heads of the crew turned towards Emme.

She glared back at him.

'I am no doxy, sir.'

Ferdinando called out to her. 'I'll have you chained up below, Mistress Murimuth. Be gone with you.'

Kit answered him, 'She was just about to go back down, Master.' He helped her to the ladder.

'Best be quick.'

She slumped to the wet floor, enveloped in fetid blackness once more, aware of hands reaching out for her and Eleanor Dare's reed-broken voice close by.

'What did you see? Are we sinking? Is there hope?'

Emme collected herself, determined to show a brave face. It would not help the others if she went to pieces.

'We're not sinking. The Boatswain has been through far worse and he's confident the *Lion* will carry us through. We're sailing out of the storm now. The seas are rough but I could see a little sunlight which must mean the clouds are thinning.'

Mistress Dare tugged at her sodden cloak. 'We will survive?'

'Yes,' Emme said.

'Praise be,' John White muttered over and over. 'Praise be.'

People hugged her beyond caring about propriety, the Governor's daughter amongst them. She could feel the hard roundness of the lady's pregnancy as her mistress embraced her, and smell the rancid stench of the lady's sickness and a trace of the sweet rosewater she used to try and disguise it: a residue of English gentility. How long would that last? How much longer would the journey take? Weeks, she knew: at least six more weeks of subsistence in the tiny cabins below deck, cramped dark and noisome; weeks of playing the maid and attending to her mistress's intimate needs when keeping anything clean was nigh impossible, of scrubbing with sand and emptying slops in the scuppers; of eating salt beef and weevil-ridden biscuit; of bruises and sickness, no heat and poor light, and constant discomfort in damp clothes and blankets; of confinement closer than a prison within the regime of the ship's bell – hours of sleeplessness punctuated by hours of boredom when not in fear of imminent death in sudden storms. They could yet drown at sea but in her heart she did not believe it.

'We'll survive,' she said, and felt sure they would as she spoke. Master Kit was with them and he had sailed around the world with Drake.

# 6

# *First Landing*

'The 22— We came to anchor at an Isle, called Santa Cruz, where all the planters were set on land...At our first landing on this Island, some of our women, and men, by eating a small fruit, like green apples, were fearfully troubled with a sudden burning in their mouths...'

> —*The entry describing the first landfall after crossing the Atlantic, from John White's Narrative of his 1587 Voyage to Virginia to which Richard Hakluyt the younger added a marginal note: 'Circumspection to be used in strange places.'*

## St Croix, the Virgin Islands
### *June 1587*

'Welcome to paradise: the Island of the Sacred Cross, discovered by Columbus on his second voyage to the New World.'

Master Ferdinando held out his hand for Emme as she climbed down the rope ladder. The little boat below floated on limpid azure water above white sand and coral that she could see clearly, right down to the bottom. The bay around her was vibrant with colour, teaming with scintillating fish, dappled by sparkling sunlight in a tireless gentle dance. She looked across to the beach and saw a ribbon of silver fringed by palms. The land beyond rose in ruched folds to distant low mountains thickly cloaked in lush verdure, and as she wondered at the life within, a string of parrots flew noisily over the shore. The scent of foliage carried on the languid breeze; she could taste it on her dry tongue and savour it as she breathed: the promise of release, fresh food and clean water. Her legs felt like jelly but her spirits were soaring. She had reached the Americas. She had arrived. After more than six weeks of sailing in stinking cramped confinement she had survived to relish this: an island garden of delight. She clambered down too quickly and almost fell onto the passengers already aboard the lighter.

'Take care, Mistress Murimuth,' Ferdinando called after her. 'I've brought you safely across the ocean and would hate to lose you to a mishap now.'

The mariners at the stern of the boat chuckled, lowered their oars and prepared to row. An excited hubbub rose from the Planters around her.

John White doffed his hat and waved it. 'See the idyll that awaits us. Let us rejoice and enjoy God's greeting.'

Ferdinando raised his hat too.

'Go blithely, sir.'

Governor White cocked his grizzled head. 'Didn't Columbus encounter some hostility from the natives here?'

Ferdinando waved airily. 'The Caribs are long gone, annihilated by the Spanish. You have nothing to fear. There is no one to trouble you here.'

Governor White almost smiled back at him, though that was checked to a twitch of the lips. His resentment of Ferdinando's bullying command at sea had been obvious throughout the voyage, made worse after the flyboat had been abandoned in the Bay of Biscay, a decision that the Governor openly stated to be wrong to everyone but the crew and Ferdinando. Perhaps now the rift between them could begin to heal since the worst perils of the crossing were over; Emme hoped so. Let there be a fresh start in peace. This place was too beautiful for grievances.

'Make way together,' Master Kit called from the helm. 'At my word: *Pull*.'

The oarsmen hauled in unison, the boat moved from the *Lion*, and when Emme looked at Kit he grinned at her.

'Alleluia!' someone cried. 'Landfall!' Soon all the Planters in the boat had taken up the shout, Emme included. She couldn't wait to get ashore, and before the lighter had been beached she clambered out with the other passengers to wade, laughing and splashing, through the warm shallows to the scorching sand. She staggered and dropped to her knees, lying amongst flotsam and the soaked folds of her skirts. She picked up fistfuls of tiny bleached shells and tossed them childlike into the air, then dug her fingers in the heaps of coral fragments, shining white against the reddened backs of her hands.

Governor White gave orders that no one appeared eager to heed: directions for building cabins, collecting water and gathering food. Many of the colonists who had arrived with Emme were wandering into the undergrowth, rustling through dry leaves and around giant roots and branches. Mistress Dare flopped down in the shade and seemed ready to fall asleep, while her husband sauntered over to Maggie Lawrence who was paddling at the water's edge with her petticoats up to her knees.

'We will have a shelter here,' said the Governor, dragging a broken palm frond to a washed-up tree trunk, though no one else paid much attention.

'Look 'ere!' a man yelled. 'Tortoises as big as cows. Come an' help me kill one.'

A shot rang out from another direction and Emme supposed one of the Planters was firing at some game fit to eat. They ought to have a feast that night. Should she make a fire for cooking? What should she do first? Whatever the answer, she felt it didn't much matter; everything would be well. She saw Kit walking towards her and stood happily, but his expression was not nearly as cheerful as she had expected. Behind Kit trooped his page and a few other mariners. She wished they hadn't come too.

'There's a pool over there,' he said gravely, pointing behind the next inlet where mangroves grew densely, spreading in islets out to sea. 'But the water is foul. Don't drink it. And don't eat anything until I get back.'

She regarded him askance. Why shouldn't she eat or drink without his permission? Just because he said so was a poor reason. She was desperate to slake her thirst and enjoy some unsalted food, and she was past caring where it came from.

'I wouldn't drink bad water whether you were with me or not. Where are you going?'

'To find water that's fit to drink.'

She noticed the skins slung over his shoulder.

'I'll leave Rob with you,' he said.

'There's no need. I have enough company.' She gestured to all the people who were milling about under the palms, a swelling number since the lighter had returned with another boatload of passengers.

128

'Rob will remain here,' Kit said firmly. 'Stay with him until I return, and try and rest. Activity will only worsen your thirst.'

'Relaxation is exactly what I have in mind.' She forced a smile though she felt like snapping back. It was not his place to dictate to her, and she would be the judge of her own thirst. Gone was the respectful friendship she had hoped would grow between them once they were on land. Had the rumours made him think she was worthless? He seemed little better than Ferdinando in flaunting an assumption of authority. But in the Americas she would choose who she answered to, even if Kit Doonan did look like a Greek hero with his long fair hair and his muscles showing all too clearly under his thin loose shirt. Looks weren't everything. She wouldn't humble herself for him.

'I hope your foraging is productive,' she said, and watched him leave with his little band of mariners trailing behind.

She took a deep breath, leant back against a palm bole and half closed her eyes.

'Mistress Murimuth, come and share a toast with me.'

She looked up to see Master Ferdinando standing over her with a straw-padded bottle in his hand and a lascivious glint to his eye. He held up the bottle. 'You have made the crossing without causing me too much trouble. I believe you have earned the privilege.'

He ran his hand around the straw jacket and winked at her. 'Spanish aqua vitae: a choice beverage that we might savour from that vantage point over there.' He pointed to a rocky outcrop a few hundred feet away. 'The place commands a fine view and an assurance of privacy. After the rigours of the voyage I would like to offer you some reward.'

She flicked at a tiny insect that was nipping at her cheek and considered his attentions no more welcome. She stood up and brushed the sand off her skirts.

'Thank you, Master Ferdinando, but I have work to do. I should not have been resting.' She watched one black eyebrow rise and his breezy smile give way to a knowing leer.

'As you wish, my dear. No doubt Ananias Dare is a hard task-master. But I think you may be confident of your position and not fear his displeasure. You must be a very special maid.' He eyed her beadily. 'I have a request from Sir Francis Walsingham to bring you with me back to England.' He cocked his head. 'I wonder why...? I think we should become better acquainted.'

He nodded to her and strode off in the direction of Maggie Lawrence who was recumbent on the beach, airing her petticoats like a giant daisy.

She hoped the wench enjoyed the brandy because it would cost her a high price – one that Emme was not prepared to pay. She glanced over her shoulder and noticed Kit's page at a distance. Rob could not have heard what Ferdinando had said, but the boy would have noticed the gentleman in conversation with her. What did Ferdinando hope to achieve? She pushed the most base possibility from her mind. His brashness had unsettled her. She had expected more circumspection from him given that Walsingham must have charged him with ensuring her safety. If he was an agent of Spain, then wouldn't he be wary of provoking any antagonism? Tact and discretion were plainly not Ferdinando's style. She would have to avoid him. Thank God he'd be leaving for England once he had delivered the colonists to Virginia. She chanced another peek at him and saw that he was looking her way. At once she wheeled round and beckoned to the boy.

'Rob, could you walk with me? Master Kit spoke of a pool nearby; I would like to see it. He said it was over there.'

She pointed to the mangroves and began pushing through the vegetation without waiting for the boy to answer. The pool didn't interest her but it was somewhere to go to that was not in the vicinity of the outcrop of rock where Ferdinando and Mistress Lawrence would be admiring the view. She ploughed on, becoming increasingly hot, thirsty and exasperated. The vegetation was almost impenetrable and she had no way of cutting through it, the sand soon gave way to swamp and the ground became a monstrous tangle of roots arching waist-high into the air. Mosquitoes tormented her and her underclothes stuck to her skin. Her dress felt so heavy she longed to rip it off, except that then the insects would be all over her. She had thought she would be alone but she could hear other colonists not far away, crashing through the underwood just like she was, calling to one another in loud voices.

'We should move away from here,' said the boy.

'But where?'

'Come this way, if you please, Mistress.'

The spindly-limbed youth veered up a slope that was even more thickly covered in a labyrinth of foliage, but then the brush began to thin out and Rob helped her up out of the trees to a shallow plateau covered in dry grass and cacti. Towards the centre was a natural basin in which shone the blue of still water, and already drawn to it were a few colonists, squatting and dipping in their hands, drinking and filling their hats, pouring water over their heads and calling for others to join them. The cool sheen of the pool could not have been more inviting; she hurried closer.

'Wait, mistress!' Rob cried after her, running to get in front, though she reached the water first.

She knelt on a coral rock shelf as close to the edge as she could get, rested her hands on the rough stone and peered over to look down. She was on the point of plunging in her face when something stopped her.

The pool had the inky darkness of great depth, and to begin with all she saw in it was a gleaming mirror of the sky, as if seen through sooted glass, with puffy clouds and dazzling sun, and a small reflection of her head at the rim, like an egg on a jagged wall. Then her focus shifted to the floating world below that seemed to emerge as if rising up from a pit. She couldn't see any fish, no turtles or other creatures, but there were strange forms that suggested life: trailing fronds that hung like loose hair, amorphous spongy matter in rich lichen shades of green and orange, and translucent globules in a stringy mesh around splintered pale sticks. Or were they bones? She lowered her head to peer more closely; then jerked back on hands and knees, catching a whiff of an evil miasma that hung just above the surface. She shuffled away, not daring to stand. Her throat flooded with bile and the smell of corruption.

The boy was still calling, 'No!'

Suddenly she heard him.

'Master Kit said you shouldn't drink here,' the boy cried out, putting himself between her and the pool.

'I won't,' she said, standing up and feeling dizzy. Then she looked across to the other colonists by the water, several of whom were coughing and rubbing their faces.

'Don't drink any more!' she called out to them, and pointed at the pool where she'd seen what was submerged. 'I think there's something dead down there.'

She turned and walked away, making for the turquoise blue of the sea by a route that did not involve wading through mangroves, doing her best to warn everyone she saw that the water in the pool was not potable. But her words seemed to fall on deaf ears, and perhaps the curiosity of those she met only heightened their determination to judge for themselves; most of them carried on towards the plateau. Where was Governor White? He should have been taking charge. She trusted that the Planters she had left by the pool would alert those who arrived to the danger. That water should at least be boiled before it was drunk, and even boiling would not induce her to swallow it. As soon as Kit returned she would get him to set up a guard. She wished he was back. How much longer would he be? Her temples throbbed painfully and her thirst was greater than ever. She even considered going back to the ship and begging for some stale barrelled water, but if she did there was a chance she might encounter Ferdinando on her own. She wouldn't risk that. Trudging on, head down, she made for a low ridge of bare rock that seemed to offer the easiest descent to the beach. At the summit were coral boulders, and, where a gap lay between them, she noticed a blackening as if made by fire. She walked closer and stared. At her feet were spiny blade-leaved plants and beyond them, near the rock, were fragments of smooth clay. She picked one up. It was unmistakably a piece from a pot, shaped and crudely patterned. She searched around and found more: the evidence of people, but who and from how long ago? She looked round, half expecting to see the strangers and noticed Rob hovering close. She showed him what she had found.

He nodded gravely. 'Someone else was here.'

'Yes. Perhaps they're still here now.'

With one of the potsherds in her hand, she stumbled down from the ridge, her feet sliding in loose sand and snagged by prickly scrub. She had never before really appreciated how important paths were to traversing land. Whoever had been here before had not left trails of any kind. Did that mean they had been gone for a long time? She thought of the word 'Canibales' as she had once seen it written on a map in the library at Greenwich Palace. Had there been cannibals on the island? She was glad they would not be staying for long, though she began to meet more colonists as she drew closer to the shore and most of them were abuzz with excitement. They fooled around like children chasing after any new wonder that caught their fancy: giant grasshoppers, bobbing honey-breasted birds and scurrying lizards with long harlequin ringed tails. The flowers and fruits they found drew shrieks of amazement.

'See the size of this!' a man shouted out. 'Big as a feckin' dog prick!' He held up an unappetising brown husk like a roasted giant bean pod.

Margery Harvie showed off another find: 'Apples! Green apples.'

As the wife of one of the senior Assistants, she commanded respect enough for the Planters to listen to her. She was also heavily pregnant, and Emme wondered at her wisdom in biting into the fruit, even though she declared it to be 'crisp and sweet as any pippin'.

The response from the colonists was beyond control. They rushed to the tree that Mistress Harvie pointed out, began tearing at its glossy branches and gorging on the white flesh of its fruits which did indeed resemble cooking apples, not that Emme was tempted to try any. What if the fruits concealed evil like the pool? With a sigh of relief she noticed Governor White approaching, and ran up to him at once brandishing the potsherd for him to see.

'I think there are people here, sir, and they have poisoned the pool we have found. The Planters should be cautioned...'

'What's this?' he took the shard and turned it over in his hands. 'Ah, interesting.' He traced the lines and pits of the geometric design scratched over the surface. 'See, the Caribs were not all brutish. There is even evidence of colouring...'

'If you please, sir,' she interrupted him, hearing cries of distress and sounds of choking from those gathered around the tree. She turned and gestured to it, seeing Mistress Harvie bent over, spitting out pith and retching.

'My mouth!' the lady cried, gasping. 'It's burning. Give me water.'

'Over here!' someone shouted, and beckoned for her to go the way Emme had come.

'No!' Emme rushed to stop her. 'You can't drink that water.'

'Get away.' Mistress Harvie barged her aside. 'I must have water. Mush...'

Her speech was becoming slurred. Emme looked on aghast at the size of her lips. Her face was swelling like dough in an oven.

'Zounds!' a man moaned. 'My tongue.' His mouth opened wide and his tongue lolled out, thick as a small cucumber and bright mulberry red. He pelted past her.

'Stop!' Governor White held up his hands, but everyone who had sampled the fruit ran round him towards the plateau. He turned to Emme and spoke curtly, tossing the shard at her feet before turning to follow. 'You should have stopped them.'

'I...?' Her jaw dropped. How could he shift the blame to her? How *could* she have stopped them? No one would listen when she tried to warn them about the pool. What would happen to them now if they drank there? A horrific vision swamped her mind, of colonists driven wild by the burning in their mouths drinking recklessly from the pool and dying in agony. She must prevent it. She turned to Rob.

'Stay here and tell anyone who comes not to eat that fruit.'

Then she hurried towards the pool, cursing the island with every panic-driven step. It was more hell than paradise; she wished they had never set foot in the place. Would Virginia be like this? She ploughed on, not looking back until she heard crashing vegetation and the rip of someone running hard behind her: Kit. There was his voice.

'Emme! Mistress Emme...'

He came racing towards her, back bent under the weight of the full waterskins on his shoulders.

'Are you all right?'

'Yes, but they're not.' She pointed ahead and blurted out what she'd seen. 'Give them water.'

He rushed on with his band of mariners following, all carrying water. There would be enough to help those who'd eaten the fruit. She began to slow. Kit would make sure they only drank what was clean. She took deep breaths. All would be well; she had to believe it. She sensed someone else was coming up behind her and turned round.

Master Ferdinando strode towards her with a look of bemusement on his face.

'I gather some of the Planters have been foolish.'

She scowled at him, disgusted by his apparent lack of concern. 'No one told them the fruit could be harmful.'

Ferdinando shrugged and raised his voice so that Governor White and everyone else gathered by the pool could hear as he approached.

'I cannot be expected to know the qualities of every plant in the Americas. You should have been more prudent.'

Kit paid him no attention but continued to minister to the suffering colonists, helping them flush out their mouths and drink from the heavy waterskins, though their tongues were so swollen that many could barely swallow or speak.

Emme rushed to assist, and Governor White also did his best to give support, kneeling to prop up Mistress Harvie who had slumped down on the grass, holding her head while Kit steadied the spout of the waterskin at her lips.

Ferdinando looked on, arms folded. 'I am surprised Governor White did not advise you to test first before consuming anything unfamiliar.'

White glowered at him. 'You assured us of safety here.'

The response was a sardonic smile. 'You have not been attacked.'

Kit eyed Ferdinando soberly. 'We need fresh water and there's none to be found here that can be easily collected. This water came from a peak several miles away. It won't be enough for everyone and it'll be difficult to collect more. I know of river mouths on other islands that would serve us much better. I'm sure you do too, Master Ferdinando.'

'Of course, but they are guarded by the Spanish.' Ferdinando stared back at Kit and narrowed his eyes. 'Or have you forgotten, Master Bo'sun?'

'I have not forgotten.' Kit moved to another of the afflicted colonists, a lanky, red-faced youth with ginger hair. 'Drink, Tom,' Kit said gently, pouring water over the lad's swollen lips.

Ferdinando raised his chin, speaking to Kit as if he deserved admonition.

'You're not with Drake now, able to strike fear in the hearts of any Spaniards you meet. We've got to hide. If the Spaniards find this gaggle,' he swept his hand to encompass the colonists, 'they'll send every one of them to the bottom of the sea, or clap them in irons to face the Inquisition.' He looked around at everyone listening and seemed to relish their expressions of shock.

Kit moved to the next colonist in need of succour and worked calmly to offer help. When he was ready he spoke to Ferdinando.

'There are savages on this island. We saw about a dozen close to dwelling places in the hills to the west.' He gestured towards green peaks. 'I think we shouldn't stay here any longer.'

'Savages!' White seized on the word, jabbing his finger accusingly at Ferdinando. 'You told us this island was uninhabited.'

Ferdinando raised his eyebrows and turned his back. 'I thought it was.' He stalked away. 'Savages come and go. They generally don't inform me first.'

Emme looked from Governor White, who was plainly seething, to Master Kit, who appeared unperturbed, though the sorry sight of the suffering colonists was enough to melt her heart. A few of them had tried to ease their discomfort by rinsing their mouths and faces with water from the pool. They had eyes so inflamed that they could hardly see, and faces so bloated that they resembled pink puffballs. She knelt down to do her best to help, taking a half empty skin from another mariner and dribbling water on raw skin.

138

Kit crouched down beside her. 'You should drink as well. You must be thirsty.'

She shook her head. She had almost forgotten her thirst. 'Let me see to these people first.'

She moved on amongst the Planters in need of relief; then, to her horror, she saw Mistress Dare in their midst. The lady must have followed the others up from the beach. She didn't seem as badly affected as Mistress Harvie and those who had sampled the fruit, but her lips and cheeks were plainly swollen, and she was dabbing at them and moaning like a cat about to be sick.

Emme went to her mistress next, offering her the water despite the way that she glared as she gulped to ease her pain. Then a tirade from her began between mouthfuls, one made almost incoherent by the distension of her tongue.

'Where were you, wench? You should have been by my shide when I needed you, not off on a fanchy of your own.'

Emme stopped pouring in amazement. Who was Mistress Dare to call her a wench? And how could the lady blame her when she had been doing her best to warn everyone about the pool, and had left the woman dozing in the company of her own father?

Governor White turned to face Emme as well, along with a growing number of those she had tended. The Governor wagged his finger at her.

'You left my daughter in her parlous condition to fend for herself in this alien place? You should be ashamed of yourself.'

Emme gasped with indignation, and shoved the water-skin against her mistress's ample bosom so forcefully that it spurted and soaked the lady's bodice and shift.

'Take it yourself if you do not wish for my help.'

She stood abruptly, intent on walking away just as Kit sprang gallantly to the lady's aid, stripping off his shirt to wipe down her clothes, and giving Emme a steely look of reproach.

'Have some consideration,' he murmured under his breath as she passed him, leaving her stunned with a glimpse of the athletic beauty of his naked chest.

Tears welled in her eyes. Her tongue was parched with unslaked thirst. Her pride smarted from unjust accusations, and she hated everyone at that moment but most of all she hated herself.

She strode on until she was out of view, kicked at a stone and stubbed her toe.

*

They would not stay on Santa Cruz for much longer, Emme felt sure. Captain Stafford had already been despatched to another island, but Master Ferdinando had seen fit to order that the *Lion* remain at anchor while it was cleaned and repaired. So now she had a third night of frustration to look forward to, running errands for Mistress Dare while trying to minimise the discomfort of living under a tent on a beach in sweltering heat, when not being drenched by torrential rain. The work might have been tolerable if she'd received some gratitude for her pains, but no, her mistress was determined to exact retribution for what she'd described as 'behaviour ill-becoming a maid', by which she meant the soaking she'd taken after the incident with the waterskin, and the affront to her dignity compounded by Emme speaking her mind. The woman was a fool to have drunk where the water was not known to be potable, especially in her gravid state, but Emme was not going to be forgiven for having reacted contrarily. She was being punished, she knew, and she was being put in her place, and if she was to preserve her guise as a maidservant then she could not complain. She would have to air her mistress's pallet, and relinquish her own dry blankets in return for her mistress's that were wet, and bring her mistress cooled boiled water and griddled tortoise steaks, and shake sand from her mistress's clothes, and tighten the guy ropes of the flimsy tent whenever the wind got up at night, and fan her mistress with palm leaves in the suffocating heat of the day. When she saw Kit Doonan walking towards her, she threw down the apron she'd been wringing out, not caring that it missed the wash bucket and landed in wet sand. What did he want? Kit had been critical when her composure had failed, and his muttered admonition to 'have some consideration' still rankled. Did *he* have any consideration for *her*?

'I am busy,' she said, putting her hands on her hips and feeling a twinge in her back as she straightened. She looked down at the dirty apron and sighed. She should pick it up and try to wash it again in sea water but it was all so much effort. She flicked back a strand of lank hair from her forehead and scowled at him. He should not even have been looking at her in such a state.

His expression slid from concern to the kind of stern gravitas she associated with being told off. It did not please her.

He retrieved the apron and tossed it into the bucket.

'I am glad to see you are working hard, Mistress Emme. I hope that will help repair your relationship with Mistress Dare. I could see that the lady was upset by your treatment of her earlier; it was ignoble of you to be insensitive to her distress, uncharacteristically so, if I may say. I would have expected better of you. Mistress Dare is pregnant and lacks your acumen; she is also your superior, given the role you have assumed for yourself on this voyage. No maid should be intemperate with her mistress. I trust that, in future while we are all together, you will show more discretion. I counsel this with your own interests at heart.'

She glared at him agape. Who was he to accuse her of being ignoble? She could barely believe what she'd just heard. Did he mean to insult her?

She raised her chin and resisted the urge to walk away.

'May I remind you that I am a baron's daughter and one of the Queen's ladies, and I do not consider it meet for you, a common mariner, to give me advice on my conduct. You forget yourself, Master Doonan. You are, by your own admission, little more than a pirate who has lived as an outlaw with renegade slaves.'

That struck home, she could tell. His eyes blazed like blue fire. She pressed the advantage.

'What makes you think that you are fit to be my judge? How *dare* you?'

He took a step towards her and spoke again, lowering his voice.

'I dare because I care for your welfare, and I am as good a judge as any man who recognises rash conduct when it stares him in the face. If you wish to be deferred to, then you cannot expect to be believed as a maid, and there is more to being a lady than enjoying the courtesy of others; tact and delicacy are other attributes I would expect.'

She felt a prickling down the back of her neck.

'Do you mean to imply that I lack those virtues?'

'Did you show them to your mistress when she was suffering after being poisoned?'

She took a sharp intake of breath, feeling rage rise up within her to the point at which she could have slapped him. But she would not. She was a lady.

'I will not be berated by you, Master Boatswain. If you wish to give a lecture then lecture your page who is too much in awe of you to do other than dumbly obey. I am not.'

At that, she turned her back on him and walked off, though she only managed a few steps before he strode in front of her. He raised his hands and she sprang back, shuddering at the thought that he might have been about to seize hold of her.

'Get away from me,' she hissed.

'I only wish for your wellbeing,' he said, though she felt the heat of his anger in each clipped word.

His lips tightened.

'It will benefit none of us now for your true identity to be revealed. If the Spaniards discover it, the results could be disastrous, most of all for you. At the least it would cause anxiety and division amongst the Planters...'

Was he threatening her? He didn't mean to unmask her, surely?

'You wouldn't...?'

'Of course not,' he gestured dismissively. 'I have sworn to tell no one, and I won't give you away. But you must learn some humility or you'll give away yourself.'

'Pah!'

She stepped aside to move past him.

'I'll not humble myself to *you*. If you truly wish for my wellbeing then I beg you to leave me alone.'

She walked on along the beach, past the place where the Harvies had set up their tent, and she determined to scream if he followed her, but he did not.

She carried on. He was nothing but a knave trying to dominate her, just as every man she had ever known had tried to dominate her, and she wanted no more to do with him.

Once she reached the end of the encampment she turned and retraced her steps. He was nowhere to be seen, thank God.

Henceforth she would avoid him if she possibly could.

*

'Did you see that?'

Kit stared down into the river, past the luminous ripples around the boat and the glowing clouds stirred up by the oars, seeing the depthless black beneath touched by a ghostly light with every movement, and the trails of fish-like streaming sparks, and the bluish yellow gleam fading to a disc under the surface where something had come close to them. Something alive. It had been shining.

He kept to his stroke, pulling hard and steadily. The current was swift and they were rowing upstream. They couldn't afford to ease or take time to marvel.

'As long as it doesn't come up under the boat,' he said.

'Could have been a sea cow,' James Lacy ventured. 'One grown monstrous. I've seen them before around St John's.'

'Keep rowing.'

It could have been a sea cow. What he had seen had seemed to swell up like an enormous mushroom from the deep, trailing bubbles and cold light: a phantasmal leviathan.

'Aren't you worried?' Lacy asked.

'I'm worried about not finding enough water.'

'Aye, that's a bother for sure.'

Lacy's thick Irish accent made the concern seem quite homely.

'We should have more barrels and boats,' he observed.

'I'd like to know how General Lane managed. You were with him, weren't you?'

Kit kept rowing without trying to look over his shoulder; he wouldn't be able to see Lacy anyway, but he was sure he remembered the man as one of those whom Drake had brought back from Virginia the year before. Ferdinando had said that they would follow Lane's route, and this was where he'd taken on water: at Muskito Bay in St John's, as they called the island of Puerto Rico.

'Aye, I served with Lane, was pressed by him in Ireland and stayed with him when he took Sir Richard Grenville's commission to set up the garrison in Virginia. Same with Denis and Darby back there.'

Kit couldn't see either man, but he knew Lacy meant the Irish soldiers who were in one of the boats behind.

'We all signed up together,' Lacy said. 'Been together ever since. Jack was with Lane too.'

Kit thought of John Wright, the Virginia veteran he'd selected for another boat, along with a seasoned mariner he considered strong enough for the work.

'I know; that's why I picked you for this.'

The four soldiers were the only men from the last expedition to join White's voyage, and he'd tasked them all with helping him get in water. They knew what to do, and it was an opportunity to talk to them. He was keen on finding out more about Lane's expedition.

'Tell me how Lane faired here.'

'Lane had Muskito Bay run like a militia camp,' Lacy went on. 'Got a moated fort and great breastworks built within a week. Those defences could have held off an army and lasted ten years if Lane hadn't torn them down.'

'Why did he?'

'Because we had to leave to go to Virginia, for the love of St Patrick, and Lane didn't want to offer the Spaniards a fortress on a plate that could have been used against us if ever we came back.'

'Like we are now,' Kit said, keeping his strokes deep and steady, thinking that collecting water would have been easy with a fort to offer protection, instead of having to creep upriver under cover of darkness against the constant threat of being spotted and attacked.

'We had more men, of course,' Lacy added. 'Hundreds to help dig the defences, fell trees and suchlike. No one had too much to do; not like now,' he muttered.

Lacy cleared his throat and an eerie low cry rippled birdlike over the water above the honking and plinking of the hundreds of frogs hidden in the mangroves.

Kit heard the cry answered and knew that Lacy's friends weren't far away. He stared downstream and thought he saw the faint gleam of their progress.

Lacy gave a grunt of acknowledgement. 'Look at us: six men collecting water for nearly two hundred and as much beer drunk in the meantime by those Planters making merry.' He hauled on the creaking oars and spoke again. 'We're leaving tomorrow, and there'll probably be less water aboard the *Lion* than there was when we arrived.'

'At least the Planters are refreshed,' Kit said, thinking of Mistress Emme's glowing face as she'd watched the sun going down behind the trees that had invaded the earthworks. He could tell she was relieved simply to have set foot again on land, despite the oppressive heat and tormenting insects. He didn't begrudge the Planters a little celebration. If she'd been more civil he would have offered to share a cup with her, but she'd already made it plain she preferred to keep her own company, and his earlier attempt to caution her with well-meant advice had met with the kind of rebuff he should have expected. He wouldn't intervene with her again. It hurt to be shunned by a woman he found attractive, a woman who plainly considered herself above him, but there it was; best to forget her if he could. She was much too haughty for her own good. Why she had come on the voyage was a puzzle; perhaps Raleigh had put her up to it, or possibly the Queen on a whim, or, more likely, the two of them together, thinking that it would be entertaining to hear what one of their own ladies thought of Virginia. But Emme would never make a settler, not with her prickly temperament and skittish behaviour. She'd probably dip her toe in the waters off Chesapeake, watch the Planters beginning the struggle to build their homes, turn up her nose and then sail back, and that would be the last he'd see of her. He wouldn't grieve. But he still cared that she came to no harm.

'I wish them no ill,' he said to Lacy.

The Irishman responded with singsong conviction. 'They'll go hungry afore long. This is no place to find game. The hunting was poor when Lane was here, just the same, the difference being...' He kept his voice low. 'We hadn't lost all our supplies.'

'Captain Spicer may yet find us,' Kit said, picking up on Lacy's concern. The colony would struggle without supplies; it was a worry he'd heard before, but fretting about it would achieve nothing.

'It's a pity Captain Stafford didn't bring back any sheep as the Portugee said he would.'

'You mean Master Ferdinando.'

'The very one, the Portugee whoreson: our Pilot whose assurances I wouldn't trust as far as spit.'

Kit heard the plop of phlegm hitting the water.

'I'd keep that opinion to yourself,' he advised.

'Too late.' Lacy snorted. 'It's already shared. Ask Denis and Darby. No man who served with Lane at Roanoke has any respect for the swine. He's not led us well so far, has he? Abandoned the flyboat with our victuals, set us on an island with savages and foul water, and thus far failed to find anywhere fit for taking on fresh food.'

'There could have been sheep where he sent Stafford. The evidence was there . . .'

'Old droppings,' Lacy cut in. 'He sent Stafford to capture sheep, and all the Captain found was shit.'

Kit pulled up his oars and dipped his hand into the water, watching a hint of light shimmer around his fingers like the palest gauze. The brilliance was gone. The bloom had faded. The water felt cooler, almost cold. It was time to test the river's freshness. Above his head trailed vegetation hanging from branches in ragged arches: trees that weren't mangroves; he couldn't tell exactly what. He felt as if he was floating in a watery maze, a branching gully almost completely overgrown, where the only visible elements were the sheen of the river on which he was drifting, and a strip of starry sky directly above him, crisscrossed by creepers as if in a bower. Had they gone far enough? He scooped up the water and drank.

It tasted clean, not brackish, a bit earthy but that was no surprise, and if he used his teeth as a filter it was really quite good.

'This will serve us,' he said, then plunged in his leather water bottle and drank deeply.

Lacy did the same.

'Let's tie up and get the barrel in. Over there,' Kit whispered, pointing, seeing a place where the shine of the river met a shelving bank in a still line. They needed somewhere to ground the boat so the barrel, once filled, could be hauled aboard safely. But the little river beach was exposed and unfamiliar. Had he been here before? He couldn't recall seeing anything like it during the past two nights of scouting for water. The river channels were a network of convoluted streams, gushing down ravines from steep limestone hills and tunnelling around mangrove islets near the sea in a matrix without clear banks. Would they be able to find the way back? Getting lost was an unspoken fear, greater than ever this night since it would be their last at Muskito Bay. Ferdinando had announced that they would weigh anchor at daybreak, and for once Kit was inclined to agree with his decision. Every day they lingered increased the chance of their discovery; the Spaniards knew the bay had been used by English seafarers before. They could easily be trapped. The water-boats should get back early so the *Lion* could leave undetected. They must be quick.

He looked round for any sign of being watched but there was none, no glimmer of light, or snapping twigs, or tell-tale smell of smouldering matchcord from a musket. Even the frogs had quietened. He beckoned Lacy on and in silence they set to work.

Not until they'd filled the barrel and stowed it, pushed off and got back under the trees did they begin to talk again, and then only in snatches. They put all their energy into rowing hard and getting into the flow, taking advantage of the current to race back downstream. Between strokes Kit listened, straining to hear the sloosh of the other boats amidst the clinking of the frogs, scouring the sheen over the water behind the black curtains of foliage but seeing no trace of movement beyond the shimmering ripples in their wake.

Lacy eased on his oars. 'Should we wait for the others?'

'Just for a moment.'

Kit pulled up his oars and they drifted in an eerie stillness. Then Lacy's haunting cry rang out softly over the water. It was swallowed without answer by the silence.

'Perhaps they've gone another way,' Lacy murmured. 'They could be ahead of us.'

'Aye. Let's carry on.'

They'd been separated before and Kit's instructions were to always keep going if that happened. The veterans wouldn't tarry. He glanced up at the sky and saw cloud drifting over the stars. It was getting darker if anything, without any hint of dawn about to break. That was good. The other boats could well be near the *Lion* by now; he visualised them appearing around the next bend. He set the stroke again.

'What brings you back to the Americas?'

He wanted to settle Lacy as well as hear his story. He could feel the Irishman's unease as much as the chill rising from the water. He'd wrap the question in a little warmth.

'You must have more mettle than most. Few of Lane's men were keen to see Virginia again.'

'There's no finer country,' Lacy answered wistfully. 'As green as Ireland, so it is, but without the bogs.'

Kit chuckled at that.

'Good folk live there too,' Lacy went on. 'It's mainly for them I'm coming back.'

'You mean the Algonkians?'

'Some of them. The ones like your friend, Manteo.'

'If the Virginians are like him they must be fair indeed.'

'I didn't say they were *all* like him.'

'But you took to his tribe: the Croatans?'

'They were kind to us, God knows; at least to me they were . . . I'd like to see them again.'

Lacy was skirting around the question, Kit could tell. He'd have to dig to tease out the truth.

'Them? Or do you mean one of them?'

'Yes, I do, so help me God. There was someone I left behind who meant much to me.'

'A woman?'

'What makes you think that? But yes, 'twas a woman I left...'

Kit breathed out deeply as he hauled again.

'I too left a woman behind once, in Panama, a long time ago. I could never forget. I understand.'

'I thought I'd be able to go back to my old life without her,' Lacy said.

'But you couldn't?'

Kit knew what it was like to try and pick up the pieces of a life. There was never any going back.

'No,' Lacy answered softly. 'I couldn't.'

'What's her name?'

'Alawa.'

'I hope you find Alawa again, Jim.'

'We'll be stopping at Croatoan to take Manteo back to his kind. I aim to find her then and take her with me to Chesapeake.'

'I'll help if I can. Remember that.'

'God bless 'ee, sir.'

'So what White has promised is true? Virginia really is another Eden?' Kit asked the question brightly, though he'd long suspected White of having a rather woolly grasp of material matters. 'In which case,' he went on, 'why did Lane and his officers spread such bad reports about the region? They made Roanoke sound cursed.'

'Perhaps it is,' Lacy replied, grunting as he rowed. 'To be sure things happened there that don't bear dwelling upon. But we're not settling in Roanoke, are we? We're going to Chesapeake where everything's much better.'

'What things happened?' Kit leant back after the next pull and paused for Lacy's answer. He'd had an inkling that something terrible had blighted the last voyage. But what? He needed to know.

'Tell me,' he said.

He looked round and saw Lacy shake his head slowly. The man's stroke faltered then picked up. He hauled fiercely on the oars before he spoke.

'Lane's way was to govern by fear. He believed in showing no weakness and setting examples. It was necessary, he said. But he repaid the Indians poorly for their trust. He...'

The boat tipped violently and rocked back. Cold light burst like a spectral firework around the hull. A dark swelling wave raced towards them from one side.

'Jesus!' Lacy cried, letting his poles fall against the tholes and grabbing hold of the gunwales with both hands.

Kit gripped his oars and leant towards the middle of the boat to try and steady it. Great bubbles rose around them bursting with light. More waves struck. They had to row or capsize, keep the boat moving forwards to stop it tipping.

'Row!' he shouted.

He rowed frantically, struggling to turn the boat into the waves. Water was flooding in; they were rocking too much. With the weight of the barrel aboard, they were already half submerged. He rowed frantically. One of his oars skimmed the surface, sprang clear and beat air. It almost shot from his grip.

Lacy seemed to wake from a stupor and took up the stroke.

They both rowed, breathing hard; they rowed until their backs were breaking. The boat steadied, bobbing on waves that broke harmlessly, slapping against its bows. Whatever had come close to sinking them moved further away, trailing a hazy streamer of thin sulphurous light. Kit watched the lustre fade and then vanish.

Darkness enclosed them. Kit shivered, drenched in spray and sweat.

'Jesus,' Lacy kept repeating. '*Jesus*. By all the saints that ever lived, that was close.' Then almost timidly he asked, 'What do ye think it was?'

'Something big; it doesn't matter. It's gone and we have to get back.'

He glanced up at the sky and saw a dull brown glow above the blackness of the trees, as if the cloud was a blind of leather that had been pulled open a chink.

'Concentrate on rowing. We've got to hurry.'

They were back in the labyrinth of mangroves, and where the branches formed tunnels it felt as though night was still upon them, but as the trees opened out the glimmer of sunlight was plain to see, like molten gold seeping through great rents in the hem of the sky.

'Pull...Pull...'

He quickened the stroke, glanced over his shoulder, and saw the bay beyond the river mouth like a pool of gold leaf, and the ship like a fletch on the arrow-straight horizon, only a furlong from the shore and at anchor as she had been left, though a top sail was uncurling.

'There's the *Lion*. She's waiting.'

'Thank God,' Lacy cried with a crack in his voice. He turned round.

'I can see a boat as well. The others must have overtaken us.'

Kit felt relief wash over him, but he kept on rowing without letting up. As they neared the ship he heard the capstan working and the rhythmic chanting of men weighing anchor, shouts from the rigging and the flapping of canvas: all sounds that told him the *Lion* would soon be making way. A low cheer followed when he got to the hull, secured the water barrel for winching and began the climb to the deck. Then Ferdinando's head and shoulders appeared over the bulwarks.

'Not before time, Master Bo'sun. Get a move on.'

'Are the others back?' he called to Ferdinando, though he could hear some of the passengers jostling to greet him and ask questions.

'Wright's boat is with us,' Ferdinando replied crisply. 'We have enough water now and it's time we were gone.'

Kit carried on climbing.

'What about the two other Irishmen. Are they here?'

Ferdinando turned his back and called to the Quartermaster, giving him orders to stow the water barrel and haul up the boats.

Kit knew it all meant the answer was no. He leapt over the gunwale and onto the deck.

'You can't leave yet. There are two men missing.'

Lacy scrambled after him and almost fell to his knees, reaching towards Ferdinando as he pleaded.

'Darby and Denis are back there. I beg you wait and send help. They could be in trouble. Something monstrous is in the river. It almost took us…'

'Monstrous?'

Ferdinando's eyes widened mockingly as a thrum of unease rose from those looking on; then he waved his hand at Lacy as if to brush an irritation aside.

'Get below or I'll have you flogged.' He turned to Kit. 'Back to your post, Master Bo'sun. I've given the order to set sail. Get this ship under way.'

'No!' Lacy interrupted. 'Master Doonan saw it too: something monstrous. Send out a search-party and I'll go with them...'

'Silence!' Ferdinando snapped his fingers and called for Lacy to be taken away.

The soldier was led down, writhing and protesting, in the grip of the Quartermaster and enough mariners to subdue him. As he was bundled below, he shot Kit a look of entreaty.

Kit turned to Ferdinando and clenched his jaw.

Ferdinando smiled grimly back at him.

'To your post, Master Doonan. My instructions have been plain. We leave at daybreak; that means now. The two who are missing are Irish Papists who were pressed into service by Governor Lane. They've probably run away.'

He turned to John White who was scanning the bay with his hand to his brow.

'Do you wish to jeopardise this expedition by mounting a search for these Irish deserters?'

White frowned and scratched his chin. 'Well, I suppose that might be difficult as well as imprudent, given what we've just heard.' He looked at Kit with a hint of accusation. 'Though it grieves me to think of men being left behind. What if the Spaniards find them? Master Doonan, perhaps you would advise as to what you think might have happened.'

Ferdinando's look darkened and he took a step towards White. 'Nothing happened except that two cowards fled. You're wasting time, Governor.'

White shuffled back a little and his eyes rolled towards Kit. 'Nonetheless, I should like to hear from Master Doonan.'

Kit sensed the whole ship's company was looking at him: mariners, soldiers and passengers – all waiting for an answer; a decision; a show of defiance or submission, some resolution to the tension between the Governor and the *Lion's* Master – an outcome that would allay their fears. Their questions rose in whispers like the buzzing of unsettled bees.

'What was monstrous?'

'What will we do?'

'Should we stay any longer?'

He noticed Mistress Emme watching him with a look of tense concern, and the Governor, frowning, glancing from him back to the sea. What would be gained by sowing more anxiety? They were in greater danger every moment that passed, especially now with the ship clear of shelter, though, God knows, the plight of the missing men was worse.

'Nothing happened,' he said. Then he squinted up to the crow's nest and looked across to Ferdinando. 'By your leave, Master, let us hear from the lookout.'

Ferdinando gave a nod. 'See to it.'

Kit called up, and the boy in the tops cried down.

'All clear!'

Kit exchanged a look with Ferdinando and knew there was nothing more to be done. He gave the orders to get the ship out of the bay while he continued to scour the river mouth for any sign of the men. There was none. He hung his head.

Then he sensed someone approach – Mistress Emme; he saw her when he raised his eyes.

'I am glad you are safe,' she said and smiled shyly.

The greeting was meant kindly; he felt it and reached out to her on impulse, grateful for her small show of support.

But then she drew back as if his shadow had burnt her.

# 7

# *Valiant Courage*

'...Only be you of valiant courage and faint not, as the Lord said unto Joshua, exhorting him to proceed on forward in the conquest of the land of promise; and remember that private men have happily wielded and waded through as great enterprises as this, with lesser means than those which God in his mercy hath bountifully bestowed upon you, to the singular good, as I assure myself, of this our Commonwealth...'

*From Richard Hakluyt the younger's epistle dedicatory to Sir Walter Raleigh, in his 1587 translation into English of René de Laudonnière's* Notable History, *urging Raleigh to proceed with his ambition to found an English colony in Virginia*

'We're lost, aren't we?'

Emme edged closer to Master Kit, keeping one hand on the gunwale so the roll of the ship would not dislodge her. In the other hand she carried a crock of pottage, sealed with a cork bung and still hot enough for her to feel the heat against her knuckles. She held the crock out to him.

'Something to warm you,' she said, hoping he would accept it despite the breach that had opened up between them. Kit might be overbearing and too cocksure of himself, but he'd been on deck for hours navigating the *Lion* through the stormy night and he must also be tired and hungry. She had brought food to the rest of the watch and it seemed unfair to exclude him, despite the fact that he still hadn't apologised for the offence he had caused her with his unjust chiding. But she could forgive him for the moment. Whether he would appreciate her goodwill was another matter; she wouldn't let that bother her. She wanted him to see the sort of person she really was, and that she certainly was not so proud as to be uncaring.

'The crew have all had some,' she said, anxious that he wouldn't think she was showing him any special favour.

He tucked away the instrument he had been looking at, and took the crock from her with a smile she could only guess at from the brief gleam of his teeth.

'Thank you.' He pulled out the stopper and inhaled deeply. 'Turtle pottage?'

'How did you know?'

She let out a small chuckle and felt him near her, as solid and comforting as an oak in a storm, and warm like a cloak of fur that in another life she might have snuggled up to, though of course she would not, and had no desire to do anything of the sort.

'Have you any idea where we are?' she asked, not really expecting him to say he did. Master Ferdinando had admitted he had been mistaken about the location of their last anchorage, and if the ship's Pilot did not know where they were, it was hardly likely that the Master Boatswain would know better.

'I think we're not far from Roanoke, don't worry.'

159

'But I do, I can't help it.'

'Is that why you're here? Couldn't you sleep?'

She hesitated, wondering whether to admit her apprehension, and then decided that she would, though it meant revealing a weakness and breaking her previous resolution to have nothing more to do with Master Kit. He must be lonely, staring at the starry sky in silence for hours on end. She would show him she could be compassionate.

'I kept thinking that the ship was going to strike a reef and I'd have only minutes to get Mistress Dare up on deck and then there wouldn't be enough room for everyone on the boats. We'd be doomed, anyway, wouldn't we?' She faltered to a pause. 'If the *Lion* was wrecked, we'd never get to Chesapeake...I can't swim,' she added, and choked back a little noise that she didn't mean to make at all, a kind of sob that she tried to turn into a laugh because she would not give way to the deep terror that was gnawing at her.

He offered her the crock. 'Have some yourself. It will do you good.'

She shook her head, and pushed it gently back, keeping her fingers away from his.

'Try not to fret,' he said. 'I expect the soundings disturbed your dreams.'

One of the leadsmen by the chains called the depth, his voice straining against the wind: 'By the mark, seven.'

Kit drank quietly from the crock.

The cool wind gusting from the north carried the faint smell of marsh and cedars. They were not far from land, but was it the wilderness around Roanaoke or somewhere more desolate?

Another call came from the darkness.

'By the deep, six.'

She could picture them: leaning out to throw down their plummets, balanced on the chain plates at the side of the hull, one hand clinging to a shroud, the other pulling up the line and feeling for the leather discs that marked the fathoms. But she could not see any of it.

She tried to read Kit's face and made out only a shadow under the stars.

'What do the soundings tell you?'

'That there's plenty of sea beneath us, at least for now.'

'But that could change in an instant.'

'It could. We could find the inlet to Roanoke Sound and a few days after that we could be on our way to Chesapeake. It's probably only a week away now.'

'Another week,' she said, and felt her heart sinking. When Ferdinando had announced mistakenly that they'd reached Croatoan, she had thought the long voyage would soon be over. That was four days ago.

Kit bent to tuck the empty crock into the netting behind the bulwark.

'You've been at sea nearly three months. I'm sure you can bear another week on this ship. Or is the company so terrible?'

'No.' She sensed he was trying to cheer her, and she smiled because he would not be able to see it. 'Some of the company I have found very congenial,' she said, making an effort to better his drollery, 'even if latterly rather over-assertive and opinionated...'

'Over-assertive and opinionated? You must mean Master Ferdinando.'

'I most certainly do not!' She put him right instantly, appalled

161

at the notion of valuing Ferdinando's oleaginous company, and the next moment regretting that she'd ever been drawn into an exchange of banter. Now Kit might suppose that she was encouraging him with quips when in fact she meant no such thing since he had not yet atoned for his rudeness.

A leadsman called again. 'By the mark, five.'

Kit looked round. She could see his head snapping back, suddenly tense and alert, his face upturned to the stars, then moving slowly down as if scanning the lightless shoreline and wide open sea. The waves beat against the side of the ship, and the roll was as great as she'd ever known it, though she felt they were moving no faster than a ponderous walk. The bleak black dunes that edged the coast like ragged braid seemed to ripple along as if trailing behind a mourner.

Kit gripped the gunwale and looked over the side. He gave a shout to the helm.

'East by nor-east.'

'East by nor-east,' the helmsman repeated, and the wind flurried the few sails that had been set as the *Lion* changed her bearings.

She imagined the sea bed sliding beneath them and hidden danger up ahead: some reef or shoal. Why else had they turned?

'Is Master Ferdinando not here?' she asked.

'He's below decks this watch.'

She was relieved but did not say so.

He reached into his pocket and took out the instrument she had seen him looking at before, like a fat metal disc that nestled in his palm: a miniature astrolabe. She recognised it from those she had seen in the royal palaces, and the one with which Ferdinando took readings from the sun most days. Was it usual for a Boatswain to have such a thing? She did not see how it could be any use without the almanacs and charts that Ferdinando kept in his cabin.

He held the instrument to the stars, squinting through the sighting pins and turning the tiny spindle.

She tugged lightly at his sleeve. She could do that without any qualms: touch a man by his clothes. She did not like to seek Kit's attention, but for once she sensed an opportunity to talk in private and he seemed prepared to listen despite their past altercation.

He lowered the astrolabe, and she faced him. There were things she felt Kit should know, concerns that she could not keep to herself any longer.

'Governor White thinks that Master Ferdinando is intent on destroying us all. He has said so to Ananias Dare in front of me. He says "our Simon" is an agent of the devil and that he'll lead us into oblivion if he doesn't run the ship aground first.'

Kit gave a sigh that sounded as if he was bottling up his exasperation.

'White should be more careful with his remarks. What benefit is there in whipping up anxiety? I'm sorry he has upset you. Has he voiced these concerns to anyone else?'

'Not as far as I know.'

'And you've not repeated them?'

She bowed her head.

'Only to you.'

'Good.'

He hunched his shoulders and turned away.

She stood beside him and stared into the darkness, seeing nothing but the gleam of the ocean below the sparkling stars, and the stern lantern of the little pinnace, like a firefly hovering at a distance, seeming to wink on and off with the rise and fall of the swell. Then another wave struck abeam and she almost lost her footing.

Kit steadied her, and she started, only to find that she could bear his arms around her so long as his face was away from hers and he did not try to grasp her hands, but then his hold loosened and he took a step back. Why did he do that? It left her strangely disappointed. Though she did not want him to hold her, his desire to do so was reassuring. But perhaps he no longer sought the kind of intimate contact with her he had done once, such as the time when he had tried to hold her hand at Durham Place. She felt both more at ease with him and more perplexed. Was he interested in her any longer?

'What will become of us?' she whispered. 'It is not only the Governor's fears that trouble me, but my own. Consider everything that has happened . . .'

She took a breath, wanting to pour out all the worries that had brought her close to despair, and talk of the seeds of mistrust that Walsingham had planted in her mind, because if Ferdinando was really an agent for Spain then the colonists were probably doomed, she could see that now, and all the setbacks that had so far dogged the voyage seemed only to confirm this was so. Yet how could she warn Kit without saying too much and coming close to breaking her promise to keep secret her task for the Queen? Would he even believe her?

'Consider what exactly?' he asked.

'Think of all the assurances that Ferdinando gave us that have amounted to nothing, all the things we have need of that he said we'd collect on the way: fruit and saplings for planting; cattle, sheep and salt; we have failed to find any of them. We sailed all around

Hispaniola without stopping once. We were meant to collect salt at St John's and that was abandoned for no clear reason. He has not guided us well, Kit. We've lost our supply boat and two experienced soldiers, and now the Spaniards will probably be alert to our plans. If we ever reach Chesapeake we'll have little food left, and it will be too late to grow crops before the winter sets in. Even if we find game we won't be able to salt it...' She pointed to the astrolabe he held in his fist. 'I hope you can use this, Kit, because, I beg you, do not trust Ferdinando to tell us where we are.'

He put the instrument back in his pocket, and kept her on her feet when the next wave struck, but again he let her go once the rolling of the deck had settled, just when she thought he might hold her a little closer.

'Have courage,' he said. 'I believe we're on the right course. I've sailed this coast before with Drake. We're following hundreds of miles of sand banks, stretched between a few treacherous capes, looking for a handful of narrow inlets to a vast lagoon the size of Wales. If we miss the inlets, there'll be no easy way back; if we get trapped behind a cape, we're likely to be wrecked. This is one of the most difficult coasts to navigate so do not judge Ferdinando too rashly. White is over-reacting to talk of being led by the devil; pay no heed to it. We must pull together and not let suspicion weaken us. Ferdinando has been cautious, perhaps too cautious, but that doesn't make him intent on undermining this voyage. The collecting White had in mind would have amounted to stealing from under the noses of the Spaniards and, poorly armed as we are, with women and children, I can understand why Ferdinando was loath to take that risk.'

'But how could he have been so wrong about the last anchorage? He's the Pilot...'

'Here.' Kit reached down to the netting behind the bulwark and pulled out something like a long hilted sword. 'Take this.'

He held the shaft out to her; it was blunt and square sided, about three feet long.

'What is it?'

'A cross staff. It's one of the easiest ways of reckoning latitude by the stars. Help me find out where we are.'

He glanced around as if to check that all was quiet then moved to stand behind her, guiding her hands gently to the staff and pointing it up towards the heavens. The contact was brief but bearable, even pleasurable. He wasn't holding her but the pole, and he was being courteous.

'Aim at the North Star, the brightest; it's over there. Imagine you're firing at it.'

His arms took the weight, and she could see the star he meant, shining intensely, fairly low in the sky, like a brilliant diamond in a glittering mantle. She leant against him, and his chest was like a bolster behind her shoulders, and his neck pillowed her head.

'Put the base of the staff to your cheek,' he said gently. 'But be careful. Hold it firmly and use the transom like a sight. It should be vertical, like this.'

He touched her right hand and led her fingers to the wooden crosspiece, sliding it along until it covered the bright star.

'Now lower the staff a little and move the transom until the North Star seems to sit on the top edge and the horizon seems to hang along the bottom.'

The staff wavered as she fought to hold it steady and position the transom as he'd asked. Her body swayed with the roll of the ship and her feet kept taking little uncalled-for dancing steps. His instructions had sounded simple, but no sooner had she got the staff aligned with the star than the horizon swung away, and each tiny movement of the crosspiece threw everything out completely. But she would not give up.

'Steady,' he said. 'Let your body relax. Move with the ship and don't hold your breath.'

How did he know she was holding her breath? She breathed out and made another tiny adjustment and then, for an instant, she was sure she had it: the star and sea were at either end of the bar.

'That's it!' she cried with a rush of triumph.

'Hold the transom there. Don't move.' He put his hands over hers and gripped the transom. 'Let me see.'

She surrendered the staff and watched him take it to the helm and the lantern that was kept there. His face lit up in planes while he bent over to take the readings. She saw elements of his features, through the frame of the helmsman's window, glowing like an illumination in hues of sepia and gold: a downcast eye, his furrowed brow, part of his bearded jaw at a quizzical angle. He was as handsome as an angel in a stained-glass window.

Then the ship's bell began tolling and he came over to her quickly. She counted eight couplets and knew the watch would be changing, the half-hour glass had been turned and the time was now midnight. At once the ship was alive with activity; men darted about, hailing one another, padding over the decks, shinning up out of hatches and scrambling down for their rest. She heard a splash and low chanting that told her the log had been thrown to reckon the ship's speed.

'Two knots,' someone shouted.

The *Lion* crept along, rolling as if drunk, waves slapping hard against her side.

'By the deep, five.'

'East by south,' Kit called out.

'Two knots. East by south,' the helmsman repeated.

She clutched at the gunwale, feeling the change in direction again. Was anything wrong? Why were they moving southeast when Roanoke was meant to lie to the north?

'Do you know where we are?' She asked with faint hope, unable to believe that her fumbling with the cross staff might have helped yield an answer.

He tucked the staff back behind the netting and took hold of the rail with his arm stretched straight.

'According to the measurement you just took and Harriot's charts, we're between thirty-four and thirty-five degrees north.' His reply was crisp, as if he wanted to have done with it. Was he hiding something?

'Is that right for Roanoke?'

'It could be, given the allowance we should make for error.'

'My hands shaking, you mean.'

'That, and the fact that the art of navigation is not exact.'

'But you are concerned, aren't you?' She moved closer to him, sensing his unease. 'You took readings from an astrolabe as well. Do you think we're still too far south for Roanoke?'

His silence answered her.

'Does Ferdinando know?'

'I don't think our Pilot would appreciate hearing observations on navigation from his Boatswain.' He inclined his head. 'Or from you.'

'I suppose he would not.'

'I take readings for my own benefit to test the little I have learnt; that is all. I wouldn't rely on them.'

'But I would, Kit. I trust you more than . . .'

A man's bellowing interrupted her.

'Master Doonan!' The voice was Ferdinando's, strident and reproving.

'Why are we sailing this course? You should be following the coast, not sailing away from it.'

She shrank against the bulwark as Kit stepped forwards on the poop.

'Look ahead, Master. See the way the waves are breaking to the east? I think that might be a shoal around a hidden bight. We could be in danger of getting caught to leeward.'

'Or it could be the inlet to Roanoke Sound and those waves could be caused by the flow out to sea. Get back on course!'

Kit moved to the steps and spoke to Ferdinando in an undertone.

'There's a treacherous cape in this region with a shape like a hook. I remember it well from my last voyage with Drake...'

'Don't give me Drake!' Ferdinando's voice cut him short, like a bullet blasting from the darkness. 'Obey your orders. East by north, and closer ashore. Would you have us sail past the channel?'

Kit turned and Emme heard the shrill blast of his whistle.

'East by north,' he called. 'Hands to the cables. Slacken the port top foresail sheet. Haul to starboard...'

His orders continued as Ferdinando climbed up from the afterdeck.

'Who's that with you?'

She edged towards the steps on the other side, thinking that she'd go down and leave by the mizzen hatch, but Ferdinando got in front of her first.

'Mistress Murimuth! I see you are up on deck again when you should be below.'

His tone was light with a hint of mockery and nothing to suggest any apprehension of impending disaster. But his confidence did not reassure her.

She stepped back towards the stern, gripping the rail.

'Do not let me distract you, Master Ferdinando. I was on the point of leaving after bringing some pottage for those on watch. I'll not trouble you, save to ask you, please, to consider the warning I've just heard, because it seems to me that those waves ahead are indeed very rough. They appear to be foaming, wouldn't you agree?'

He loomed closer and put one hand behind his back. She imagined it bunched tight in the shape of a fist.

'The sea is as disturbed as I would expect at a confluence,' he said loftily. 'We are looking for Port Ferdinando, a passage named after me because I discovered it. No one knows this coast as well as I. We cannot risk missing the only safe way into the sound because we are too far away to spot it.' He brought his fist down onto the rail, close to her hand, making her spring back. 'Now I think I have justified my decisions quite enough. I shall be . . .'

A blinding beam of light cut him short, lighting him up like a spectre. He stared back, blanched white and startled.

The Bo'sun's whistle made her jump again; then she heard Kit's voice, urgent and insistent.

'About! Hard to starboard. Turn about!'

'Hard to starboard,' the helmsman called, and the ship heeled as the whipstaff slid. Emme grabbed hold of a shroud, almost losing her balance. Canvas slapped and timbers groaned. The *Lion* turned against the waves, hull shivering as if kicked.

'More sail! All hands! Spill and set sail!'

Kit's orders rang out and men dashed to respond, darting up rigging, yanking at furling gaskets, freeing the sails to catch the wind from the land.

'Haul the main halyard. Due south...'

'South.' The call was repeated. 'Turn about.'

Ferdinando leant over the gunwale, looking to the source of the light, and Emme saw the stern lantern of the pinnace, much closer now, and another lantern swinging wildly as if in a signal.

'Stafford!' Ferdinando called. 'What mean you?'

Stafford's voice rippled back almost drowned by the roaring sea.

'Turn away! Shoal ahead.'

Emme stared at the place where she had seen the foaming waves. Beyond them was another bank; she could see it rising like a cliff, a line of black above the seething white of breaking surf, a line which cut across the course they had been sailing. From the sea jutted a long timber like a skeletal accusing finger: the mast of a wreck on the shoal they could not see.

Ferdinando took up Stafford's shouting.

'Away! Shoal ahead!'

Orders streamed from him as if his commands all along had been to sail away from the shore.

'Due south. Full sail.'

'Due south,' the helmsman affirmed.

The sea churned beneath the *Lion* and tossed her about like a feather caught in rapids, but Emme sensed the danger had passed; they were already sailing away from the ferment. Thank God for Stafford and Kit's quick thinking. Her legs felt weak and she wanted to go down below and make sure everyone was all right. If she saw Kit she would thank him; she hoped to catch sight of him. But the first man she saw was Ferdinando still on the afterdeck. She worked her way past him and as she did he turned his back.

He spoke to her, even so.

'It is as well my orders were obeyed at the last.'

*

Kit felt behind his back and touched the hilt of his ship-knife, blunt at the point but honed razor sharp at the sides. He moved his free hand to his chest and over the strung charges on his cartridge belt, the looped match-cord at his hip, the strap of his provisions bag with his water-bottle, tinderbox and victuals; powder horn and bullet pouch on his right side; sword at his left. In his right hand was the stock of his flintlock caliver, its long barrel heavy against the padding over his shoulder, its curved butt smooth in his palm, trigger lever nuzzling at his jerkin. His scalp itched under his helmet and he was sweating in the glare of the sun. Was he ready to go? He looked across at the other men waiting to board Stafford's pinnace from the deck of the *Lion*: forty in all, as many as the pinnace would hold. Were any of them ready? They did not know what they would face. This was as close to Virginia as he'd ever come with Drake: anchored outside the channel that led to Roanoke Sound. They were to look for the fifteen men led by Master Coffin that Sir Richard Grenville had left to guard the fort. But could fifteen have survived where Lane's garrison of hundreds had failed? Jim Lacy should know since he'd been through whatever had finished it, but the Irishman would say nothing about that, and he didn't look very comfortable about going back. When Kit spotted him, he made the sign of the cross over his chest.

Governor White blustered about, rooting through papers in a satchel that was in danger of disgorging. Ananias Dare hovered nearby brandishing the flag of the new City of Raleigh. Why was he bringing that? There'd be few to impress and it would only get in the way. But a day's carrying it on march should knock the swagger out of the man; he wouldn't suggest it be left behind.

He turned to Rob, at his side keen and eager, armed with knife and pistol: weapons that were light but effective if used well. The boy had learnt diligently, and Kit had few qualms about bringing him. Better to keep him close than leave him with Ferdinando out of sight. Was Rob afraid? Kit's gaze flicked to the dark purity of the boy's face, the crimson scarf around his woolly locks, and the trappings of soldiering that he wore like trophies: bandolier and wide sword belt. No, Rob was too young to be fearful, too caught up in the moment, and too sure that with his master he'd be safe.

'Ready?' he murmured.

'Yes,' Rob answered, checking his natural smile, concerned to show he had the seriousness of a man, while some of the Planters who would cross to Roanoke japed and laughed like schoolboys.

Manteo clapped Kit on the shoulder and Kit looked him in the eye. He stood impassively with his tribesman, Towaye, a quiet shy man who had served as his manservant with a diffidence that had made him seem almost invisible when they were in London. Both had abandoned all trappings of English dress. They wore deerskin breechclouts and fringed aprons over their thighs, carried bows and quivers, and sported feathers in hair cut to a roach from front to back. On the right side, their scalps were shaved so their eyes would be clear for taking aim with bow and arrow. Their upper bodies were bare, save for necklaces of bone, and markings over their skin in great whorls of white and red-ochre. They seemed to have grown in stature with the casting off of their shirts. Kit was proud to be with them and count them as his friends, but he noticed the way that a space had opened up between the two of them and the Planters on deck. Kit moved to fill it.

'You'll soon be home,' he said to Manteo.

'*Kupi.*' Manteo nodded, smiling. 'Yes, my land is close.'

Kit breathed deeply, catching the scent of pines in the warm breeze. He scanned the line of dunes nearest the inlet: a strip of sunlit white sand topped with soft green beach grass. It could not have looked less threatening: Manteo's home, but a wilderness for the Planters, further from England than they had ever been before – a wasteland to men like the farmer, George Howe, who had given Rob an apple from his orchard outside Moor Gate. Kit cast his eye over those assembled while White began calling them to get aboard the pinnace. He knew some of their histories and recognised the signs of their apprehension. He was pleased to see those he had chosen standing calmly in the main: men like Jack Tydway, the debtor from New Gate gaol, and Tom Humphrey, the Christ Church foundling. He stepped out to join them; then Mistress Emme pushed forwards from the crowd looking on, her lovely chestnut hair blowing in ringlets about her face, her dark eyes wide and shining. She spoke to him earnestly.

'God keep you and hasten you back.'

He gave her a bow, touched that she had singled him out for a farewell, even if he couldn't understand the reason. Was it because she hoped he'd tell her first about what they found at Roanoke? He could hardly believe she was truly concerned about him, though the last time he'd been close to her some of her frostiness seemed to have thawed. He'd felt her responding when he showed her the cross staff, or had that been artifice? She'd made it clear that she considered him beneath her: 'a common mariner', she'd said when they'd had their falling-out at Santa Cruz. 'Little more than a pirate who has lived as an outlaw with renegade slaves': that was what she really thought of him. In the heat of anger her prejudice had been revealed, and it had wounded him all the more because of what that meant for Rob. She would never consider the boy as other than inferior, and she would always see him in the same light, a friend of slaves and no better than one of them. She would have scorned him if he'd tried to woo her in England, so why was she being attentive to him now? Perhaps she thought that this was behaviour expected of maids. She was trying harder to appear like any serving girl, though it was obvious that her natural disposition was to be aloof and distant. Even so, he was drawn to her. She was undeniably beautiful, and he could do nothing about finding her attractive, only recognise it and be wary. He expected she wanted reassurance. She was plainly anxious to get to Chesapeake, and that, more than likely, was because she couldn't wait for the voyage to be over. As a lady used to palaces, her illusions about adventure had probably ended months ago. She must be desperate to return to court. He'd try and reassure her.

'We will only be gone a few days. Not much longer, now, Mistress Emme. You will be at Chesapeake soon.'

She brought her fingertips close to his hand and spoke softly but urgently.

'Then you will stay with us, won't you, Master Kit? You won't go back to England?'

Her intensity surprised him. Why should it matter to her? Maybe she wanted to be sure he wouldn't disrupt the rest of her journey. Perhaps she sensed his attraction to her and wished to avoid it.

'I will stay,' he soothed. 'But you will return.'

'No!' She suddenly took his hand and as quickly let it go. 'I shall be part of the new colony.'

He gave her a kindly smile, supposing that she still wanted him to believe the fiction that she would remain to serve as a maid like Maggie Lawrence and the other wenches.

'I think you will go back.' He lowered his voice for her alone. 'I know Walsingham's orders. I found out when he made me swear to tell no one who you really are. Ferdinando will make certain you're on the *Lion* when he sails for England. I know you've agreed to this because Sir Walter has asked you. I expect he wants you back for your lady's report.'

She shook her head, and bent her face close almost as if she meant to kiss him, but of course she did not. Then she looked up at him with imploring eyes.

'I will not leave Virginia. Believe me . . .'

'I must go.'

He gave a quick smile, stepping back, and looked round to the file of men still waiting to board. There were only about ten left.

Fleetingly, she touched his arm.

'Please be careful, Kit.'

She held something out to him and, not wishing to offend her, he opened his hand to receive whatever it was. She dropped a small object onto his palm. It was an oval nut.

'This comes from the finest oak in Richmond Park,' she said. 'I'd like you to have it for luck.'

He smiled at her and placed the nut in his pocket. The gift pleased him very much, probably more than she would ever know.

'I'll save it to plant at Chesapeake.'

He turned once to see her waving before he climbed over the gunwale and down to the pinnace. Ferdinando was nowhere to be seen, a surprise but not a disappointment. Perhaps he didn't want to be present when White was giving the orders.

The Quartermaster unhitched the hawser, and the pinnace began to drift away. Kit settled in the stern and had the oars passed to the men on the benches. They would row through the shallow passage; he could see that the race from the outflow would make entering it difficult. They were fully loaded and low in the water; they would need to be cautious.

'Let fall!' he called for the oars to be lowered and for the oarsmen to prepare. 'Make way together at my word.'

The oarsmen waited, eight on each side, their oars held level over the water, resting steady in the tholes.

Kit looked to Captain Stafford sitting at the helm with his usual poise, long legs stretched out, right hand on the tiller, left arm draped casually along the guard rail. Kit's respect for him had grown after the incident at the cape when Stafford's timely warning had averted certain disaster. The Captain was another veteran of Lane's expedition, one of the few to have sailed to Roanoke before, and Kit trusted him. Stafford touched his hat; then the Quartermaster called from the *Lion*.

'Message from Master Ferdinando: Those colonists put ashore needn't bother coming back. He'll not take anyone to Chesapeake.'

'What?' White spluttered. He half stood but Stafford pulled him down.

The pinnace rocked and drifted further away.

'Hold water!' Kit called, watching the mariners he'd selected slide their blades vertically into the sea while the Planters who were rowing slapped their oars down and flicked up spray. He glanced over his shoulder and saw the gap between the two craft was still widening. The rope ladder had already been pulled up, and no one was left at the rail.

'Come back, you bugger!' one of the Planters shouted.

'We're not staying here,' someone else yelled across.

White flapped his arms about as if he meant to fly back to the ship. His voice was shrill with indignation.

'What's the meaning of this?'

'Back astern!' Kit called to his mariners, and they promptly rowed backwards to return within hailing distance. 'Now hold.' He gave the commands as best he could to keep the pinnace near the ship.

Stafford raised his voice.

'Quartermaster, explain yourself.'

A crewman came on deck, looked down and left. Moments later, the Quartermaster reappeared.

'Master Ferdinando says that the summer is far spent. The Planters must be put ashore at Roanoke or not at all.'

'This is insufferable,' White blurted. 'Sir Walter Raleigh's instructions were to sail to Chesapeake.'

Stafford stood, holding onto a shroud.

'Fetch Master Ferdinando.'

'He will not come,' the Quartermaster replied. 'Those are his orders.' He turned his back.

White pulled off his straw hat and dashed it against his knee, crushing its brim in his hands. He tugged at his hair and screwed up his eyes, making a noise between a howl and a groan of agony.

'This is treachery. Treason! Our Pilot cannot countermand Sir

Walter's express orders. You will take us back to the *Lion*, Captain Stafford.'

Stafford inclined his head and raised his brows.

'I fear that if you take your men back aboard then Master Ferdinando will take everyone back to England. Is that what you wish?'

'No it is not!'

Kit ordered the men on the starboard side to row slowly; they would turn a rough circle while the debate was thrashed out, though he felt in his gut he knew the way it would end. White wouldn't want to risk having the whole expedition aborted. He heard Lacy muttering under his breath, 'Typical of the Portugee swine. He wants us all dead.'

White turned to his son-in-law. 'Ferdinando gives me no choice. He's a malicious, incompetent scoundrel...'

Dare frowned, hunched his shoulders and spoke low, but still loud enough for Kit to pick up. 'Is it so terrible here? At least this is somewhere you know – and we've arrived in one piece. If we sail for Chesapeake there's always the risk that Ferdinando will lead us to our graves.'

White shook his head and sighed. He glanced towards Manteo sitting near Kit at the stern. 'I suppose we have allies in the Croatans...'

At the mention of his tribe's name Manteo smiled across at him. White forced a smile back.

'And it is late in the year to be planting crops,' Dare went on. 'Ferdinando is right in that. It's almost the end of July; if we go on to Chesapeake we won't arrive until August. Perhaps he has a point...'

White gave a strangled moan of exasperation. 'But this is not what was planned! I know what this is about; Ferdinando wants to go privateering. That's been his intention all along: to get rid of us as soon as possible and then hunt down Spanish ships to rob them of their gold. Isn't that right?' He raised his voice and looked straight at Kit. 'Master Boatswain, are you going to abandon us here so you can go chasing after Spanish galleons?'

'No, Master White.' Kit didn't take any time to reflect; he didn't need to. He knew his answer already. All that had been uncertain was when he would declare his hand. 'I will stay with you.'

'I see,' White answered with a sudden softening in his tone. He looked around and put his crumpled hat back on his head. 'Good. Well…' He fiddled with his satchel strap as if caught in indecision as to whether to set the bag down between his feet or shoulder it ready to get up and leave. He left the bag where it was and called back to the *Lion*.

'Did you hear that, Quatermaster…?'

Fortunately for White, the pinnace had just about completed a full turn and was once more close to the ship. He bellowed at the first mariner he saw on deck.

'Your Boatswain will stay with us!'

The man made himself scarce and Kit got his oarsmen ready to row hard. There'd be no more circling. He caught Stafford's eye and Stafford gave a nod.

The Quartermaster came back to the rail.

'A message from Master Ferdinando for the Master Bo'sun: He says he'll not have you on his ship again.'

Kit said nothing. Some of the oarsmen muttered in sympathy. Lacy spoke to him in an undertone.

'I'll not leave you, sir. I'll stay too.'

'Thank you, Jim.'

White waved his hand. 'Let us get underway, see how Roanoke fares, and pay our respects to Master Coffin.'

Stafford called back to the Quartermaster.

'We'll return for the rest of the Planters in a day or two. Tell Master Ferdinando that, and be sure that he is waiting.'

Kit gave the order to make way.

'At my word, together: Pull!'

The oarsmen hauled in unison and the pinnace surged away.

So this was it. He'd be going no further aboard the *Lion*. This was where he would stay. He had reached Virginia and his journey's end. He hoped he would see Mistress Emme again and that Ferdinando would, at least, let her set foot on Roanoke Island, but he wasn't sure about that. It might not be safe. He stole another look at Lacy and saw the shadow of fear over his face. She must not leave the ship if there was any risk. He hauled, and bent forwards, pushing, and leant back, pulling again. He clenched his jaw and glanced at Rob: his son, all he had left.

The *Lion's* guns fired in farewell and the shock of the detonations sent a shiver down his spine. The blasts rumbled to silence and the sweep of the oars that took the pinnace through the channel and into the unknown.

\*

The musket volley thundered over the water sending great flocks of birds rippling up into the air. Gulls, cormorants and pelicans rose up in waves, wings thrashing, wheeling and mewling as they streamed past the pinnace in patterns that seemed alive; then they dropped down to the lagoon, filming the surface in the distance in fluttering patches of black and white, their screeching fading until all was quiet.

Kit looked at the trees above the low sandy cliffs. The pines, oaks and cedars led to a wooded rise beyond, but he could see no sign of the fort on Roanoke that Stafford had said was there, no building of any kind, no smoke nor sound of people.

John White sat in the bow with his hand shielding his eyes. 'They cannot have set a lookout,' he observed. 'It's quite possible that Master Coffin could have taken his men foraging elsewhere.'

'That's true,' Ananias Dare piped up. 'They can't have been expecting us.' He stood unsteadily and waved the great flag of the City of Raleigh.

Stafford hailed him from the helm. 'Sit down, if you please, Master Dare.'

To Kit he spoke more gently. 'We'll sail round and come in from the north. There's a fair anchorage in a wide bay on the east side of the island, but the approach is very shallow, like everywhere around Roanoke: barely greater than a fathom, and in the bay no more than a few feet. We'll use the leeboards and go easy. Time to tack, I think.'

Stafford pulled on the tiller and Kit gave the orders to bring the mainsail round, hauling on the lee brace as he did. 'Brace about! Slack windward sheet and haul the leeward. Make all!'

They both ducked when the boom swung over, and so did everyone else astern of the mainmast; they'd soon learnt the essentials of sailing gaff-rigged. But there was barely a puff of wind to fill the sails, and, once they began to drift on the next tack, the silence settled as still as stone. The view ahead was a perfect expanse of pure smooth blue: azure sky mirrored in turquoise water – a sea of glass.

'Hoay!' Ananias Dare called out. 'Is anyone there?'

His shout seemed to land in felt. There was no answer, and even White hissed at him to hold his peace.

Manteo, sitting at the stern, took out a hook and line and began to fish, so did Towaye and Rob along with several of the Planters who were crammed together in the bows. Soon the pinnace trailed lines like darning threads, and they had their first catch: a small blue fish from a vast shoal that slid by, crystal clear in the sun-bright water, as if the hull was gliding through a shower of pieces of eight. More followed, along with one like a bass with a spot near the tail. Manteo pulled it aboard.

'*Manchauemec*,' Manteo proclaimed. 'A young one. It's good to eat.'

'We'll get a fire going when we're ashore,' White promised. 'We'll grill the fish in the open and eat well tonight.'

'No more cold pottage for us,' someone remarked and patted White on the shoulder. 'Sweet bully-rook, thank Christ!'

Kit looked about, seeing more fish shoaling, even leaping from the water, and birds without number flocking over the lagoon. How had Lane's men ever run short of food in this place? He squinted across at the island and thought he saw the shapes of fields over the slopes, though there was still no sign of people; the clearings, if that's what they were, seemed overgrown and desolate.

Suddenly Rob cried out and Kit turned to him in a flash. The spool he held span in a blur, making a whoosh like a whipping top as it unwound out of control.

'Let go!' Kit yelled, but it did no good.

Rob tried to catch hold of his line and jerked back his hand. He tried again, blood streaming down his wrist.

'It's big!' he shrieked. 'A huge fish. Help me!'

He leant back, tugging on the spool which had wound itself out, and the fish he had hooked jumped clear out of the water in a jagged arc of silver. Writhing and thrashing, it plunged back, spraying water, almost yanking Rob overboard though Kit held him fast, grabbing hold of him by the waist.

'Drop it!' Kit shouted again.

'No! I've got it hooked. Just hold me . . .'

'It's dragging the ship. Let go!'

The fish was taking the pinnace with it, even under sail. The thing was a mass of twisting muscle, shooting into the air then plummeting into the water, splashing and spiralling, swerving wide and carrying the pinnace onto another tack.

'Cut the line,' Stafford called.

The next instant Rob toppled back, all resistance gone. The spool span and slowed, and Manteo sheathed his knife.

'That fish is best to leave,' he said.

Rob glared at him, clutching his bleeding hand. 'But I had it. Why didn't you help me?'

Manteo passed over a strip of leather. 'Bind your hand. The fish was too big.' He looked across at the island and the lengthening shadows over the water. 'We should get ashore.'

'He's right, Rob.' Kit rubbed his back. 'We've got enough fish, more than we can eat. We'll hunt for that kind another day.' He looked at the cut. It was deep. He should have warned Rob to let go if he hooked something big, told him to secure his line first on some part of the ship: tie the end round the rail, not try to hold the thing in his hands. The boy could have lost his fingers.

The water settled to glassy stillness, and Stafford got the pinnace back on course. They furled the sails and used the oars, took soundings by the rod and crept through the bay. The bed of the lagoon was only feet below them and every so often the hull ground against a shoal. They reached a small natural harbour as the sun was going down. A narrow bank of sand led to low wooded hills, and, just above the waterline, as far as the eye could see, were flat brown swathes of cord grass and rushes.

White led the Planters ashore but no one was waiting to greet them. There was no path, beacon, shelter or remains to suggest that anyone had ever been there, not that Kit could see.

White turned to Stafford. 'You're sure this is the place?'

Stafford looked about, took off his hat and mopped his brow. 'As much as you are,' he said. He scanned the water; then pointed to a log at an angle protruding a few feet from the surface in a tangle of weeds.

'That's one of the mooring posts. Odd there's only one left.'

'Very well. We'll camp here tonight and proceed to the fort in the morning. There's no reason for Master Coffin to have taken any interest in this anchorage, not without a vessel bigger than a boat. Hardly surprising that it's been neglected.'

'Good,' said Dare. 'Let's cook the fish.'

It didn't take the men long to start a fire and set up a few canvas shelters. Rob found a lizard and dropped it down Tom Humphrey's neck. Tom then found a crab and put it down Rob's breeches. That seemed to restore Rob's humour since he was able to retaliate in kind with something larger. The sun sank to a shimmering red disc like a boss of molten metal plunging behind the dark shield of the land. Fireflies began to glow and cicadas started to trill. The smell of spruce and pine hung resinous in the cooling air. Kit walked along the bank and then to the edge of the trees. Manteo followed him. They both probed and scraped, examined and pondered, picking over driftwood and shells, pinecones and roots. Every so often one of them would find something that would make them both crouch down, heads together.

'A button?' Kit asked, fingering something black, round and smooth which seemed to have a hook on the back.

'A nut,' Manteo answered, shaking his head and smiling in the shadows. 'Like a walnut.'

From the camp came the sound of singing and the smell of fresh grilled fish. The beach glowed orange in the flicker of firelight, and the water was motionless with a gleam like pewter in which the ship seemed grounded, black and lifeless, a broken skeleton of angled yards and cable.

Kit found something else, a pale domed carapace. He blew away the sand and held it out to Manteo.

'A turtle shell?'

'Yes. You are right. Here is a leg.' He flourished a little white bone and they found more as they searched.

'Another turtle,' Kit said, brushing sand and dirt from a discovery which he could feel was domed, though broken, even more than the first. He passed it to Manteo along with another piece that seemed to fit by its side. He rooted around and found something else that was small and hard, shiny and ridged. He held it up in the fading light.

Manteo was quiet.

It was a tooth – unmistakably; a human tooth.

Manteo hunched down beside Kit and dug with him. They exhumed part of a jaw in which three teeth were embedded. There was no doubt.

'This is a man,' Manteo said. 'This is his skull.'

Kit scraped in the sand. The limbs, when he found them, were far less damaged. He unearthed whole leg and arm bones, ribs and pelvis. But the skull was smashed to fragments.

He made a neat pile of the teeth.

'Whoever this was, he didn't die a natural death. Beasts wouldn't pulverise a skull and leave the rest intact.'

Manteo nodded, scrutinising a femur. 'There are no teeth marks. A bear would have chewed the bones, so would a wolf. They would have broken them for the marrow, probably eaten them.'

'So the man's head was crushed by the people who killed him?'

'Yes, so I think.'

'Beaten to a pulp – as if they wanted to destroy his face.'

'Yes, beaten in that way.'

'Can you tell how long ago this happened?'

Manteo fished around the grave site and Kit did the same. They both looked for other clues: a trace of fabric or metal, some relic of weaponry or clothing, anything other than bone.

'A long time,' Manteo answered. 'Maybe a year, not much more; the bones are not decayed. But not recently. There is no flesh or hair . . .'

'There are no clothes either.'

'They could have been taken.'

Kit nodded. The Indians prized the clothes of foreigners, so if Indians had murdered the man they probably would have stripped him. Suppose the bones were those of one of Coffin's men. But was that likely? Was he jumping to the worst conclusion? The body could have been that of a savage killed in some tribal skirmish, or any one of those left marooned on the coast of Virginia over the years; he'd heard talk of slaves abandoned along this shore, both African and Indian, even of a few men left behind when

187

Lane's garrison was evacuated. He rummaged in the dirt, feeling the grains of grit between the pads of his fingers. He came across another tooth, a smooth enamelled molar broken off from its root. Was there a way of distinguishing English teeth from savage? He supposed there wouldn't be.

He delved again and touched a thin strip of something metallic. He held it up to the vestiges of light. It was brass, a tiny elongated cylinder, fatter at one end than the other: an aiglette of the kind that a man would have at the end of the laces on his doublet or sleeves.

He passed the find to Manteo. 'It's an aiglette, like this.' He held out one of his own laces.

It wasn't fancy or very valuable, not gilded or jewelled, but the sort of tag that a soldier might use. He imagined the man brought down, perhaps clubbed or struck by an arrow, the clothes ripped off him as he lay dying, the lace torn away and lost in the dirt to later rot and leave just its capping behind. He watched Manteo push the aiglette over his palm.

'This was no Indian,' Kit said. 'I think he was English, most probably one of Coffin's men, murdered not long after being left here.'

Manteo nodded. 'Yes. I think so too.'

'We must warn the Governor.' He stood and looked down at the remains. 'We'll show him what's left and I'll give him the aiglette.' He held out his hand and Manteo pressed it into his safekeeping.

'The Secotans will have done this,' Manteo said.

'The Secotans.' Kit looked up at the black woodland. 'I wonder where they are now.'

# 8

## *Manner of Wars*

'Their manner of wars...is either by sudden surprising...most commonly about the dawning of the day, or moon light, or else by ambushes, or some subtle devises...'

—*From an account of the 'natural inhabitants' in Thomas Harriot's* Brief and True Report of the new found land of Virginia *first published in 1588*

### Roanoke Island, the new found land of Virginia
#### *July 1587*

'You need not go.'

The wind thrummed through the *Lion's* rigging, and drove rolling waves against her hull, making the ship strain against her anchor lines, rocking with a sickening motion. But Master Ferdinando smiled.

Emme regarded him askance. 'Of course I must go. Mistress Dare will require help in establishing her new home on Roanoke, and her time is almost come. She needs me now more than ever.'

'Is her comfort so important to you?' Ferdinando took hold of the main halyard and leant over her. 'I think, considering your friends, that probably it is not.'

What was he getting at? She supposed he meant to unsettle her by inferring that he knew more than he did. She would not rise to him.

She turned aside and looked down at the pinnace she was meant to board. It bobbed up and down, knocking against the side of the ship, already fully loaded with the last of the Planters to be taken ashore: the old men, women and boys. She saw the anxiety in their wan faces. They were waiting for her.

Ferdinando took her arm as if to help her to the rail, and she tried to wrench away from him but to no avail. His hold meant she could not easily proceed further and the constraint made her flesh creep. He stood in front of the boxes placed to form steps over the bulwarks, released her and gave her a sly look.

'I mean those who are concerned about your safe return to England. They would not want you lost on this island.'

'I do not intend to be lost.' She took a few steps to skirt past him. 'I shall serve the Dares and Governor White in the new City of Raleigh. I will not be difficult to find.'

He took hold of her again and she shot him a fiery glance, standing rigid until he let go of her.

His lips twisted into another subtle smile.

'But you will not stay on Roanoke for long. When I am ready, you will leave.'

'Most generous of you, considering that you have told all the other Planters that they are not to be allowed back aboard this ship.'

He stood by the rail, speaking in an undertone that followed her, low and unhurried as she negotiated the steps.

'I shall allow Governor White back and possibly one or two others. Someone must return to England to report to the venture's patrons. I would rather not have that responsibility – or need to explain your absence.' He inclined his head, confident now of her attention. 'So do not expect to remain here for more than a few days.'

She turned to him before climbing down. 'I expect nothing, Master Ferdinando, least of all anything from you.'

She did not look back at the ship; she had no wish to ever see it again. She fixed her attention on the line of white dunes and the turbulent channel that led to the lagoon. The pinnace was crowded, and everyone was thrown together in the rough passage through the inlet, tossed from side to side, soaked through with spray, and bounced to bruising against boards and netting. But the water calmed to blue serenity once they were through to the other side, gently rippled by a soft breeze, and she caught her first glimpse of the island that would be her home in Virginia. There it was – Roanoke: a low band of hazy green that gradually spread over the horizon during the long hours of their approach, and rose to give the promise of gentle wooded hills and land fit for farming. The whole island was less than twelve miles from north to south, and four miles from west to east, so Captain Stafford told her, but to circle it almost completely, as they did to avoid the shallowest water, took most of the sultry morning.

When they arrived the sun was high, and the distant line of dunes fringing the sea shimmered as if melting into the heavens. She was wilting in the heat and concerned for her mistress, but they were soon led into the shade of trees, and offered water by those sent to greet them. Kit's page welcomed her with a bunch of sweet grapes, then escorted her and Mistress Dare along a trail fragrant with juniper. The lady walked slowly, but Emme was happy to savour the delight of everything around her: the sunlight filtering through moss-draped branches that made the trees look as if they were trailing long beards, the antlered deer feeding in sheltered glades, and the flowers that grew wherever the canopy thinned out, climbing over the undergrowth in glorious abundance – blush pink briar roses and bindweed with blooms like purple trumpets; passion flowers and red columbine; dainty plants covering the ground that sported florets like horn-shaped jewels. She lost sight of the sea but could still smell its freshness mingled with the tang of the pines. And almost everywhere she looked there were great oak and walnut trees; fruits and nuts that were ripe or growing; grapes on vines in patches of sunshine; small plums and orange fruits that Rob assured her were safe to eat. They proved to be delicious, like medlars wrapped in mantles of paper.

How to marvel at wonders without name? She could only relish through her senses like a child before mastering language: enjoying the sight of a bird like a flame in the trees, a vivid flash of vermilion; see gourds like luscious melons, and flowers taller than she was with heads like radiant suns; touch the little leaves of the creeper that moved when she brushed by, feel them closing under her fingers; smell the bark scented of cherries; and hear the song of a sparrow that would have delighted the Queen.

What would the place be like in winter? She tried to picture that, reminding herself of the season and that now, in the height of summer, she was probably seeing the island at its best. Come the winter it would be colder and everything would die back. In the autumn there might be hurricanes, the wrecking storms that Kit had told her about. But Roanoke was sheltered by the ribbon of dunes; some of the oaks must have stood for a century or more. The island was further south than England and surely the winters could not be any worse. She doubted that snow ever settled or water thickly froze.

It was not that she saw only good as she walked, because she recognised things that could hurt and prove a danger: stems and fruits covered in spines; the webs of spiders, some of monstrous size; ant trails leading up tree trunks to giant nests hanging from high branches; a black snake like a whip that slithered into the shadows. But these were dangers she could understand and they did not frighten her. They only reinforced her perception of manifold variety, a land as fascinating as a gem splitting light, revealing more and more the closer she looked.

At the settlement, when they reached it, her delight was compounded for there were houses intact: good timber-framed cottages built on two storeys, brick walled on the lower level with lath and daub up above, better than many she had seen around London. They had chimneys and tiled roofs, wooden shutters and solid doors. There were not enough houses for everyone, but at least the families would have a roof over their heads, and more cottages were being built; she could see the studding posts in place. Creepers and ivy had grown over the houses still standing, but the Planters who had gone ahead had already cleared away the worst. Repairs were well underway. Men were up ladders, nailing back timbers, plugging with mud and patching with lead. Sounds of sawing and hammering rang round the clearing. There was a well with a winch at which the women gathered to draw water for themselves, the men and boys. They cut up calico for partitions and made rush pallets to serve as beds. Emme saw a kiln trailing smoke, and a forge with a roaring furnace. A smith was at the anvil, stripped to his waist, pounding iron and dripping sweat. Men were felling trees and hewing wood, heaping up dirt from a collapsed earthwork and dismantling the ruin of a burnt building inside.

'This is the fort,' Rob announced to both Emme and Mistress Dare. 'The Governor has ordered it rebuilt.' Then he pointed to the cottage nearest the broken wall of earth. 'This is your house for now. It will be shared by the Governor and Master Dare.'

'Thank you, Rob,' said Mistress Dare. 'It looks perfect.'

She leant on Emme's arm and walked over to her new home, pausing by the well for a drink on the way. Emme could see the Governor with Kit deep in conversation outside the cottage and Ananias Dare looking on. All three had their backs to her. She could hear them talking while her mistress refreshed herself, taking a ladle from the bucket.

'I think they should be told,' Kit said, his words just discernible from where Emme stood.

'Not the women,' muttered Governor White as he scrutinised a curling document. 'There's no need to alarm them. Whatever happened, it was nearly a year ago.'

'You will say nothing?' Kit seemed surprised; his tone was incredulous.

'Keep quiet about it,' Ananias cut in.

White mopped his brow.

'What would be gained?'

Mistress Dare finished drinking and waddled eagerly towards them.

Kit turned and saw her, and immediately the three men fell silent.

Emme considered asking them what they had been talking about but decided not to for her mistress's sake. If indeed the lady might be alarmed, it was probably better that she didn't know.

Master Dare greeted his wife first, putting his arms around her and kissing her lovingly in a way that made Emme feel somewhat better disposed towards him.

'Welcome, my dear,' he said. 'Let me show you inside.' He led her to the threshold with his hand over her rump.

Emme narrowed her eyes and caught sight of a swept dirt floor, a joint stool and trestle table, and a ladder leading upstairs. Perhaps Mistress Dare would have the luxury of giving birth on a bed; she might even have her husband's full attention for a while.

Governor White turned to Kit, rolled up his paper and touched it to his cap.

'I must see how the work goes at the fort.'

Kit gave a short bow. 'I'll help with the felling. There's much to be done.'

The Governor nodded and walked away, his lips drawn tight.

'Master Kit.' She raised her hand to stop him following.

He smiled wryly at her.

'Mistress Murimuth. I hope you will be happy here.'

'I am sure I will be. I am enchanted by Roanoke already. The work you have done here is . . .' She searched for a word that would encapsulate her gratitude. '. . . Magnificent,' she said, and smiled apologetically. She hoped he understood.

'Magnificent?' His eyes twinkled as his smile stretched to a grin. 'Thank you. But we have all worked hard, and the work has just begun.' He inclined his head. 'I doubt it will ever end.'

'I suppose it won't. I...'

She looked round and noticed Rob and whatever she had thought to say was suddenly gone from her mind.

Kit put his hand on the boy's shoulder.

'Go and help the woodsmen, Rob. I'll join you in a moment.'

The boy darted away, and Kit gestured for her to walk with him to the back of the house. They stood in the shade, facing the forest, against a cob wall without windows, and by their feet were piles of vegetation that had been cut from the building. Beyond were ox-eye daisies and cow parsley taller than they were, flower caps like the lace bonnets of tall ladies bowing in the sun. He pulled off his woollen hat and tucked it in his belt, then pushed back his hair with a sweep of his hand. He must have been labouring, probably hewing wood. She could see a band of dirt across his forehead and that his shirt was so sweat-soaked it concealed very little, from the open ties at his neck, where she glimpsed tight springs of golden hair, to the bulge of his chest muscles and down. She looked up quickly with a twinge of embarrassment, and took in his shadowed face as he leant against the wall. His tanned skin was glowing, and his chin newly shaved, so she could follow every angle of his lean strong jaw and every contour of the perfect shape of his mouth. Her gaze moved to meet his, and the blue of his eyes seemed alight as if charged with pale fire.

He held his hand out, open towards her.

'What did you want to say?'

She brought her fingertips to his hand until they were just resting on his palm, breathed deeply and closed her eyes. She could bear this kind of touch, and it was what he wanted, wasn't it? Hadn't he reached for her hand once? She longed to sense again that he still had regard for her, despite the hot words that had passed between them weeks before. She wished them forgotten, and she no longer needed an apology, because Kit had earned her gratitude by delivering her to this island safely. She only hoped he didn't think she despised him. He had been solicitous with her off the cape when he had shown her how to read the stars, and she wanted to show that she welcomed that kind of consideration, all the more so since they would be together in the New World for some time. They should be good companions.

She looked at him again.

'I wanted to thank you for helping us arrive here safely. I am more glad than I can say to be in Virginia at last, and able to look forward to building my future in this place. This is my home now. I will never go back to England.'

'But you must.' A crease deepened between his brows. 'This land may not be as hospitable as you think. Remember Lane's soldiers couldn't wait to leave, and the fate of Coffin and his men remains uncertain. We do not know what has happened here...'

He turned towards the fort, though nothing of it could be seen from the seclusion of the overgrown garden.

'I know,' she said, thinking of the blistered black timbers she had seen being dragged from the earthwork. She tipped her head on one side and regarded him quizzically. 'Perhaps something that might "alarm" me, something that happened "nearly a year ago"?'

She looked straight into his eyes and saw that he was troubled, as if a deeper shadow had drawn over his face.

'I overheard what you were saying to Governor White,' she explained. 'But, Kit, I do not care. Whatever it was makes no difference to me. It is over. This is where I will stay.'

He cradled her hand in both of his very gently, as if it was made of glass, and the sensation was not unpleasurable; she enjoyed the feel of his delicate touch. He was being attentive as she had hoped, and she sensed he might not have lost his tender feelings for her. But had she confounded him? He seemed not to know what to do.

'You are one of the Queen's ladies,' he said. 'I know you have promised to return…'

'The Queen has many ladies. I doubt my absence will trouble her much.'

Then the set of his jaw hardened and his tone became more insistent. He squeezed her hand a little as he spoke, and that made her tense, but she did not pull away.

He spoke firmly.

'Your duty is to serve the Queen, above all others. You cannot remain here. You must carry out whatever tasks have been entrusted to you and then you must return as Sir Walter has asked…'

'No, Kit.' She brought her fingertips close to his mouth, as if she meant to close his lips. She would have liked to, but she did not touch him. She spoke softly. 'I was one of the Queen's ladies in another country, not this one which is now mine – and yours. We have a whole new realm here – ours for the glory of our Queen and God: a virgin land in which we can build new lives, freely and fairly without fear or censure.'

He sighed and bowed his head then looked away towards the trees.

'It is a fine country, I will grant.'

'It is beautiful.'

He held her hand as if in prayer, between his two palms, bringing it close to his heart. Poor Kit, she felt his concern; he was only trying to protect her. Perhaps also, she hoped, he did not really want her to go.

'But consider what you have undertaken,' he reasoned, 'what is expected of you back in England.'

She looked at him levelly.

'All that is over. It is part of the past I have left behind. We are here to start again, and it does not matter what you were or I was, here we are washed clean. I am a woman, nothing more or less, and you...'

He drew her to him, bringing his face close to hers, whispering as if his words might easily destroy them both.

'I am a man who fears he loves you.'

She tipped back her head and half closed her eyes. She felt herself shaking though she tried to hold still.

'Do not fear it because I do not,' she said.

It was a lie.

She felt his lips meet hers, soft and sensual, then urgent and hard. His arms enfolded her and his hands held her head, pressing her closer, not letting her go, and her response was to shiver like an animal overpowered, submitting to him completely because, at that moment, she did not want him to move away. She surrendered to her passion for a man whom she loved: the finest man she had ever met, better than all the courtiers in all of London, and all the mariners who sailed the seas, and all the gentlemen, and all the lords. He was an angel in her arms, Gabriel brought to Earth, and she did not care about anything else except to have him close by her, his smell on her skin, his taste in her mouth, and his touch overwhelming her, bringing tears to her eyes.

Then someone called for him and the kiss came to an end.

He seemed to sense what she yearned for and hugged her tenderly before he left.

*

Kit watched Emme helping with the supper, chatting with the other women by the open fire, keeping the lid on the cauldron in which the crabs were boiling, those that had been caught that afternoon along with the clams and mussels which would make a dainty feast. There was even the promise of fresh bread, baked in the oven he'd helped to build, made with the flour from Spicer's flyboat which had reached Roanoke safely three days ago much to the Planters' relief. This was contentment indeed: the sight of the woman he loved more than he'd thought he could love again, the smell of hot bread along with the aroma of steaming crab, his son by his side, part of a community taking root: the City of Raleigh, now with everyone together, and enough supplies to see them all through their first winter in Virginia; his body aching from a day of fruitful labour, his stomach craving to be filled, but his heart brim full. He was in a land where he could shape a future, build a house, till the soil, make a home, and, though the work was hard, the land was bountiful with much of the promise that White had described, certainly deer and fish aplenty. Perhaps he could believe that Emme might stay, and accept what she'd told him: that she would not go back, despite her promise to Raleigh which must have been made with the knowledge of the Queen. Perhaps he could convince himself that with him she would be safe. He was sure he could look after Rob, so why not Emme as well if she chose to remain? Had he imagined dangers where none really existed? White's Planters had been on Roanoke for over a week and they'd not seen a single savage apart from Manteo and Towaye. Why fear what a broken skull might mean when in

London the cemeteries were full of such things? There was nothing else to suggest that anything sinister had happened to Grenville's men, nothing apart from the damage to the fort, the burnt timbers and broken earthworks. But a violent storm could have caused all that: fire from a lightning strike and the wash of heavy rain. The cottages had survived intact, so why not conclude that Coffin and his men had moved elsewhere of their own volition? Maybe they'd left on a long hunting trip and were now on their way back, about to appear at any moment. There might soon be an explanation, and if Emme freely wished to stay, without any persuasion on his part, if she truly cared for him as she'd led him to believe, then why shouldn't he contemplate a future shared with her?

Look at her: cheeks rosy with the sun, chemise rolled up above her elbows and open at her pretty throat, down to the beginning of the crease between the full roundness of her breasts. He'd take that thought no further, but observe how she moved, and spoke and smiled. Didn't she seem happy? Her laughter was like sunshine, brightening everything around her. Even one of the old dames laughed along with her as well, and the woman's usual scowl would have frightened a ghost.

Emme was a lady, at ease in the palaces of the Queen, who was prepared to turn her hand to anything she encountered. She was undaunted by hardship and what was strange and fearful. Few people suspected she wasn't used to keeping house, though he'd seen her puzzle the Governor with the shrewdness of her questions, and her mistakes often caused amusement. Take the time she tried to find wood for a dish when told to bake venison in a coffin, which she plainly didn't know should have been hard pastry. But her mistress was too unimaginative to think that her maid was any more than incompetent at times, and Emme had learnt to accept criticism with good grace, and to ask when she wasn't sure then make up her own mind, and, in this new land, she was as good as most in making use of what she found.

She was cheerful and resourceful, clever and unassuming. Her faults he could accept. If she was headstrong, then wasn't he too? If she was over-bold for a woman, then he considered that a virtue. He'd never met her like, nor would he ever again. She could never displace what his Ololade had meant to him, but Emme was not the same and his love for her was different, fresh and sharp, keen enough to hurt. Maybe the time had come for him to laugh again and join with Emme in the enjoyment of this New World. To each was its season, and there was a time to let go, just as there was a time to love, and sometimes love more than once in the span of a man's life. Perhaps, for him, a new time was beginning. He did not know what would happen next, but he'd relish his good fortune in being with Emme in this place, treasure the affection she had shown him and savour her with his eyes. She was beautiful and she roused him. O, she roused him. When she began to sway in a mime of dancing, to some private joke she was sharing with her friends, he had to look away to let his blood cool.

He turned to White sitting beside him on one of the tree trunks round the fire. The Governor was hunched over his pocket desk with an air of rapt concentration, hair ruffled, tongue tip just showing between the line of his lips. The lid of the box lay open in his lap to reveal a sheet of paper and an array of mussel shells each aglow with a different pigment. In his right hand he held a tiny brush, and in his left was an oyster palette on which he was mixing colours, dipping his brush into another shell half full of water, then blending the hues on the mother-of-pearl. Kit leant over and saw that he was working on a life-sized limning of a striking yellow butterfly, about a child's hand in size, striped black on its forewings, but rather tattered and clearly dead. Manteo had it resting on his knee, wings spread between his fingers.

White pointed to the lower areas of the creature's wings, parts that looked much battered, as if pecked by birds.

'Does the frilling continue here?' he asked Manteo.

'The wings have tails. They are like this.' Manteo gave a little sweep of his finger.

'Curling? Hmm . . . Is this right?'

White mixed a very watery grey and drew a small curved elongation to one lower black border.

'Yes, I think so,' Manteo nodded.

White dipped his brush in a shell smeared with a residue of black and gave a small grunt; he'd obviously run out of pigment. He proceeded to place a smooth piece of round crystal on the log by his side; then he took a small paper envelope and poured out a tiny amount of black powder, and sprinkled it with white powder from another paper wrapping.

'What's that?' Manteo asked, peering over.

'The black is from charred cherry stones and the white is gum Arabic; it's the best binding for limning,' White added, shooting Manteo a smile. He tapped the picture with his little finger. 'That earth yellow you gave me has worked very well.' He passed his finger over the vivid wings. 'As good as the best ochre from Italy.'

'I am glad.' Manteo grinned back.

Next, White added a few drops of water and began to grind the mixture to a black paste with a small ovoid stone.

'Let me hold that for you,' Kit offered, placing his hand around the crystal.

'If you would,' White said, glancing up and raising an eyebrow, as if he'd noticed Kit beside him for the first time. 'Keep it steady.'

Kit did as he was asked while White tempered the mixture, then picked up most of it on his index finger and smeared it inside a shell. After examining the colour, White seemed satisfied, wiped his hands on a cloth, and picked up his brush again ready to give his butterfly black wing tails.

'And do the tails have blue spots, like these?' He turned to Manteo and indicated one of the rows of indigo roundels within the lower borders.

'No. But I am not sure.' Manteo frowned; then he smiled broadly. 'You know the *mamankanois* better now than I do.'

'What did you call it? Could you say that again slowly?'

'*Ma-man-kan-ois*,' Manteo repeated, enunciating each syllable.

'Thank you, Manteo.'

Kit watched White paint the tails then write the butterfly's name in sepia ink beneath the image. He respected White for that. The Governor made no attempt to give the creature an English name, or describe it after himself as some sea captains liked to do with lands they had found or features, like Ferdinando's port.

'The likeness is good,' Kit said with genuine admiration, and he was conscious of White's pride. This was his genius: he had a gift for recording life. He could imagine White making notes on all the plants and animals of Virginia, painting and naming every single living thing: all the birds and fish and trees and flowers, and all the kinds of savage people, their homes and curious ways.

'You could spend a lifetime on limnings of all that is new here.'

'I could,' agreed White, inclining his heavy head, 'and with great contentment.'

Kit smiled back, warming to him more. He'd seen White's paintings before but had never appreciated the work that went into them. Perhaps this was how White envisaged his days playing out: in making volumes of notes to be sent back to England, observing the New World for the enrichment of the Old.

He looked round for Emme, wanting to show her the picture, certain it would charm her. It was as vibrant as a jewel, with the quality of an illumination in a rare Book of Hours, but better, in his view, because it was so true to life. He did not need to look far for her; she was heading towards him with little Georgie Howe at her side, her hand in his.

'Master Kit!'

'Mistress Emme!'

They spoke together and he laughed, but whereas he had begun joyfully he could see she was concerned. Her expression was grave and her tone unusually serious.

She beckoned him aside.

'Georgie cannot find his father.' She bent down and put her arm round the boy. 'Make sure I have this right, please, Georgie.'

Emme looked up at Kit and he squatted down beside her, eye to eye with Georgie who couldn't have been more than about seven years of age.

Emme spoke gently. 'You were out with your father, and about a dozen others, catching crabs in the lagoon, along the sands and shallows. You were with your friends and you thought your father was with Master Harvie. That's all correct, isn't it?'

The boy nodded emphatically.

'Yes. Please find him.' Georgie pulled timidly on Emme's sleeve.

'We'll find him, but we must be clear about this first. You came across Master Harvie but he did not know where your father was. Master Harvie told you he thought your father might have come back here. But he is not in your house and no one knows where he is. Since the sun is going down, you're now worried.'

'Yes, Mistress Emme. You need to come with me.' Georgie took hold of her hand again and tried to pull her away.

Kit put his hand on Georgie's shoulder and noticed that the boy's eyes were puffy and close to running with tears. Probably the boy had been weeping while he searched, getting more upset the harder he looked. The boy had no mother alive, so more than likely the boy's father was the only close relative he had left.

'I found his clothes,' Georgie said. 'I can show you where they are.' He danced from foot to foot as if on the point of running ahead.

'You left them?' Kit asked.

'Yes. He'll need them, won't he?'

Kit nodded and spoke to Emme, but not so quietly that the boy couldn't hear.

'Stay here and save something for us. Georgie will need a meal when he gets back; so will his dad. I expect George the elder has fallen asleep in the sunshine and if he wakes up now he'll find everybody gone. Don't let the man wander off if he arrives while we're searching. Keep him here.'

Emme looked uncertain.

'Can't I come too and help? I could look after Georgie.'

'It would be better if you waited. Actually, no . . .'

Kit looked at her trusting face. If anything untoward had

happened to George Howe he didn't want Emme to be put at any risk. But she could keep the boy company while he searched with Manteo. If they needed to follow a trail he'd rather the boy wasn't involved; tracking was best done by a few without distraction. He gave her a nod.

'Thank you. I'd like you to come with us.'

He stood straight and patted Georgie on the back. 'We'll be as quick as possible; try not to worry. And you must stay with Mistress Emme. Now I ought to tell the Governor . . .'

He looked across the clearing and caught sight of Dyonis Harvie, another of the colony's senior men, an Assistant like George Howe, whose distinguishing features were a diminutive frame and stubbly cheeks so burnt by the tropical sun that his face put Kit in mind of a strawberry. Harvie was a sober Kent yeoman with a scatter-brained pregnant wife. Kit doubted he had any skill at tracking, but Manteo would take care of that, and Harvie had seen George Howe last. He pointed him out to Emme.

'Ask Master Harvie to come with us too.'

A few words with Manteo ensured that he followed discreetly. White seemed unperturbed, and waved Kit away, as if he was more bothered by the interruption than that one of his Assistants was missing. He'd started a new painting of a blue-legged crab based on one of those just caught, though it had been cooked pink which plainly presented him with a difficulty. Kit left him peering at it and frowning.

Kit tagged behind Emme who was hurried on by Georgie as fast as she could trot in her petticoats and skirts. Harvie and Manteo strode after them. They wound through the woods until they could see the shore to the west where the dunes shelved down to mud flats and reeds, and the sun flared over the water that led to the mainland a good three miles distant. It shimmered in the heat. From the bank where they stood, the vast unexplored continent looked no more than a faint line: a wavering streak drawn with one of White's squirrel-hair brushes. To the south the reeds stretched in a brown blanket full of holes, reaching to the horizon in a rough wind-combed haze.

They all stopped with the boy and looked down at what he showed them: a pair of shoes and a heap of clothes – breeches, jerkin and hose.

Manteo bent and smelt them.

Harvie bit his thumbnail. 'He must still be in his shirt tails,' he said, as if that was a singular puzzle. He gestured to the water's edge. 'That's where we were, spread out along the shore. Young Georgie here was with a few other boys, and his father was near me until he walked off over there.' He pointed to the reeds. 'I thought he'd gone back to his house when he didn't reappear.'

'Dad!' Georgie called out, funnelling his hands around his mouth and shouting as he had done all the way through the forest. 'Da-ad!' But the answer was the same as it had been before: the whisper of the wind in rustling leaves, nothing more. He started to run down the slope, but Kit had anticipated what he'd try to do and sprang forwards to hold him back.

Emme caught up and hugged the boy tight.

'Stay close to us, Georgie.'

'Let us search carefully,' Kit said to him. 'We need you here to look out. If you see your father, then shout. That's important. You understand?'

Georgie stared at him, bewildered.

Kit took hold of the boy's shoulders. 'If we're down in the reeds, and he walks another way to the trees, we won't see him. So you must watch for that and let us know if he does.'

Georgie nodded, sniffling.

Emme beckoned for the boy to sit with her and they huddled together facing the sun, their backs to an eroded bank trailing grey roots and brambles.

Kit walked back up to Manteo and Harvie. He could see that the Indian was scanning the land, water and sky. He would not rush him. He caught a trace of his smell: tangy, animal and earthy, a mix of the cedar oil he used to keep the insects away, the deerskin he wore round his loins, and the pigments that marked his skin.

Manteo held out his bare arm and pointed with one finger.

'We should go over there, about two miles.'

'Have you seen something?' Kit kept his voice low.

'The *nahyápuw*. Look.'

He pointed high in the sky at a soaring great bird, as big as an eagle, almost completely black against the light though its head showed a flash of white.

'And see there, coming down...'

Kit saw carrion-birds slowly circling, flecks in the distance, wings like boards with splintered tips, repeatedly appearing then disappearing as they wheeled in huge spirals.

'Vultures. At least I think that's what they are.'

He turned to Harvie who nodded. 'Let us see what's there.'

They walked down to the shallows then waded through the water. It was only a few feet deep at most, close to the rushes and reeds, the mud not too thick, mixed with shells and sand. Oystercatchers screeched around them; beyond that, all was quiet.

The water lapped gently, sheltered from the breakers behind the ocean banks, and the wind had settled leaving dark clouds in billowing bands not far above the horizon, around which the sun shot brazen rays and lit up the hammerheads in shades of orange. For over half an hour they splashed through sea grass and sludge until Kit's feet had lost sensation, and the air felt cold above the water, and still the vultures circled, not seeming to settle, and the eagle soared overhead, sometimes lost in the clouds. But gradually they drew closer and, bit by bit, Kit could see where some of the vultures had perched on dead branches sticking out from the level of the reeds, and he noticed that their heads were red as if stripped raw of flesh.

Manteo crept forwards cautiously, and so did Kit, eyeing the reeds and rushes that rose above their heads, and the sentinel vultures crowding together on the branches, and the water out in the open. Without any prompting they all crouched low. The trees were lost to sight. Soon all they could see was water and reeds, and then a black mass of vultures all rippling together like one giant scaly creature rising, hissing from the marsh, fragmenting before their eyes as the birds beat into the air, wings flapping ponderously.

Kit charged to the place where they'd been feeding, heedless of the noise he made and the soaking. He saw something like a manikin that had been used for target practice: limbs straight as poles, body bristling with arrows. It was floating belly uppermost in a few inches of water, the remains of a white shirt fanning out around the chest. The stomach was torn open and the head submerged. Blood turned the water red. He looked over his shoulder and saw Harvie edging forwards.

'Is this George Howe? Is this his shirt?'

'Yes.'

Harvie doubled over to be sick. He turned his back, spat and coughed, then bowed his head with his hands on his knees.

'It was all he had on, knotted up between his legs like that.'

Kit touched Manteo's arm.

'We'd better look more closely.'

They waded nearer, and Kit didn't want to see but knew that he had to.

By the body floated a long stick, forked at one end, bobbing about on the ripples they created. Kit picked it up.

'George must have been using this for crabbing. It's undamaged. He can't have had a chance to try and defend himself.'

Manteo took the stick and used it to poke around under the body.

'He would have been struck by arrows first.'

Kit counted. 'Sixteen of them.'

'Then...' Manteo gave a grunt as he pushed up under the head. It emerged in a pulp, streaming blood.

Kit gagged and turned, clapping his hand over his eyes. 'Let it drop.'

Manteo lowered what was left on the stick.

'His head has been smashed. They will have used clubs and swords of wood. This is the way of the Secotans. They will have scalped him to show their people. Maybe they sought revenge...'

'Revenge for what?' Kit looked round, appalled.

Manteo spread his palms.

Kit shook his head. How could Manteo know? It couldn't have been for anything that Howe had done. Whatever the explanation, what had happened was clear. George Howe had been murdered.

He looked at the torso, already bloated. All that was left of his stomach was a gaping hole.

'He's been disembowelled.'

'The birds will have done that,' Manteo said calmly.

Kit cast around for anything else that might offer clues, but there was nothing, not even a trace of the crabs Howe was collecting. Whoever had killed him probably took them. Kit looked across to the mainland, above which the sky glowed red as if the sun had torn itself going down. Was that where Howe's murderers had come from?

'The Secotans will have come from over there,' Manteo said quietly, as if he had heard Kit's inner question. 'Dasemonkepeuc. It means "land pushing into water". It is the nearest village to Roanoke. It is now home to the tribe which used to live here. They are all friends of the Secotans.' He stared across to the west. 'They will have come in canoes and hidden in the reeds.' He glanced back at Kit and gave a lop-sided smile. 'They will not be here now.'

Kit breathed out deeply. It was small comfort that the Secotans appeared to have gone away. When would they come back? He felt as if he was dragging a colossal weight and could go no further. He could barely move or think straight. What would happen to the colony now – to Georgie and Rob, to Emme and all his plans for the future? He looked back at the body and spat bile from his mouth.

'We can't leave him for the vultures.' He turned to Harvie. 'We must bury him.'

Harvie shook his head. 'How can we without a shovel or spade?'

'We'll drag him ashore and bury him in the sand. We can dig a grave with branches.'

'It'll be dark before we're finished.'

'Even so, we must do it. We can come back tomorrow and bring weights to put over.'

'I'll dig,' Harvie said simply, and waded towards the shore.

Kit looked at Manteo. 'Can you pull up the body?'

'I'll do that, and I'll help Master Harvie.'

'When I come back with the boy...'

Manteo clapped his arm. 'Master Howe will be buried. Do not worry.'

Kit began the long wade back to Emme and Georgie. When he saw them cuddled together he was glad that Emme was there to soften the blow he was about to deliver because, sure as he stood, he did not know how he could have broken the news to the boy if he'd had to do it by himself.

Georgie ran to him first. He made the boy settle then took Emme aside and told her softly away from Georgie's hearing. He spared her the worst, and, when it was done, he watched Emme go to the boy. Then, while she spoke to him, he sat and clasped his hands around his knees, waiting for the child's cries that came and rose and tore him inside out. Afterwards Kit led them to the place where Howe lay in his grave, not far from the reeds where he had breathed his last.

He took off his hat and held it in both hands.

'Earth to earth,' said Dyonis Harvie. 'Rest in peace, George Howe. Blessed are the dead which die in the Lord. So saith the Spirit; they rest from their labours.'

'Amen,' Kit murmured, and opened his eyes to see Emme saying the same, her cheeks streaked with tears, the boy pressing against her, sobbing and shaking. Her skirts were wet through, and darkness covered her like a cloak.

Somehow he had to tell her that she could not stay on the island. It was not safe.

He put his arms round them both.

As Emme swept she heard a man whistling outside, and she began to hum softly to herself, picking up the tune of 'Greensleeves' that was so much part of her growing up it sent a tingle down her spine. She was in a cottage that could have been in England, for it looked much the same as many she'd seen on her father's estate, and little around her was any different to anything she could have witnessed there: the sunshine slanting between the wooden bars of the open window, the smell of wood smoke and baking from the bread oven, the sound of someone chopping logs and a cockerel crowing, the rustle of rushes under her feet as she moved over the packed earth floor. Their City of Raleigh was a piece of England entire. She almost sang out loud:

> Greensleeves was all my joy,
> Greensleeves was my delight;
> Greensleeves was my heart of gold,
> And who but my Lady Greensleeves.

Then she realised she might disturb Governor White and she carried on working as quietly as she could, sweeping carefully around the knick-knacks stored under the trestle table at which he was bent over another painting. There were gourds and pieces of coral strewn haphazardly around the struts, along with twigs, bones and feathers, a sloughed snakeskin and large pink-and-white scallop shells, the stump of a beeswax candle and bits of material crumbling to what might have been charcoal and chalk. She bent down and attempted to push together the collection into a neater pile against the wall, then stood up quickly when a large yellow and black spider crawled from the heap. The creature scurried over a stick that had a tooth fixed to one end, polished and bound with waxed thread. She retrieved this and placed it with the brushes and quills on the table.

The Governor did not look up. His hand moved over the paper, to his water-shell and oyster palette and back to the page on which he was working. She carried on brushing around his feet with the broom, and wondered whether pretty yellow-flowered broom would one day grow in Virginia. She could imagine it blooming on the sandy soil round about. Would the people who came after her ever miss things that could never be brought over? Deep snow, perhaps, and stone churches. There was no stone on the island; their church would have to be built from timber and daub. There would be no headstone for George Howe.

'Greensleeves' faded from her mind.

Governor White stretched out his hand to his palette again and a pencil of black lead fell from the boards, breaking into pieces as it hit the floor.

'God's blood!' he muttered.

She stooped to pick up the fragments then saw him looking at her.

'Oh, it's you.' He sighed and gestured to the clutter around him. 'Forgive me. This table isn't big enough.'

'If you will allow me,' she said, and stacked up all the loose brushes, quills and pencils into a large leather jug that she placed on the clearer surface, giving it a brisk wipe beforehand. By the jug was a small bunch of freshly picked blue flowers just beginning to show signs of wilt.

'And shall I put these in water?' she asked. When he nodded she placed them in a pottle which she half filled with water from the ewer.

His attention moved from the flowers back to the jug.

'There's my burnisher,' he observed with obvious satisfaction, picking up the stick with the tooth that she had found. 'I was wondering where that had got to.'

She smiled back. 'If you would lift your feet, please, sir.'

He raised his legs, stiff as pokers, and she swept underneath.

'I am glad you are here,' he said, lowering his feet by degrees once she had finished. 'I have received a note from our Pilot requesting that you return to the *Lion*.' He tapped a letter with a broken seal that was also in danger of sliding to the floor.

She resisted the urge to take hold of it, and supposed he was talking about a message from Master Ferdinando, since 'our Pilot' was how John White now referred to him; he was no longer 'our Simon'.

'I find this perplexing,' said Governor White, ruffling his hand through his hair, 'not least since our Pilot has refused to allow any other Planters back aboard.' He picked up the sprig of leaves he was painting, turned it about and examined it closely. 'Apart from myself, of course. He would not dare deny me access to the ship. But you...?' He looked at her askance, one brow raised.

She lowered her eyes and carried on sweeping. How much did he know about who she was? She was not sure, and she had no wish to tell him any more than she needed to.

He coughed, probably to attract her attention since she was no longer looking at him. 'Our Pilot says that Sir Walter Raleigh wishes you to return to England.'

Did John White remember her from Richmond Palace? Could he recall her being introduced to him as one of the Queen's ladies? He'd never mentioned that he recognised her, and he gave no sign of doing so now. Though it seemed strange that someone so observant about leaves and flowers could be so inattentive about the features of a face, yet that appeared to be the case. Perhaps she had been of no interest to him at court. She glanced up and saw that he was staring at her and frowning.

'I realise you are known to Sir Walter. It was his request that secured your position in this household and my agreement not to raise any enquiry. But I wonder...'

She kept her gaze fixed on the floor.

'Have I seen you somewhere else?...I mean before you joined us?'

'I have worked for Sir Walter at Durham Place; that may be the explanation.'

She teased her broom around the heap under the table.

'Ah, yes,' she heard him say. 'Well, I've not mentioned this to Ananias or anyone else because I would not wish your special...dispensation to create any resentment amongst the rest of our company.'

'There will be no resentment,' she said brightly. Then she stood and placed a shell lined with dry blue pigment on his table, another casualty of his untidiness. 'I will stay.'

'Stay? No, no, you don't understand. You cannot stay, not if Sir Walter wants you back.' He pushed his forelock from his brow, and scratched his scalp at the same time, an action that left his hair looking even more unkempt than usual. 'I would have thought that you would be only too pleased to return after what has happened...'

'You mean the death of poor Master Howe?'

'Most unfortunate. It leaves us with an unwonted dilemma...'

She turned to the fireplace and began to sweep out the hearth, answering him while her back was turned.

'It is because of Master Howe's death that I am determined not to leave. His son, Georgie, needs looking after. I mean to do that as well as tend to your daughter. She will soon want a maid's help more than ever to care for her through her birth, and afterwards once she has a baby to nurse.'

She was also determined not to leave Master Kit, but the Governor didn't need to know that.

She rattled about with the irons and wondered whether John White had even noticed that little Georgie Howe had taken refuge in his house and slept last night on a pile of rushes, wrapped in a blanket close to the place she now cleaned.

Governor White shuffled on his stool. 'Indeed, that is all true.' Then he tapped the letter again. 'But this cannot be denied.'

She regarded him directly for the first time.

'Did Sir Walter ask you to ensure I returned?'

The Governor's face clouded. 'No, no, he did not. I wonder...' He looked away and towards the open window. 'I never have trusted that Portuguese swine. Tell no one I said that,' he added quickly. 'So...' He picked up the letter and waved it about then tossed it next to the jug and pottle. 'I have notified you of his request and that must suffice for now. No one here is going to return to England until we have determined our position in relation to the savages. Sir Walter will want news about that, and about what has happened to Sir Richard Grenville's men; we should try to find out more about both matters. Sir Walter should at least have a written report...Our Pilot must wait.'

He rubbed his hands together and added a note to his drawing, speaking as he scratched with his pen.

'Manteo tells me that the sap of this herb can cure poison arrow wounds. *Wisakon*, that's what he calls it: a most useful physic. There is much to be learnt from the savages, and much of value in what grows here naturally, not to speak of what *could* grow here with transplanting and nurture.'

She looked hard at him, since his attention was on his writing, and noticed that his hair was beginning to thin over the top of his head, though the rest was surprisingly thick for someone who must have been well over two score years and had endured the hardship of the last Roanoke voyage. He spoke calmly despite the recent tragedy of George Howe's death. Was John White extraordinarily resilient, or so locked in his own world of discovery that he did not appreciate the threats around him and the fears of everyone else? Did he still think that the Indians could be trusted?

'If the Indians attack us,' she began, 'I am sure that such a cure would be a help. And, in view of Master Howe's fate, perhaps we should expect—'

He interrupted her. 'The savages also use the silk of the seeds to make soft covers for the privy parts of their virgin maidens.'

'Really?'

He teased out some of the downy seed tails from a pod at the end of the sprig and studied them carefully as if envisaging the effect.

'Mmm...'

'If we are attacked,' she persisted, 'then...'

'Oh, I don't think that's likely in our City of Raleigh.' He made an airy sweeping motion with his quill. 'We are too great a number for the Secotans to dare confront us. But we must not be complacent, or careless like George Howe, and wander off into the wilderness for miles unaccompanied.'

Her jaw dropped. 'You surely don't mean to suggest that Master Howe was at fault in making his murder possible?'

'Perhaps not "at fault", but he should have been more cautious. Some savages will take advantage if they perceive weakness, just as small children will when left unattended.'

'You said they were naturally gentle when you spoke about them in England; I heard you...'

'Indeed they are, but who knows what may have occurred in their encounter with Master Howe, what grievance, old or new, might have provoked them to unnatural violence.'

'*Grievance*?' She turned from him to hide her shock. A maid's place was not to take issue with her master. She must not argue or appear judgemental, but she could hardly credit what she had just heard him say. She tried to keep the indignation from her voice. 'What grievance could have justified such brutality against an innocent man?'

'I do not say justified. But Governor Lane's relations with the savages here were... not as comfortable as they might have been towards the end of his stewardship. Incidents may have occurred of which I was not fully aware...' He wiped his hands on a rag and peered at his palette, holding a tiny brush close to a bright green colour. 'Is this the correct green, do you think? I have used tender buckthorn berries for the hue.'

She gave a little shudder of exasperation and moved closer to see what he was doing. 'The limning looks perfect.' She meant it. The picture was exquisite. But what of the Indians? Should they be feared now? She certainly feared them even if he did not. She tried another tack.

'You said Sir Walter would want to know the disposition of the savages towards us. What will you tell him?'

He tipped his head on one side, but still considered his oyster palette, as if he was more concerned about his colours than anything else.

'We need to know more, don't we?' His gaze flicked up to her. 'Perhaps we should ask for a parley, approach in peace without seeking redress. But if we are to be avenged for Howe's death, then surprise is the better tactic: a sudden attack and show of strong force...But these deliberations are hardly a fit subject for your hearing.'

'On the contrary, I thank you for sharing your thoughts. It is a comfort to me to be kept informed.'

'Good.' He reached over and patted her hand. 'In our new city I hope we may share more. For leaders to share is also to unburden. So, think on this question: love or discipline – which is the best way to correct a child? With the Indians who are our neighbours, do we embrace or chastise them? My Assistants are divided over the issue. Master Harvie urges that we answer their crime with punishment – forestall any further outrage with a decisive raid.'

A chill ran through her.

'You would take other innocent lives?'

'It is a quandary, as I said.' He looked hard at her. 'I must say, you ask searching questions for a maid.'

She turned back to the crude chimney place and busied herself with shovelling up the ash from the hearth.

'I am only concerned for the welfare of our city.'

'As are we all, and must trust in God to guide us, and give thanks for the manifold mercies he has shown us in safeguarding our city thus far.'

'Yes, of course. But what will you do?'

'*Do*…? To react in haste is often to err. I am considering. Should I note the use of this herb by savage maidens, do you think?'

She glanced over her shoulder and saw him staring down at his picture.

'Your page is already quite full.'

'Hmm…'

He put his pen aside and took a blue flower from the spray she had placed in the pottle.

She tipped the ash out in a bucket and moved to stand near him. Then she picked up the pottle and put the rest of the flowers on one side.

'Have you spoken to Manteo's people to find out what they know? They are still our friends, aren't they?'

He nodded.

'I am thinking of sending a delegation to the Croatans, but that would mean despatching Captain Stafford in the pinnace. Their island is some sixty miles distant, a long way south of Port Ferdinando; such a mission would take at least a few days. Or do I send Stafford to the mainland to raid the nearest village before the savages run away? That village, Dasemonkepeuc, is almost certainly where Howe's killers came from.'

She gave a small sigh of despair. Could he not decide upon anything? She remembered Walsingham's advice when she had been given leave to join the voyage in the presence of the Queen.

'I once heard someone say that to act on knowledge is better than to act on conjecture.'

'True indeed. Perhaps we should talk to the Croatans first. Yes.' He held up the flower and pointed at it with his brush. 'Look at the beauty of this gentian, the depth of the blue, purple and pink. See how its petals are patterned like a star...'

A knocking at the door stopped him short. She turned to see Ananias Dare show his head round the frame.

'My wife would like something to eat and drink, if you will, Emme.'

'Certainly.' She moved to attend upon her mistress and take her a cup of fresh water first.

The question still turning in her mind was whether the Governor had decided to do anything at all.

As she left the threshold she noticed Kit standing outside, not far from the door, and he looked so fine her heart gave a lurch. He stood like a soldier with a caliver on his shoulder and a belt of cartridges across his chest; powder horn, shot bag and match-cord hung by his waist. A sword was at his hip and in his free hand he held his helmet.

Whatever Governor White might be thinking, it looked as if Kit had already made up his mind.

He saw her and beckoned, and her pulse quickened as she neared him, though his expression was sombre.

She wondered what he had to say.

# 9

# *Indian*

'Speak of me as I am...
... Of one whose hand,
Like the base Indian, threw a pearl away
Richer than all his tribe ...'

—Othello *by William Shakespeare, Act 5, Scene 2*

Kit led Emme to the clearing behind the house, the place where he had kissed her when they had been alone together last, where the flowers and weeds grew tall and the shade was deep by the rough blank wall. Would he kiss her again? She kept close to him, half fearing and half hoping he would. She yearned for another kiss yet she remained nervous of his touch. Kit was the only man she could bear to hold her since Lord Hertford had shamed her and left her defiled. Her guilt was like a shadow in a sealed locket around her neck. What if Kit wanted to do more than kiss her? She did not know whether she could bear it. And if he wanted to do more, then shouldn't she confess? She needed to be sure of him, certain he would be true to her, though in her heart she already knew. She needed to hear it: some affirmation to give her comfort, albeit that her body was melting just through being beside him, weakening and trembling, thirsting for an intimacy as dangerous as fire. Yet the look on his face was confusing. He seemed forbidding, as if his mien was a book that had been shut and bound closed.

He propped his caliver against the wall and spoke softly without touching her.

'We are going to Croatoan to speak with Manteo's people. Captain Stafford and most of the Assistants agree on this. I am about to tell Governor White.'

'The Governor was thinking about doing exactly that,' she said with as much confidence as she could project. 'He told me.'

'We need to act now. I'm sure he'll agree.'

She looked at him, waiting for him to meet her gaze though he seemed reluctant to do so. Perhaps he was abashed. Maybe what he intended to say was of such importance to him that he found the saying difficult. Was he about to declare his love, not just now but for ever? Would he suggest that they live in Virginia together and set up house as man and wife? Would he pledge his troth to her? Would he say what she most longed for and feared? When his eyes found hers she smiled a little.

'I will go too,' she said.

He smiled back at her; she saw it. His smile was there for her; then it was gone in an instant. She longed for him to show some affection: take her hand, caress her cheek, put his arm around her shoulders; it need not be much. Her desire for him was so great that she felt the heat of it spreading and flowing through her like a star-burst spraying light. She bit her lip and clasped her hands together, hoping that the shade would hide her blushes. She looked back at him and saw him frowning and that his features were on the cusp of giving way to emotion, as if a struggle was going on inside him between passion and reason. Then his angel-blessed face set hard as sculpted stone.

'I would like you to come with us,' he said.

Those words were music to her even if his expression was per-plexing. She reached out to brush her fingers against his free hand.

But he did not take hold of her. He broke contact and clasped his belt.

'Once we have spoken with the Croatans we will return to the *Lion*. Stafford will report to Ferdinando and prepare to sail back to England. You must go as well...'

'No,' she blurted out, seizing the leather of his sleeve. 'I will not. I am staying here...With you,' she added, feeling tears welling up and the words dying in her throat.

He prised her hand from his arm and stood apart from her. The set of his face was grim.

'You cannot stay; it's too dangerous.' He took a deep breath and bowed his head, not looking at her, as if he did not trust himself to look at her.

'I thought at first there might be a chance – for us – despite who you are and your duty to your true mistress. But not now. Not after what has happened to George Howe. The savages...'

'That was just one incident: a misunderstanding.' She reached out to cling to him, then hesitated as he drew back. She bunched her hands into fists. 'How could the Indians know that we come in peace? Once you have spoken to them, and made clear that we bear them no ill-will – that we can forgive…'

'No.' He cut her short, and the authority with which he spoke came from years of being obeyed. She felt it, and it silenced her.

'Listen to me,' he said more gently. 'Things have happened here that have turned the savages against us. I don't know everything, but I know enough now to realise that you would not be safe here. Howe's fate could be yours…'

He turned away from her but she glimpsed his face crumpling. He put his hand to his eyes and his voice tightened. 'I could not bear that.'

She took a step closer and reached for him again, tentatively and with unsteady fingers. She placed her hand on his cheek and felt the wet of his tears. A lump formed in her throat and she knew that she too was weeping. Tears flooded her eyes.

'I do not care. I wish to stay. Georgie needs me and so does Mistress Dare. More than that, I wish to be here with you. This is my choice.'

She put both her hands to his face, lightly and gently, turning him to look at her.

'We can forgive and begin again. I cannot believe that the Englishmen who were here before us can have done anything so dreadful that it has made enemies of the Indians forever. We must have courage…'

He shook his head and grasped her right hand. 'Try to understand. White never meant to come back here, not to set up another colony. The plan was to go to Chesapeake because the savages there appear to be well disposed to us. That is no longer true here; some of them now hate us, I mean the people who used to live on this island: the Roanokes and their allies, the Secotans. I'm sure of that now.' His face darkened. 'I saw what they did to George Howe.'

'But why?' She was trying to understand and could not. All she knew was that she was crying for his love, for the love he was trying to hide from her, for the love that might heal her. 'What have we done to hurt anyone?'

'Not us – Lane. I'm still trying to find out what happened, but I believe Lane abused the trust of those who once dwelt here. He drove them from their homes and taught them to hate us. They were led by a chief called Wingina who was killed on Lane's orders along with many of his followers not long before Lane left. Wingina was their *weroance*, like a father to them all, and Lane had him murdered. I knew that before I set sail. I did not realise what the consequences for us would be. I had thought that Lane's troubles would not be ours.'

Kit hung his head and held open his arms, and she moved until she could wrap her arms around his waist. That felt so lovely. When he embraced her she did not recoil. Her fear of him was gone; only the fear of what he might say to her remained.

He nestled his brow in the crook of her neck. 'I am sorry,' he whispered. 'I should have told you before.'

She clasped him tight, aware of all the pieces of weaponry that hung about his hips, feeling the knife under his padded jacket, and the helmet that he held against the small of her back. She did not mind. He was close to her. She did not want him to ever leave her.

'So now they have no leader?' she murmured, hoping that at least this might be some help.

'That may make our position worse.' He kissed her neck then raised his head, giving a sigh before speaking as if the weight of what he had to say was a burden he could not escape.

'When Manteo first came to England he did not come alone; another savage came with him, a man from Roanoke called Wanchese. This man learnt our ways, just like Manteo, but whereas Manteo grew to love us, Wanchese resented his abduction and loathed our intrusion upon his homeland. When Manteo and Wanchese were taken back to Virginia, Wanchese rejoined his people to counsel them against us. He did not return to England again; he wanted nothing more to do with us. Manteo has told me this. Our fear now is that Wanchese leads the Roanokes and perhaps some of the other tribes who are allied with the Secotans. If he leads them, it will be against us.'

She hugged him. Nothing he had said really worried her; her worries were all about whether she could hold onto his love. He had wept for her and she had touched his tears. She did not need more reassurance that he believed he loved her now. But would he love her if he knew of her shame? Would he ever make her his wife? Or would he insist she went back to England? She would not go if he did. What he had told her about the Indians seemed no more than conjecture: possibilities that were as remote as death, real but distant when life was for living. Nothing was beyond hope.

She moved her hand to his chest and felt the heave of his breathing: life of her life. What could she say to give him faith?

'But you cannot be certain about the enmity of the Secotans. Let us go to Croatoan where the Indians are friendly and find out what we can, and, if the news from Manteo's people is that the colony is at serious risk here, then we can always move to Chesapeake…'

'That would be difficult.' He cut her short. 'There are nearly six score of us, three times as many as the pinnace can take aboard, and whilst the winds and currents would help us north, they'd make getting back here by sea almost impossible. We don't have the craft on Roanoke to relocate so many people, and, even if we did, the passage would be risky, through swamp and little known territory, or chancing wrecking hurricanes off shore. We'd have no shelters waiting for us and no crops sown for next year. Our supplies might last us through the winter, but then we'd go hungry unless the savages helped us. We'd need to work with them in setting fish traps and finding game, learning what was safe to eat and finding our way around the land and rivers. Life would be hard…'

'Shhh.' She raised her finger to his lips. 'You've said enough. We should not consider Chesapeake unless there is no alternative. But we do not know that yet. We need to speak to the Croatans.'

'We will do that,' he murmured, nuzzling her neck. 'I see no reason why you should not come too, since Manteo's people are our allies and we will rejoin the *Lion* afterwards. Then you must stay aboard for the voyage back to England.'

'Perhaps.' She snuggled closer to him, determined now that she would never leave, neither would she fight with him.

'You…must…go,' he said, bending over to kiss her, smothering the words against her mouth, pressing his lips against hers as if the strength of his kisses would force her to comply.

She arched her back and had no will to protest.

*

'You'd better put this on.'

Kit tossed over a leather brigandine, the sort of old-fashioned surcoat covered with plates and studs designed to protect against arrows, though Emme doubted whether it would be much use against bullets and honed steel. But the Indians didn't have firearms, she remembered, they didn't even have metal, and the coat would probably be more comfortable than the plate armour some of the men were wearing; she had dreaded being made to don a corselet in the sweltering heat. She ran her fingers over the rusting iron embedded in the stiff cracked leather that had rubbed through in places to expose a crumbling under-hide. It had probably been made in the reign of good King Harry, and for how many years afterwards had it knocked about in a ship's hold? She found a patch where the leather was stained black and there was a hole the width of her thumb. Had blood soaked it once?

'Is it yours?' she asked Kit.

'Yes,' he said, strapping on his helmet and handing her a similar morion. 'Put this on too.'

She obliged and immediately felt as if the weight of the pieces was crushing her. It was difficult to breathe and her head was cooking, but the garb also gave her pride. She was one with the men, almost indistinguishable at a distance. Even her skirts had been split and sewn so they resembled a sailor's galligaskins – to help her run if needed, as Kit had advised. Most importantly, by wearing the armour she knew she would not be left on the pinnace as she had feared at first. She would land on Croatoan with Captain Stafford and Kit, and she would be with them to meet the Indians who had been trailing them for miles, too far distant to hail as they followed in their canoes. Though the armour was only a precaution, since Manteo's people were their friends, she still felt glad of its protection, as if Kit was all around her, with his steel-clad hands cradling her head, and his leather-coated body shielding her front and back. The smell of him was in the fabric: strong and raw, hot and salty. She was tired but not afraid.

'We'll soon be ashore,' he said. 'Stay with me.'

Of course she would. She could not wait to move after more than twelve hours on a hard bench, with only a sheet of canvas to screen her from the sun, and rationed water to drink, and little privacy at the heads. They had left before dawn and were arriving with dusk, but the breeze and calm water had helped the pinnace over the sound, and they had covered the vast distance in less than a day and a night. Now the strongest men were rowing, Kit amongst them, leading the stroke, and the sands of Croatoan were clearly visible above the reeds, rising up to a low line of trees. They had passed the inlet that separated the island from the long sand banks of Hatarask and the channel leading to the open sea.

'Bring in your oars!' Kit called, giving the last order to the rowers before the pinnace slid ashore, and Emme made ready to disembark along with the seventeen men who had been selected for the parley. She watched them stand unsteadily after the pinnace bumped aground. Stafford made his way to the bows, and Ananias Dare picked up the standard of their city which he liked to flaunt wherever he went. Manteo followed, holding his bow and quiver, with nothing covering him but his breechclout and paint.

'Bring all your weapons,' Kit called again. 'Leave nothing behind.'

He jumped down before her with his caliver roped to his back; then he held up his arms for her. But she looked down at the water, only a few inches deep, and waved him aside. She didn't mind getting her feet wet, and she'd rather he watched the Indians who were emerging from the trees at the top of the slope from the beach, standing in line along the crest of the bluff. The Indians following in canoes were also drawing close.

Kit looked round and unslung his caliver, ushering everyone onto the sand, apart from the three who had elected to keep guard over the craft. She was glad not to be with them; their wait would probably be long and tedious.

Stafford formed the men into a square, four wide and four deep, pikes in the centre rows, firearms forward and rear. He placed himself in the vanguard, with Dare behind him, and positioned her in the middle, though she had no pike, only a sharpened knife. Kit moved behind her and scanned the Indians all around; they were increasing in number. They drew their bows and waved their spears and made a strange ululation that grew louder and louder. It set the hairs prickling at the back of her neck. What was happening? The Croatans were their friends – so why the show of hostility?

She glanced at Manteo and saw that he was calling, hands circling his mouth, though none of the Indians seemed to hear him amidst their whooping.

'Ready arms!' Stafford called, and the men at the front and back of the square brought their firearms into position.

'Fix matches!' Kit shouted, and the smouldering lengths of match-cord that every caliverman carried were fastened into the locks of their weapons and cocked ready to fire.

'Open your firing pans,' he ordered.

She heard clicking as the pans were opened, already charged with priming powder.

'Guard them!'

Fingers were placed over the powder. A spark from the burning match-cord and the weapons would discharge. They were already loaded and ready to fire at any moment.

She could not believe it; this encounter was supposed to be peaceful. Why were the Indians showing aggression? There would be a bloodbath if the guns fired.

'No!' she murmured, ducking her head on instinct and putting her hands to her helmet. She prayed everyone would stop.

The ululation intensified, rising in pitch. She shrank under her armour and her scalp shivered cold.

Kit's face was a mask: eyes narrowed, mouth rigid.

'Present!' Stafford called.

All the calivermen brought their firearms to their chests, just under the right shoulder.

'Aim!'

They took aim. Kit fixed on one of the Indians coming up from behind.

Suddenly she heard a shriek above the blood-chilling noise. The ululation stopped and, as one, the Indians fled. Those at the top of the slope disappeared into the trees; those on the beach ran and ducked down into the reeds.

'Hold fire and advance!'

Stafford led the company in formation up the rise of white sand, pikes waving as boots slid, but they all arrived at the brow intact and with nothing fired.

The landscape before them was as pretty and peaceful as one of the Islands of the Blessed.

Manteo darted forwards, crying out.

'Ahoy! *Wingapo! Pyas!* Come here, it is I, Manteo!'

He stood alone with his arms held wide as if inviting anyone who could see to shoot him in the chest, but none did. Then a solitary savage ran out to seize him, and others followed all crowding together, until she could see nothing of Manteo for men who were pummelling one another and jumping up and down.

Was Manteo being beaten or were they embracing? She could not tell until Manteo emerged with a group in procession and they all beckoned for Stafford's company to follow. Others came nearer to usher them on, smiling and waving, and Stafford gave the order for the calivers to be put up.

'Tell them we come in peace,' he called out to Manteo. 'We wish to affirm our friendship and ask for news. We will hurt no one.'

Manteo spoke earnestly to those around him, and nodded as they answered.

'My people welcome you with glad hearts,' he said. 'They ask only that you do not take their corn for they have very little.'

'We are here to give, not take,' Stafford replied, gesturing for Manteo to interpret. 'We have presents for our friends of Croatoan. We have English flour and beans. We also have tools of metal: hoes and billhooks, hatchets and axes, knives and fish hooks. We have glass beads and brass bells, looking glasses for the ladies and dolls for the children. We would like to show these gifts to your leaders.'

He spoke more quietly, for Manteo alone. 'I would like to talk with your mother, Manteo.'

Manteo spoke with his people to a chorus of whoops and shouting.

'Come,' he said, beckoning Stafford on. 'You must come to the place of council.'

He led them through open groves of low tress through which the breeze carried the clean smell of pine sap and ocean, and in every bright clearing there were small plots of peas and Indian corn in various stages of growth, and patches of ground where vines and pumpkins grew, and deep pink briar roses bloomed in the brush, and blushing convolvulus twined under small fruiting plum trees. Before they had gone very far she saw her first Indian house, like a little longbarn covered over in hides, with rolled rush matting above an open side revealing the wooden laths of its simple framework, and an arched barrel roof that was curved at both ends. The house nestled amongst trees behind the shelter of higher ground and around it threaded paths worn to silver laces in the sand. Then she saw other houses as she looked further, so much part of the woodland that she barely noticed them at first, not close together but scattered wherever there was space between the tree trunks. She saw a shining pool of water and skins stretched on frames, mats being woven and a dugout hollowed by burning. The deeper they advanced, the closer the dwellings stood, until they assumed some semblance of a village with a cleared space between them and a log fire in the centre. Drying racks and storerooms lay between larger longhouses with sleeping platforms. Posts were arranged in lines, with large-leaved tobacco plants growing between them, and others in a circle, their tops carved with the faces of men, as if at rest but open eyed.

Kit kept by her side, and stooped to ruffle the ears of a little dog that barked at him then scampered near, tail wagging furiously. A small girl tugged at Emme's pantaloons, and Emme picked her up and placed the girl on her hip, laughing with her as she did. The girl was almost naked, but for a pad of moss at her crotch held in place with long leather cords, and a necklace of pearls which she pushed against Emme's mouth, giggling as she tried to force a pearl between her lips. For her efforts Emme kissed her stubby fingers and then her smile-dimpled cheek.

Many more Indians surrounded them, drawing them to mats that were being spread around the central fire, inviting them to sit beside large bowls that were filled with food. Berries and pottage were set out, stewed meat, fish and nuts, along with gourds of water and small piles of fresh fruit. Everyone was thirsty, tired and hungry, exhausted after the tension of their initial encounter. She watched hopefully as Ananias Dare strode forward and planted the city standard firmly in the ground. She was ready to sink down with Kit onto one of those mats.

'Good,' Manteo said, squatting down and grinning broadly. He spread his arms in welcome. 'Now please sit and accept the hospitality of my people.'

Stafford set down his caliver and helmet, crouched beside Manteo, and gestured for the rest of the company to do the same.

'But your people are short of corn,' he said, raising his brows to Manteo. 'It is not right that we should eat much. Let us offer our gifts first.'

Stafford opened a bag he had with him and began to display some of the things he had brought, as did Kit and several of the other men. The tools and adornments were arrayed in shining rows, along with small sacks of flour, bread and pulses. Stafford spread his palms.

'These are for the Croatans, given in friendship.'

Manteo swept his hand towards an elderly woman who advanced with dignity, speaking quietly as she did.

'My mother says we accept in friendship and give to you in return.'

The lady sat down opposite Stafford, slowly and with genteel caution that suggested some stiffness in limbs that must have once moved gracefully. Her face was kind, marked by blue tattoos across her cheeks that followed the upward sweep of an open smile. Around her long, greying hair was a circlet of leather, and about her body was a deerskin mantle, fringed and finished with dainty polished shells. The garment was gathered at the shoulder so it covered most of her breast. Her skin was deep brown and wrinkled, banded with markings around the upper arms and neck. She wore a necklace as well, one made of glass beads similar to those which Stafford had brought. When she smiled, to Emme's surprise, she showed a full set of teeth.

Stafford rose up on one knee and bowed to her respectfully.

'I am honoured, once again, to meet the mother of my friend, Manteo. Alsoomse, great lady of the Croatans, my *weroanca*, Queen Elizabeth, sends you greetings from England across the ocean.'

Emme's eyes widened. So this lady was a leader; that shouldn't have astounded her, but it did, even more than the sight of the bare-breasted maidens who gathered near, and the deerskin aprons they wore which covered their pudenda but not their buttocks, or the actions of the man behind Alsoomse who danced around as if possessed, wearing only a breechclout with a pouch swinging at his side from which he took herbs that he threw into the air. Stranger still, a small black bird flew close by his ear throughout all his leaping, and the puzzle was why it did, until she realised that the bird was dead and fixed to his hair by a network of threads.

On either side of Alsoomse squatted men of great age with the aura of priests, and their arms solemnly folded under rabbit-skin capes. They conversed in low voices, then the lady spoke and Manteo translated.

'We are sorry that we did not receive you properly. Your kinsmen have attacked us when they have mistaken us for enemies, therefore we are cautious.'

Stafford frowned.

'That should not have happened.'

Alsoomse raised an arm across her breast and touched her shoulder lightly, a gesture that seemed placating.

'It is forgiven,' the lady said through Manteo. 'The attack took place on the mainland where your kinsmen did not expect us.'

One of the elderly men leant over to her, his arms still under his cape. They spoke together, heads bowed, then Alsoomse looked up.

'We will show you what they did.'

She summoned a young man with feathers in his hair and he left at speed, dodging around the crowd. When he returned it was with a woman, and between them they carried an older man on a hide-and-wicker frame. The frame was lowered in front of Stafford so he could see the man's withered legs. Emme saw them as well, and the scar of a bullet wound when the man was turned and uncovered: the neat round entry hole in his back, and the pale puckered skin over the wide tear of its exit. He must have been shot from behind.

'When did this happen?' Kit asked.

There was more consultation, then the answer came.

'Over a year ago, in the time of new growth.'

Stafford leant forwards and cupped his chin, one elbow on his knee. 'Some recompense should be made.'

'It must have been Lane,' Kit whispered to Emme.

Stafford spoke again to Manteo's mother.

'Let this wronged man have first choice of our gifts.'

'That is fitting,' she said, as her son translated with a nod of approval. 'We ask you, please, for a token so that a mistake of this kind will not happen again.'

Stafford turned to Kit and Dare. 'The request is reasonable, but what can we give them?'

Dare shrugged his shoulders.

'We've nothing spare but the gifts, and a few beads in their hair aren't going to be much use; there must be close to a hundred of them. Whatever we offer won't go far amongst so many.'

Emme looked round and caught sight of the standard hanging in all its glory behind the place where Dare sat. She glanced at Kit and saw him looking in the same direction. They shared a wry smile, then Kit stood and took hold of the flag.

'No!' said Dare before Kit had even uttered a word. 'You cannot!'

Kit rubbed the fabric between his fingers as it hung spread between top bar and pole. The colours were magnificent in their flamboyance, quartered between the arms of the new city, Raleigh, England and the Crown. At the top left was a red cross on white with an antlered deer in the first quarter; then came the alternate red and white squares of England, four in all; below were the Queen's three gold lions passant on a red ground; lastly were Sir Walter's arms of lozenges argent and gules: silver diamonds on red running in a diagonal line from top left down. The emblazoning had all been sewn in silk with a trim of crimson sarcenet.

Kit smoothed it down. 'What is the motto of our new city?'

Dare narrowed his eyes suspiciously. '*Concordia res parvae crescent*. You should know that.'

'Which means?'

'Work together to accomplish more – as we are doing,' Dare added, raising his chin.

'Well said,' Kit remarked. 'I think that answers the question of what we offer. If we work together with these good people we will achieve far more than if we kill them by accident.'

Emme suppressed a smile and noticed Stafford doing the same.

Dare looked outraged.

'We cannot destroy the standard; it represents the honour of our endeavour. The colours of England are in this silk.'

Stafford coughed. 'Perhaps we could consider using the edging cloth. Some substitute may always be found later.'

'An excellent suggestion, Captain.' Kit unsheathed his knife. 'Let's waste no more time debating. There should be enough here to make a strip each for twenty adults. They can wear the bands around their heads whenever they venture from this island.' He looked to Manteo. 'Will that meet the request?'

Manteo gave a nod of agreement. 'It will serve and be much valued. Your flag will honour us.'

'So, to work.' Kit cut away at the fine fabric while Dare turned aside in disgust. Once finished, Kit gave the material to Manteo for division.

Manteo placed the sarcenet reverentially beside his mother.

She stroked it and seemed well pleased.

Manteo spoke for her.

'My mother says now we will feast. Tomorrow we will meet in council.'

'That is good,' said Stafford. 'We have questions to ask. One of our men has been brutally murdered. We wish to know who was responsible.'

Alsoomse conferred with her son who answered for her.

'My people have heard of this.'

Alsoomse turned to the bird-man and took a pipe from his hands. She drew on it deeply until smoke streamed from her nostrils, then she spoke again and Manteo translated.

'Your questions will be answered tomorrow.' At that, she closed her eyes in a way that made clear that the conversation was over.

The pipe was offered to Stafford and he took it and smoked. Emme looked at the bowls and hands of the Englishmen who were already helping themselves, digging into the meat and wolfing it. Only Kit and Stafford beside her showed polite self-restraint, while she picked up a gourd and saluted Alsoomse before sipping at the water slowly. Then the old lady drank too and, when Emme began to eat, so did she, picking at hulled corn from the same large flat bowl, until gradually everyone settled to eating their fill, enjoying the taste of Indian cooking: the nut-roasted venison and sassafras-thickened stews, the broiled fish and corn pottage with berries, seeds and fruit.

The one question Emme had for Manteo, as she settled to replete contentment, was why his people had said they were short of corn when the display of bounty suggested they had plenty to spare. Their recent harvests had been poor, he explained.

'The rains have almost failed this year as they did the last. Our watering ponds are nearly empty. The corn that has grown is small and we will have a hard winter.'

'So why be generous like this?' She gestured to the feast.

Manteo licked his fingers.

'This is our way. We share what we have when we can, and set nothing aside from one year to the next. We do not hoard so there is no resentment.'

She frowned as she sucked at the tender corn from a small boiled cob, trying to understand. What he had told her seemed charitable but also foolish. Were there no grain lofts in their village?

'But what if you have a good year and there is a surplus?'

'Then we destroy it,' he said, and smiled at her.

Kit leaned over, plainly having overheard.

'The Croatans live for each day, share freely, care for one another without reservation, live simply and modestly, indulge in nothing to excess, know no jealousy and strive for harmony with the world.' He took the baby corncob from her fingers that she'd been about to pop in her mouth and ate it while he looked at her, eyes twinkling mischievously. 'They are savages.'

She stole a cherry-like fruit from in front of him, but he didn't seem to mind, and she gazed at the fire which had been fuelled to blazing and was sending sparks into the darkening air. In time she hoped to better understand. They could learn much from the Indians, but what could they offer in return that would not change them forever? With metal and writing and the word of God Almighty they would be different people. But for the present she was content, and the sound of drums beating quickened her pulse, and the brandy that Stafford had brought flamed sweetly in her throat, and she settled back against Kit when the night fell completely, watching the Croatans dancing, shaking leaf wands and gourd rattles, driving their bodies to exhaustion, leaving to rest only to return and dance ever harder. Then, when her eyes began to close, he led her to the largest longhouse where they had been given a platform to sleep, and he settled her against the matting that served as a wall, and lay down beside her with Stafford on his other side and the rest of the company beyond, the ones that slept at all, and there was no contact between her and Kit that night beyond the touch of their hands. Still the drums beat and the Indians sang, but what she heard in her dreams was the sound of his breathing: like rain in a drought on a field of new corn.

*

Dew cooled the dusty earth, and the shape of forms emerging in the burgeoning light were hazed blue as if misted over, though there had been no rain despite the thunder in the night. The new dawn broke cloudless with a breathless radiance like limpid amber. Emme walked close to Kit, in procession with Stafford and the rest of the company, all trooping to the place of council like a train of armoured angels in a ghostly garden of delights. Most of the Indians were already assembled, judging by the thrum which rose from the clearing, and when she rounded the last longhouse there they were, seated on mats opposite Dare's tattered flag. Manteo and his mother sat cross-legged in the forefront, and on either side were the fur-caped priest-men along with elders of both sexes all murmuring together. She glanced round and saw Dare and Harvie take their places by the flag; the rest of the company followed, though one man arrived late. She saw him hurrying pell-mell past the tobacco plants, still buckling on his belt while hitching the caliver on his back. A young Indian woman ran after him holding his helmet in outstretched arms. He took it from her and jammed it on his head. The man was small and dishevelled and pulled a rueful smile as he joined Stafford's party.

'Who's that?' she asked Kit quietly.

He stifled a chuckle. 'One of our Irish soldiers by the name of James Lacy. I think he's been reunited with someone he's been looking for.'

'Ah.' She watched the woman who had followed settle with her own people, not far away; her eyes never left the soldier, and his eyes never left her.

Emme's attention moved to Alsoomse and the rest of the Croatans gathered round: the heads of families, the old and the young; some of the women had babies with them or stocky infants clinging to their backs. The bird-man was there again, waving his hands over a steaming bowl and muttering some kind of incantation, standing still as a heron until, with a cry, he tossed in a substance which dissolved in white smoke. At that, he clapped his hands, then whispered to Alsoomse while the little black bird swung over his ears. A moment later he sat and Alsoomse spread her arms. Manteo translated for her.

'*Win-gan-a-coa*, Captain Stafford. Welcome to our council, people of England. We are here to answer your questions.'

Stafford stood and bowed.

'We thank you for your kindness, *weroanca* Alsoomse, great lady of the Croatans. We thank you for the feast you have given us, and your loyalty to England.' He looked to Harvie who gave a nod. 'You know that one of our company has been murdered. It happened within a week of our arrival. Our man was killed in cold blood. He was struck by Indian arrows and so viciously beaten that we only knew him by what he wore. Can you tell us who did this?'

Alsoomse listened to Manteo's interpretation, beckoned to a young man and sat back.

'Achak will tell you,' Manteo said.

The youth was barely above a boy, probably only a year or two older than Rob, but he stood proudly with a feather in his roach. A tracing of tattooed lines emphasised the thrust of his rounded chin. His voice began low but ended high and quavering, the voice of a boy eager for approval, excited but fearful of losing face. Manteo spoke for him.

'He says he heard some of the Roanokes say they had seen the white man's scalp. Wanchese has it now. His people killed the white man.'

Dare and Harvie muttered together and Emme saw that Harvie was shaking with anger. Dare pounded his fist against the ground.

'Enough!' Dare shouted. 'We should attack right now.'

Stafford raised his hand to silence them.

'Where did you hear this?' he asked the youth.

'When he was fishing near Roanoke,' Manteo answered. 'He was hailed by men from Dasemonkepeuc. They were watching the Englishmen on the island, hidden in the reeds in their canoes. They boasted of the killing. "Your friends will soon be gone," they said. "The white men have lost their power."'

Stafford turned to the old lady. 'Are you sure that Wanchese was behind this?'

'*Kupi*,' she said, and Manteo nodded, putting her next words into English. 'Wanchese now leads the people of Dasemonkepeuc, those who once lived on Roanoke. He became their *weroance* after your kinsmen killed Wingina.' She took a puff from a pipe that the bird-man offered her. 'Perhaps the spirit of Wingina will now rest.'

Dare grabbed the hilt of his sword and Harvie rose to his feet.

'This is preposterous!' Harvie called out. 'There was no justice in Howe's killing. What had Howe to do with that savage's death? He was innocent and defenceless. His murder must be punished. I say we do that now.'

'Settle down, Dyonis.' Stafford motioned for him to sit, and, slowly, Harvie sank back to his mat. Stafford spoke so that only those nearest him would hear. 'Remember the Croatans are our friends and not responsible for Howe's death. Let us find out as much as we can before rushing to do anything.'

He smiled at Alsoomse and gave a nod to Manteo.

'We thank our friends, the Croatans, for this news and would like to know more. Can anyone tell us what has happened to the Englishmen who came to Roanoke after I left with Governor Lane?

Fifteen were garrisoned at the fort a year ago, yet we can find no trace of them.'

Manteo translated and Alsoomse bent her head to speak with her priests and elders, then she spoke to her son and he addressed the whole assembly. In time a man stood up. He looked like a hunter with well-muscled limbs and a quiver on his back. He wore his hair in a spiked roach and had a necklace of curved teeth.

'Come forward, Nootau,' Manteo said.

The hunter walked into the centre of the circle.

'This man saw what happened,' Manteo told Stafford. He gestured for the man to proceed.

The hunter pulled a hide and a metal knife from his belt which he held up like trophies. Manteo translated as he began his account.

'Nootau used to trade skins for blades with the white men at the fort. He was there last year when Wanchese drove them away.'

'So they are alive?' Stafford asked eagerly.

'Some of them may be, but he is not sure. He saw two of them killed and many others wounded.'

'How did he see this?'

'He hid when the Secotans came, and he watched from the trees.'

'Did the Secotans attack the fort?'

'Yes,' said Manteo as the hunter began to mime out the action of shooting with bow and arrow. 'The warriors of Secotan and Dasemonkepeuc attacked together; about thirty of them. They were led by Wanchese.'

'That's it!' Dare jumped up and seized the standard, brandishing it in one hand and drawing his sword with the other. 'This Wanchese must be stopped. He's probably spying on our city right now, preparing to strike while we're away.'

Kit sprang to his feet and took hold of the standard with both hands. He pushed the shaft down then held it against the ground. 'Sit down, Ananias,' he said softly. 'Hear the man out.'

Kit exchanged a glance with Manteo who spoke to the hunter in his own language. The man resumed talking and Manteo carried on interpreting.

'The Secotans used trickery. Two approached the fort at first and asked for a parley.' Manteo turned to Stafford. 'Nootau thinks that Wanchese was one of them. This man was big, with cheek tattoos like arrow heads, and he had a gap here.' The hunter pointed to his front teeth and Manteo did the same, pushing his thumb nail between them.

The elders nodded and murmurs rose. Manteo added his own verdict. 'This is Wanchese.'

The hunter carried on speaking, acting out the action of his story as he described it.

'These two men appeared unarmed,' Manteo said. 'But they had weapons concealed under their cloaks. The rest of their warriors were hiding in the woods. Two Englishmen came out to speak, and the Secotans looked as if they wished to embrace.' The hunter held out his arms. 'But when the first soldier was received then Wanchese drew his sword and smote him a death blow to the head.' The hunter whipped out his arm and slashed it down and next clutched the back of his head and dropped heavily to the ground. 'As soon as the first Englishman was struck then all the Secotans rushed out in ambush. The soldier left standing fled back to the fort, and those at the fort ran into the strong-house where all the weapons and food were stored, but the Secotans set this place ablaze, and the soldiers were forced to abandon the fort taking only what they held in their hands.'

The hunter enacted an intense sequence of running and firing, miming the shooting of bows and the loading of muskets, the ferocity of the fire, which must have been fuelled by the gunpowder in store, and the panic of escape in total disorder. Throughout it all, the bird-man cavorted in a manic frenzy.

Stafford leant over to Kit and spoke under his breath. 'Well, at least that clears up another mystery – it accounts for the fire damage to the strong-house.'

'Yes,' Kit murmured. 'What we've found is beginning to make more sense.'

Manteo turned back to the hunter as he described the battle that followed.

'The fight went on: first this way, then that. One of the Englishmen died after being struck in the mouth by an arrow. A flaming wildfire bolt killed one of the Secotans. Many were wounded, but the English were hurt most. The Secotans could hide behind the trees and shoot with their bows, but the English could not hit back with their muskets. Their power was fading. Their...*mantóac* left them.'

'*Mantóac*?' Stafford eyed Manteo keenly. 'What is that?'

'It is that which is beyond man,' Manteo tried to explain, his hands moving erratically. 'It is the wisdom of the gods.'

The bird-man generated another cloud of white smoke, and the hunter crouched low and mock-fired a bow and arrow, then he fell down writhing and clutched at his thigh as if impaled. He ended his account on his knees, clawing at his ribs. Manteo made it intelligible in English.

'The white men left alive ran down behind the fort to the little creek where they kept their boat. They rowed away, though many were injured. They stopped for four others who had been collecting oysters along the shore, then they all fled to a tiny island near the passage by which your ships now wait. A few days later they left.' Manteo slowed and looked hard at Nootau; then he spoke to Stafford. 'Nootau does not know where the Englishmen went.'

The hunter drew himself up and waited, chest heaving.

Alsoomse gestured for him to return to his place.

She regarded Stafford sympathetically then bent to confer with her priests and elders. Afterwards she signed for the bird-man to bring the pipe. She spoke after puffing on it and offering the pipe to Stafford.

Manteo stepped forward again.

'My mother says we would have helped your kinsmen if they had come to us. But they did not come. We do not know where these men are now. No one has heard anything of them since.'

'I see.' Stafford turned to Dare, Harvie and the rest of the company. His gaze took in everyone, Emme included.

'We only have two choices,' he said. 'Either we attack the Secotans now on the basis of what we've just heard, or we offer them the hand of peace and hope to move forwards in amity.'

'No!' Harvie blurted out. 'You cannot forgive what they've done and forget about it as if it never happened.'

Stafford continued with what he had to say. 'We cannot both talk with the Secotans and expect justice for Howe's death, or the attack on Coffin and his men. The Secotans will never hand over Wanchese for execution. Either we subjugate them in conflict, or we draw a line under past wrongs in order to live with them in peace – if they will accept a peaceful co-existence.'

'Never!' Dare spat, red faced, eyes flaming. 'What peace can be founded on such villainy?'

Kit turned to him. 'A peace that offers some hope for our colony. It is not a question of what is right, but what is possible.' He held Dare's eye but kept his voice low. 'This is a colony of men, women and children: ordinary people of all kinds. We are not all soldiers. To attack must be a last resort; it may well plunge our city into war – a war we may well lose because the Secotans outnumber us.'

Emme nodded and looked at Stafford. 'We should at least allow the Secotans the chance of living with us in peace. We should talk to them. I believe that this is the course that Governor White would advise. I am sure he would not wish to see any Indians killed unless there was no alternative.'

Stafford wiped his brow.

'Since the Governor is not here I must decide.' He looked everyone in the eye, one by one. 'If we attack precipitously then the way of peace will be closed to us for certain, so let us try for peace now and if that fails then let us reconsider.' He squeezed Harvie's shoulder. 'We will have justice in the fullness of time.' Then he patted Dare's shoulder as well, though Dare shrugged him away. 'We will have honour too.'

He stood and addressed the lady Alsoomse. 'Can you deliver a message to the leaders of all the villages in this region, in particular the *weroances* of Secotan and Dasemonkepeuc?'

She inclined her head and answered through her son.

'Yes,' Manteo said. 'We speak with the Secotans, though they are not our friends. We can deliver a message to the *weroances* of all the nearby villages.'

'Good.' Stafford sighed then stiffened and spoke decisively. 'Please tell the *weroances* that we wish to offer our friendship. We will forgive all past wrongs against us, trusting that English men and women may live peaceably with their neighbours in Virginia. We invite all the chiefs to Roanoke to a council to affirm this peace, and we look forward to welcoming them seven days from now, or to receiving their answers if they are unable to come. Could you send this message?'

The old lady listened to her son's translation, bowed her head, and turned to confer with her priests and elders; then she placed her arm across her breast.

Manteo spoke for her.

'We will do our best to send this message and to bring the *weroances* to you in seven days as you have asked, or to tell you what they say if they do not come. But we cannot speak for the Secotans.'

Alsoomse said more and Manteo added, 'My mother says they may not answer.'

Then the old lady closed her eyes.

Emme looked at Kit, sensing that the meeting had come to an end, and, when Stafford bowed to take his leave, Emme curtseyed before the great lady and drew Kit aside to be alone with him for a moment.

They stood beside a hide-covered shelter, and the sky was a halcyon blue behind the shaggy pines and windswept oaks, but Kit's expression was like a heavy cloud, dark and remote.

'We have another day together,' he said. 'We'll leave now, and we may draw close to Port Ferdinando by nightfall. The next morning we'll return to the *Lion*. Then you must leave.'

'But why must I? Why only a day?' She smiled at him with tears in her eyes. 'Why not a lifetime?' she asked softly, not daring to say any more, hoping beyond hope that he would now get down on one knee and offer his hand, and pledge to wed her if she would only take him, which of course she would with a soaring heart, and then they would never be apart in this land or any other. But all he did was stroke her cheek with the tips of his fingers.

'You never yield, do you?' He shook his head slowly as if he saw her as an enigma, but his look was also admiring; his eyes glistened as he beheld her. 'You really think that there is still hope, that after everything you've heard about the barbarity of the Secotans – the murder of Howe and his scalping; the ambush on Coffin, and the pitiless rout of his men – you think that our City of Raleigh can survive alongside these people.'

'Yes,' she said quickly, taking his hand and kissing it. 'Yes, I do, with all my heart. More now than I did before, because we have offered them peace.'

He gave a soft hollow laugh, and his look, once it was over, was even more troubled than before.

'They will not accept our peace,' he said. 'Why should they when what they want is not to live with us, but to drive us from their land?'

'You cannot know that. Once the Secotans appreciate the benefits we can bring them, and come to accept that we will do them no harm, then they will welcome us. They will grow to love us as we will love them.'

'O, Emme.' He put his arms around her and pressed her head to his chest, kissing her hair. 'If only that could be true.'

'It will be true if you believe it enough to make it happen.'

He took a deep breath and she felt it shudder through him.

'But I cannot believe it,' he said, and his voice cracked as he uttered the words. 'You cannot stay here.'

She held him to her, and sank into his kiss, and did not say that she would never leave him, and that nothing he could do would make her go, because to argue would have been pointless, and anyway she could not speak for the emotions that choked her throat. He said no more either, but the taste of tears was in his bittersweet kiss, and the pain of loss was in the tightness of his hold.

*

Captain Stafford had Master Ferdinando with him. Emme caught sight of Ferdinando's slick black curls under his gaudy cap and the crimson doublet he liked to wear. The Pilot jumped down into the bows of the pinnace and moved to the foremast where he waited, one arm raised to lean casually against it. His Quartermaster and a line of burly crewmen stood, arms akimbo, looking down from the *Lion* to which the pinnace was moored up abreast. Stafford alone advanced towards the stern, climbing over the crowded rowing benches to reach the place where Emme sat with Kit in front of Manteo and Towaye. Kit shuffled over to make room, and Stafford sat next to him with Emme on his other side. The Captain spoke quietly to her.

'Master Ferdinando is now ready to sail back to England and bids that you accompany him. I too will return and can assure you safe passage. There is far more risk to you in staying here in Virginia. I am about to go to Roanoke to deliver my report on the Croatans. I shall inform the Governor that you are on the *Lion* in readiness for the voyage back to England. There is no point in your returning to Roanoke only to have to leave immediately. You should stay here, out of danger. I gather from Master Ferdinando that Sir Walter Raleigh has charged him with your safe return to London. My advice to you is to board the *Lion* now without any fuss. The rest of the Planters have no such dispensation, as you know; they must stay here.'

Emme bowed her head.

'Thank you Captain Stafford, but I have already decided not to leave our colony. I shall return to Roanoke and nothing will make me change my mind.'

'Very well.' Stafford gave a resigned nod and looked from her to Kit. 'You are sure of this.'

'Yes.'

Kit interrupted, addressing Stafford directly. 'She will go.'

He leaned forwards in front of Stafford and whispered to Emme with urgent entreaty. 'You must go. I beg you, Emme, do not make this any more difficult for both of us. For the sake of the esteem in which I hold you, please go: live and enjoy a full and happy life in England. I will always...'

'What's the delay, Stafford?' Ferdinando's strident voice stopped Kit short.

Emme looked round to see Ferdinando working his way closer. Stafford got to his feet and stepped aside as Ferdinando waved him away. Ferdinando took his place and put out a hand to keep Emme where she was. He gave her a supercilious smile though he also appeared irritated. With his other hand he drummed on his knee.

'Quite the Amazon, I see.' His tone was mocking as he scrutinised her apparel.

She held her tongue. She was aware of Kit on Ferdinando's other side, hands on his knees, head bowed. Though he faced forwards, his gaze was fixed on the Pilot. She could see his eyes burning from under his lowered brows, stare narrowing out of the corner of his eye. But Ferdinando seemed not to notice; he ignored Kit completely.

'The *Lion* awaits you, Mistress Murimuth.' Ferdinando made an airy gesture towards the ship. He shifted nearer when she made no sign of getting up. 'I gather from Captain Stafford that you have expressed some reluctance to leave the Planters. Have no qualms about your preferment. I am sure you will prove yourself worthy of deliverance once you are safely back in England.'

She turned away from him and looked back to the white dunes of Hatarask and the channel leading to Roanoke.

'Spare your breath, Master Ferdinando. I am not leaving. I have decided to remain in Virginia.'

She heard something else above the sigh of the waves, the drum of rigging and the grinding of the ships' strakes: a sharp intake of breath. Perhaps the sound came from Kit though she could not see him.

Ferdinando put his arm behind her, not actually around her but close to that. She was wedged between him and the side of the pinnace, facing the sea and long shoreline. She twisted away from him.

He rubbed his leg against hers in a way that made her feel sick. She squirmed to escape contact with him, but he bent over in front of her. As he smiled, his lip curled.

'Your leaving is not a matter of choice for you, Mistress Murimuth, so please reconsider. The only choice you have is whether to leave with dignity or under restraint. I will not hesitate to carry you away forcibly if need be.'

His eyes flicked to the Quartermaster and his mariners lined up on the *Lion*. Some of them were stripped to the waist. They all seemed to be leering at her.

She chanced a glance at Kit and saw that his face had darkened, though he remained perfectly still. She turned back towards Hatarask with a sinking heart. No one was standing up for her, but she would never leave willingly. She kept silent.

Ferdinando brought his hand to her arm and gave the flesh a squeeze as if he was testing her plumpness.

'So do not be coy, dear maid, I am looking forward to your company on the homeward voyage, as I am sure you are looking forward to mine despite your show of diffidence.'

Her skin crawled where he touched her. She shrank away from him clasping her arms together over her chest and squeezing against the side as much as she could. If she had to be dragged away in chains then so be it, let the fault be Ferdinando's for so ill-treating a lady, and let it be Kit's for doing nothing to stop him. Why wasn't Kit coming to her aid?

She turned her back and replied without looking at him. 'I have already told you I am not leaving. I will have nothing to do with you because I am staying in Virginia.'

His anger was palpable; she could feel the stiffening of his body as he pressed against her, along her thigh and lower back. He snapped his fingers and summoned the Quartermaster.

'Get this woman aboard the *Lion*,' he called out. 'Bring rope and a gag and half a dozen men. She wishes to be treated like a *puta* in need of chastisement, so we shall oblige.'

While the Quartermaster bellowed orders she heard Ferdinando's breathing and felt his mouth close to her ear.

'It will amuse me to teach you some obedience once you are back aboard my ship. A maid should know her place.'

He took hold of her shoulder, pinning her down painfully. Even if she had wanted to jump overboard, now she had no chance of doing so. He had her trapped.

'And do not think you can complain to Raleigh on your return,' he whispered. 'By defying me you are also opposing him. Sir Walter expressly requested that I bring you back; I will do as he has asked.'

She writhed, but he kept hold of her and pulled out his kerchief, dangling it in front of her.

'If you scream I will stop your mouth.'

She stilled and heard a succession of thuds. Then she looked forwards and saw the Quartermaster and his men jumping one by one onto the pinnace.

Stafford leant over and tapped Ferdinando on the arm; he looked appalled. 'I am sure this is not necessary.'

'Well, I am sure it is,' Ferdinando snapped back, wrenching round Emme's arms and crossing her wrists behind her back. She felt a rope passing over them, pulling tight and burning her skin.

'Enough,' Kit said softly.

Ferdinando froze.

She twisted round and saw that Kit was holding his pistol to Ferdinando's neck, but so well concealed under his cuff and the collar of Ferdinando's shirt that only those closest could have noticed it.

'Manteo and Towaye are behind you,' Kit murmured.

She turned a little more, glancing down towards the shiver of movement behind Ferdinando's back, and glimpsed the Indians with their knives drawn, hilts angled upwards, blades nestling under Ferdinando's doublet.

Stafford stood facing the Quartermaster with his back turned. If he had seen anything of what Kit was doing, he was not going to interfere.

Kit spoke very softly.

'Now let her go, Master Pilot.'

Slowly, Ferdinando released his hold on Emme; his eyes were no longer upon her, but on Kit, boring into him.

Kit glared back. 'Tell your men to return to the *Lion*.'

Kit cocked his pistol. She heard the click.

Ferdinando flinched. 'Back,' he blurted out, waving away the Quartermaster and his crew. 'Get back to the ship.'

Manteo gave a little jab and she saw Ferdinando arch his back. His eyes widened, though he kept them on Kit.

'We have had a change of plan,' he called out. 'The lady will join us later.'

'Stand,' Kit ordered, barely above a whisper. 'Go back to your ship and do not make me shoot you. Stafford will join you once he has spoken to White.'

Ferdinando rose with a face like thunder. Kit withdrew his pistol and folded his arms, but she knew that under his sleeve his pistol was still trained on the Pilot. Kit watched Ferdinando like a hawk as he clambered back to board the *Lion*.

'Cast them off,' Ferdinando barked, watching as the mooring ropes were untied and thrown over to the pinnace.

'As you wish, Master Ferdinando,' Stafford called up to him. 'I will return with the Governor's report.'

Stafford gave the order to make way, and Kit called for oars and the stroke. As he turned to face Emme and began to row, he looked at her with grim seriousness.

She beamed back at him. They would return together to Roanoke and their journey would continue. Kit would come to be glad that she had not left him, only give her time to convince him. But his expression seeded a doubt, and the shame that never left her cast a shadow over her heart.

Would they be together for much longer?

# 10

# *Revenging*

'...The Governor having long expected the coming of the
weroances...seeing that the seven days were past within which
they promised to come in, or to send their answers by the men
of Croatoan, and no tidings of them heard, being certainly also
informed by those men of Croatoan that the remnant of Wingina
his men, which were left alive, who dwelt at Dasemonkepeuc,
were they which had slain George Howe, and were also at the
driving out of our...Englishmen from Roanoke, he thought to
defer the revenging thereof no longer...'

—*The entry for 8th August from John White's Narrative of his
1587 Voyage to Virginia*

'We must attack. We have no choice. We've offered peace and it's
not been accepted.'

Ananias Dare thumped the trestle table as he made his points,
setting it rocking on the dirt floor inside the Governor's new strong-
house. John White leant away, stiff backed and tight lipped, while

the other Assistants around the table all bent forwards, and everyone else looking on stood motionless, packed against the daub and timber walls. Emme peered over Manteo's shoulder, determined not to miss a word, suppressing the urge to shout out that they did have a choice; no one was forcing an attack – let the colony not begin with warfare.

Dare banged the table again. In the candlelight his face looked like an angry demon's, red and fiery with sickle shadows above his eyelids.

'A full week has gone by and not one *weroance* has come or sent a message to us. If we do nothing the savages will believe we are powerless. They will think they can attack us with impunity. We cannot survive under constant threat of annihilation, unable to hunt or fish for fear that our men will be picked off one by one – unable even to grow crops for fear that there will be Indians lurking, waiting to pounce on our women and carry them away. Are we to go abed each night wondering whether our city will be torched while we sleep? To have any hope of continuance we must demonstrate our strength: show that we will not tolerate any interference; that we must be respected, and that crimes against us will be punished.'

'Well said, Ananias,' someone interjected amongst a general muttering and clapping in support.

'I agree,' Dyonis Harvie said, getting to his feet while Dare sat down. 'I think we owe it to the memory of good George Howe to avenge his death and do what we can to bring his murderers to justice.'

Governor White raised his hand, though he remained on his stool at the head of the table.

'No one can accuse us of not trying to live with the savages as friends. We have offered to forgive and they have turned their backs.'

He sounded weary, Emme thought; he seemed to reek disappointment. She saw dejection in the way he pulled down his hat and hunched his big shoulders. He must have hoped for a celebration of friendship with the Indians, not the hostility that Dare was espousing.

'They despise us, that's why.' Dare waved his finger. 'They think that we have neither the will nor the means to oppose them, and that they can do whatever they please: kill all of us or worse. Are we going to let them scalp every man, rape our women and make slaves of our children?'

A shiver of disgust ran through the assembly.

'We cannot allow that,' Harvie said amidst a chorus of 'No' and 'Never'. He continued firmly. 'To make the savages respect us we must avenge Howe's murder and the driving away of Coffin and his men. We must strike back hard.'

He sat down. White pinched the bridge of his nose, shielding his eyes as he did, head bowed, appearing deep in thought; then he nodded as though he'd reached a conclusion.

'I suppose a punitive strike may be in their interests as well as ours in the long run, if it leads to peace. But would it be possible to attack decisively so as to demonstrate our superiority once and for all? What do you say, Captain Stafford?'

White raised his shaggy brows towards Stafford with a look of abject appeal. The Captain stood near Kit and took a step forwards as the nearest Assistants turned to face him. He could move no further in the crush. Stafford gave his answer with the elegant assurance of a prowling cat.

'We could launch a surprise assault on Dasemonkepeuc which appears to pose the greatest threat to us. The village is hardly more than three miles away. We could sail over in the pinnace under cover of darkness and ambush Wanchese's warriors at dawn. We have enough calivermen to scare them witless with musket-fire.'

'Crush them,' Dare cried out. 'It's the only way. Sweep the village clean of them.'

Stafford hooked his thumbs in his belt, a confident stance that reflected his aura of dependability. Emme did not doubt that Stafford could do as he claimed; he was an experienced soldier and sea captain, whose service with Governor Lane meant that he knew what the colonists faced. But he would go back to England with Ferdinando; he would not stay with the Planters like Kit. If he took action against the Indians, he would not have to live with the consequences.

'But are you sure that would be right?' She spoke up without even meaning to, and then was acutely conscious of everyone looking at her, Kit included, who had barely exchanged a word with her since their return. He was plainly vexed that she had defied him in refusing to leave, but she felt sure that his annoyance would soon fade if she left him alone. Her interruption wouldn't have helped. She turned in some embarrassment to Governor White.

'May I speak?'

White inclined his head graciously, and gave her a concerned smile.

'Every citizen may voice an opinion, man or woman, gentleman or maid. We will disregard no one. But I and the seven Assistants here will decide on the course to be taken. The government of this City of Raleigh rests upon my shoulders and theirs. We will not abrogate that responsibility.'

'Thank you, Governor White.' She turned to address everyone around the table and as many others as she could. 'I ask you please to reflect upon the way our offer has been communicated. We have asked the Croatans to be our messengers. I do not suggest that they have not informed the *weroances* as they promised. But remember that the Croatans have openly stated that the Secotans are not their friends. Would the Secotans trust an offer delivered by their adversaries?'

'Maybe not,' Harvie answered. 'But can we trust the Secotans?'

Dare waved his hand dismissively. 'What would you suggest, Mistress Murimuth: that we send an emissary to treat with the Secotans face to face?'

Harvie nodded. 'Do we assume that they will receive one of our own messengers with dignity when they murdered Master Howe without any provocation?'

'The question is unhelpful,' Dare said, and to Emme's chagrin some of the other Assistants muttered in agreement. 'Let's move on.'

Kit alone sprang to her support. 'It might be that a direct approach would be fruitful. I would be prepared to try and talk with the Secotans.'

'You would talk with Wanchese?' Harvie asked, raising his brows.

'Yes.'

A ripple of astonishment passed through the crowd. Feet shuffled and people pressed forwards. Private debates began in low voices, behind hands and at the back of the crowd.

'No, Kit,' Emme interjected quietly. 'I did not mean . . .'

Manteo cut across her, frowning and clearly discomfited. 'You may trust my people. The message will have been delivered.'

She was mortified; she had never meant to upset Manteo, nor to suggest that Kit should take any more risk. She only meant to try and avert conflict by suggesting a reasonable explanation for the silence of the Secotans, one that did not presuppose that they meant to kill every colonist.

Manteo thrust out his jaw defensively. 'The *weroances* will have been asked to come.'

Dare rounded on him accusingly. 'But even your mother is not here.'

'She may have thought that coming here would serve no purpose if the Secotans refused to respond.'

Harvie turned and fixed Manteo with a pointed stare. 'Which will have left the Secotans believing that they need not fear us because we have sued for peace and have been ignored.'

'Good,' Dare asserted. 'We can catch them off guard and so terrify them that they never trouble us again.'

The general hubbub became louder.

White clasped his hands and frowned. 'If the Secotans can indeed be frightened without too great a loss of life, then I suppose ...'

'We need to act quickly,' Harvie said, 'or the element of surprise will be lost.'

'Strike now,' agreed Dare. 'Strike tonight.'

'I am ready,' another Assistant asserted.

'But we should first properly consider the risk...' White began.

Emme did not hear any more. Kit raised his hand as if about to speak, but, before he could say anything, Stafford had taken hold of his arm and ushered him outside. She followed them to the doorway, beyond which they stood facing the new triangular palisade and the gateway to the central clearing.

Stafford spoke to Kit in an undertone but she could still pick out the gist of what he was saying.

'I think we should leave this to Governor White and the Assistants. They are the ones charged with the running of this colony.'

'Yes,' Kit answered, bending his head so that she saw his handsome face in profile, dark against the light of the fire, his chiselled lips closed as he mulled over what Stafford had said; then he spoke again.

'You are right. This is a cup I will gladly leave in White's hands. I'll wait for his decision, and then support it whatever it is.'

Stafford held Kit's shoulder briefly; then he slid past Emme to return inside. He did not seem to notice her, and Kit appeared lost in thought. Manteo came out seconds later and she launched into an apology, wishing now that she had kept quiet at the meeting.

'I have faith in you and your people, Manteo; I hope you believe that. I never meant to suggest otherwise.'

Manteo's voice was warm though she could barely see him to look for a smile.

'We are still friends, Mistress Emme; be not troubled.'

But she was troubled. More people emerged, spreading out between the strong-house and the fortified earthwork that surrounded it. The bank was topped with tall pointed stakes so close together that they formed a black curtain away from the rushlights. The colonists who moved to the shadows to talk in private became lost to her sight. Kit remained by the outer wall of the house, squatting on his haunches, drawing shapes in the dirt with his knife, plans of attack for all she knew. She did not question what he was doing because the rest of the mariners and soldiers soon gathered round him: Lacy, Wright and Stafford too, about ten of them in all – the men who would have to fight if White decided to attack. Manteo and Towaye formed their own group of two near a corner of the house. The women made a third group and the young men another. The Planters were breaking apart and reforming in smaller units of like kind. All were huddled together and glancing over their shoulders. Soon only White and the Assistants were left inside, and it seemed as if she was the only one outside who was left alone.

She wrapped her shawl about her shoulders and wandered over to the gate to look at the fire left smouldering in the middle of the clearing. It would be pointless trying to sleep. How long would White take to decide? They could be debating all night; White was not a man to be hurried, and she could not imagine him making up his mind very quickly, not when the issue in question was of such significance for the future of the colony. She considered drawing closer to the fire and sitting on one of the logs where at least she might find a little warmth and get away from the cool breeze blowing in from the sound. But all of a sudden the door to the strong-house flung open and Stafford was summoned back inside. He entered and shortly afterwards re-emerged. She moved closer as he strode over to Kit and the soldiers, knowing in that instant that the decision had been made. White must have capitulated. If he'd persisted in his arguments for caution and restraint there would never have been such a swift resolution. There would be an attack. Stafford confirmed it when he spoke.

'Get ready. We're leaving at midnight. Twenty-four men will be led by myself and Governor White. We've nearly two hours to prepare. We'll be sailing in the pinnace and landing at Dasemonkepeuc.'

One by one, Stafford clapped the men on the back, tasking them by name, listing the weapons each should bring, and one by one they left.

She yearned to go too, but she knew without asking that Stafford would never consent to that, and neither would Kit. This was a business for men. It would be violent and bloody and some of them might not come back. Images of horror welled up in her mind, indescribable and fragmented, seeded by everything she had heard about the ferocity of the Secotans: a sword thrust from under a cloak; a club smashing open a head; an arrow tearing into a mouth – possibly Kit's mouth. She moved closer until she saw him clearly. She could barely speak.

'God go with you, Kit,' she said in a voice like a stranger's, shivering as if with cold.

He ushered her round to the shadow at the side of the stronghouse. She felt they were alone but did not care if they were not. Would he now declare his love then ask her to marry him, so that with her promise he would be strengthened for what lay ahead? What was there between them apart from stolen kisses, a few tender words and others more divisive? There was only the desire deep inside her that burst into flame whenever she saw him, or heard his voice, or slept and dreamt of him, or came close enough to touch, as now, inhaling his smell of leather and salt, his arms caressing her back, and his body against hers, breathing life between her lips while the spirit of love beat inside her, until her fingers were sparkling and every delicate point of contact was consumed in sensation: face and neck, shoulders and back; and his touch set her alight, and her breasts ached against his chest. She would never let him go and then the moment would never end.

He drew breath, still kissing her.

'I have something to ask you.'

'You do not need to ask. If you wish my answer to be yes then that is my answer.'

He kissed her forehead gently.

'Let me ask you anyway, so I am sure you understand fully. You should know...'

'What, Kit? What should I know?'

She prompted him as he fell silent and in his pause all she heard was Stafford giving orders.

'...More water – and pitch. Bring a cask...'

She kissed him where his jerkin was unbuttoned, and his collar ties were loose since the day had been very hot. With her lips she found a little of the wiry hair that curled over his chest. What more could she do? He only had to ask and she would say yes to him. Why was he hesitating?

He held her shoulders, peeling himself apart from her. Where they had been together she felt suddenly chill.

'I have a son,' he said.

'I see.'

She did not see; she had said she did without thinking. She did not understand. What did he mean? Did he want to confess to having fathered a bastard? It wouldn't matter to her if he had; she would still love him.

'Was he born out of wedlock?'

'Yes, in a sense, though his mother and I were married in a way.'

'Married? You are telling me you have been married?'

'No. We...It was not marriage as you would recognise it. I...'

'You are not married now?'

'No.'

She put her arms around his waist and smiled though he would not see it. As long as he was not married now, she did not care.

'I am glad you have a son, Kit. You must be proud of him.'

He stroked her shoulders as he held her and she felt him relax a little.

'I am proud. He is a fine boy. He is here with us. He...'

She heard him struggle while her mind span with questions. How could Kit's son be 'here with us'? Who was he?

'Tell me, Kit.'

'...He does not know that I am his father.'

How could the boy not know that Kit was his father? He was making no sense.

'What are you saying? Who is this son?'

Kit took a deep breath.

'Rob is my child.'

'Rob?' She stood motionless with shock. 'But he's your page, he's...'

'He's a blackamoor, yes. His mother was a runaway: a slave from the Guinea coast who escaped from the Spaniards, as I did in Panama. We lived together as man and wife, though a priest never blessed us. We stayed with the Cimaroons...'

'The outlaws you told me about?'

'Yes, the fugitive slaves who roamed the mountains. For a while I was their leader. But when I heard that English ships had arrived, I left the Cimaroons to try and find them. That led me to my brother, and together we returned to England with Drake. At the time of our parting, the woman I lived with was expecting my child. That child is Rob. I found him years later when I returned to Panama.'

She felt something cold settle like lead in her stomach.

'You went back for this woman?'

'Yes; I loved her very much. But my Ololade was killed by the

271

Spaniards long before I could reach her. Her son is all that she left me – *our son*.'

She should have been weeping for him but she could not. She felt sick.

'Why are you telling me this, Kit? What does it have to do with me?'

He still held her shoulders, but beyond that they barely touched; she must have edged away from him. She held herself upright while inside she was sinking. People were calling in the distance. Stafford's commands rang out, and in her mind they were like stones smashing apart all her hopes, as if her dreams had been made of porcelain and now they were shattered, and the shards were cutting her as they fell at her feet.

Kit's voice seemed ragged.

'I beg you to care for Rob if anything happens to me. Remember he does not know he is my son. Do not tell him unless you have to, but if you do, then do so gently.'

'Kit, *you* should tell him, not I.'

She pulled away from him, pushing him back, unable to hide the anger that welled up inside her. This was not for her to do; she hardly knew the boy.

'Go to him now and take your leave of him properly, as his father.'

She folded her arms and clawed at her sides while tears of rage spilled uselessly from her eyes. 'Why do you burden me with this?'

He stepped nearer again and reached for her. She backed away but he grabbed hold of her, circling her with his arms and embracing her so tightly she could not break free. Panic welled inside her. She struggled to escape as he pressed a rough kiss to her lips, a kiss forced upon her just as he had imposed the knowledge of his son, a knowledge she could not forget.

'I am sorry,' he said. 'Watch out for him, please.'

He let go of her and waited for her answer: the reassurance he needed that would unburden him for the fight.

Bitterness almost choked her, but she gave a nod.

'He is but a child.'

Kit reached for her again, but dropped his hand when she shied away from him.

'If the time comes…' he began; then he finished quickly as Stafford called out his name. 'If you need to speak to Rob then tell him that I love him.'

She barely saw him walk away. He was gone in a blur. She almost ran after him, but then she heard the splash of oars and she knew it was too late. She walked aimlessly away. Kit meant everything to her even though he had cut her to the quick. It was clear to her now that he cared for his son most of all, and that if his lover was still alive then that woman was the one he would be with. Kit Doonan would not have looked twice at Emme Fifield, lady-in-waiting to the Queen. So what did that make her? Nothing. She was less than a concubine and a dusky slave. Perhaps he had only ever shown her affection in order to persuade her to look after his boy. But she had been sure that he cared for her. He just didn't care for her enough to ask her to be his wife. Well then. She wiped at her cheeks and eyes. She would prove herself worthy of his love, even if she no longer knew whether she could love him as she had.

She found herself by the fire though she'd hardly noticed that she was walking. Not far away was the canvas shelter that Kit shared with Rob. Suddenly she knew what she would do: find Rob and tell him that his master had left with the Governor and Captain Stafford, explain their mission, then invite the boy back to the Governor's house to help her with Mistress Dare while the men were away. The resolution stopped her tears – better to act than to mope. She bent to call the boy's name. It would be kinder to speak to him now rather than let him wake up alone. She cleared her throat.

'Rob.'

Her voice sounded strong, but in her heart she was still weeping, sure that Kit would never love her as he had loved the mother of this young man.

She felt her own love had died.

*

It was an ugly dawn for an ugly business. The first show of light glimmered sickly yellow behind a thick pall of cloud. Kit rubbed at his eyes, unable to focus on much beyond the black blur of reeds stretching to the weak shine of water. From where he lay, flat against the ground, everything was mist-hazed, low in the distance and foreshortened. The mounds of bark-covered shelters rose between him and the sound like the humps of a coiled beast, six that he could make out: a village of maybe ten families. But the only evidence of habitation was the smell of dung and drying tobacco, a thin plume of smoke, and the vague suggestion of feathered Indian heads, three of them, close to the source of the smoke. He saw one of them move.

He kept still, hearing rustling as Stafford and his advance party crept forwards. Soon the Indians would sense them and react. He positioned his caliver ready to fire, blew softly on the match-cord and checked it was secure on the serpentine. If the savages didn't hear Stafford's party, they would scent the acrid smell of smouldering saltpetre. At any moment they would dive for cover and reach for their bows. If they tried to escape through the village then they wouldn't get very far; Kit and the rear-guard had all the longhouses surrounded. In a way he hoped the savages would run. He was glad not to be leading the attack – glad not to be there with Stafford, Dare and Harvie because he knew what they would try and do: take aim on one of those unsuspecting warriors and shoot him before he had a chance to even see who they were. They were stalking the Indians as if they were game. This was not the way Drake would have done things. Sir Francis would have fired a warning volley and called for the savages to submit. This was a raid by stealth with the aim of killing in the same way that George Howe had been killed: an eye for an eye. An Indian would lose his life who probably had nothing to do with Howe's death, just as Howe had been murdered who had nothing to do with the death of the old Indian chief, or with Lane's depredations, whatever they were. He hoped it would end there.

Kit tensed, waiting for the piercing crack of musket shot that would surely come. Whether the Indians broke first, or Stafford's party fired before they were alerted, there would be at least one shot, and the shot from Stafford would bring down a savage; then Kit and the rear-guard would drive everyone from the village, and those left alive would be so terrified that they would flee to spread the word about the fearful might of the English. It was possible. It was also possible that afterwards there would be peace. Maybe the leaders of the Secotans, Wanchese, and the *weroances* of all the neighbouring tribes, would come to Roanoke to discuss terms by which everyone could live in harmony, English and Indian together. He had to believe it. He fingered the firing lock of his caliver and blinked to clear his eyes. It was possible that Rob might grow up free here and live a long life full of contentment. It was possible that Emme might still care for him though he had felt her coldness when they had parted. Dreams. Without dreams there could be no endurance. Sometimes it was better not to think too far.

He was glad he was here, able to act, rather than wait back at Roanoke wondering what would happen. Action would wipe everything from his mind. He wanted to move and let impulse take over, not linger in suspense, hearing the muffled click, click as White fiddled with his firearm, and the soft sibilance of Manteo's whispered prayers. At least those two were safe. If he did nothing else he would keep them that way. White must be preserved as the colony's ambassador to safeguard the future with Raleigh's support. Manteo must not be put at risk; this was not his fight, and he had played his part in guiding Stafford to Dasemonkepeuc. For the sake of the safety of the Croatans, Manteo must not be seen as one of the attackers.

Kit nosed the muzzle of his caliver further between the stalks of long grass. What would he do when the shot came? Move forwards to shield White and Manteo then try to protect the Planters from any counterattack – sacrifice his life without hesitation if that would be of any use; there no longer seemed much point in worrying about his own preservation. Ever since he'd been a prisoner of the Spanish, sure that any moment he was going to die, he had ceased to much care about clinging onto life.

But he'd never been less concerned about his own survival than now. He had done as much as he could and disappointed those who meant most to him. He had failed Rob as a father; the boy did not even know who he was. Emme was right: he should have told Rob the truth before. Perhaps he had always been chary of facing up to Rob's reaction. What if the boy hated him for taking him away? Rob had cause to resent the fact that he had only accepted him as a page, never acknowledged him as a son – never openly shown him a father's love. Rob might well loathe him for keeping secret the fate of his mother. Why had he done that? The boy would want to know. Rob could blame him for abandoning them both. He had failed Emme too: upset her so much that he had felt her recoil. He had shocked her, he could tell. In her eyes he was shamed. He had fathered a bastard by a blackamoor and hidden his passion for a slave, a passion he still felt, though, in a different way, he loved Emme even more. Now he had lost her affection as well as her respect. She was a good woman who would do as he had asked her out of kindness. He could trust her to care for Rob in his absence and keep him with her if he died; at least he was sure of that. But he could no longer hope for her love without reservation. She was a lady who should have been on her way to England, away from danger, back to the Queen. Ferdinando was not fit to protect her, but Emme could yet sail back with Stafford and Spicer in the flyboat and come to no harm. Once this business was over, he would make sure she did – and he would tell Rob the truth.

He raised his head slowly to see more. The rustling had stopped. Stafford must be in position. Lacy and Wright would be ready, poised to advance at his signal and flush out any savages left in the village. Most of the veterans were in the rear-guard, hidden in the marsh-grass behind the shelters. The Planters with Stafford would have the glory of the attack. This would be the vengeance Dare and Harvie had wanted. May it be quick.

The black reeds did not move under their blanket of mist and umber cloud. All was shadows and dark mire, a bleak insect-ridden wilderness. He supposed that if he had felt constrained to abandon a home on Roanoke for this miserable slough then he would have been resentful, maybe to the point of laying down his life to drive the intruders away. But the Planters had nowhere else to go. Roanoke had been deserted when they arrived, and if the mainland was as vast as the reports of earlier explorers suggested then surely there would be room for Indian and English to live side by side.

There was no going back. He would not abandon the colonists to please the Secotans or anyone else. If he had to kill to preserve the City of Raleigh then he would.

He took aim at one of the heads. Even from where he was, about two hundred paces away, he could have toppled one of those Indians. But he held fire. Let someone else do it. He levelled his caliver and kept his aim. The light spread like water soaked up by the grey rags of cloud. The Indians were eating; the man he had fixed on raised something to his mouth. No one else emerged from the longhouses, though Kit had expected to see more of an assembly as the sun seeped over the horizon. There was only a suggestion of other people in grey forms beyond the fire: shapes that moved beneath a pale sheet of mist. He waited, ready to do what he had to.

He felt the smooth stock of the caliver against his cheek and thought of Emme. His lips brushed the warmth of the wood under his hand and he remembered kissing her, the times when she had yielded and accepted his touch, when they had melded together and she had seemed to be offering her love. A tiny wisp of smoke rose from his firing lock, and he saw the sway of her walk in its drifting motion, her back turned, fading away from him. She was with him even now, though he did not wish her to be. He heard the shot he had been expecting and still it made him jump. It was as loud and sudden as a thunderclap, setting a flock of birds rising in raucous frenzy. He saw one of the Indians fall, thrown to one side, crumpling as he hit the ground. The others who had been eating sprang to their feet and ran off like foxes, twisting and turning as they plunged into the reeds. Someone screamed loud and high, more a woman's scream than a man's, but there was no time for reflection. Shots followed in an explosion of sound. Crack, crack: the blasts reverberated over the water and bounced back deadened from the cloud.

Stafford's men gave chase. Kit saw their helmets and shoulders bobbing black above the reeds. They were charging towards the sun: shadows against the first rays of light. They splashed into the shallows, firing as fast as they could load.

Kit turned to White and Manteo.

'Stay here until it's over.'

They both nodded. This was what had been agreed.

'Now!' Kit shouted, baring his teeth as he ran to the first long-house, knowing that Lacy and the others would be following, swarming into the village. He stormed the doorway, but all he found inside was darkness, a moment of fearful blindness in which he attuned to the silence, and the mouldering damp of a place lived in and left. He ran outside and looked back towards the gunfire. Stafford's party was invisible behind the billowing smoke from their matchlocks lit by streaks of flame before each new discharge. His ears rang with the noise.

'Empty,' Wright called from the next shelter.

'All's well,' Lacy confirmed. 'There's no one here.'

His men spilled into the space between the dwellings. There was no trace of the Indians beyond the remains of their early meal: the smoking fire, scattered bowls, and soup soaking into the dirt which a few chickens were already pecking at, and a dark pool of blood. The man who had been shot must have crawled into the reeds. No one was left. Kit had only seen three Indians for certain, so where were the rest? Had they spotted the pinnace and fled in the dark? He looked from the village to the shore and the thickening blanket of smoke. They could be waiting in the mist. He waved his men on.

'Run. Stafford could be heading into an ambush.'

Ahead lay a trail to the water through cord grass and rushes. He loped as fast as he could, weighed down by his weapons, feet sinking into mud. The sulphurous smoke swirled around him. Shouts became louder: voices he struggled to recognise, distorted by tension.

'After them!'

'Over there!'

Figures moved in the cloud: grey shapes, running into sight and as quickly disappearing in the haze. An Indian sprang up before him and darted away like the wind, naked but for an apron of hide. He raised his caliver and took aim, firing pan open, fingers curled around the trigger, but something held him. He froze watching the Indian receding, back bent almost double under a writhing burden. He could hear screaming like a mewling infant's. Then he realised why. The Indian was a woman and her burden was a child.

'Stop! Hold fire!' he called, as an Indian began yelling hysterically. The man's language was unintelligible but one word was clear: 'Stafford.' How did he know Stafford's name?

The man yelled again: 'Sta-ford.' He carried on gabbling, edging forwards, arms waving in supplication, legs bent in terror. He was cowering and pleading, plainly unarmed.

Stafford held up his pistols then lowered his hands to his sides, pointing his weapons to the ground.

'Come forwards slowly. No one will shoot you.'

Another report exploded in the depths of the cloud and the man started wailing again, sinking to his knees.

Kit called out. 'Stop the attack! There are women and children here. Look at the band round this man's head; I think these are Croatans.'

Stafford groaned. 'Oh Christ.'

'I'll fetch Manteo,' Kit said, already turning to dash back. He'd noticed the material circling the man's roached scalp: a ragged strip – woven cloth, not rawhide or twine. It was too dark to discern colour, but he guessed it would be red: the crimson of the sarcenet from the City of Raleigh's flag. But if the Indians were Croatans, what were they doing at Dasemonkepeuc? He raced through the empty village, calling for the Governor and Manteo, leading them back when they answered and explaining to them on the way.

'There's been a mistake. Come. We need you.'

'What mistake?'

'A savage has been shot. He may be a Croatan. We have another savage who called Stafford by name. There.' Kit pointed as they approached.

Manteo ran to the man, arms outstretched.

'Enato!'

As they embraced they talked and wept.

'This is my friend,' Manteo declared, face wild with anger. 'You have attacked his wife and child.'

'What is he doing here?' Stafford demanded, wiping at the sweat running down his face. His expression was sombre. The wounded

Indian had been found dead and was dragged out from the water's edge near Stafford's feet. He had been shot in the back.

Manteo called out in his own language and more Indians crept from the reeds. He turned to Stafford.

'They were here collecting food.'

The reproach in Manteo's voice was plain to hear. He put his arm around his friend, Enato.

'This man knew you from the council meeting. He was there. He thought you wanted peace.'

Stafford looked mortified but said nothing. He offered his water-flask to Enato's child: the girl that Kit had almost killed. White wrung his hands. He seemed dumbstruck by the enormity of what had happened and paced around the Croatans, observing them and their injuries, shaking his head.

Manteo moved amongst his people, taking them into his arms one by one. A young woman was amongst them, a maiden bleeding from a bullet graze across her shoulder. When Lacy saw her he leapt to her side.

'No! Sweet Jesus, Alawa. What have we done?'

His eyes were wide with shock. As he pulled Alawa towards him, her blood smeared his hands. The Croatans tried to push him away, but Lacy would not let go of her.

'I'm so sorry, Alawa, so sorry.'

She murmured and fell against him, then spoke softly to her people, and what she said must have been enough to calm them, for they left her in Lacy's care and let him use his shirt to bandage her.

Stafford clasped Lacy's arm. 'It's just a flesh wound, Jim. She'll live.'

He looked at Manteo. 'Have any others been badly hurt?'

'No,' was Manteo's answer after he had conferred with the Croatans. 'But my people are afraid. They came to Dasemonkepeuc because they had heard that Wanchese had left after the Englishman's murder to escape your revenge. At Croatoan there is little food, so they came here to collect what the deer and birds would have eaten. Now they wish they had not. A good man is dead: a man not yet a father. His mother's tears will never dry.'

Stafford put his pistols in his belt and spread his hands.

'Tell your people that we will make recompense to the dead man's family. We will gather all the crops we can find here and share everything amongst your people. We invite everyone back to Roanoke to rest and receive proofs of our friendship. Our remorse is heartfelt.'

He stepped towards Manteo, arms wide, and, after a moment's hesitation, Manteo received his embrace.

Manteo took a step back and raised his chin. 'It is done. Had my people come to Roanoke as you asked then they would have known better; this would not have happened.'

Manteo turned to leave and Kit moved closer to touch his shoulder.

'Generously said, Manteo. We value your loyalty.'

Manteo shook his head and pulled away. 'You English put me on an arrow tip. Whichever way I turn, it is sharp.'

Kit watched him go to join his own people and help carry away the body of the man who had been killed. They tied him curled over like an unborn, and placed him in a canoe ready for his last voyage. Another canoe was filled with all the food in the fields and shelters, everything ripe that could be garnered: corn, tobacco, pumpkins and peas. When they finally left Dasemonkepeuc it was together,

Englishmen and Croatans sitting side by side in the pinnace. The canoes were towed behind.

As Kit rowed he looked at the dugouts jouncing over the wind-ruffled water and thought of what they held: the body of a friend and the food of their enemies. Death and life; the colony had brought both – little boats bearing the remains of so much hope. It was a sorry return for the Planters' desire for vengeance and a show of might. The Croatans had been given yet more reason to be wary of the English, and the Secotans had been shown no cause to be fearful. What prospect was there now for the colony's future? The Secotans had driven away Englishmen before. Why should they hold back from driving them away again? Wanchese had shown himself to be ruthless. Sooner or later there would be war. To survive at Roanoke, the colony needed protection. Raleigh should send soldiers: a garrison of at least the size that Lane had commanded. There had to be enough strength of arms to secure the peace, enough to deter any prospect of attack. A messenger should be sent to petition for help: someone whom Raleigh would listen to, maybe even someone who would have the ear of the Queen.

Emme had to leave for England, out of danger. It hurt to think of parting from her, as if a knife was twisting in the pit of his stomach, but he'd been reconciled to it before, and hadn't he lost her anyway?

She must go back.

*

Manteo knelt before Governor White and raised his hands in an attitude of prayer, looking as fine a Christian as any Kit had seen in an English church. White held out a mantle of black velvet trimmed with ermine and placed it over Manteo's shoulders, then he read from a parchment before everyone looking on: all the Planters and

Croatans who had been brought back from Dasemonkepeuc, and the mariners from the *Lion* who had come to Roanoke to collect water.

White spoke boldly. 'Know ye that by these presents we do advance, create and prefer our right trusty and well-beloved Manteo of Croatoan to the state, degree and honour of Lord of Roanoke and Dasemonkepeuc...'

With his hands over Manteo's, White completed the investiture.

'Do you, Manteo of Croatoan, swear to become our liege man of life and limb, and in faith and truth bear unto us to live and die against all adversaries?'

'I do,' Manteo answered.

White opened his hands as if releasing a dove.

'Arise, Lord Roanoke.'

Manteo stood, and White placed a gold ring on his index finger and handed him a mace ornamented with silver bearing the insignia of a crown and an antlered deer.

'May you serve our city faithfully and watch over this fiefdom steadfastly as the vassal lord of Sir Walter Raleigh.'

White beamed at Manteo and the Indian grinned broadly back. When Manteo turned the whole assembly cheered and clapped, the ship's trumpeter struck up a fanfare, someone began beating a drum and the Croatans gathered around Manteo to touch the symbols of his authority. Soon everyone was making merry, singing, dancing or enjoying the feast prepared in honour of the occasion. The wine was broached that had been reserved for this: a toast to Lord Manteo and the fulfilment of the last special duty with which White had been charged by Raleigh, though Manteo should have been lord here while White settled the region of Chesapeake. Kit raised his cup too – in tribute to Manteo and Roanoke and the founding of the colony in hope of true permanence: the derelict cottages made into homes, the strong-house rebuilt, the fort repaired and the earth-works fashioned again in great arrowhead buttresses – a celebration of everything achieved despite the setbacks and misfortunes: the fields sown; the forge, kiln and ovens built; the water-well restored, and all that was now clean and working – in praise of their commu-nity and endeavour, and their friends, the Croatans. Kit drank deep, and allowed himself, just for a moment, to feel that he was part of something good that might be of some lasting benefit to his son and England, and perhaps even a new nation. Then he caught sight of Emme threading towards him and instantly his heart lurched.

She looked lovelier than ever, possessed of a quiet dignity that seemed to have grown in her since his return from the ill-fated raid, though they had both kept their distance from one another and he supposed that was as well. It would make her leaving easier. The agony of seeing her and being apart from her would not be his to endure for much longer. The departure was imminent; Ferdinando was ready. In truth it was probably Emme who had kept Ferdinando close offshore and the *Lion* riding at anchor over the three weeks since their arrival. Ferdinando was waiting for her. He had caulked and refitted the flagship and the flyboat and his men had nearly fin-ished reprovisioning. All the supplies for the colony had now been brought to the island, down to the last bean and nail. The colonists had written their letters and prepared their tokens for friends and family back in England. Emme had written as well; perhaps she still believed that she was going to stay. Kit had seen her letter on White's desk: one addressed to her father that Emme would have meant to be seen by Raleigh and the Queen. She had probably explained why she would not be returning. Well, if so, she was mistaken. However much he admired her courage, he would make sure she was on the flyboat when Spicer and Stafford left for England. He just hoped to God he could persuade her to go of her own volition and not see her dragged away to be locked up in the hold. He no longer under-stood why she might want to stay. It could not be because of him, not since his revelation about Rob and Ololade. Somehow he had to convince her that the colony depended on her going back and appealing for help in person to the Queen. That might be easy, but he still suspected it would be hard. He needed to be prepared with compelling evidence that would sway her, and as yet he didn't feel ready for a battle with her over leaving. So he turned aside as she neared him and stared fixedly at the fort, though even then his eyes were drawn to her like needles to a lodestone. He felt the pull of her and kept his face averted.

She spoke to him coolly.

'Kit, I should be grateful if you would help me bring out one of the Governor's chests which he would like to be taken aboard the *Lion*.'

'Later,' he answered her abruptly, knowing that there wouldn't be any 'later'. He cast about for some excuse to move away and saw it in the shape of Jim Lacy at the palisade gates.

'There's someone I need to speak to urgently, if you'll forgive me.' He gave her a perfunctory bow and strode off, but not before he'd noticed a flash of distress in her beautiful face. Why was that? Did she regret having spoken at all?

Lacy was happily swigging from a leather tankard when Kit clapped his shoulder and ushered him back behind the palisade.

'A proud day for us, Jim.'

'Aye, sir,' Lacy said, lurching a little. 'But the wine's back there.'
He jabbed a thumb towards the gate and gave Kit a grisly lop-sided
smile.

'I've some brandy to share once we've spoken.'

'Do we need to speak first?' Lacy winked.

'Yes, we do, and you must tell me the truth.'

Lacy's face fell a little as he wiped at his mouth. His eyes narrowed.
'About what?'

'Lane. What happened while he was governor here? What did he
do to set the Secotans against us?'

Lacy frowned and glanced back to the gate then stared at his feet.

'Begin with Wingina,' Kit said. 'How did he die?'

'You could ask Captain Stafford,' Lacy suggested. 'He was with
Lane as an officer; he'd give you a fine report.'

Lacy turned as if to leave but Kit barred his way.

'I already have asked him. Stafford was on Croatoan looking
out for relief ships when Wingina met his end. White and Harriot
weren't with Lane then either; I expect they were left on Roanoke,
and maybe it suited them to concentrate on their record-keeping
rather than on what Lane was doing. But you were with him, weren't
you?'

Lacy took another drink and his troubled eyes slid from Kit back
to the packed dirt at his feet. He nudged at a pine cone with the
scuffed toe of his shoe. 'Yes, I was with Lane when the old chief was
killed, and I was with Lane all the way up the Moratico and back
which was where the trouble really began.'

'What trouble?'

The look Lacy gave Kit was bloodshot and anxious. He seemed
to shrink inside the shirt Kit had lent him.

'Lane wanted gold and he'd stop at nothing to get it.'

'That led to trouble?'

Kit resisted the urge to shake the truth out of the old soldier. He waited while Lacy stepped back into the shadow by the palisade, and then moved to keep close to him. Lacy leant against the rough-hewn stakes.

'Lane went scouting-like, first north to the land of the Weapemeocs, then west to the Choanokes, mightiest of all the savage tribes around the sound. Last spring we travelled up the Chowan as far as the city of Choanoke ruled by the crippled king Menatonon. He welcomed us with respect, but Lane took him prisoner and made a hostage of his most favoured son. This boy, Skiko, was sent back to Roanoke in irons to ensure his father's co-operation.'

Kit grimaced, thinking of Rob. He'd have killed any man who tried to make a captive of him.

'A poor way of securing loyalty.'

Lacy shrugged before carrying on. 'Lane didn't care. He wanted to be feared. He thought that if the savages weren't cowed then they'd kill us.' He cast Kit a tangled look. 'Maybe he was right.'

'What happened to the boy?'

Lacy shook his head and looked down. He pushed the pine cone into the loose dirt by the stakes. 'No matter what ransom was offered for Skiko, Lane wouldn't let him go.'

'But when Lane left, what then? Skiko wasn't brought back with us, was he?'

'No.' Lacy kicked the cone away. 'I don't know what happened to him.'

Was that the truth? Kit wasn't convinced, but he wanted Lacy to keep talking.

'Go on. What did Lane do with Menatonon?'

'He milked him for information then demanded a ransom for his release. Menatonon told him there were pearls of rare purity to be found to the northeast, and that there was a land of mountains and gold far to the west. He called this place "Chaunis Temoatan", and said that to reach it we'd have to pass through the land of the Moratucs. That was where we went: west – thirty men in four boats rowing up the Moratico against a powerful flow. Lane's plan was to prevail upon the savages living by the riverside to provide us with victuals along the way, but not a scrap of food could we find. We saw the smoke from fires, but every village we reached was deserted and stripped bare. Lane blamed Wingina for that. He believed that Wingina had forewarned the Moratucs that we were enemies, and told them not to help us in the hope that we'd starve to death. We nearly did. We were reduced to eating our dogs. Only the promise of gold kept us going. We travelled so far in such extremity that we seemed close to losing our minds. In the end we heard singing and believed that at last we'd be received in friendship. Like a chorus of angels, so it was. But Manteo warned us that what we heard was a battle song. Sure enough, a volley of arrows was our greeting, though none caused us real hurt. We scattered the Indians with bullets, but we'd had as much as we could take. The next day we turned back.'

'You all survived?'

'We did. The journey home was much faster. In a day we'd covered what had taken us four days against the current. Once we got back to the sound, we fell on the fish traps of the Weapemeocs and were able to relieve our hunger.

'Lane must have been pleased to show Wingina he still lived.'

Lacy raised a mottled eyebrow. 'Lane felt cheated. We all did. We'd been through purgatory on that journey and all for nothing. Wingina was shocked to see us alive, but he could also see that we'd suffered, that we needed to eat or we'd die.'

Kit frowned, eyeing Lacy closely. The Irishman's sun-reddened face was a mess of blotches, scars and freckles. The look he gave Kit was shifty but not mocking. Lacy seemed scared, if anything. He avoided Kit's gaze and looked down again.

Kit pressed him harder.

'Didn't Wingina think you needed to eat?'

'Wingina's father, Ensenor, believed we were in league with the gods and couldn't be killed. Even if we were killed, the old chief thought we'd only return to haunt his people and hurt them more. That was why we were pale: we were already ghosts. Ensenor told Wingina to treat us kindly-like and give us what we wanted.'

Kit still couldn't see how this amounted to the 'trouble' that had led to the Secotans' entrenched hostility, but he'd tease it out. Lacy was opening up. The Irishman took another swig from his tankard and offered it to Kit.

Kit drank with his tongue blocking most of the wine; then he wiped his mouth and handed the tankard back.

'So did Wingina continue to show friendship after Lane's return?'

'For sure, Wingina seemed more eager to be our bosom friend than ever. A delegation arrived from the Choanokes and the Weapemeocs offering tribute and to recognise our good Queen Bess as their supreme *weroanca*...'

Kit seized on that: a glimmer of hope.

'So these tribes are well disposed to us?'

Lacy scratched at his neck.

'In return they wanted Skiko's release. But Lane wouldn't give them the boy, not straight away. It was his way of controlling Menatonon.'

Kit clenched his jaw. If Lane had sent the boy back before he left then there might be a chance of rekindling friendship with the Choanokes. He hoped to God that he had.

'But this delegation persuaded Wingina to help us?'

'Yes. He couldn't oppose us as well as his father and those two mighty tribes. So he went out of his way to show cooperation: planted corn for us and built fish traps. A wily bastard he was.'

'Why a bastard?'

'We were hungry. We'd run out of provisions, and this was April; the corn wouldn't be ready to harvest until July. We relied on Wingina's people giving us food. Lane knew it and he didn't like it. Wingina knew it too. He tested us gradually, finding our weaknesses. He never did trust us, not like his father.'

Kit wasn't surprised, not after Lane's behaviour with Menatonon, but he made no comment about that. He wanted to know what Lacy thought.

'Why the lack of trust?'

'Wingina believed that we were killing his people with invisible bullets. He asked Lane why he did it – why it was that in every village we visited the savages began to die not long after we left, though we raised not a finger against them. Lane said we'd done them no hurt and wished them no harm. But there was some cause for Wingina's suspicion.' Lacy looked at Kit with the credulous wonder of a good Catholic shown a miracle. 'The savages did die: scores of them, in village after village. Even the Roanokes on the island began to die.'

Kit sighed. He'd heard of this from Harriot, but even Harriot could give no explanation.

'A tragedy.'

'For the savages it was. Maybe it was the will of God; that's what Drake's preacher told us on the way back to England.'

'So if Wingina thought we were killing his people, what did he do about it?'

'He left. He moved his chief village to Dasemonkepeuc, that was after his brother and then his father died. They'd always counselled peace. In their stead, Wanchese became Wingina's most trusted advisor, and Wanchese hated us for bringing death to his island. He warned that all the Indians would be wiped out if they didn't drive us away first. His views were no secret; the Croatans heard of Wanchese's proclamations in council. Wanchese knew we weren't gods. He'd seen how we lived in England. Wanchese persuaded Wingina to stop giving us food. Our worry then was that we'd starve before our corn ripened. The upkeep of the fish traps was a strange art to us, and we'd hunted out all the deer on the island. Our food became such shellfish and berries as we could scavenge. We were tormented by the memory of the search for the gold in the west. The final blow came when Lane found out about Wingina's plot to destroy us.'

'What plot?'

'A conspiracy led by Wingina and the Secotans involving all the foremost tribes in the region. They planned to launch an attack with a force of over seven hundred bowmen together with at least that number again from the outlying tribes. Once we'd become suffi-ciently weakened through hunger, then they'd strike.'

'I suppose Lane saw the withdrawal of food as a sign that the plot was being put into effect.'

'He did, and when he learnt that the outlying tribes were on the point of assembling, he decided to attack first.'

'How did he find out about all this?'

'Through Skiko...'

'Skiko!' Kit struggled to hide his disbelief. 'Skiko, the boy held hostage?'

Lacy regarded Kit cautiously. 'The same. He confided in Lane because he wished to befriend us just as his father had done.'

'Did Lane tell you that?'

'Yes. Maybe the boy hoped to win his freedom that way.'

'Maybe.' Kit didn't argue; he wanted Lacy to continue. 'So what happened?'

'We were ordered to gather up all the canoes on Roanoke and kill any savages we found on the island. Lane wanted their heads.'

'You decapitated them?'

The Irishman nodded, grim faced.

'We dealt with as many as we could get hold of. Some fled into the woods, but we crossed over to Dasemonkepeuc under cover of darkness before they could reach the mainland and raise the alarm. Then Lane asked to speak to Wingina. He said that he wanted to complain about the release of Skiko...'

Kit cut in quickly. 'Had the boy escaped?'

'No. Lane only said that to persuade Wingina to receive him in the village.'

Kit's smile faded.

'The ruse worked?'

'Yes. All twenty-five of us marched in. Then Lane gave the signal for attack: '*Christ our victory.*' With those words we all opened fire. Many of the savages were killed outright. Wingina fell as if dead but it was just a feint. When our backs were turned he got up and ran away. He was wily, like I said. It was Lane's manservant who finally tracked him into the forest and slew him. He brought back Wingina's head with which Lane was singularly delighted. We collected many more heads that day and left them for the savages as a warning. That was Lane's way of showing them how we deal with traitors.'

Kit did not ask how the heads had been left but he could guess. Lacy shuffled uncomfortably from foot to foot. Kit turned to the pointed stakes around the palisade, still raw and leaking sap which had become black with trapped flies. He must not push Lacy too hard.

'What of Wanchese?'

'We didn't find him. Either he escaped or he wasn't there.'

'But he'd have seen the heads on returning to the village.'

'He would; they couldn't be missed.'

'And was the boy Skiko then let go?'

'I told you, I don't know. Drake arrived a week later and we all left after the wrecking storm which carried away the ship that Drake was going to give us. We didn't know then that Grenville's supply fleet was close. We thought that Drake offered us at least a good chance of staying alive.'

'But the boy was in the fort when you left?'

Lacy turned to him with sweat beading over his sunburnt skin.

'Why do you keep asking after that boy?'

Kit gave Lacy a wry smile. 'I'm curious, that's all. I have a boy too. By a savage,' he added. 'But that's another story. Tell me yours first.'

Lacy sucked air through his broken teeth, and then shot Kit a look of concession. 'Skiko wasn't in the place where he was usually kept when we left, and three of Lane's men didn't make the final roll call. It's possible they'd been sent to take the boy back to Menatonon. I never found out.'

Kit balled his fist and pushed his knuckles against his brow.

'Dear Christ, I hope he lived.'

'So do I, by all the saints. We never meant that boy any hurt. I hope those men left behind are still alive too, and those of Coffin's company who survived Wanchese's attack. But it don't look good for any of them, do it?'

'No, it doesn't look good.'

Lacy drank and handed Kit the tankard that he'd almost drained empty. Kit finished it in silence. He looked back at Lacy, feeling the Irishman's remorse though, heaven knows, the damage that had been done was not Lacy's fault.

He beckoned for Lacy to follow him and left the fort for the central clearing.

Once he reached the shelter he shared with Rob he asked Lacy to wait by the entrance, then he rummaged inside for the brandy he'd promised. He found the keg by his sea chest under a pile of possessions he'd never use: spurs and a bridle, nether-stocks and a ruff. He pulled out two sleeves with lace cuffs and handed them to Lacy along with the keg.

'Alawa might like these,' he said, thrusting the sleeves into Lacy's hands then placing the keg at his feet.

He didn't wait for Lacy's reply. He'd seen Emme walking by.

'Mistress Emme!' He paced towards her, not sure what he'd say, but knowing he had all the information he was likely to get. He was more certain than ever that now she had to go.

She looked at him with wide dark eyes that both appealed and drew away. The next moment she had turned her back on him, and he felt the sting even while he accepted that her distancing would make his task easier. She no longer cared for him; he was sure of that now, but he still didn't know how to begin talking to her. How to gain her attention? Should he reach for her? He never knew. She was like an unbroken filly, calm one moment, bucking the next, as unpredictable as the wind and as volatile as quicksilver. Sometimes he felt as if she could not stand to have him touch her, but there'd been other times when she'd seem to yearn for his caress. That was all in the past. She would not wish for his comfort now.

He walked in front of her.

'I have something to say to you,' he began, and gestured for her to follow him to a place where they could be alone, round the back of the Dares' house facing the nettles, the spot where they'd spoken before.

'You should know the truth of what has happened here ...'

She kept a step away from him and looked down.

'What truth?'

# 11

## *Leave-taking*

'If thus thou vanishest, thou tell'st the world
It is not worth leave-taking.'

—Antony and Cleopatra *by William Shakespeare, Act 5, Scene 2*

'Emme!'

The cry brought Emme running, cutting into her brooding over what Kit had told her about Roanoke's dark secrets. The future looked bleak, but her fear for it was forgotten at the sound of Mistress Dare's scream.

Emme found her mistress doubled over, the floor wet beneath her skirts, and she knew that the lady's time had come, her waters had broken, and she must now play her part in earnest to help her mistress be delivered.

Gone was any nicety. She did not baulk when Mistress Viccars waddled in, one of the older dames and a mother, who started giving orders as soon as she arrived to fetch extra bedding, boil water, take away soiled sheets and a chamber pot, bring cloths and candles, prepare the swaddling bands, thread a needle with catgut, and lay out the instruments that might be needed to assist with the imminent birth: scissors, bowls and two long-handled spoons. Emme had no idea why the spoons could be useful, but she did as she was told, and she made sure her mistress had plenty of broth to give her nourishment between her moments of distress, when she gasped and strained, and Emme knew the lady's womb was tightening like a fist, harder and longer with each racking spasm.

This was a woman's greatest trial, the ordeal that had to come before the fulfilment of her life, if it did not end with her death or that of her baby. Emme was glad to help and observe, though some of what she witnessed made her stomach turn over, and her dread of the worst made her mind reel with prayers. One day, she too might suffer in agony before giving birth. If that happened, please God, may she not be alone.

All night her mistress laboured, writhing, sweating, and pleading for mercy. By the first grey trace of dawn she was weakening, but her contractions were becoming greater. Emme was startled from a fitful doze by a piercing screech of pain.

She shook the old dame awake, took her mistress's hand, and wiped her brow with a sponge dipped in cool water. Mistress Viccars grunted and felt between the lady's legs, shooing Ananias Dare away when he poked his head round the door, telling him to go back to bed.

'Four fingers wide,' the dame announced to Emme. 'Nearly there.'

What was four fingers wide? Emme guessed with a shudder, and tried to give her mistress some comfort.

'All will be well. Breathe deeply and slowly.' This was something she had learnt from talking to the mothers. They had told her that when the pains came, a woman should fill her lungs then let out her breath by small degrees. She found herself doing the same to help her mistress along, taking in great gulps of warm steamy air amidst the fug of bodily intimacy and the smell of sweat and blood.

'Oh, God,' the lady cried. 'Help me.' She bent forwards and bore down.

'Push,' Emme encouraged her. 'Push harder.'

'The child is coming,' Mistress Viccars said. 'You must pant now, Eleanor.'

Another spasm took hold of the lady, and she clung onto Emme as if to drag herself off the mattress.

'Hold her down,' the dame instructed, while she worked with her hands where Emme had no wish to look, and her shadow loomed in the guttering candlelight over the spattered canvas screens.

Emme held her mistress against the bolsters, feeling the lady's muscles locking hard in another straining push.

'Pant, don't push!' Mistress Viccars cried. 'If you push now, you'll tear.'

'Pant!' Emme repeated, and heard little gasping sobs as her mistress tried to obey.

The sound that came next was like a net of fish spilling open, a slithering wet gush of squirming release. Her mistress moaned and cried in torment.

'I'm splitting,' she wailed.

Emme turned in horror, seeing Mistress Viccars hold up a baby by the ankles that was blue and greasy as if covered in lard. Was it alive? It didn't move. The next moment, the dame slapped its buttocks and the baby began to cry.

'A girl,' she announced. 'A fine little girl.'

The dame wrapped the infant in a swaddling sheet, and placed her on her mother's breast, guiding the babe's quivering mouth to her mother's swollen teat.

'Welcome to the world, little one.' She stooped and gave Mistress Dare a kiss. 'God bless you, Eleanor. You should be proud. What will you call her?'

'Virginia,' Mistress Dare murmured, weeping and stroking her baby's little head. 'We'll name her after her birthplace. Please tell Ananias that his baby has arrived. I hope he will not mind that 'tis not a boy.'

'He will be a fool if he does,' Mistress Viccars replied, and delivered the afterbirth while the babe was suckling. Then she cut and tied the cord, showing Emme how, and wiped Mistress Dare down, while Emme changed the sheets and tidied away the spoons that had not been required.

What would Ananias think? Emme wondered as she went to fetch him. Would he be as happy as she was? She felt a rush of elation to have been part of such a miracle, despite the ordeal from which it came, the mess and the pain; she was sure she had never witnessed anything quite so beautiful before.

\*

The storm still bowed the lolling pine tops but the rain had eased, and Emme needed release from the confinement of the Dares' house, so she took the baby outside, wrapped up securely in a shawl, and sang a gentle lullaby while she rocked the bundle in her arms, and paced around the clearing that would, one day God grant, be the child's city square. Little Virginia Dare was only a week old and already she'd turned her mother's life upside down, and Emme's too, demanding to be fed at all hours, coaxed, winded and soothed, insisting on those essentials that everyone around her took for granted: warmth, nourishment and a place to sleep, the reassurance of the familiar and the comfort of human touch. Emme felt sure that the lullaby was one that her own mother used to sing to her; it came without effort from the depths of her earliest memories, and as she murmured the song softly, with the babe against her breast, she felt what it meant even though the child was not her own.

Lullay mine liking, my dear one, my sweeting
Lullay, my dear heart, mine own dear darling.

The newborn had narrowed her world and opened everything out. For a week she had barely ventured beyond the lower room of the Dares' house, the place where she looked after the babe when her mistress was resting, where she slept, ate and washed; cooked, mended and prayed, often sharing with others, and attended to all the chores that could not easily be done outside on days like today, and yesterday and the day before, when the wind tore around as if it was trying to scrape the island bald.

The babe tied her to this patch of earth, to this windswept island and makeshift home, yet in Virginia was the wide future with the promise of the new land in her name: the first child of English parents ever born in the New World, and already not the last since, only days later, Mistress Harvie's child had also been born. This was the start of the next age, the first generation of the new country, and who knew what America would be like in generations to come. Perhaps, where there was now wilderness, there would be roads leading to fair cities, and farmland and villages: a land of peace and plenty for the blessed children of tomorrow. It was her privilege to be here now, holding that future in her arms: precious, vulnerable and perfectly lovely. God keep Virginia safe.

She was still humming the lullaby when she felt a tugging at her skirts and looked down on the thick mop of hair belonging to young Georgie Howe, so blond it was almost white. Maybe he and Virginia would grow old together in this place. Maybe they would love and marry and have golden-haired children of their own, though, at that moment, Georgie plainly had other concerns on his mind.

'Have you seen my marbles, Mistress Emme? Rob says we can play cherry pit since it's too windy for fishing.'

She laid her hand on the boy's shoulder.

'The bag is hanging on a nail by the logs under the eaves. It was getting wet where you'd left it by the path.'

'Gramercy, Mistress Emme.' He looked up at her and grinned, wrinkling his nose at the bundle she carried.

'You won't be leaving us, will you?'

'No, Georgie.'

She made an effort to put the boy at ease. He was still coming to terms with the loss of his father, and most of the time his insecurity kept him close to her. He slept on a pallet by the Dares' hearth, and in the day he would often come for titbits from Emme's cauldron, or to see if she had anything for him like the marbles she had baked from balls of rippled red clay. To most of the Planters he seemed like a well-settled boy, happy and full of mischief, but she understood his needs, remembering what it was like to lose a mother, never mind a father as well. So when the storm had raged at its height two nights ago, she'd let him pull his pallet beside hers, and when the *Lion* had been swept out to sea, she'd tried to comfort him with her

303

own inner confidence. The *Lion* would return, she told him, and the Quartermaster, whom Georgie hated, and all the other stranded mariners, would leave for England, along with the Governor or one of the Assistants, and then soldiers would come to make sure everyone was safe, and they would carry muskets and be almost as brave as Master Kit, and, no, she would not go back with the sailors on the ship.

'If anyone tells you differently they are wrong,' she said to him. 'This is my home now.'

But she'd not said that to Kit.

She ruffled Georgie's hair and watched him scampering to the cottage, then, out of the corner of her eye, she noticed movement within the palisade. Men were emerging from the strong-house where most of their meetings were held. She saw them milling about in huddled groups, just as she'd often seen them before after recent assemblies. There was Kit standing with Ananias Dare and Dyonis Harvie, heads together, talking earnestly. Kit glanced across at her and the flash of affinity sparked between them, then he turned aside as Harvie spoke.

She walked closer, rocking the baby in her arms. When Manteo passed through the gateway she moved forwards casually and showed him the sleeping baby.

'Have they reached a decision?' she asked quietly.

Manteo gave her a wry smile.

'Master Cooper has changed his mind and said to the Governor he will not go to England. Again the Governor has been asked to sail back. He alone can do this, the Assistants have told him. He must alert Sir Walter Raleigh because the city needs help. He must ensure that relief is sent here and not to Chesapeake.'

'He has agreed?'

Manteo shook his head. 'He is thinking about it. Always he is thinking.' He shrugged apologetically and strode on.

Emme glanced back and noticed Master Cooper deep in conversation with several others. She counted all seven Assistants close to the walls of the strong-house, sheltering from the wind, and several other men besides who must have been involved in the debate. Only the Governor seemed to have been left inside, and doubtless he was deliberating over what to do next. The colony was in crisis, and again White was dithering. He should have been overseeing the strengthening of the defences instead of getting mired in interminable discussions about who should summon help. Kit had told her what he had learnt about the atrocities committed under Lane's stewardship. The violence had shocked her, but she was not so horrified that she was prepared to abandon those who'd come to depend on her help, particularly Georgie and the baby.

She held the baby to her shoulder and rubbed her tiny back while she walked, mulling everything over. She could never hope now for a future with Kit, not since it was obvious that she'd never mean as much to him as the Cimaroon woman who'd been as good as his wife. She and Kit were unmatched in every way. How she'd ever supposed they might be married she did not know. It would never happen. She could say that to herself and be sure of it for a while, begin to make plans for a future without him but near enough to see him settled and follow him through the advance of years. She could reconcile herself to never being wed, never bearing his children, never sharing his bed. But then grief consumed her: an overwhelming ache for all the promise she had lost, for the man who could never be replaced, the one who had touched her body and soul, the only one with the power to release her from her shadow of guilt.

Burying her face in the baby's blanket, she gave a small stifled sob, then she looked up and straightened her back. She would stay in Virginia and see the endeavour through, to the next generation and beyond if she could. Kit might have supposed she'd be persuaded to leave by convincing her that she'd be doomed if she insisted on remaining, but if so he'd failed. Governor White would be able to petition Raleigh just as well as she could, and here she could be useful. The colony was her life now. Despite its blighted start, the blunted hope and endless toil, the settlers' bold dream was hers: of building a better country in this raw new land. Having come so far, she wasn't about to give up. She would remain at Roanoke, not as one with Kit, but near him. He must accept that this would be so.

Let him think she was ready to go. She hadn't protested against Kit's plans for her, but neither had she promised to do what he wished. That had bought her more time; it had kept her in Kit's confidence and allowed her to act freely. Kit had been reluctant to tell the rest of the colonists about the horrors of the past for fear it would weaken them and destroy their morale. She had agreed with that. What good would it do to give them reason to expect disaster? He had tried to alert the Governor but he'd seemed reluctant to believe the worst. He was a man blinded by his own vision, far more concerned with the minutiae of observation than with recognising evil in the wider picture. She and Kit would keep the knowledge to themselves, along with Lacy, Wright and Manteo who already knew what had happened.

She walked calmly back to the Dares' cottage, and settled little

Virginia back with her mother since it was time for her next feed, then she filled a ewer with water, pulled her shawl over her head, and crossed back to the fort. When she entered the strong-house, she found what she'd hoped; the Governor was alone.

John White had his head in his hands and a mass of papers strewn around him over the table by which he sat. A candle stump stood on a saucer in a congealed mound of wax. A board-backed clasped Bible lay near an inkhorn and quills, while indentures and other documents were strewn around the Governor's elbows. His hair sprang in tufts between his long knobbly fingers, and his brow was a mass of furrows. She picked up some discarded pewter: an empty cup and a plate that bore the remains of a meal, around which a fly buzzed in circles. The only light in the room came from around ill-fitting shutters that rattled with each gust of wind. The Governor sat in shadow, unmoving in the sultry heat.

'Would you like something to drink?' she asked gently. 'Some water, perhaps?'

'Water. Yes.' He rubbed his forehead with the heel of his hand. 'Thank you.'

She filled the cup from the ewer and brought it to his hands, making sure that he took hold of it before she began tidying around him.

'Have you now decided to return?' She asked the question blithely while getting the table top into a semblance of order. 'Our city needs a champion back in London who will bring aid from Sir Walter. I hope that will be you.'

White heaved a fretful sigh.

'Our city also needs a Governor here in Virginia, and I would be failing in my responsibilities if I left the Planters now.'

'You would not be failing them, if I may be allowed to say so, sir; you would be answering their prayers. No one carries more influence with Sir Walter than you do in this enterprise. If you took our plea to England this would be the greatest service you could give us, so I believe, Master White.'

He waved his hand dismissively.

'But I cannot leave my daughter and granddaughter here while I return to safety – and with you as well. That would render Eleanor quite bereft. She needs support.'

'She has her husband,' Emme countered lightly.

'Ananias is a bold man, but not accustomed to caring, and, without anyone else to help her, my Eleanor will be more dependent on me than ever.'

The evidence of this caring was not something that Emme had noticed in any practical way, but she supposed that Mistress Eleanor must have found her father's presence comforting. She did not dispute the point. She inclined her head meekly.

'I could always remain and look after her,' she said. 'Please hear me on this, sir.' She continued quickly as White groaned. 'I know that Sir Walter has asked for my return; probably he wished to hear an account of life in his city from a woman he knew and trusted. But, if I remained here, wouldn't that give him yet more inducement to send help? I would gladly go back with the relief ships that I am sure Sir Walter will send. By staying in the meantime I could be doubly useful. I could help Mistress Eleanor as dry nurse to little Virginia, and I could help give another incentive to Sir Walter to come to our aid. I am certain he would not object to my being here a few months longer, considering the unforeseen circumstances we have encountered about which you could enlighten him. You could ensure that Sir Walter and the Queen heard only the truth about what has happened.'

'Ah, yes, the truth.' White bent his head lower and raked his fingers through his hair, sighing again before raising his eyes with a look of torment.

'There is no doubt that if the reporting is left to others it might be open to misinterpretation. I have found this before, not least after Governor Lane's return.'

'Indeed,' she remarked with an encouraging smile. 'You are the patriarch of this enterprise, trusted by Master Harriot and others of influence who have ventured here before. Sir Walter will heed you. The fate of this city is in your hands. You could take news of our plight to London and the highest in the land. You may justly say that the pride and honour of England now rests with this city's continuance.'

'Yes, verily...' White looked hard at her. 'Well spoken for a maid.'

She busied herself with more tidying. 'I say only what I have heard from others.'

White cleared his throat.

'Well, I could account faithfully and put the case for relief. Yet...' He picked up a quill and rolled it back and forth between thumb and forefinger. 'No, I cannot. What will people think if I go back? They will point at me and say: "There is John White who persuaded good English folk to leave everything for a new life in Virginia and then forsook them in their hour of need." They will say I never meant to stay here.'

'I am sure they would not say that, for you are manifestly a self-less and virtuous man, and it would be clear to everyone from the reports that you left for the common good, not only your report but Master Ferdinando's also...'

'That swine. I don't know . . .' White shook his head.

Perhaps mention of Ferdinando had been a mistake. Emme racked her brains for something that would sway the Governor: something to protect his reputation since that was plainly his chief concern.

'What if all the Assistants swore to a document that you could take back to England stating that it was their desire, not yours, that you should return to seek help. They have begged you to plead for Sir Walter's assistance, have they not?'

White threw up his hands.

'They have most certainly. Their importuning knows no bounds. I have tried to encourage others to go in my stead but no one will do it. If I had some proof of this with which to silence any mischief-makers who might seek to malign me, then possibly . . .'

'Yes?' she murmured hopefully. The Assistants had lost faith in him but he could not see it, and nothing would be gained by pointing that out. How to convince him that leaving was the right thing to do? She put the quills in a neat pile under a shell.

White's eyes rolled up to her above dark pouches as heavy as a bloodhound's.

'But what of my possessions?' He winced as if the thought had nipped him. 'What of my furniture and instruments and chests of books and charts? Some of my finest work is in my chests. It is too late now to carry them to the ships. The *Lion* has been caught up in this cursed storm, and the flyboat is already fully loaded and in position behind the bar. The ships only wait for the mariners who've been left here by mischance, and for whoever is going to take our report to Raleigh. And for you,' he added pointedly.

She opened her mouth but held back, resisting the urge to

observe that much trouble could have been spared if he'd had the chests moved before.

He pulled out one of the quills and began stripping the remains of feather-down from its shaft. 'When the storm eases enough for the *Lion* to come close to shore, and we hear that the ships are ready to embark, then the pinnace will take the mariners and passengers across, no more. There'll be no room for baggage.'

She tried to soothe him, wondering what she could say that would impress him with a sense of urgency. They could be attacked at any moment by the Secotans, yet he was fussing about his chests. The sooner he was gone, the sooner help could be sent. He could leave now in the flyboat. Why even wait for the *Lion*?

'Your possessions will be safe, sir. I am sure you can trust us all to take care of them. Your daughter and I will see to that. I treasure your work as much as anyone.'

'But if you leave Roanoke, what then? My chests are heavy and would be difficult to transport if the relocation is up rivers that only small boats can navigate. If the Assistants decide to head for Chesapeake, as we originally planned, what would happen to my things then? How would I know where you were?'

Emme hid an inclination to roll her eyes and bang something down. How many more excuses could the Governor come up with? Increasingly she felt that this is what his arguments amounted to. White wanted to return to give a good account of his actions, but she also sensed his fear of failure; he couldn't bear to reach a decision.

She picked up a napkin and wiped the table clean.

'Be not troubled about finding us. We could easily agree signs with which we could alert you if we moved to another place, and tell you where we had gone. Through a signed document, the

Assistants could swear to safeguard all the belongings you leave behind. You could depart in good conscience knowing that this is the wish of all the Planters and with proof to that effect. They would see you as their saviour. Furthermore, let us not forget that Master Ferdinando has offered to receive you aboard his ships. Whether he would allow any Assistants to board is uncertain; he has previously denied them all that privilege. Once our Pilot returns – *if* he returns as I hope he will...'

White snorted and flicked ineffectually at the fly. 'He'll come back once he's ridden out the storm. His Quartermaster and half the crew are still here on Roanoke. The swine won't leave without them...'

She seized her chance. 'Then you would be best placed to leave quickly without objection when he does. I beg you, sir: be ready to go for the sake of this city and its hundred and more souls, including your daughter and new granddaughter.'

White was silent. He placed the stripped quill neatly on the cleared table boards where a sliver of light cut tangentially across it. At length he spoke wearily. 'I will consider all that you have said.'

'Thank you, sir, for listening, though I am but a maid, and God bless you for all that you have done in founding this city. Virginia will be a testament to your vision as much as your observations and charts and most beautiful limnings.'

He made a noise that acknowledged he'd heard her but that was all. The wind whined outside and rustled the papers she had stacked under another weighty shell. Beyond that, nothing moved, though she fancied that White was closing his eyes.

She crept out quietly and made for the clearing, searching for Kit amongst the Planters repairing storm-damage to the buildings. After spotting him on a roof, she caught his attention when he came down by waiting near a swaying ladder held in position by two men. She wouldn't keep Kit or press him to do anything. She would be brief.

'I think the Governor will leave,' she murmured. 'But he must be offered some written proof that he is acting at our request and exonerated from any censure.'

She outlined the terms of the document that White had intimated he would accept, and was gratified to see Kit nodding and looking very pleased with her.

'We can do this,' he said. 'We have nothing to lose by trying.' Then he regarded her steadily in a way that made her think he might have tried to take hold of her if they were not in the middle of the town, surrounded by a throng of busy people.

'Now are you ready to go?'

She gave him a tight smile.

'As ready as I'll ever be.'

A warm flurry of wind snatched at her shawl and sent it whipping behind her as something clattered to the ground.

He turned to look and she stepped away. She had to get back to her mistress.

'You will be safe,' he said, calling after her.

She dodged around rippling puddles until the wind dropped suddenly and the sun blazed out; then the muddied earth steamed and she was dazzled by mirrored light.

Somehow she would keep near Kit and then, she was sure, everything would be all right.

*

This was a morning for setting sail. The sky was an intense blue with streaks of white vaulting under the heavens and a perfectly clear horizon. A sweet warm breeze blew fresh from the southwest and the gulls were crying: 'Come away. Come away.' If he was to choose a day to be at sea then this would be it, with the call of freedom pumping through his veins, and the longing firing his blood: to hear again the slap of wind filling canvas and the thrum in the rigging, the creak of timbers and the deep booming in the hull, to feel the surge of a ship rising and dipping beneath him, the bows cutting through waves, leaping into life, full of the power of the skies.

From the shallow cliffs near the fort he looked out over the sound and saw the white trail of a wake and a small tawny sail. He recognised the pinnace instantly and was not surprised: Stafford was returning from Hatarask. Almost certainly that meant that Spicer was ready to leave in the flyboat, and probably the *Lion* was now offshore. Stafford would be coming for the mariners and whoever had been nominated to take the report back to Raleigh. The Governor would be leaving since he'd accepted that he should go. It meant that Emme would leave as well while he stayed behind. She'd be gone from him for good and, more than likely, he'd never sail the high seas again. A pang of remorse formed a lump in his throat and, though he tried to dismiss it, he could not shake his sense of loss. It was with a heavy heart that he turned to spread the word in the city. Everyone had to be ready who was going to leave with the ships. He had to be sure Emme was prepared and that might yet prove a trial; he still wasn't convinced that she had accepted she was going. But the time for debate was over. The ships wouldn't wait.

Perhaps his fears had been unfounded. When he alerted Emme to the probability that Stafford was coming to collect her, she thanked him for the news and left to prepare for the voyage. He got ready as well, since he'd agreed to sail the pinnace back to Roanoke after Stafford boarded the *Lion*.

White caused the most difficulty by continuing to vacillate over whether he would leave to summon help. It took further entreaties and a public rendering of the memorandum to which all the Assistants had set their hands and seals to get White reconciled to packing his bags. When Stafford brought the pinnace into the nearest mooring, a little creek close by the sandy bluff behind the fort, White was ready and waiting for him.

But Emme was not.

Kit looked at all the colonists gathered to bid White farewell and Emme was nowhere to be seen, yet the urgency was great, just as he'd supposed; Stafford confirmed it. Ferdinando was anchored off Hatarask and would brook no delay. He wouldn't take the risk of getting caught in another storm. The flyboat was beyond the sandbar and the ships would sail before noon.

He had to ask Stafford to wait.

'Mistress Murimuth should be here. I'll go and fetch her.'

Stafford frowned but gave a nod. 'Look lively about it, Kit.'

That set White into another bout of temporising.

'But Mistress Murimuth is staying here, that is what I understood from her. If she is not staying I may need to reconsider...'

There was no time to remonstrate; Kit left Stafford to do that. He ran back to the Dares' house where he found Emme as he had guessed. She was sitting by the crib, gently rocking the baby, and she couldn't have looked less ready to go on a voyage. He clenched his jaw.

'Get up now!'

She didn't even glance at him but gazed down at the infant and carried on rocking the cradle.

'Hush,' she whispered. 'Virginia is sleeping.'

He strode over and hauled her to her feet. 'You are going,' he growled, letting some of his anger bubble out. He strengthened his grip on her. How could she do this?

'You said you would go. Now is the time. You are jeopardising White's departure. Ferdinando will not wait.'

'I am jeopardising nothing,' she said meekly, turning her head and looking at him with dark eyes, soft as a doe's, and her look only inflamed him more because he knew she was deliberately appealing for his compassion, showing him a woman's weakness. But he would not give in. She had to go now. He wrenched her towards the door.

She went limp in his hands, almost falling at his feet. He staggered in trying to hold her up. He would drag her away if he had to, pin her arms behind her back.

His hands tightened and he felt her begin to shake. That stopped him instantly. He didn't mean to hurt her, only get her to leave. In a wave of remorse he released his hold, but his anger still raged inside him.

She backed away.

'Listen to me,' she murmured. 'Governor White will not go unless I stay. I have agreed to look after his granddaughter. He knows that with me here Sir Walter will have to send relief; the Queen will make sure of that. Accept it, Kit. Let me be, and go and see the Governor on his way.'

The rage passed through him and left his hands clutching at air. She was throwing her chance away and all he could do was watch. He turned from her, choked with fury.

'Very well, but I consider your defiance a poor repayment for my trust. You deceived me.'

'I told you no lies.'

'But a lie was what you let me believe.'

He marched out and didn't look back. She had disappointed him and the tragedy of her fate would now be bound up with his. The chances were that, when relief finally came, *if* it came, they both would be dead. So be it. He had done his best to spare her.

But the suspicion still haunted him that he could have done more.

The wind was blowing stronger when the pinnace finally left. Stafford stood at the helm while Kit led the stroke and the mariners helped to row, and White still protested his reluctance to depart, arguing that he might yet remain even as Stafford gave the order to get underway. The Planters waved everyone off with a fanfare, and the pinnace left Port Ferdinando only two hours later, the flow being in their favour. After seeing White aboard the flyboat, the pinnace took Stafford and the mariners across to the *Lion*. Once there, Kit had the satisfaction of hearing Ferdinando vent his exasperation over Mistress Murimuth being left behind, an anger directed at the hapless Quartermaster. There could be no going back for her with the wind getting up.

Kit was left on the pinnace, with Rob and a few others who would stay on at Roanoke, briefly in command at the fringes of the ocean. He looked out to the northeast, to the crossing he would not make, then back to the ships that would undertake the great journey. He saw the *Lion* set sail and watched the flyboat prepare to follow, the men at the flyboat's capstan labouring to haul up the anchor, backs bent as they strained to push round the bars, two to each of the six spars, turning the drum by degrees. But then disaster struck as fast as a bolt from the heavens. The next instant they lay crippled, limbs shattered and broken; blood flooded the deck; screams rent the air.

He told Emme what had happened when he got back to the island.

'One of the capstan bars broke. Those remaining spun round so fast they knocked the men down like skittles. The anchor must have snagged and the strain was too much. Even a second attempt wouldn't shift it and that led to more casualties. In the end, Spicer cut the cable and lost the anchor to get away – not good for a ship without a boat, since all the tenders have been left here at Roanoke. Ten of the crew were badly injured, and some of them most likely won't last out the crossing. Only five men and Captain Spicer were left fit enough to work the ship.'

'Will they continue?'

'They have little choice if they're to get White back to England without any more delay. Ferdinando wants to go privateering once he reaches the Azores.'

Kit looked at her, hair haloed by the light from an open window, sitting at the table in the strong-house where White used to preside over meetings. They were in a room that seemed curiously peaceful after the heated arguments he'd heard in it recently, fists thumping the boards where now her hands gently stroked the wood-grain. He was still cross with her, but in an aimless way that left him more annoyed with his own lack of foresight. He should have anticipated what she'd do; perhaps deep down he'd always known she would try to stay. He was also, if he was honest with himself, exceedingly pleased that she had not left, and even more pleased that she seemed eager to talk. At least she'd not been caught up in the disastrous start to the flyboat's voyage. Perhaps good fortune had saved her from something worse than the present danger. Though the Dares' baby and Georgie were undoubtedly the real reasons for her remaining, he still cherished the notion that maybe she cared for him a little, despite his chequered past, and his revelation about Ololade which must have upset her, and the anger he had shown her which he should have kept under control. Her determination to defy him and stay on Roanoke had been both brave and selfless; he could not fault her for that. In truth she humbled him.

She pursed her lips and tipped her head on one side. The simple clothes she wore suited her, though only a few months ago he'd admired her in ruffs and finery. He liked to see her in blue home-spun with a shawl over her shoulders, the fabric loose about her and shaping her fine figure without wires and ties and all the para-phernalia of display. She looked like the goodwife he'd once dreamt of coming home to, before capture and escape to live as an outlaw and then as an adventurer. He'd make a poor husband now. But he must concentrate on what she was saying.

'Haven't you noticed?' she asked him.

'Noticed what?'

'Misfortune seems to have dogged our enterprise with everything that Ferdinando has had a hand in. Consider all that has happened: the abandoning of the flyboat on the outward journey; the poison-ing of the Planters on first landfall; the failure to take on board salt or find any livestock or fruit; the loss of the two soldiers at St John's; the near wrecking off the cape to the south, and Ferdinando's refusal to take us to Chesapeake. Don't all these instances suggest to you that he's been intent on our destruction all along?'

Kit put his elbows on the table and cupped his chin, studying

319

her closely from the place where he sat opposite her. Did she really believe that Ferdinando was to blame for all their trials?

'I'm not convinced of that.'

'I am. He's a snake. Consider his behaviour towards me. What would he have done if I'd been at his mercy now?'

'I cannot forgive him for offending you, but I don't think he'd have seriously hurt you. He might have tormented you, that I will grant, which is not to excuse him.'

'But why torment me?'

Kit wondered how much to share with her. *Everything*, whispered one inner voice; *Be cautious*, whispered another. Her mouth was irresistible, soft and sensual, vulnerably full in the upper lip. Whenever he looked at her lips he was seized with an urge to kiss them. He took a breath.

'Perhaps Ferdinando has been trying to disguise who he really is, just as you are now.'

Her expression registered puzzlement in one tiny line between her arched dark brows.

'That makes no sense to me. Who do you think I am really? Who *do* you think Ferdinando is? Sir Francis Walsingham alerted me to his suspicions that our Pilot is an agent of Spain. I believe that must be right. It's the only explanation that accounts for everything that's gone awry when Ferdinando has been involved. Perhaps he's been responsible for even more than seems obvious to me now.'

He ran his finger along the oak grain on the table top just as she was doing, but in the opposite direction. He brought his finger to rest a fraction before they touched.

'I think you are much more than you seem, even though I know a little of your past; who you really are I think you do not yet know yourself. I believe the Queen agreed to your coming on this voyage, and it is the Queen who insisted that you return.'

She bowed her head and spoke softly.

'That is right. It doesn't matter now.'

'It does,' he said. 'She will be annoyed to have been defied.'

'But she will encourage Sir Walter to send help...'

'Only if she considers it in England's interests to do so. She will not send a fleet to rescue one lady, even one of her own.'

She looked upset and he moved his fingertips to rest lightly on hers, hoping to give her some comfort.

'As for Ferdinando, if he is a Spanish agent then why did he stay to help the colony for so long? Why offload all our supplies and then wait close to shore? Even after a storm blew up, he didn't abandon us and leave for England. He beat up and down the coast and waited it out, then came back to escort the flyboat on the start of her homeward journey.'

'Perhaps he was espying on us and wanted to be sure of what we were doing.'

'Maybe. But why would the Spaniards want us here rather than at Chesapeake?'

Her frown deepened, and she moved her hand away slightly, beginning to trace a small circle with her finger, watching the pattern forming, not looking at him.

'Because some of the Indians are hostile here? I don't know. I agree it doesn't seem rational, but I'm sure there'll be a reason; we just don't yet understand everything. That Ferdinando is working for Spain will only be part of the explanation.'

'But Ferdinando didn't know the Indians were hostile around Roanoke, only Lane knew the full extent of that and what he'd done

321

to cause their hatred. But he kept quiet about it because it didn't reflect well on him.'

She raised her eyes straight to his: two brown pools full of warmth, wide, open and inviting.

'So what is your conclusion?'

He would hide nothing from her.

'I can think of one person who wanted us as far south as possible.'

'Who?'

'Drake. I heard him say as much. He wanted the colony further south to provide a base for harrying Spanish shipping and stopping their advance north from Florida. If Drake wanted us here and not at Chesapeake then Walsingham would have wanted it too.'

'Walsingham?' He saw her shock: the hand raised to her mouth, the blink, her eyes opening again a little narrower, more guardedly, the awareness sinking in. 'No,' she whispered, drawing out the denial then rushing on. 'It was Walsingham who told me that Ferdinando was suspected of spying for the Spanish. It was Walsingham who acceded to my request to join this enterprise and who made that possible.'

He flattened his hand on the table, palm down, motionless: no more drawing lines and circles. This was what he knew.

'Bluff and double bluff. What matters most to Walsingham is the safety of the realm, curbing Spanish expansion and keeping the Spaniards guessing. He and Drake saw the strategic advantage of a base here, even further south if that could be achieved, but they also wanted the Spaniards to think we were heading for Chesapeake. By misleading the Spaniards they could hope to avert the risk of Spanish attack. If the Spaniards were ever to find and destroy us – worse still, take over our base here – that could lead to Spanish control of the whole of this coast. It would make England's claim to Virginia impossible to sustain.'

She shook her head slowly.

'I still can't believe it.'

'Follow it through and see how this supposition explains so much of what has occurred: Ferdinando leaving the two Irish veterans at St John's who thought we were heading for Chesapeake; his nervousness in the Caribbean: not wanting to do anything that might alert the Spaniards to our presence which could have led to confrontation and capture – and possibly, through him, the discovery of our true objective; his trying to find an anchorage behind the sand banks further south from here.'

Her eyes flashed.

'That foolishness almost wrecked us.'

'He did not intend for us to be wrecked. He took a risk, thinking that he'd be able to navigate a way into the river mouth behind the bight, but it proved more difficult than he thought.'

Emme placed her fingertips to her cheeks, her hands over her chin and most of her mouth, and her lips formed a tiny 'O'.

Kit went on.

'It also explains why Ferdinando was so desperate to take both you and White back. This was what Walsingham had told him to do.'

'But why was he so odious to me?'

'To keep up the pretence that you were only a maid: just a woman he found attractive and thus would allow back on his ship.'

He could tell that she still did not believe it, would not want to believe it.

'But why abandon the flyboat in the Bay of Biscay?'

'I don't think that could be helped. There was a storm and the ships became separated. Spicer might have been captured by the Spaniards. Ferdinando couldn't run the risk of the *Lion* being captured too.'

'Then why did Walsingham ever let me come on this mission?'

He heard the defiance in her voice. She must have considered Walsingham her protector, someone she could depend upon. Maybe she yet thought of him in that way.

Kit regarded her steadily, waiting for her to take her hands away from her beautiful face, to look at him directly.

'You helped sustain the interest of the Queen and that in turn secured Raleigh's backing. None of this would be possible without the funding from Raleigh's purse. The Queen would never have paid for it; the risk is too great for her to gamble a fortune on the Virginia colony from the stretched resources of the Treasury.'

She placed her hand beside his.

'Perhaps you are right. I am beginning to believe that you usually are.'

She touched his hand and the contact opened something in him, a floodgate to feeling he'd been trying to hold back, because he could be sure of nothing now where she was concerned: a woman he had tried to distance who had persisted in remaining close, a woman who could touch him physically but who might be removed by a gulf as wide as the sound in the secrets of her heart.

'I don't think we will ever know for certain,' he said. 'But now Ferdinando is gone, and it may be some time before help reaches us from England. We must make the best of what we have.'

She smiled at him. 'And you must make the best of my being here.'

He couldn't help but smile back. 'I will try to, though I would much rather that you had been safely on your way to England. You defied me.'

Why had he said that? He no longer cared that she had opposed him.

Her smile became mischievous.

'I would defy you again if I had to.'

As she spoke, he leaned closer to her over the table, tipping his head on one side, thinking that he really would like to kiss her. But would she let him?

A loud rap at the door denied him the chance to find out; it left them both sitting upright swiftly. Kit found some papers to leaf through that had been quaintly stacked under a large shell. He was thumbing through them when Dare and Harvie entered.

'We have a request for you, Master Doonan,' Dare began.

Harvie followed.

'All the Assistants are in agreement in Master White's absence.'

Dare carried on, and so they continued, one after the other.

'We need someone to take advice from the Assistants and act on our behalf after due consultation regarding matters of importance.'

'Someone to arbitrate where there is contention.'

'As well as assume ultimate responsibility for the proper governance of this city, its defence and preservation.'

Dare handed him another piece of paper with a flourish.

'This sets it all out.'

'We have decided to appoint you as acting Governor,' Harvie explained, red faced.

'If you agree,' Dare added.

'We pray that you will,' Harvie said, as if the words were stones in his mouth.

The two gentlemen stood back and regarded him soberly. Kit glanced at Emme and saw that she was beaming at him with a look full of pride. These men, who had scorned his advice, both new fathers, now wanted him to lead the colony on which their children's lives depended, and, in a way, their request was no great surprise. He had been asked to lead before when he had joined the outlaw Cimaroons, and now, just as then, he would not turn from the challenge.

'You are certain?' he asked.

'Yes,' they said.

He gave a nod. 'I thank you for this honour.' Then he raised his right hand, presenting Dare and Harvie with the flat of his scarred palm. 'I swear to fulfil the office you have bestowed on me to the best of my ability, so help me God.'

That dealt with, he smiled and spread his arms wide.

'There is much to do. Let us meet in an hour's time to discuss what is needed.'

Dare and Harvie mumbled their thanks and left, heads high.

He turned to Emme who seemed to be glowing with joy though he could not rightly understand why. Leading the colony could well be like leading the Spartans against the forces of Xerxes. They might have little hope.

'Do I have your support?' he asked.

She looked back at him with a smile that seemed to beckon him to ask for more.

'Yes, Kit, you do.'

He moved to sit beside her.

'May I kiss you?'

She moved towards him in answer, and he brushed his lips

against hers, brim full of love for her, not merely aching desire. If only she could be his. If only she could accept him as he was. He spoke without thinking beyond what filled his mind.

'If I could offer you a settled future here I would ask you to be my wife.'

She placed her hand on his arm, eyes bright with tears.

'If only...' She shook her head and then clung to him, words tumbling from her as if the chance to say them might never come again.

'Ask me anyway. Ask me now, in this moment we can be sure about. We can never know what lies ahead.'

'If I ask you...' he breathed, halfway to kissing her helplessly, praying that she would not turn him away.

She answered anyway.

'I would say yes, but you should know...'

Thank God. He poured his love into his kiss without waiting to hear more. Whatever she was about to say didn't matter. Nothing could make him not love her.

As the kiss ended he looked at her: his Emme, sweetest of women, light of his heart.

'You have told me enough. I pledge myself to you, body and soul, to love you and no other, and to marry you when the time is right – when we may rest without fear.'

She kissed his hands in return.

'I pledge myself to you in like kind. I will love you till the day I die.'

'Speak not of death but only of life. I shall love you every moment I have on this earth, more with every breath, deeper with every dream, further through all I may endure.'

She held him as if she might drown if she let him go.

'What will become of us?'

He clasped her to him, nuzzling her neck, wanting to tell her not to worry, all would be well.

'Whatever happens, we will be together.'

That was the truth.

Emme found Kit in the same room at the strong-house when she returned with fresh water for the meeting. He was bent over the large table studying a chart of some kind.

'What are you looking at?'

He answered without raising his head.

'It's a map that I copied from one that Harriot had in London. I'm trying to think about what I'd like to be decided before hearing opinions from everyone else.'

She set down the ewer and pewter cups she had brought, and moved over to him, thinking that she would like to slide her arm around his waist and that this might be acceptable since they had promised themselves to one another. Surely she could do that now, because he'd said that he loved her in words so beautiful she'd thought of nothing else through every minute since. She felt lighter than air, a galleon in the sky, her doubts cast aside like ballast thrown overboard. He loved her after all, despite his passion for the Cimaroon who had borne him a son; that was all in the past. In the time that was left to them he had promised himself to her. This was their new beginning, their new life in a new land. So why shouldn't she take hold of him? She moved nearer and reached out, then hesitated with her hand only inches from his back. They were not yet properly betrothed. All he had promised was to marry her when the time was right, and when would that be? Wasn't this only as much as Lord Hertford had promised before forcing himself upon her: a sop to gain her trust? Had her longing for Kit addled her wits? She drew back her hand, feeling her yearning for him like a wound, deep, hot and pounding inside her. But she must be cautious. He didn't yet know the truth about her, despite her trying to tell him. It was as if he'd guessed and wanted to pass over the possibility. Even if he'd meant every word, his promise might fade once he knew she was not untouched. She wanted to talk, yet she must not trouble him now, only leave him to think, because the colony depended on his decisions being right.

Quietly she stepped away and gazed at the chart. What was it telling him? There was Roanoke with the City of Raleigh at the northernmost tip. She identified their domain easily as the only large island inside the outer ribbon of sand banks, and it was shaded deep pink, as were parts of the ribbon and a few other tiny islands, but the rest, including all of the great unexplored mainland interior, was edged blue and mostly blank. The sparse dots of native settlements were ranged along the shoreline, beside the sound or the broad rivers that fed into the great lagoon. Roanoke was on the edge of a vast wilderness and the island looked very small.

'What does the map show you?' she asked.

He put his arm around her, and the gesture set her blood racing again because it mirrored the way she wished she could have touched him, but still he did not look up. He swept his hand over the map and pointed at areas as he referred to them.

'We have friends to the southeast, enemies to the southwest, and tribes of uncertain allegiance to the north.'

She frowned, sensing the precariousness of their situation; it was probably much worse than she had previously supposed. In truth, she realised, she had been living in a bubble, concentrating on Kit and those who depended on her, rarely thinking further than the limits of their city, a city that seemed more established with each day that passed. But beyond was the unknown and enemies were not far away. She struggled to comprehend what they faced.

'Let me try to understand this better, if you don't mind explaining.'

Kit turned to her with his ageless perfect face, fair and earnest, his eyes the blue of untroubled skies, and she felt utterly helpless because the burden of protecting the colony was now his, and she knew he would lay down his life for that, yet she did not want him dead. She wanted him alive and with her always. Could that ever happen? He looked at her sagely and she felt like weeping when she should have been most happy.

He placed his hand over hers on the map.

'I don't mind, Emme; it will help me to talk things through.'

She shuddered, desperate to believe that he would find some hope for her, something in the map that would assure her they would survive together.

'Begin with the Croatans,' she said. 'They control the string of outer islands to the east, don't they? All these – including Hatarask and Croatoan?' She drew her finger along the ribbon of sand banks.

'That's right. Then the Secotans are here, to the southwest; this is their principal settlement, also called Secotan.'

He pointed to a place way to the south, below a huge lake. The distances were so vast that it was probably as far removed from Roanoke as Northampton was from London. He carried on talking and she did not interrupt.

'There are at least three other villages allied with the tribe, one of which is Dasemonkepeuc which was, until recently, inhabited by the Roanokes led by Wanchese. But, as you know, when we went there nearly three weeks ago, that village was deserted.'

Where had Wanchese gone? Was he now with other tribes trying to incite them to attack? She looked at the mainland coastline to the west of Roanoke.

'This is shaded a muddy purple.' She pointed to the indented shore. 'What does that mean?'

'It means that my skills as a mapmaker are not very good.' He gave her a wry grin and she sensed he was trying to keep her confident and lighten her mood. 'It was pink,' he said. 'I used some of Manteo's plant dye and washed over it in blue.'

'I suppose that signifies it may now be hostile?'

He gave a nod.

'The areas washed red belong to us or our allies. The regions edged blue may be opposed to us.'

She turned back to the map feeling drained by a rush of despair. The whole of the mainland coast was edged blue or purple. What could they do?

'Tell me about the Roanokes,' she asked, still searching for a ray of hope though she was sure that, if there was one, then Kit would find it first. Perhaps the Secotans could be persuaded to talk even if the Roanokes were intent on enmity. 'Are they vassals of the Secotans?'

He tapped the paper.

'That's difficult to be sure about. Even Manteo is uncertain about the balance of power between them now. The Roanokes may rule the Secotans, though they are smaller in number. All we can say for certain is that the Secotans and the Roanokes are very much in league. An enemy of one will be the enemy of the other.'

A shiver of apprehension ran through her. The Secotans were their closest neighbours and far greater in number than they were, even with the Croatans. The City of Raleigh could be overpowered despite their firearms and artillery and defences and learning; Kit didn't need to tell her that.

She gazed back at the map and noticed the way the sunshine caught it, raking across from a small window and bathing the upper part in honeyed brilliance, the kind of intense brightness she'd sometimes observed before a thunderstorm. For a moment everything was motionless. The map was captured in light. Kit's hand rested in shadow beneath the tiny image of a small sailing vessel, a craft like the pinnace approaching the confluence of two river mouths. This was a sight she would not forget, she knew it as she watched. They were details to look back upon for what they symbolised and where they might lead. She sensed everything imprint on her memory. She and Kit were together in the New World: a good man and a lady of unremarkable birth, part of the first English colony founded to last and perpetuate. Perhaps, in her dreams, they'd be the first English couple to be married in the New World. Whatever they did next would set the wheels of fortune turning, not just for themselves, but for their companions, for England and the new America. It was a moment to treasure, a moment of peace, a moment for reflection: the quiet before the storm. But it could not last. The ship on the map faced a choice of two rivers, to go forwards or go back. They, too, would soon have to decide. Nothing stood still. The thunderclouds were gathering and the chill wind of fear was blowing outside. Should they try to find shelter where they were, or go somewhere else?

Above the ship were two names, the only names she could read: 'Weapemeoc' and 'Choanoke'. She pointed to them.

'So which tribes are to the north? Would it help to know whether they might support us?'

He pointed to the same names then described areas far around them.

'Indeed it would, and I believe that somehow we need to find out. The Weapemeocs and the Choanokes occupy these regions. They offered allegiance to the Queen when Lane was in command here.' He turned and smiled at her, giving her hope at last. 'If the northern tribes are willing to accept our friendship then our position may not be so desperate.'

She looked from the north to the southwest of the sound.

'Are they stronger than the Secotans?'

'They would be if they joined forces, and the support of the Choanokes alone would probably be enough to deter the Secotans from troubling us any further. From all that I've heard, the Choanokes are the mightiest tribe in this region with as many as three thousand warriors paying homage to their chief.'

*Three thousand.* Allied with that number they would be a force too great for the Secotans to overwhelm. She smiled back at him.

Kit squeezed her hand and she did not pull away.

'When Lane was Governor, that chief was Menatonon.'

'Menatonon offered Queen Elizabeth allegiance?'

'He did, but of course that was at a time when his son was held hostage by Lane. As an honourable soldier, Lane should have restored the boy to his people before he left, but we've no idea whether he did, whether Menatonon is still alive, or whether the Choanokes would now wish to befriend us despite Lane's earlier coercion.'

'But if there is a chance of fostering friendship with the Choanokes, we must take it, surely? What alternative do we have?'

Kit looked at her steadily with blue eyes that questioned her. 'We could move to Chesapeake.'

She shook her head. 'You know we'd be at risk of attack while we left in our boats and, even if we arrived, we'd have to start all over again with building houses and tilling the land.'

He pointed back to their island. 'We could remain here behind our defences, reinforce them and venture nowhere except with strong force of arms.'

She looked down sadly and again shook her head. 'We would be destroyed slowly as we ran out of food.'

He turned away. She heard him and raised her head to see him standing with his back to her, hands on his hips, looking out of the little window. His shadow fell over the map. His voice was soft. 'We could hope that the Secotans now leave us alone.'

'Do you really believe that's likely?'

'No, I don't. Not in view of what they did to Howe and Grenville's men.'

That horror; she had tried not to dwell on it but it was locked in her mind. That horror could be theirs.

'They hate us, don't they?'

He faced her, silhouetted against the light; the sun burnished his golden head.

'With justification, considering that Lane murdered Wingina and many of the Roanokes without warning, and under the guise of friendship.'

She clutched at another straw. 'Would they listen if we approached them directly?'

'I doubt we would ever have that chance. The cycle of revenge has become too entrenched. The violence and mistrust between us and the Secotans has been so great it will take more than a lifetime to heal.'

She looked at him but his face was lost in shadow. 'So the Secotans will attack?'

He answered without expression. 'Yes.'

'The only question is when?'

'It is. They may pick us off slowly, one by one as we search for food, or they may attempt to overpower us quickly in one concerted assault. I'm sure they will not simply ignore us, not as we are: patently isolated.'

He was telling her they were doomed, but doing so with such calm that she did not scream or wail or cling to him in desperation. He was Gabriel the messenger, showing her the truth and filling her with the strength to face it. She rose and moved over to him, feeling both his warmth and the heat of the sun.

'Friendship with the Croatans will not be enough to save us?'

He put his arm gently around her shoulders and she felt no urge to pull away. She welcomed the reassurance he gave her.

'That did not stop the Secotans before; why should it now?'

She rested her head against his chest. There was only one course that seemed open to them. 'Then shouldn't we try and forge another alliance – one that will make the Secotans wary of upsetting us?'

'Yes.' He stroked her hair. 'If that's possible. But remember that White's invitation to all the tribes to come to Roanoake and agree to peace passed completely unanswered.'

She wrapped her arms around him as she had wanted to do all along. 'Maybe we must go to them. We could send a delegation to the Choanokes.'

Then she realised what he had done: he had got her to suggest what he had already decided upon. He planned to leave her on this mission and she felt suddenly queasy. She turned away from him, her thoughts clouding over. He had said he would stay with her and straightaway he meant to go. He might not come back. All their promises would be for nothing. She tried to swallow her hurt, reason clearly and not selfishly. They both had to do what was best, not for each other but the colony. She looked back at the map and saw the word 'Choanoke' in a patch of sunlight. She pointed to it. 'Is this where they are based?'

'Yes.' He slipped beside her, circling her waist with one arm and indicating the river by the settlement with the other hand, tracing a course to it from their island.

'The city of Choanoke is on the Chowan river. The way to reach it would be by boat, travelling north and then west to the head of the sound, here.'

She looked hard at the map and knew it was based on one she'd seen before: a map of White's that he'd examined, several times, spread over the table in the Dares' house. But something was different; she tried to identify what had changed. She stared at the divide between the two rivers, the place where Kit's fingertip had come to rest.

'I remember seeing the symbol of a fort there on a chart that White consulted not long after we arrived. I'm sure it was about where you are pointing. The fort stood out to me because it seemed so odd. There's only one fort here, isn't there? The fort we're in now. Why would White have marked another fort where none existed?'

Kit kissed her lightly on the cheek, then held her from him just enough to look her in the eye.

'Perhaps there was once a plan to build a fort there. Think hard.

336

Was the fort you saw shown here, between the mouths of the Chowan and the Moratico?'

She glanced back to check where he was pointing. 'Yes. I think it was.'

Kit gave a nod. 'There was a patch on the chart I copied in roughly this area. It may well have masked a similar symbol. So we may suppose that both Lane and White once thought that the construction of a fort there would be feasible. That must have meant their relations with the Choanokes were good at one time.'

She appreciated why Kit would want to believe that; she wanted to believe it too, and that friendship with the Choanokes could be resumed. But the altering of Harriot's map she could not understand.

'But why hide what they had planned?'

'Because they didn't have time to carry the plan out. Drake arrived unexpectedly when Lane's garrison got into difficulties. Lane and his men left, and the mainland fort was never established. The charts were later altered to keep them accurate, all except for the one that White kept for his own personal use, and there was no need for him to change his own map; he knew the fort had never been built.'

'If that is right, there must still be a good chance that the Choanokes could accept our friendship.'

He smiled at her but she saw sadness in his eyes. He wanted her to believe that there was hope, but perhaps, in his heart, he knew there was none.

'A chance,' he said, 'but maybe not a good one. If Menatonon's son was not given back, the Choanokes could now be determined on vengeance against us.'

She sought to shore up his spirits just as he was trying to bolster hers. 'But they have not attacked us yet, not like the Secotans.'

'No – which suggests that the chance is still worth pursuing.' He pulled her closer to him. This was where he would tell her he was leaving; she braced herself for it.

He took a deep breath.

'I am considering asking Dare and Harvie to strengthen the defences here; we should at least have a wall of tree trunks around the houses. I could go to Choanoke and sue for peace. I'd only need a few men: Manteo to interpret, maybe Jim Lacy and Jack Tydway – strong fit men willing to risk their lives for this chance – not so many as to appear threatening to the savages. We might return with an alliance that will ensure the safety of our city, and if we fail then our prospects will be no worse than they are now. I'll advise Dare and Harvie to lead everyone to Chesapeake if I'm not back in a week.' He looked at her and she knew he was asking for her approval. 'The mission would be risky, but it would be better than doing nothing and waiting to be attacked.'

She met his eye. He must understand that she meant what she was about to say. 'I will come with you.'

A flicker of worry passed over his face.

'No. *No*,' he said again, shaking his head. 'You must stay here to look after Georgie and the Dares' baby. They will need you if the colony has to move.'

She raised her hands to his shoulders and gripped them firmly. 'The baby has her parents, and Master Harvie will keep an eye on Georgie. Remember what you told me: "Whatever happens, we will be together." If I go too, the Choanokes will be assured that you are not leading a war party; the sight of a woman should stay their hostility. If I remain, I could be killed if the city falls while you are gone.'

That point meant much to him, she could tell. He flinched and closed his eyes. 'Emme. Emme...'

'I would be safest with you. I have decided, Kit. If I am to die here, I will die with you.'

A look of pain creased his face.

'You will be in jeopardy either way; that is true...' He pressed her to him and whispered against her neck, his voice close to breaking. 'I wish it were not so.'

'But it is, and I will not leave you.'

He held her tight and she could feel his longing as strong as hers was for him, but a thread of uncertainty kept them apart, perhaps hers alone, but maybe he had doubts as well. They were like two strands of a cable not yet twined fast together.

He released her gradually.

'If you come then so will Rob.'

'Very well, he is your son. A woman and a boy together should give the Choanokes cause for reflection before they shoot anyone down.'

He winced and bowed his head, then turned suddenly in response to a commotion at the door.

She had already seen the hats of some of the Assistants passing by the window, and she knew they were arriving for the meeting. She touched Kit's hand.

'Now you must say what you will do. They are here.'

He kissed her quickly.

'I am ready.'

She kissed him back on the cheek.

'So am I.'

# 12

# *Dead Men Returned*

'...We had taken Menatonon prisoner, and brought his son
that he best loved to Roanoke...it made Ensenor's opinion to
be received again with greater respect. For he had often before
told them...that we were the servants of God, and that...they
amongst them that sought our destruction should find their own,
and not be able to work ours, and we being dead men were able
to do them more hurt...and many of them hold opinion, that we
be dead men returned...'

—*From Ralph Lane's* Narrative of the Settlement of Roanoke
Island 1585–6

The wind had dropped and the talking was over. Emme looked
from the prow of the pinnace to the six men rowing at the limits of
their strength, sweat-streaked faces glowing in the last rays of the
sun, expressions dead with exhaustion. The breath whistled from
them as they bent to haul again, their oars creaked in the tholes,
the water rippled by, but in the lull before the next stroke she heard

something she could not place, a sound that might have been the breeze in the rigging or sighing through forest leaves, except there was no breeze, and the nearest forest was over a bowshot away. The sound was more like singing than anything else, haunting and ethereal, a melancholic wave that endlessly rose and fell, though there was no one to be seen, and the nearest shore was so distant she could only just make out the trees at the water's edge, rising straight from a haze of river mist, their roots bulging in mounds as if they had grown out from graves, their branches trailing moss like tattered shrouds. How could voices travel so far? Perhaps all she was hearing was some trick of memory, a singularity filling the quietness with noise from inside her head: singing and chanting, prayer and laughter; voices from the past, some recent, some long gone; sounds of all kinds that formed part of her history. But mostly she heard the voices of those who meant much to her, voices from palaces and places she'd once thought of as home. She heard her father and the Queen, and she heard Kit speaking again, just as he'd done that afternoon, when the wind had filled the sails and carried the pinnace effortlessly north and west, and they'd travelled past the drums of the Weapemeocs, almost to the head of the sound, making for the region where two rivers met. Their journey had been fast until the wind had failed, and the need to row had put an end to talk, and the sun started to sink, and they'd begun to doubt whether they'd reach Choanoke before night engulfed them.

'Tell me about your childhood,' Kit had asked. 'I'd like to know everything. You had an older brother, didn't you, like me?'

'He was my stepmother's son by an earlier marriage, not a real brother in blood. I hated him at first for taking away my father's attention, but I suppose, thinking about him now, it was not his fault that I felt unwanted. I missed my mother. I was only six years of age when she died; he came to Fifield not long afterwards...'

Emme had spoken freely as Kit had asked. She'd told him about all the inconsequential incidents that had made an impression on her in growing up, about her games and her pets, as much as she could remember about her mother, and her father's kindness before he grew cold towards her. She spoke about the foal he had given her that he'd allowed her to name.

'I wanted to call her Quince Jelly Biscuit because those were the nicest things I could think of when I was very small. My father laughed and agreed to Quince as a name, but my pony was always Quince Jelly Biscuit for me. I'd call her that when no one was listening. Her favourite treat was pippin pie.'

Kit had smiled, listening to her, close enough for her to feel him.

'Not quince jelly or biscuits?'

'No, I should have called her Apple Pie.'

Kit was the first person she had told about her pony's name. She told him that as she told him everything that had mattered to her, and much that didn't, just as he told her his stories, about his father who beat his older brother and was drunk most of the time, about the favouritism that he wished had never been his, the mill that was meant for him, which now belonged to his sisters' husbands, because everyone had thought him dead after his capture by the Spaniards; his mother who'd died of a broken heart believing him dead; his brother, Will, who had always tried to look after him; and the fall in the forge that had left him with the scar over his palm.

What were they doing in telling these stories? She felt she knew, though neither asked the other why. The stories were a testament to each of their lives, full of the irrelevancies of memory that had shaped them as people: unique, inconsequential, meaningless to everyone except themselves, but now meaningful, because, for each of them, in the telling was their essence, and in sharing they were giving, becoming part of the other. These were memories known to no one else, memories that would otherwise be lost if they died, leaving their lives to fade like the play of light on a wave. But now Kit's stories were in her heart, and hers were in his, imprinted for so long as the other would live. They would be with one another always, and if they both should die then, surely, they would be together wherever God placed them next.

'Remember I love you,' he had said. 'The more I learn about you, the more I am with you, the more I love you. No matter what we face, wherever I am, I will never stop loving you. Always remember that.'

'I will remember,' she had said, wanting to throw her arms about him and sob out her bitter secret. But there had been others very close, Kit's son amongst them, and Kit had charge of the tiller, and she had feared to distract him. Her answer had been just a murmur.

'I will always love you.'

She meant every word, but would he really always love her? Would he love her when he knew the truth?

*You have not told him everything.*

That was another voice she heard, her own voice deep inside.

*You have not told him about your shame.*

Could she? *How* could she? She did not know where to begin. All she knew was that he would find out if and when the time came for him to take her as his wife, if there was ever peace, if he meant what he had said. When they were joined in body, then he would discover her secret.

*He thinks you are untouched and that is a lie.*

She had told him everything except her greatest hurt, but, every time she tried to confess, the words dried up and her tongue would not work. She could not tell him now when she might so easily be overheard; that was her present excuse. But she was also afraid. What man's love could survive the knowledge that another man had been before him where he should have been first? The single flower that had been hers to offer had already been picked and thrown in the dirt. She should have been a maiden for Kit; he was perfect and she should have been pure, yet she was pure no longer and now never could be. However hard she tried, whatever she did, nothing could bring her maidenhood back.

*If you die now he'll never know.*

Perhaps she was destined never to tell him. If she died before he took her she would die a maiden in his eyes. Maybe that was what was meant to happen; if that was so, then even in death she would find sweetness.

She looked towards him where he rowed, now sitting alongside Manteo in the stern of the boat, his face drained by exertion, but still vital and handsome. Her gaze took in everyone, seeing her friends as they might appear to strangers: a curious mixed company, motley, travel-worn and weary. There was Rob and Tom Humphrey, Jim Lacy and Jack Tydway, Manteo and the man she loved – a young Cimaroon and a lanky foundling, a scraggy soldier and a burly gaolbird, an Indian who was a gentleman and a privateer who was betrothed to her; then include herself, erstwhile lady-in-waiting, wearing pantaloons and a plated brigandine. What would savages make of them? Curious, perhaps, but of little consequence. They carried few arms, and little of any value beyond the tools and trinkets that Kit had brought along as gifts. Yet they also carried the hopes of England, of Sir Walter Raleigh and the Queen. Probably, almost certainly, they were heading for destruction, but she was not afraid. She feared for the Planters in the city, for Georgie and Virginia – prayed for them all to live. But with Kit she felt invulnerable. Nothing could hurt her so long as she could cling to a belief in his love; without that now, for her, life would not be worth living. Merely looking at him gave her sustenance; he was manna for her eyes. She feasted on the sight of him, as much as she could see: from his golden hair swept back from his brow to the strong angles of his short-bearded jaw. Maybe he sensed it. He looked up and smiled at her, and in that instant everything cleared. She heard all the sounds around her: the lapping water and creak of wood, and the singing that seemed to be coming from the mist.

He heard the singing too. From the glance that passed between them, she knew it at the same moment. A shimmer of anxiety troubled his face. She turned to scan the nearest shore, dark below the coals of the sunset in the west, but nothing was visible beyond mist and water and ancient moss-draped trees.

She moved from the prow to the stern, climbing over the benches, and Kit called for the rowing to stop.

'Do you hear it?' she whispered to him.

'Yes.'

The singing wavered through the silence as they drifted slowly back downstream, enigmatic and poignant, unearthly and lonely.

Kit turned to Manteo looking more worried than ever she'd seen him.

'What kind of singing is that?'

Manteo answered in an undertone.

'It is a song of welcome.'

Kit's shoulders relaxed.

'They won't attack?'

'Not yet. They are welcoming us back from the dead.'

*From the dead.* What did that mean? She moved closer to Kit.

'Do they think we are ghosts?'

He held her hand.

'Yes. But that should help us.' He gave her hand a squeeze. 'Ghosts cannot be killed.'

He spoke to everyone as they turned to face him. 'We'll anchor mid-river tonight and set a double watch: two hours on, four off. Rob and I first, then Tom and Jim, then Jack and Manteo. In the morning we'll hear what the Choanokes have got to say beyond singing us lullabies.'

There was a ripple of muted chuckling before the men began to row the pinnace back and away from the shore. The anchor was dropped as darkness closed, leaving only black shadow and the starry sky, and the grey sheen over the wide water. Emme sought some privacy under an old sail thrown over the boom, shared a meal of corn biscuit and dry venison, then settled in the prow where Kit led her to try and sleep.

'I have this for you,' he said, pressing something like a small string of beads into her hand.

'Pearls,' he explained. 'But only black. I bartered for them from the Croatans.'

She didn't ask what he'd given for them, and she didn't mind that they were black. What did that matter now? They felt as smooth and flawless as any she'd ever seen.

'Will you help me tie them on?' she asked, holding the pearls in

346

place then drawing his hand to her wrist 'Tie the string fast. I never want to take it off.'

He did, and then she bade him wait while she took the knife from her girdle and cut at the lace of her left cuff. Once it was free, she gave the strip to him.

'This is for you. I'm sorry I have nothing better.'

He held out his wrist to her. 'Tie it on for me and make the knot tight.'

She did as he asked and they held one another quietly. The gifts would be their love tokens in pledge of their promises. Nothing more needed to be said.

He kissed her cheek in a tender way that no one else would have noticed under the cloak of the night.

'Now try and rest.'

'You know I will not.'

'Count the pearls until you reach the end.'

She smiled to herself at that, since now there was no end to the loop they had made. But that is what she did, running the pearls through her fingers one after the other, imagining arrows raining down like the shooting stars in the heavens, only to vanish as completely because she had the pearls in her grasp and each was full of the shielding power of his love. Even so, the singing troubled her and sleep would not come, but sometime before dawn she must have sunk into a dreamless doze because she woke with a start to find Kit stroking her shoulder.

The singing had stopped.

\*

They approached the city as the mist fled wraith-like from the water and early sunbeams filtered between the cypress trees. The light had a quality that Kit had observed before in cathedrals, slanting down from unseen openings, hazed as if through the smoke of candles, entering a vastness framed by countless pillars that were buttressed tree trunks reaching to inestimable height, their branches bearing tattered flags of moss that gleamed golden where the sunbeams struck. Fur-cloaked priests led them along a path like a cloister, the view framed by the arches of creepers, the passageway trailing through courtyards of swamp, shining under the few rays that penetrated so far, black in the shadows, or crusted by weed glowing green like mown grass. Their first sight of Choanoke was the brightness of a clearing around a low hummock of higher ground, then the palisade that surrounded it, over twice the height of a man: an impenetrable wall of tree trunks driven into a depthless mire, their tops hewn to spikes. The entrance was a double ribbon of stakes leading to the outermost dwellings, mostly bow-framed huts covered in skins or rush mats, some of which were rolled back to air raised sleeping platforms. Beyond these was an inner palisade with another concealed entrance, and behind this wall were great longhouses, and a higher building on stilts with a curious terrace-ridged pointed roof. To this place the priests led them. Kit reckoned the number of the city's inhabitants as he followed the cloaked men up a ladder to the high floor inside. There must be close to fifteen hundred; he'd counted seventeen longhouses, each large enough to house sixty people, along with at least a score of smaller shelters. The whole place was so well protected that it would take an army to overpower, but the strength of the defences suggested the Choanokes feared attack. They must have enemies amongst other savage tribes; perhaps that would help the City of Raleigh.

Kit looked round at the others before entering the gloom within the strange building. No one spoke. They all looked apprehensive, Emme most of all. Her shock-wide eyes revealed fear bordering on terror. He wanted to soothe her but something about the eerie silence held him back from uttering a word. This place was sacred, he felt sure. It smelt of death.

Once inside, the mats that had been raised for them were lowered back down. The darkness was blinding, and, in the time it took for Kit's eyes to adjust, he heard nothing but ragged breathing. No one moved. Gradually he made out forms in the shadows: ghostly shapes revealed by a spectral luminescence that somehow managed to seep through the covers, stripped of colour and reduced to shades.

He saw bodies. Many of them. Before him was a long row of men laid out side by side, legs stretched to an unnatural length, faces shrivelled around empty eye-sockets, lips parted like gaping slits baring the smiles of skulls covered in masks of leather.

Emme gasped and gripped his arm.

He covered her hand.

The priests began to sing, deep and low with powerful resonance, voices rising in wailing harmony, circling in pitch, soaring in mood. The song was uplifting and infinitely sad. They seemed to direct it at something, then Kit saw what that was: a man attired completely in black apart from a blaze at his breast, sitting, ankles crossed, knees apart, his dress accentuating his shoulders as if he was wearing a padded doublet, open at the chest, and with a black hat on his head of the high-crowned kind that he'd seen no Indian wear. Was the man Spanish? English? Was he alive? He merged so completely into the shadows that Kit could hardly discern him. His face was invisible.

Manteo came close, bringing his own smell of hide and resin. He placed his hand on Kit's shoulder and whispered into his ear.

'This is Kiwasa, guardian of the dead. He watches over former kings.'

'*What* is he?'

'He is between our world and theirs.'

'Does he see us?'

'Yes, though his eyes are wood.'

'Ah.' Kit exhaled. 'He is a statue.'

Kit stared harder at the manikin, imagining the thing was moving, head turning as he edged nearer. He must have imagined it; no statue could move unaided. Emme was still with him, clutching his sleeve. He felt her shivering and murmured reassurance.

'It's just an effigy. This place is no more than a wicker tomb.'

'The smell...'

'The smell of mortality; it could be worse.'

She huddled closer as the singing enveloped them. Suddenly it ended.

A hand slid over his throat as fur brushed his cheek. The pressure on his throat was slight but it made his blood run cold. He imagined the hand tightening, two hands strangling him.

A priest spoke quietly.

'He wants you to tell him the message,' Manteo said.

'What message?'

'The message that you hear.'

He heard nothing. The priest was silent, waiting. Why him? Why the question? He closed his eyes and steadied his breathing. Quell his fear. Nothing could be achieved without trust. Empty his mind, black within black. He spoke what he thought.

'There must be an end to mistrust.' He turned to Manteo. 'Tell them that.'

Manteo translated, and the priests spoke softly between themselves.

Perhaps the message was what he most wanted from the Choanokes, perhaps what he hoped they wanted. It seemed to satisfy the priests; they said no more and ushered everyone outside.

The priests led him on towards a huge longhouse at the heart of the clearing. The others trooped with him, Emme on his left side, Manteo on his right; Rob followed with Tom Humphrey, Jack Tydway with Jim Lacy. They marched inside the immense barrel-roofed structure and assembled at the centre before a line of seated elders. Scores of people were at either end, all crammed together, squatting cross-legged; there must have been several hundred all told. Light streamed in from the side Kit faced where the middle strips of matting had been rolled up to the roof. The elders sat with their backs to this light, their faces in dark shadow as they gestured for everyone to sit. Kit took his place opposite on a wide row of mats, and Emme joined him, soon followed by the others. They spread out their gifts, mostly tools and beads, things that the Choanokes might find useful and prize, and all the while Kit searched for someone who could be Menatonon, but there was no sign of a cripple amongst the cloaked and aged men. He cast a quizzical glance at Manteo but his friend shook his head.

'He is not here,' Manteo murmured.

Kit spread his hands and fixed his attention on the elders.

'We come in peace in hope of friendship. We offer these gifts of steel and glass. If the *weroance* Menatonon is here, we ask to speak with him. We wish to renew our alliance with the great tribe of the Choanokes.'

The elders conferred amongst themselves, roached heads bent

together, occasionally glancing over their shoulders. Smoke rose from their pipes to writhe like transparent snakes in the sunbeams above. None of the elders was distinguished in dress beyond the fringed deerskins they wore like the robes of the ancients. They had no tattoos or ornamentation, no strings of pearls or emblems of leadership. Were any of them *weroances*? It didn't seem likely. They looked uncomfortable, as if they were waiting for someone else to take charge. Kit saw one of them puffing on a pipe and staring into the shadows at the north end of the longhouse. He looked there too. There was someone approaching. A hum of anticipation rose from the people all around; then, at a single word of command, everyone got to their feet. The elders stood, and Kit motioned for his company to stand also. Absolute silence fell as a figure strode forwards, passing through the crowd which opened up before him, forming a passageway to the place where Kit and his party waited.

The man was magnificent, tall and strongly built with the sinuous grace of an athlete, clothed in nothing but a breechclout, but covered in tattoos from head to toe that flowed around the lines of his powerful muscles. His hair was shaved either side of a spiked and feathered roach, and at his chest was a great square pendant of burnished copper. There was copper around his neck and in bands around his wrists. When he smiled, as he drew closer, Kit saw a gap between his upper teeth.

'Wanchese!' Manteo croaked, stiffening at Kit's side.

Kit groaned inwardly, sensing their chances crumbling. What was Wanchese doing at Choanoke if not fomenting trouble for the colony?

The warrior eyed Manteo suspiciously, and spoke in English. 'Still fawning before our enemies, Manteo? There is no place for you here. I can speak for myself and the Choanokes in the tongue of the English. I can tell everyone at this council the truth of what is said. We have no need for your meddling.'

Kit spoke up. Manteo's position had to be recognised.

'We would like Manteo to stay so there is no misunderstanding. He can put your words to us in the tongue of the Choanokes for the benefit of those assembled, and you can do likewise with our words to you.'

Wanchese inclined his head.

'Very well, Englishman. I will know if he lies.'

Manteo's translation followed, hoarse but defiant.

With his arms spread wide, Wanchese welcomed Kit and his company and turned to include everyone.

'Greetings, English, ghosts from the spirit world.' His eyes narrowed as he addressed Kit directly. 'You must know you cannot speak here with the *weroance* Menatonon. He lies now in the House of the Dead.'

Kit swallowed with an effort, looked at Wanchese and saw their ruin. They were surely finished. Menatonon was dead, and Wanchese, their known enemy, now commanded the respect of the Choanokes who had once been their friends. What hope was there left?

But he would not abandon the course they had embarked upon, not yet, not with the lives of Emme and his son at stake. He would see it through until he could hope no longer.

'We grieve to hear of the death of Menatonon,' he said, projecting as much authority as he could. 'My name is Kit Doonan, and I speak for the City of Raleigh at Roanoke, and the English, my countrymen. Our greetings to you and all the people of Choanoke.'

Wanchese bade everyone sit, and settled opposite Kit on a mat in front of the elders. The smell of sweat and smouldering tobacco pervaded the air. But Wanchese did not smoke, nor did he offer a pipe to Kit. He stared with eyes like glowing embers.

'Menatonon spoke to you, the priests tell me. He told you there must be no more mistrust between us.'

'Wouldn't that help everyone?'

Wanchese calmly placed his hands on his outspread knees. His posture reminded Kit of the idol Kiwasa. Against the light he seemed almost as dark. The warrior half closed his eyes and inhaled. When his eyelids flicked open again it was to glare straight at Kit.

'Menatonon died broken after you English took his best loved son.'

'Skiko was not sent back?'

'No one has seen him since you English took him away.'

Kit bowed his head. Lord, what had they done? Damn Lane for his arrogance and for handing the good citizens of Raleigh a chalice poisoned by cruelty. He understood Menatonon's suffering; it would be his if Rob was taken from him to live out his life as a hostage, a misery he remembered all too well. He wanted to turn around, to reassure himself with a glance that Rob was still alive and behind him. But he did not move. Thank God for the boy's colour; Wanchese would never recognise him as his son. But Rob's fate, and Emme's, now depended on healing the hurt that had been done, and all he could offer was remorse. He looked up.

'Skiko should have been released and returned to you. We apologise for his loss.'

Wanchese shook his fist.

'Apologise! You think that is enough for destroying the great *weroance* of the Choanokes and his son? He offered you friendship and tribute and in return you tore out his heart.'

Kit raised his scarred palm and turned slowly to take in all those gathered round, from the savage faces crowded together at one end of the longhouse to those at the other, some of them pooled in light, most cast in shadow, the whites of their eyes gleaming: hundreds of people he had to convince through filtered words and unasked for gifts with little to aid him but the way he spoke, the distance between them made greater by deep suspicion. How could he reach them?

'We apologise sincerely,' he said. 'That is the truth. This company, and those of us now at Roanoke, had nothing to do with the taking of Skiko.'

A sneer curled the warrior's lip.

'Neither did I have anything to do with the offers of peace made by Menatonon.'

Kit turned again to all the Choanokes assembled.

'There have been wrongs on both sides.'

Then he spoke directly to Wanchese, looking him in the eye.

'You murdered one of our best men at Roanoke, a man innocent of any offence against you.'

Wanchese's sneer twisted to a baleful smile.

'His offence was to be English, as is yours. You English have proved you cannot be trusted. You bring us tainted gifts and evil ways. You invade our lands and kill us by stealth.' He raised his voice to a shout. 'You must all die.'

Kit sat motionless as a shiver shot through his spine: the chill barb of hatred. Wanchese would never accept the offer of friendship he brought. It was too late to try and reason with him; his ears had been blocked by the blood spilt in the past. Their only hope now lay in direct appeal to the Choanokes despite Wanchese's malign influence. He would have to try. He spoke to the elders and the people looking on, a task made harder by the sunlight that bathed him but left most of his audience in the shadow behind the walls. He felt the power of his own conviction, strong as the light, but he could not gauge the effect of his words.

'I pray the Choanokes will think differently. I accept that some of the English who came before us did not act as honourably as they should have done. But we too have suffered wrongs. The Englishmen who came to Roanoke before us were brutally attacked. Many were killed though they had done no native here any harm. Now one of our own men has been murdered by the Secotans. I say the time has come for peace. The Roanokes and the Secotans have had their vengeance.' He spread his hands, palms flat. 'Let us call an end to enmity and move forwards in friendship.'

He picked up some of the gifts that had been brought: a knife and a scythe, their blades flashing in the light, a lodestone and a nail that flew to its surface, a magnifying glass that he angled so it sent rainbows over the walls. Some of the Indians gasped; he heard their wonder. Perhaps others had seen such things before.

'We can bring you tools of great use, medicine and learning. When we are resupplied, we can bring you animals for breeding: horses and cattle that will ensure you never go hungry, tobacco better than any you have known.' He held up a single large papery brown leaf from Hispaniola, one collected from his own voyages. 'Good *uppowoc*,' he said, 'new crops, delicious fruits. Let us share for the benefit of us all...'

'Share?' Wanchese interrupted. 'Would you share your weapons, Kit Doonan?'

The challenge came as no surprise to Kit. He knew it had been a rule of previous expeditions never to give the savages arms of war, yet to deny the request would undermine any prospect of the peace he sought. How could the Indians be expected to overcome their mistrust of him if he didn't demonstrate his trust in them first? He could be overpowered anyway along with everyone in his company. Better to give freely than be stripped. He unbuckled his sword belt and laid it complete with scabbard and broadsword on the mat in front of Wanchese.

'Take this as my gift to you.'

Wanchese smiled slowly. He picked up the belt, unsheathed the sword and held it up to the light; then, very deliberately, he reached across the space between them and brought the point to Emme's throat.

She did not move, but Kit sensed her fright. Her eyes were fixed unblinking on the blade. Her hands stayed frozen halfway between her lap and her throat.

Kit responded carefully without any show of undue concern. He had to keep control, but in his mind he was calculating his moves: the lunge he would make if Wanchese drew back to strike; the reach for his dagger; the thrust into Wanchese's guts with the over-balancing charge. He wouldn't hesitate, and he knew Lacy and the others would be with him as well. But Wanchese remained poised, not moving, only smiling.

Kit raised his hand. 'I have given my sword to you in friendship.'

Wanchese lowered the sword and sheathed it unhurriedly then placed the scabbard back on the mat. 'Give me your firearm as well, friend.'

This was the greater test. In firearms lay the best advantage the

English had. The Indians had no hope of making such weapons, and even the use of a firearm was an arcane mystery to most. Kit had placed his caliver on the mat by his side like all the men in his company. He picked it up and put it in front of Wanchese. Out of the corner of his eye he noticed Lacy's hand move to his belt.

Wanchese sat stock still. 'Load the piece first and set the match.'

Kit did so in silence, as fast as he could so the complex steps would not easily be remembered, though he felt that nothing escaped the warrior's attention. Surely none of it would have been new to him. Wanchese had been to England and back with men from two expeditions; he must have seen a caliver loaded before. Kit closed the priming pan and handed the piece to Wanchese along with a length of match cord attached to the serpentine.

Wanchese lit the match with one of the elder's pipes and opened the pan; then he levelled the caliver straight at Kit.

There was a ripple of movement. Most of the Indians cowered, some gasped. Those nearest ducked to the ground.

The men in Kit's company gripped their sword-hilts.

'Don't move,' Kit commanded them, his voice low, not taking his eyes from Wanchese. 'Say nothing.'

Wanchese cocked the caliver and took aim. The muzzle hovered only inches away from Kit's forehead. The shot, if it came, would blow his head off.

'No!' Emme sobbed, quiet as a whisper, and Kit knew she was weeping.

Wanchese rocked with laughter, tipped back his head and fired.

The blast left ringing silence, a thick cloud of dust and smoke, drifting fragments of matting, and the stench of scorched hair and sulphur. Kit turned in a daze and clapped his hand to a burning pain in his scalp. He saw a hole ripped out of the wall high in the rush screens behind him. Screams gradually penetrated his deafness. Emme was crying with her eyes half closed and her lips drawn between her teeth. Her face was rigid but trembling; tears streamed down her cheeks. He wished she had not been so upset. He wiped his brow and saw that his fingers were black.

Wanchese laughed louder and brandished the caliver above his head.

'See how the power of the English is now mine.' The look he gave Kit was gloating.

'You wish us to share, Kit Doonan? We will exchange women: one of yours for one of ours. I will have the one you have brought.' He jabbed the caliver towards Emme before tossing it down. 'You may choose.' He gestured to some of the women looking on and spoke to them in their own tongue.

Manteo leaned closer to Kit and whispered. 'He is ordering them to go to you.'

The women rose and stood before Kit in a line: six maidens of savage beauty with pearls around their necks and blue markings across their cheeks. Their breasts were exposed, unsuckled and firm, the nipples were soft cones. Kit saw Emme glance towards him and he shook his head.

He looked back at Wanchese.

'We do not share people. This lady is not mine to give.'

Emme murmured without moving. 'I will go with him.'

'No.'

'If it is what he wants and will bring peace...'

'No.' Kit spoke to her in an undertone. 'It won't bring peace. He is having sport with us. You must not answer him.'

He should have expected Wanchese's interest. Emme was lovely to behold, far more lovely than the young women before him, and she must have looked intriguing to any man, with her soldier's garb and armed to fight. But Wanchese would not have her.

The warrior beckoned using one long muscular arm and a single curling finger. 'She wants to come to me, Kit Doonan. Let her go.'

Wanchese smiled at Emme, though Emme looked back at him stone faced and with her eyes half shut as if to blank him from her sight.

He chuckled softly. 'She likes what she sees.'

She closed her eyes and bent her head.

Wanchese reached out to stroke her hand. 'Come, lady, I will treat you well.'

She pulled back with a start, and Kit thrust out his arm like a barrier before her. 'No. I cannot give her to you.'

Wanchese met his eye. 'Then let her decide.'

In the silence that followed, Kit sensed the expectation. How could he answer in fairness if he was not seen to allow Emme a choice? Slowly he withdrew his arm.

The warrior beckoned again. 'Come to me and be my *weroanca*. Let our union show the trust between our people.'

She turned to Kit and spoke softly. 'Give me leave to go with your blessing for the sake of everyone else.'

He gave the same answer under his breath feeling hollow to the core of his heart. Sending her to Wanchese might help for reasons that were right, but he could not do it. 'No.'

'Come!' Wanchese boomed, raising his voice for every Choanoke to hear. 'Let there be an end to mistrust.'

Kit's blood pounded hot in his veins. Wanchese had cornered

him with the love he felt for Emme; the warrior must have sensed it. But the taking of people was wrong, however it was done. It had been wrong for him, wrong for Skiko, and it would be wrong for sweet Emme to be handed to this man as a sacrifice. He would not let her go.

'You do not need hostages to be able to trust us and we ask for none to trust you.' He turned to the patriarchs sitting behind Wanchese. 'I appeal to the elders of the Choanokes. Will you accept our offer of peace and alliance?'

They heard Manteo translate the question then averted their eyes, bowing their grey heads to confer with one another, their shoulders hunched as if they wished to shrink from the need to answer. After a silence in which smoke from their pipes coiled like warring phantoms floating above them, one of their number spoke up in a tremulous voice.

'Wanchese now guides us. You English have offered peace before; then you have taken and killed us in ways that cannot be seen. We must protect ourselves. You withhold the woman Wanchese asks for as proof of your trust. How can we trust you? Wanchese will give you our answer.'

Wanchese smiled again, triumphantly. He looked from them to Kit and his eyes narrowed.

'Let me tell you something, Kit Doonan. The elders of the Choanokes invited me here for a council of war. They heard of your coming and they sought my advice. "How can we rid ourselves of these English?" That was what they asked me. "They keep coming and coming. We drive them away but they come back again." My answer is this: "*You must kill them all, because only the fear of us will keep the rest away.*"'

So this was the decision that Wanchese was working up to all along, and now it was the Choanokes' answer: the end of the colony. There was no hope of peace. All of the English would be wiped out, every man, woman and child. Nothing would stop Wanchese. Kit felt sick. He'd never even get back to Raleigh to warn the colony. He'd be killed along with Rob and Emme and everyone else he'd led like lambs to the slaughter. But perhaps Wanchese might hesitate if he thought his own people would be put at risk. It was a chance, very slim, and one Kit didn't like to take. It was a feint, but he had no choice.

'If you kill us now then your people will suffer. Our friends on Roanoke will destroy your settlements of Acquascogoc and Pomeiooc if we do not return. Those are their orders. If we do not return before the next sunset then they will attack. While you are here you cannot protect your villages; remember that. So let us go, Wanchese. We have come in search of peace, and we wish your people no harm, but if you kill us then there will be war.'

Wanchese's proud face darkened more. The light seemed to stream from behind his great crested head and shoulders. His eyes burned with hatred.

'Now we see your true intent. Do you think to frighten me with such talk? Your threats are pitiful. It makes no difference to me whether we kill you now or later. I will take your woman when your city is destroyed and she will pay for your insolence.' He raised his arm as if to sweep Kit away. 'Go back and tell your people to prepare for death. Wait in fear, for in your agony we will savour our revenge.'

Kit silently let out his breath and kept his expression impassive; Wanchese must not see his relief. They had been given a reprieve but it would not last. Could he gain any more – a chance to escape?

'Let us consider another way. Suppose we were to leave and trouble you no more; would you give us safe passage?'

Wanchese gripped his knees and laughed. Then he fell suddenly quiet and eyed Kit with contempt. He got to his feet and stood, towering over Kit, punching the air as he pounded out his message. His voice was like thunder.

'There will be no safe passage. You must die. All of you. We are the mighty nation of the Choanokes, the Secotans, the Weapemeocs and the Roanokes, and we will not rest until our land is cleansed of you and all invaders. For the misery you have brought us, for your lies and treachery, we give you death in return.'

Kit rose also and eyed Wanchese levelly. He turned to the elders who gazed up at both of them with fear blanching their faces. He asked a simple mild question. 'Is this what you want? Death?'

The elders muttered together before one of them gave their answer, doleful as a knell. 'There must be an end to mistrust, Menatonon has spoken. We must trust in death.'

Wanchese took a step nearer, close enough for Kit to smell his sweat, close enough to take Kit's neck in both hands and break it. Kit knew that was what he wanted to do.

'Trust me when I say this. We will burn your city to the ground and everyone in it. If you try to flee then we will drown you. We will send your spirits to the pit of endless weeping.'

Kit spoke to Wanchese and everyone else. 'This is your choice, not ours.'

Wanchese swept his arm towards the light. 'Go and do not anger me more. Thank me for my mercy to you now. I could take your woman before your eyes and tear the skin off this pretty boy's face.'

He pointed straight at Rob, sending another chill barb through Kit's spine, but then his fury settled back on Kit. 'I will not do either yet because I have the honour of a warrior and a *weroance*, not an Englishman and a general. I will let you go and we will meet again in battle. Once I have your head then the fruits of victory will be mine.' He lowered his voice. 'Or you may wish to kill yourselves first and suffer less pain.'

Kit kept his head high. He would show no fear and his company would preserve such pride as they had.

'We will go, but should you attack us then you will destroy all hope of the peace and friendship we now offer you.'

Wanchese spat at his feet.

'Until the day of battle, Englishman. You can offer us nothing.'

\*

'They will attack, that is certain, and they will attack soon.'

Kit scanned the faces of the colonists all turned towards him: expectant, sober and anxious. This was not what they wanted to hear, and it hurt to dash their hopes. But they must know what confronted them.

'We were followed most of the way back by Choanokes and Weapemeocs in war canoes. Wanchese may well have been amongst them. You can hear their drums now. They are gathering at Dasemonkepeuc.'

A ripple of unease passed through everyone gathered in the strong-house and out to those crowding around the wide open door. Kit sensed the mood swaying, balanced between support and disillusionment. These good people had been let down by White and they had looked to him for leadership; now he was presenting them with disaster.

Jim Lacy spoke up. He was still wearing the bandolier he'd worn during the expedition to the Chowan. He stank of swamp, and his face was streaked with mud and sweat; none of the company had had the chance to even wash their faces after getting back. Lacy spoke as if he was ready to thump anyone who argued with him.

'It was always Wanchese's intention to destroy us. Nothing Master Doonan said could have changed that.'

Kit was grateful. The mood tipped back towards him; he felt it as he swept his gaze over everyone crammed into the room, taking in those bunched up on benches or standing in the crush around the walls, along with the Assistants sitting either side of him behind the long meeting table. Dyonis Harvie and Ananias Dare waited quietly for him to continue.

'The Choanokes and the Weapemeocs now follow Wanchese. They will give him the warriors he asks for, so will the Secotans. There could be thousands pitted against us. That force will only grow as outlying villages send more men.'

Harvie slumped forwards cupping his brow in one hand, his voice drained of emotion.

'Our city will fall.'

'Yes, it's inevitable.'

Kit felt the collective shock, as if everyone listening had been punched in the stomach. This was the end of the City of Raleigh at Roanoke; they must accept it.

'The army Wanchese commands is too great for us to oppose even with firearms and artillery, and our ordnance doesn't amount to much.'

Lacy was more specific.

'One saker cannon, two falconets, four fowlers and three base guns: mostly small pieces.'

Kit clasped his hands on the table and spoke calmly. This was how a captain must feel when he has to give the order to abandon ship: sick to his soul but determined to see everyone to safety in any way possible. He had to keep a steady hand however much he was grieving. He would be parted from those he most loved. He would be the last to go, if he left at all.

'The savages will overrun us eventually by sheer weight of numbers.' He spread his hands and clenched his jaw. 'I am sorry. I wish I could have brought you better news.'

Ananias Dare leaned across to put his hand on Kit's back in a comradely fashion.

'At least we have some warning. You have given us a chance to prepare.'

That meant a lot, that hand on his back, and from Dare of all men. He'd not expected it. A lump rose and caught in his throat.

Harvie looked broken, his face ashen and aged. 'How can we prepare? All we can do is pray.'

Kit went through the few choices they had left; they had no time to debate and he wanted to forestall any argument.

'We can strengthen our defences and try to repel the savages for long enough to survive until help arrives from England.'

Harvie's expression sparked with hope. 'Could the relief fleet get here that quickly?'

The brightness in him soon faded; he must have known the answer.

'No, in truth; I don't think it could. We might hope to hold out for a few weeks before Wanchese amasses his army to full strength. But

Raleigh's relief fleet won't be here for at least another five months. We will all be dead before the ships reach us.'

'We could surrender,' Dare suggested tentatively.

Manteo stepped forward from the place where he had stood in shadow against the wall.

'If you surrender, Wanchese will have his revenge by torturing every man to death. The Secotans have perfected the art of inflicting pain. They use sharpened shells, scraping away skin and muscle to the bone bit by bit. Your women and children will be taken as slaves. It would be kinder to kill them.'

A hush settled as Manteo's warning sank in. Some of the colonists began to weep, Margaret Harvie amongst them, sobbing into the shawl she'd wrapped around her baby while pressing the infant to her breast. Most of the men stood stiffly, bunching their fists. One of the older ones crumpled and sat down heavily on a bench. This was the end for the colony. They each must have envisaged what that would mean at the hands of Wanchese. For Kit, the vision was an apocalypse.

He raised his voice. 'The city must relocate; there's no alternative.'

Now was the time to set out the plan he'd been forming throughout the return journey, the only one he could think of with a fair prospect of keeping the colony alive.

'There's a chance if we move quickly, before Wanchese mounts an attack. The colony must leave tonight, under cover of darkness. If you go in Indian dugouts and cloaked like savages, then it's quite possible that Wanchese's watchmen will not be aware of what is happening, particularly if I and a few others give the impression that the fort is still fully manned. I'll make such a show with cannon shot and fireworks that the savages will think we're being entertained by demons. It should hold their attention for long enough to allow everyone else to get away.'

Lacy stepped forwards. 'I'll stay too. You'll need a gunner who knows a few tricks with black powder.'

Jack Tydway moved to stand by him. 'And I. You gave me my freedom, Kit Doonan. This is the best use I can make of it.'

Kit regarded them warmly. They looked like brutes, travel-stained and ill-kempt, but they were both utterly loyal. 'Thank you, both of you.'

Tom Humphrey joined them, smiling awkwardly, tall and gangling. He brushed back his quiff of ginger hair with long bony fingers.

'I too. I never knew a mother or father. This city is my family. I've no one else to leave behind. We only have one death; I'll make mine a good one.'

'Spoken like a soldier, Tom,' Lacy murmured.

Harvie shook his head sadly. 'You would be certain to die, all of you.'

Kit met his eye.

'Better for four to die than a hundred and more. Take the city north, Dyonis. Your journey will not be easy but at least you'll have a fair chance. Go north behind the sand banks and through the swamp to Chesapeake Bay. That's where we were always meant to be. The journey may take you a week in canoes but Englishmen have done it before, Thomas Harriot for one.' He turned to Manteo who gave a nod. His friend had already said he would help; he was the only one Kit had confided in. The plan depended on Manteo's support, and on the use of the dugouts belonging to the Croatans who had come to Roanoke to trade. Manteo had agreed to everything; his friend had never failed him.

'Manteo knows the way. He will go with you as your guide and help you begin on good terms with the friendly tribes in the region.'

'I will,' Manteo confirmed.

'There are enough canoes here for everyone if baggage is kept light. The rest of the Croatans will return to their island in our boats. They will go now, in daylight, so their departure is clear to Wanchese's lookouts. This will be our fight, not theirs. The pinnace will have to stay here. It would be an obvious target for Wanchese's men, useless in the swamp, and it's too small even to take half of you. I'll scupper it before the savages get their hands on it.'

Dare stood as if he was ready to march straight out and down to the shore. 'If we're to leave tonight, we must get ready now: collect our belongings and stow what provisions we can.'

Kit rose also, glad that Dare needed no more encouragement.

'Yes, you should go.' He spread his hands to include everyone. 'We are agreed on this course?'

'Aye,' said Harvie. 'I'll lead the city north. God bless you, Kit.'

They embraced briefly for the last time, and Kit made his final request, speaking softly so his words would go no further. 'Take Rob and young Georgie Howe and look after them both.'

'I will.'

Rob moved near. Perhaps he'd guessed what Kit would be asking. 'I'm not leaving you, Master Kit. I'll stay with you too.'

Kit smiled proudly at his boy, the son who still did not know him as his father. He would tell Rob before he left.

'No, Rob. You must go and start a new life with the city.'

Rob squared his shoulders and stared back defiantly. 'Nothing you can say will make me go.'

Harvie patted Rob on the back and gave Kit a look of resignation.

'Your page is old enough to make up his own mind. We cannot have unwilling passengers.'

Harvie bowed his head and trudged away, plainly beyond taking on another burden.

Kit took hold of the boy's shoulders and tried to shake some sense into him. 'Rob, go, I beg you.'

'No, I will not. If you are to die for this city then I will die with you. That is my choice.'

Kit felt hopelessness engulf him. What could he say to make Rob go? He saw him as he was: a fresh-faced youth, eager and determined not to be denied the chance to prove his worth. He realised the boy had already given his answer; it would have been his at Rob's age. 'So be it.'

Tears pricked his eyes. He had never meant for this to happen. Rob had to live, so did Emme. He looked up as Dare took him into an embrace.

Kit hugged the man back. 'Take care of Mistress Fifield. I would have wed her if I could.'

Dare murmured his agreement, as if the news was no surprise. It made no difference now who knew that Master Doonan and Mistress Fifield had been destined to marry.

'I consider her part of my family,' said Dare. 'I'll look after her.'

But Emme was there at Dare's side, refusing to go as Kit had feared.

'Thank you, Master Dare, but I will stay as well. Forget about me and care for your dear lady and your child. I can do more good by helping with what needs doing at the fort. Six of us together might convince Wanchese that everyone is still here, any less and the risk to those leaving will be too great.'

Dare shuffled, frowned and shot Kit a look of bafflement. 'I am sure Master Doonan's plans do not require the sacrifice of a woman.'

Emme raised her chin. 'My decision is freely taken.' She took hold of Kit's arm. 'No one can force me to go.'

Dare nodded and smiled sadly. 'I understand.' He gave both her and Kit a short bow. 'We are indebted to you both.'

Kit turned to her and bowed his head, lost for the words he needed to keep her from him. 'Emme, not you...'

She took a step back. 'There is no more time. We must act: you to make ready the defences here; the rest of the colony to embark in the canoes. I will help them, but I will not leave you.'

He could not stop her; he knew it deep in his core. He'd witnessed her determination before. She would stay however much he pleaded with her, and she was right, there was no more time to waste in argument. He was torn between love, admiration and a grief that threatened to unman him.

Then he raised his voice to reach everyone who remained.

'God speed all of you going north!'

More quietly, for Emme, he had another message.

'Heaven help the rest of us.'

# 13

# *Love Alters Not*

'Love alters not with his brief hours and weeks,
But bears it out even to the edge of doom.'

—*William Shakespeare, from 'Sonnet 116'*

Kit watched anger spreading like heat over Rob's shock-frozen face, his eyes blazing in the gleam of lantern light, his fists clenching as his body stiffened.

'Why didn't you tell me before?' the boy asked.

Kit had told him almost everything about his life with the Cimaroons, the love he had found with the boy's mother, her death when Rob was too young to know and the boy's adoption by the couple he'd believed to be his parents. He had tried to shield Rob from any stigma, but why had he kept up the pretence that the boy was his page even after arriving in the New World?

*Why?*

Kit bowed his head and shook it. The question was one he had dreaded, and he did not know how he could answer.

'I wanted to spare you.'

'Spare me? You mean you were you so ashamed you could not recognise me as your own?'

Kit reached out to Rob but the boy moved away, his dear son in whom he could not have been more proud.

'I have never been ashamed of you. I only wished to protect you.'

Rob's voice broke as he turned his back.

'Protect me from what?' His words trailed away into another shrill question. 'How did my mother die?'

'The Spaniards killed her.'

'*How?*'

There it was. There was no evading it now.

Kit spoke softly.

'She was burnt alive as an example because she had escaped as a slave, lived with the Cimaroons, and blinded a soldier who tried to rape her. The Spaniards tied her to a tree and set it alight.'

Rob's shoulders began to shake, and Kit put his arm around the boy as gently as he could, and held him close while they wept.

*

Emme did not know for how many hours she had stared at the calm waters of the sound, only that the sickle moon had risen and was now falling behind drifting clouds, and the deep dull booming of the war drums had never stopped, neither had the explosions of gunfire and fireworks from the fort behind the trees, though the intervals between the blasts were growing longer, and the flares of brilliant white and orange light had ceased to send the deer bounding through the reeds. Each time darkness returned, the stillness was absolute. She'd watched the canoes bearing the settlers northeast across the wide waters, until the last was swallowed by the night mists rising, sliding like a speck over the pale grey sheen before slipping into the slit where the horizon met the sky. Gone from her forever now, she would never see those friends again; she would not know where the new city would be sited, or how little Virginia Dare would grow up, or what raising a family in the raw New World would be like. Their lives were lost to her as the sands of her own life were trickling away. War would begin the next day: that was the message carried by the drums; Manteo had told her, as he'd told Kit and the others remaining on the island before he left. She could not expect to see another sunset and neither should they. But their work was done, and what mattered most for the city and England had already been accomplished: the Planters had left Roanoke without being pursued.

From the point where she stood sentinel, she could see across to Dasemonkepeuc, and, though the village was veiled in dark-ness, the surface of the water was clearly visible. Not one canoe had left the mainland since night had fallen; she was sure of that. The savages must have been entranced by the spectacle of fire as Kit had hoped, while from Dasemonkepeuc, no one could have seen the exodus taking place on the other side of the island. Their little company had succeeded in what they meant to achieve. She should go to Kit and reassure him that their deaths would not be in vain. All she and Kit had left to do was to squeeze a lifetime that should have been theirs into the space of a few shadowed hours. Shivering, she drew her shawl tighter. She needed to be with Kit. She had to be with him at the end. She was not sure that she could be brave in the face of death, but with him she would try.

She skirted east along the edge of the reeds until the shore became a beach that she followed round. Then she took the well-worn track leading to the tree-covered bluff, and from there she looked down on the pinnace, anchored close offshore, and up to the sandy knoll on which stood the fort. For an instant everything flashed white and amber as sparks streamed from a fire-arrow shooting high overhead. The fort pulsed orange, its palisade like a rusty saw-blade jutting up from the bare cliff face. A thundering report made her duck and she looked up to see the arrow bursting in a ball of violet flame, sparks spraying in all directions, fading to nothing as they fell over the water. Ears ringing, she hastened towards the fort as it merged once again into a silhouette with the trees, black against the sky but hazed by clouds of thinning smoke. The stench of sulphur caught at the back of her throat, and the sharp taste of nitre was acrid in her mouth. Her pulse raced though there was as yet no reason to be afraid; that would come on the morrow. She was blind again in the dark. The only light was an orange glow, one that became more distinct as she edged along the track. The light emerged from a tracery of leaves, about head height, by the trunk of a tall tree. It came from a lantern hung on a branch, and beside it were two men. One of them was Kit. She saw him as she negotiated a bend in the path, but then she stepped back. The other was Rob.

They were deep in conversation and something about the intimacy of their stance made her reluctant to intrude. They stood face to face, one perfectly proportioned beside the other as slim as a wisp. Through the foliage, she saw the gentle way Kit put his arm around Rob's thin shoulders. The boy bowed his head and turned aside. She watched Kit catch hold of him. Then they embraced as if they were fighting, eyes tight closed as though to hold back pain, arms clamped around one another, crushing out breath. Kit's hand circled the boy's back as he shook and sobbed. She looked away.

Kit must have told Rob the truth. He must have told him he was his father and what had happened to the boy's mother, about his life with the Cimaroons, and the search that had led him to the discovery of his son. Would Rob understand why Kit had not told him before? Would he forgive? It looked as if he did, and they seemed to have found some reconciliation for the hours left to them on the turbulent earth. Let them be: Kit, the father who, for the love of his son, could not let his love show; Rob, the son who, without knowing, would not be parted from his father. Would Rob now realise that his father had tried to spare him? Kit had brought his son to the New World to find a better place for him to live; instead, he had brought him face-to-face with an early death. What could they do now? Their only comfort was that they would be together at the end, and had shown the greatest love by laying down their lives for their friends. She longed to embrace them both.

She wiped at her eyes.

Rob turned aside. In another stark flash of light she saw him clearly, heading towards the houses behind their new defensive wall, his expression loaded with feeling but resolute and contained. He was there, then he was gone. The next blast slammed through the forest and the light dulled and guttered. Before the fireball burst, he was engulfed by darkness. She looked back at Kit sensing their lives playing out as haphazardly, blazing in intensity before flickering into oblivion.

The lantern on the tree still cast its paltry glow and by that she saw he was chiselling away at the bark, carving out letters as high as he could reach: 'CRO'.

'Are you leaving a message?'

She walked towards him, and he gave her a smile of welcome,

though the streaks of tears were like rills over his smut-blackened face.

'This is for White,' he said. 'It's to tell him those of us left here will be going to Croatoan if we can. Before we leave, if we're attacked, I'll mark the signs with a cross to show our move has been forced. He'll know what that means; it's what we agreed.'

She watched his hands fall to his sides.

'Aren't you going to finish it or tell White the others have gone to Chesapeake?'

'There isn't time, and I'd rather White go somewhere safe to begin with. We don't know where exactly Harvie will site the new city.' He slid nearer like a sleepwalker. 'You saw nothing?'

'No. The Planters were not followed.'

'Thank God.' He let out his breath against her neck as he took her into his arms, and his touch was tentative as if he felt it might break her.

She nuzzled against him, her lips brushing the prickles of the stubble above his throat.

'You have told Rob?'

'Yes.'

He swallowed, and she sensed it as the resonance of his answer flowed through her, wrapped up in a sound like a low deep groan.

'That is good,' she said softly. 'You have done all you can.'

He shook his head slowly, his rough cheek rubbing against her.

'It's not enough, either for Rob or for you.'

She held him tighter.

'It is enough for me to be with you now.'

'Come inside,' he said, taking her hand as if they were children, and he was urging her to go with him to some place of secrets. 'We have a few hours before daybreak and everything is ready beyond the wall.'

He drew her to the clearing around the tree trunks that had been felled and stacked to form a star-like barrier around the houses in a great ring that connected with the palisaded fort. He guided her by the light of his lantern, circuiting ditches and earthworks, bole-walled curtains and pointed flankers. They reached the gate at the east by which was another carved sign on one of the tree trunks in the wall: 'CROATOAN'.

'Might we get there?' she asked, pointing to the letters as they passed.

He paused and kissed her hand, and she knew he did not want to tell her there was no hope. Perhaps the signs were there to give the others strength, perhaps they helped Kit keep alive the belief that there was always a chance for those he loved.

He pressed her hand to his heart.

'I think we should say goodbye to one another, somewhere quiet.'

They entered by the gate, and Kit barred it shut just as another ear-splitting detonation sent her cowering against the wall. A fire-arrow followed that flooded everything with silver light, and when it burst, somewhere far over the water, the sparks were gold.

Kit put his arm around her, leading her across what had once been the city square, now made almost impassable with upended tables, barrels and other objects heaped together.

'The boys are enjoying themselves.' He pointed to the fort and his tone was almost bantering. 'Jim and Jack are warming up the saker while Rob's helping Tom with the fireworks. Do you like the colours?'

She guessed he was trying to buoy up her spirits and she answered playfully.

'Yes, very pretty. Where did you learn how to make them?'

'From Drake's gunners, and Jim Lacy knows a few tricks. Iron filings made the gold you saw just now. The fireworks are only gunpowder in a paper casing wrapped around a stick and lit with a quick match. We've used all the prayer books we could find for cartouches.'

She pulled a face, though he probably couldn't see it. She hoped her voice sounded suitably shocked. She was too numb for much humour, but it was always better to laugh than to weep when work needed to be done.

'I hope our prayers are heard and we're given a little help.'

He squeezed her hand and gazed back at the fort. She felt his mood shift, as if he was quietly thinking everything through.

'The cannon fire should keep Wanchese's warriors away from the north shore. The savages will come at us from the west: the quickest crossing from Dasemonkepeuc; then they'll creep through the forest as soon as there's a glimmer of light.' He turned round to look at the mounds of earth that served as gun platforms behind the crude wall. 'We'll hold them off at first with our falconets and fowlers; after that, we'll fall back to the fort.'

'You expect all the houses to be lost?'

'Yes.' He ushered her on around the obstacles. 'Everything will be lost; it's only a matter of time. All we can hope to achieve is a chance to get to the pinnace while most of the savages are here on land.'

'So we do have a chance?'

He pulled her closer to him.

'So small you should forget it.'

He led her to the Dares' house, a place she barely recognised because everything nearby was so changed, the vegetation smashed down and most of the furniture piled up outside in a great barricade in front of the fort. Everything valuable had been buried, he told her; all White's chests and the belongings the Planters had left behind, they had all been sealed in a trench and covered over. The room downstairs in the Dares' house was empty but for scattered pots and crocks and the ladder leading to the upper floor which Kit climbed ahead of her.

The room upstairs felt strange, barely touched, almost as she had left it: pallets screened with canvas, clothes spilling from an abandoned chest. She took a few steps to the open window and looked out. On the timber sill, under her fingers, was the place where Rob had scratched his name, that time when he had stayed with her after Kit had left him on his first foray to the mainland. 'Robert Little' – she felt the letters and looked out at chaos: the disintegration of everything they had sought to establish in founding the city. But Kit was still with her, vital and alive; they had a few hours yet.

He put the lantern on the floor where it cast light through the shutter slits in expanding crescents over the walls. The glow filtered through the screens as if they were gauzy drapes in some fire-lit pavilion. It made the room seem warm, a place of safety in the midst of turmoil. Then he took something from his belt purse that gleamed as he held it out to her: a ring, a tiny, thin, gold ring. She looked at the lobe of his left ear and realised where it had come from.

She stared at him in confusion, wondering what he meant by it. They had already exchanged tokens, and the ring was plainly too small for a finger. The association with marriage slipped instantly into her mind, but she dismissed it as quickly. That could not be what he intended; he'd already said that marriage would be for the time when they could rest without fear.

'Your earring?'

He nodded, smiling bashfully, then reached for her left hand and placed the little ring against her fourth finger.

'Big enough to fit over the tip and that will have to do.'

She stared at her hand in shock, and then at him. He'd picked out her wedding finger. Did he really mean to wed her? Now? Here, with the blasts of cannon instead of wedding bells and Wanchese's warriors about to fall on them?

He smiled more broadly and took a thong from his jerkin which he dangled in front of her. 'You can tie it around your neck afterwards.'

'Afterwards?'

'After we are wed.'

There, he'd said it: *he meant to marry her now*. Her heart swelled fit to burst. She wanted nothing more, yet she stood petrified, looking down at the ring in the palm of his hand as if it had the power to cast her into hell. She could not wed him on the basis of a lie. He did not know that she was not a maiden, that there was another man in England who had already taken and claimed her.

He nudged the ring with his finger, looking down at it thoughtfully. Then he gazed up at her with a sweet shy look on his handsome face that was covered in sooty dirt and streaked with sweat and tears.

She began to cry, reaching for her handkerchief to wipe him clean, trying in vain, then dabbing at her own eyes though the linen was black.

He pulled a wry face and used his thumb to wipe at her cheeks.

'I would like to marry you now, Emme. I wish to be one with you before I die. Wherever we are when the sun goes down tomorrow, we should be together, completely, man and wife.'

She wept. She loved him. More than her aching heart could bear, she loved him. But how could she tell him that she was not pure? If they were to be together as man and wife, here, in this room, then he would discover her shame, and he would go to his death believing she had deceived him. He would hate her. She could not do it.

She sank down on one of the pallets, turned from him and covered her eyes.

He sat quietly beside her.

'I know this should have been better for you. We should have had music and a procession and all the pomp and ceremony fitting for one of the finest ladies of England. You should have had a beautiful dress. This ring should have been bigger.' He made a sound like a chuckle that caught in his throat. 'We should have been in a grand church before a priest, but our vows will be known to God. Surely that and our love is what matters most...'

'It's not that,' she sobbed, 'not any of that. I need no trappings to be your wife when in my heart I already am. It's...' Tears blinded her. She could not speak.

He put the ring back in his purse and placed his arms around her gently.

'What is it? The time for talking honestly with one another is now. So tell me, Emme; there may not be another chance. Let there be no secrets between us. Whatever troubles you, I am sure it will not trouble me nearly as much. Nothing could make me love you less.'

'I...' she struggled. How could she begin?

With a soft kiss on her brow he reassured her. Then he tensed and drew back a little. 'You're not already married?'

'No, not truly. I mean...'

She wiped at her eyes and saw him looking at her, frowning.

His voice hardened. 'What do you mean by "not truly"? Were you promised before you promised yourself to me?'

'Not properly, not in faith . . .'

Grief consumed her. She could not go on. Everything was falling apart: her hopes, the city, his love; she felt it all disintegrating around her.

He let go of her and looked down. 'I suppose you are trying to tell me that you have already lain with a man.'

'Yes,' she said, fighting the impulse to hide behind more weeping. She had to tell him the truth. She held up her head. 'A man took me against my will, after some jesting which I considered to be of no consequence, but he said it amounted to my promise to marry him.'

Kit looked stricken. 'He raped you?'

'Yes. He said it would join us as man and wife, even without a priest.'

He hung his head. 'O, God. O, my dear Emme.'

He looked up and met her eyes and she saw a great hurt in him that she longed to heal, but she also knew that the hurt was her own. His manner was grave. 'You did not promise yourself to him knowingly and freely as you did to me?'

'No, never. I loathe him. I would never be his wife, duchess or anything else.'

'*Duchess?*' He gave her a sad half smile as if it pained him. 'This rogue was a duke? Who? Are there any dukes left?'

She blew her nose and wiped her eyes. Nothing she said now could make any difference. Kit would know the whole truth, and perhaps, at least, they could part as friends.

'The Earl of Hertford, Edward Seymour, son of the Duke of

Somerset and first in line to the dukedom when that title is reinstated. The lord who was imprisoned for getting Lady Catherine Grey with child.'

'That scoundrel! He should never have been released from the Tower.'

He turned to her and took her hands, kissing them gently. 'Forgive me for my hard questioning.'

She cried silently. 'Forgive? You do not need forgiveness. It is I who needs your compassion.'

'For what? What wrong have you done? Is a lamb to be blamed for the cruelty of the wolf? No, Emme.' He held her again and looked at her intently. 'You are the best of women, the lady I wish to marry, and if I am the first to whom you have freely offered your love then I will be privileged above all men alive.'

He fumbled in his purse and took out the ring once more. 'So will you be my wife?'

She drank him in, sight, sound and smell, the salt and the sea. They would never be parted in this world and the next. 'Yes. Oh, yes.'

She held out her left hand for him and he placed the little ring on the very end of her fourth finger.

'With this ring I thee wed; with my body I thee worship: and with all that I have I thee endow. In the name of God. Amen.'

He looked at her.

'It is done. I think we may kiss.'

Dear God, but she wanted to kiss him, though she feared to. She pressed her lips against his like a desert traveller falling on an oasis whose mouth is too parched to drink. He was the essence that gave her life meaning, her soul's milk and nectar; he was strength and sweetness, her rock and her succour; the fire of her desire. He made her complete, but he could also destroy her. Why fear that now? She put all her longing into her kiss, and when they drew back to breathe she whispered against his chest. 'I should have told you before.'

'And I should have told Rob before.' He rubbed her shoulders. 'We have both wrestled to set down the burdens we have carried from the past. But now they are shared; you are released and so am I, undeserving though I am.'

'No, not undeserving, the most admirable of men, my angel...'

'Hush.' He put his finger to her lips. 'Let me show you how much I love you. My body is yours to serve you in devotion to my last breath.'

He rose and unbuckled his belt and all the accoutrements of war, stripped off his jerkin and shirt, kicked away his boots, peeled off his hose and galley breeches until he stood before her almost naked, and the sight of his body in the lantern light was enough to melt her inside. He was perfect and powerful. She could see every muscle under his smooth bronze skin, and the curling hair that glistened like filigree over his legs and chest, and in a dark line down from his navel over his flat stomach. She bowed her head. What could she offer him but her innocence, her softness never fully seen before by a man?

He reached out to her and drew off her shawl, untied her bodice and sleeves, ushered her to stand and took off her kirtle as she slipped out of her shoes. With his hands under her shift he rolled down her wool stockings, and the touch of his fingers around her bare thighs made her tremble with terror and longing. At that point he broke contact and waited, with his hands close to her hips but not touching. She was shivering, she knew, but she could contain that if she tried. She peeled off her own shift, and he got down on his knees before her, like a supplicant to her modesty, raising his palms as if in veneration. Then she drew his hands to her breasts, arched back her head and let him continue. His hands reached up as his head sank down sending sensation shooting through her, and together gradually his hands slid over her breasts as his mouth moved up over her legs, kissing and caressing.

She knew him fully as more explosions made the small room rattle, filling their bower with flashing light and leaving a fuzz of drifting smoke, but they seemed distant and insignificant. Her being was with him, around him and through him. She could appreciate nothing else.

When they rose and dressed, and kissed, and moved to look outside where the birds were beginning to sing in the still black sky, she once again found the place on the sill where Rob had scratched his one-time name, then she asked for Kit's knife, and scratched through 'Little', and beside it wrote 'Doonan'. Kit smiled and inscribed his own name too, and so did she, not 'Emme Fifield', or 'Emme Murimuth', or even 'Emmelyne Seymour, Duchess of Somerset', never that, but the woman she was now and would be forever, the woman she was always meant to be: 'Emme Doonan'.

# 14

# *Burning*

'...There we espied towards the north end of the Island the light of a great fire through the woods, to the which we presently rowed: when we came right over against it, we let fall our grapnel near the shore, and sounded with a trumpet a call, and afterwards many familiar English tunes of songs, and called to them friendly; but we had no answer, we therefore landed at day-break, and coming to the fire, we found the grass and sundry rotten trees burning about the place...'

*—From the entry for 17th August from John White's Narrative of his 1590 Voyage to Virginia describing his return to Roanoke*

'Are you ready?'

Kit squatted down beside Emme, looking through the upper gun port in the palisade above the roofs of the storehouses around the fort. His gaze swept over the wall of tree trunks which stretched from the cliff top southwest in a crooked curving line, beyond the belt of ground cleared of trees that had been reduced to huge logs and dragged together to form the star-pointed ramparts, to the dark woods that rose at its edge and disappeared into the haze where Wanchese's warriors would be lying in wait. He was sure of it. He did not need to hear or see them. The first hint of dawn was brightening the sky, and he looked over the dormant forest imagining the men like fleas in the pelt of a beast that could spring into life at any moment. He drew back and scanned the dirt platform where Emme sat by the bronze falconet, taking in the heap of one pound shot for the cannon, ramrod and wadding, powder barrel and scoop, reamer and the linstock for firing that she held like a spear, shaft down beside her, the slow match smouldering at its tip.

'You know what to do?'

'Yes,' she said quietly, appearing dwarfed by both munitions and defences: a slight, soft woman in the midst of weaponry that could butcher a whole company of men, clad like a soldier in brigandine and helmet.

'You must bring the match to the touch hole slowly,' he said. 'Then you must wait for the smoke that will tell you the priming powder had taken hold. After it catches, stand back smartly and cover your ears. Don't get behind the gun. Don't bend over the touch hole or the blast will burn your face. Don't bring your match to the touch until you hear the other guns firing. There will be a delay between ignition and discharge; you must expect that.'

'I understand,' she said.

He didn't doubt it. She was quick-witted and stout-hearted and he knew he could depend on her. He should leave her to check on the others, but leaving was hard. This might be the last time he saw her. Just as he'd come to know her, they had to part. She was his Emme whom he adored almost more than he could bear, so rare a lady he didn't know how he could have been favoured by the love she had shown him. She was like a comet passing Earth: a wonder to admire and expect to lose in a stream of fading light, except that last night he'd possessed her fully, and the treasure of her body had been his as a gift. Now all the shying away she'd previously displayed he could properly understand, because of the hurt that had been done to her by that earl he'd like to run through. No chance of that now, no reason and no need. Emme was his wife and she'd never be another's.

He turned his head to kiss her, and thank God he could do that without her pulling from him. There might not be another chance.

She put her arms around his chest, plate armour and all.

'God bless you, husband,' she murmured.

'God bless you, wife.'

That had to be their farewell. He turned to go before resolution failed him and he stayed to die by her side, but then defeat would be inevitable and, if he put his plan into place, at least she would have a possibility of escape, however small. He turned from her, and started to bound down the dirt slope; then he gave her one last instruction over his shoulder.

'Don't try and load the gun to fire again.'

If she answered, he didn't hear her. He had to trust her not to attempt such a thing. He had told her to leave for the pinnace as soon as the firing began, and she had said that she would. She must get across quickly in the tender once the savages attacked. One shot, then go: that was what she had agreed to do. He paced around the strong-house to the place where the great nine-foot saker pointed out from the cliff top over the sound. There was Lacy in the shadows, busy recharging the gun, loading one of the five-pound balls into the muzzle, ramming and wading it home. He'd ask Lacy to make sure Emme left.

Lacy moved to the breech of the gun and took hold of the linstock left propped against the strong-house wall. The gun overlooked the water through a gap in the palisade, and, from that vantage, Kit could see the pinnace lying below to the east, and the clear expanse of the sound above which the morning star twinkled in an indigo sky. Near the horizon, over a band of grey cloud, the blue was beginning to lighten. Nothing moved but the rippling breeze and a flock of sea-birds rising and wheeling, dropping back further away to settle again in pale streaks. The scent of pines and saltwater was in the breeze, and something sweet like the aromatic spicebushes that grew to the south-west, and from all this Kit sensed the way the wind was blowing. Under the canvas that screened the gun overhead, Lacy's face was barely visible, but Kit caught the gleam of his eyes when he spoke.

'Nothing to report, Master Doonan.'

'Good. Keep firing to the west without haste. When you hear the rest of us in salvo, get Mistress Emme to the pinnace.'

'Aye, sir.'

'Give us five minutes to join you, no longer. Don't wait after that. You must leave for Croatoan.'

'We will. God speed you.'

He clapped Lacy's shoulder and strode back. As he left the closed palisade, he heard the boom of the saker firing again, and the much quieter splash far off as the shot hit the water. He picked up the ladder he had used to scale the inner defences, and carried it with him as he negotiated the barricades between the houses, follow-ing routes he knew well, doubling back and circuiting through the maze of partially concealed pathways.

The bastion he reached first was the position to the east manned by Rob. It was guarded by a fowler behind one of the projections in the wall of tree trunks. The gun was an old iron breech loader, about eight feet in length but narrow in bore, mounted on a stock with two wheels, firing stone shot covered in lead. It couldn't fire far with any accuracy, but it could be reloaded fast. Kit cast his eye over the spare chamber, ready charged, that lay near the rear of the stock by a small pyramid of round shot. He gave a nod of approval and clapped the boy's shoulders.

'All set?'

'Yes, father.'

It felt good to be called that. He patted Rob's back.

'Don't fire until you hear the other guns.'

'I'll wait.'

Rob nodded and straightened his back. He stood with his smouldering linstock, looking every inch the battle-ready soldier, helmeted and armed, his chest and back protected by a steel cuirass. His son seemed to have grown on the voyage, no longer a boy but a man. Pray God, Rob would live to talk about this day in years to come. Pray he'd die quickly if he didn't see the day out.

Kit looked through a gap between the tree trunks that served as a crude gun port at the bastion's point. He peered along the long barrel ringed with wrought iron hoops, and saw the forest beginning to flood with colour. Dark greens lightened to purples as gold rays streamed from below the rim of the sky. Rob would be firing straight at the sun, but he didn't need to aim, only ignite the primer. The gun was pointing point blank. Its two-inch shot would rip through foliage and shatter on impact with anything solid, tree or man. After that...

'Once you've fired the gun then you must leave.'

'Not without you,' Rob answered resolutely.

'With *or* without me.' Kit pointed to the ladder which he'd left by the outer wall and his voice hardened. 'Use that to get over the palisade; then make for the pinnace with Mistress Emme.'

He spoke again as he left. There was no more time for reasoning with him. 'I'm relying on you to do that.'

He raced to the next bastion, past all the weapons that had been left ready to hand: pikes and bills; longbows and boxes of arrows; crossbows with their strings winched back; quivers full of fire bolts specially prepared by Lacy, swollen behind their arrow heads, their shafts wrapped with gauze packed with a mixture of nitre, sulphur and charcoal. There were a few loaded calivers, as many as they had left, and low braziers of smoking coals, well away from the gunpowder kegs. The position was unmanned but another fowler lay ready, its powder chamber locked in place, loaded and primed. More weapons were stacked at the foot of the wall: an axe and another crossbow, fully cocked; fire bolts, arrows and a longbow. He moved on and found Tom Humphrey with their third fowler; the fourth guarded the closed entrance gate.

'Ready?'

'Yes.'

'God be with you. Fire at my command then get behind the palisade. Use that to climb over.' He pointed to a ladder lying nearby.

The lad started to speak, but Kit left before he could hear him. Something was happening. A noise rose from the forest that was more than just the dawn chorus. There were other sounds mixed in, bird calls he could not place and a persistent soft rustling.

He rushed past a base gun at a crouch and reached Jack Tydway in the bastion furthest west just as the sun flared orange over the tops of the trees. Kit took one look at the falconet by which Tydway stood ready then tipped back his head. A sound passed over him like the whoosh of the wind gusting through leaves.

'Take cover!'

He knew what it was before he saw the arrows raining down.

'Fire!' he yelled, roaring out the command as he ducked back to the nearest gun, snatching up a linstock left smouldering a few paces away. He held the match to the touch hole while bobbing down near the wall. There was a fizz as the primer caught, and louder noises as the reed arrows struck, clanging against metal, thudding into earth and wood, all mixed in with other sounds: the ululation of countless voices and a deep rumbling vibration. He saw the blast before he heard it, the gun kicked back in billowing smoke, the tree trunks shivered releasing clouds of dust, and the ground shook as if in a thunderstorm, sending shock waves through his feet. Another blast followed, and another in quick succession; then his ears succumbed to the pain of the noise, and all he heard was ringing, and all he saw beyond the gun was smoke filling the clearing, and traces of flame in the wood, and the shadow forms of savages running. Scores of them streamed towards him through the haze before the glare of the sun, their bodies almost naked or made strange by wicker armour. His nose filled with the stench of sulphur and his eyes watered, stinging, and he knew that most of the guns had fired but that the charge of the savages had barely been checked.

'Back!' He ran round behind the bastions, past Tom and Rob, calling out to them. 'Get back now!'

He snatched up one of the crossbows and a quiver, lighting a fire bolt by the nearest brazier, putting it in place on the stock, tight against the nut, and taking aim near the gate through the port for the unfired fowler. The bastion was still clear of the worst of the smoke. Only drifting wisps interfered with his vision, and the savages running forwards to hurl themselves at the wall, springing one upon another, scrabbling to get over. Shots rang out and a man screamed nearby, but he must not look, only concentrate on the forest beyond the belt of cleared ground, and the foremost trees at the outer edge. Some were already ablaze; others were smouldering, blown to stumps by explosions. He took aim at a pine that remained intact and sighted on the black ring of pitch around its trunk, and the pitch-covered powder keg that he'd tied near its base. He let out his breath and pulled the crossbow trigger. The string twanged in release and the bolt sped away, trailing a straight line of fire for about fifty paces. Seconds later, the trunk burst into a crown of yellow flame.

He moved to the gun, set a match to the cannon's touch hole, waited for ignition, and ran to the next position. The blast came as he reached the bastion where Rob had been only minutes earlier. The boy was gone but something moved: a savage by the gun, bent over a pool of blood. Kit sprang forwards as the man wheeled round. The warrior had picked up an English axe that he swung to strike in a flash of steel. All Kit could do was charge, using his helmet like a ram to knock the man off his feet. The warrior crumpled sideways and Kit drew his sword. The reverberation of gunfire shuddered through them, earth and wall. One thrust and the man was dispatched; a twist, and his blade was free. Another blast rocked the defences, and the smell of burning sap hung bittersweet in the air. The light through the gun port was tinged the orange of flickering flames. He could hear the forest roaring.

'Get to the fort! Get away!'

He hoped no one would be left to listen who could understand; the others should be making for the pinnace by now. Most of the incendiaries he'd set at the edge of the trees were well ablaze in a ring of flame. He reached the bastion facing south and saw raging fire beyond the clearing, but men were still scaling the wall.

He grabbed another bolt and set it alight, took aim over the last unfired gun at one of the few pines intact at the edge of the wood. He put his finger near the trigger, released the lock, prepared to fire, then turned as a shadow fell over him, the shadow of a man like a carrion bird settling. The warrior leapt from the rampart, armoured front and back, the wicker of his breastplate forming wings over his shoulders. Kit shot him on impulse, impaling him through the chest, turning his armour into a torch. He gritted his teeth against the man's screaming and used a linstock to fire the gun. The shot brought down the tree.

A shout made him turn again.

'Kit!'

Someone was calling him.

'Here!'

He looked along the walkway curving round behind the wall and saw Jack Tydway staggering towards him, stumbling around the body of a savage through clouds of gun-smoke. Across his shoulders was one of their own, head hanging down, the shaft of an arrow sticking out from his neck.

Not Rob, let it not be Rob.

'It's Tom,' Jack gasped.

Savages were rushing up behind him, whooping and swinging cudgels heavy enough to brain a man at a stroke. Kit darted past to bring them down, using his pistol then his sword. They were dealt with quickly, but others followed in their wake, creeping round from the west by the tree trunks.

'Hurry,' Kit urged, though he could tell Jack was moving as fast as he could. His clothes were soaked with Tom's blood.

'Is anyone left that way?'

'No,' Jack grunted.

'Rob?'

'Haven't seen him.'

Kit felt a surge of relief, but only for an instant. More savages were closing, warriors from the first wave before the fire took hold, men who'd got over the wall.

He grabbed at weapons as he passed, used them and threw them down. There was no chance to reload. He shot a warrior climbing over the wall, sending his blood spraying in an arc. Two more were felled with bow and arrow. He hurled an axe, shot more fire bolts, threw a brazier and struck with a caliver that he wielded like a club. In the narrow passageway through the barricades he covered Jack's back with his sword. But the savages were too many, and they followed him inside the labyrinth, despite the barrels, crates and anything else he could drag across his tracks. His friends would be done for if they got any closer. Kit slowed and stood his ground.

'Carry on, Jack. Get Tom to the pinnace.'

'And you?'

'No matter. Go!' He shouted again at the top of his voice as he crouched behind an overturned table and loaded one last shot. 'Go!'

This was where he would die. He'd done what he could and his strength was waning. He'd give Jack a few more minutes. When the next savage ran into view, he fired his pistol and saw the man's legs crumple. Another warrior appeared, and he drew his sword, preparing to lunge. But there were others behind, too many for one swordsman. He said a quiet goodbye to Emme; then he stood, arms wide.

'Come on!'

A shot rang out, and two of the savages fell heavily, mid charge. At the point of leaping towards him, the first man was knocked back as if by an invisible fist, with a force that struck him in the middle of the chest. In falling he took down the man behind, a man who lay writhing, splattered with the blood of his comrade and with his own blood pouring from a hole under his collar bone. The shot had been fired from the side. Kit looked across and saw the helmet of a caliverman crouched behind a pile of furniture heaped between two houses. The chase slowed to a crawl. The nearest savage turned and fled.

'Who's there?' Kit called out as he began to edge back. There might be a chance to reach the fort after all. Had Lacy come down to help him? But surely Lacy wouldn't have left Emme. He looked from the savages at a standstill back to the caliverman who was loping towards him, bent low, carrying a firearm, lithe as a panther. It was Rob, ashen-faced where he was not black with gunpowder. He held his caliver out to Kit with a hand that slightly shook.

'It's loaded,' Rob said. 'I took two from the wall.'

Kit flashed the boy a smile and grasped the weapon firmly. He cocked the piece with his match and levelled it at the place where the savages had sought cover.

'When I fire we run.'

The boy nodded mutely.

Kit fired and took the recoil then threw the weapon down. They ran, hurtling over the ground, racing around obstacles, taking the side paths and turning the corners that would take them to the fort, leaping over the trestles and other objects positioned to hinder pursuit. Looking over his shoulder, he saw no one behind.

'I think we've lost them,' he gasped, and when Rob slowed in confusion he pushed the boy on, though the boy's young legs soon took him ahead at a pace.

The palisade loomed above them, shrouded in drifting smoke, and above the stakes there were helmets and a ladder sliding over. Shouts rippled down through the noise of the fire, crackling and popping and continued blasts in the distance. No one had left for the pinnace; he saw three people up there, and one of them must have been Jack. He heard Emme calling.

'Take the ladder. We're dropping it for you.'

The ladder fell and bounced then Rob picked it up, leaning it against the wall. Kit took hold at the foot.

'You first.'

Rob hesitated.

Kit glanced round, sensing they'd been followed. Something rippled along the passage by which they'd come.

'Up, for God's sake!'

He shoved Rob against the ladder and drew his sword.

The boy started to climb and Kit followed fast.

He held on with one hand, looking back as a savage rushed towards them and a band of warriors emerged from the shadows, whooping and brandishing great sharp-bladed cudgels. They charged in a mass. The leader aimed a blow at Kit's legs. Kit blocked it with his sword, but the blade shattered on impact and the man swung again. Kit scrambled higher, bumping against Rob.

The boy reached the top and was hauled over by his belt. Lacy grabbed the ladder just as it was struck from below. The blow almost dislodged Kit. It smashed through one of the rails and swung the ladder violently to one side, but Kit clung on, and Lacy had hold of an upper rung.

The savage leapt for what was left of the ladder and swiped upwards, shaving the cudgel past Kit's ankle. Kit drew up his legs, lunging for the top, hearing a thud: the cudgel dropping down. Then he felt a stab of pain as a hand caught his heel. The grip was like a grapnel, holding him back. He couldn't get any higher. Hands from above reached for his arms. Someone from the fort was pulling at his back, but he couldn't shake off the weight dragging him down from below.

The man's grip dug deeper. Kit kicked with his free leg and another hand grabbed his ankle, then the calf of the other leg. The man was crawling up his body, calling out.

'Come back to me, Englishman. I wish to say goodbye.'

Wanchese. It must be Wanchese; no other warrior spoke English who was not a Croatan. He did not need to look down. He could not. His head and shoulders were over the palisade, his chest between the spikes. His legs were in Wanchese's grasp, and the Indian's whole weight was bearing down on him, twisting and turning, racking his body. Then the pain became searing in the back of his calf. Wanchese was biting him, sinking in his teeth.

Emme yelled, leaning over them.

'Take that for goodbye.'

He couldn't see what she did, but a terrible scream came with the sudden release of his legs, one that ended with the thud of something heavy hitting the ground. She pulled back quickly as he was dragged over the parapet, and he was aware that she was drawing in a pike, sliding the long shaft, foot by foot, through her hands. When she set it on the walkway, there was blood on its point.

They embraced for no more than seconds. He held his wife and his son, Jim Lacy and Jack Tydway: friends as good as brothers; they all clung to one another.

'Where's Tom?'

'In the strong-house,' Jack answered. 'I don't think he'll live.'

Lacy ushered everyone on.

'None of us will live unless we move now.'

Kit got to his feet painfully and peered over the wall. The body of Wanchese was gone, but he could see warriors trying to scale the palisade using the remains of the ladder and balanced upon one another. Lacy ran along the walkway at a crouch and returned with two longbows and a sheaf of arrows. Kit took a bow and they worked together, loosing enough arrows at the savages to keep them at bay for a little longer. But there would be more, and he knew their lust for vengeance would be stronger than ever.

Half running, half limping, he got to the strong-house with the others, and as one they lifted Tom and carried him to the gun port at the back of the fort. Lacy unbarred the place and opened the gate and they scrambled down the cliff, feet sliding in trickling sand, trying to soften the jolts for Tom.

The tender boat was just big enough to carry them all over, and the pinnace lay reefed as if for a jaunt on the lagoon, except for the swivel guns on her stern rails and the base gun at her bow. Thank God he'd got her ready.

They piled in and weighed anchor, using oars to get underway, with four men rowing and Emme at the tiller until they were clear to set sail. Then she tried to nurse Tom in the well of the boat, though his chances looked bleak. The lad had lost too much blood; his skin was white and his eyes were glassy. Emme spoke to him gently, but she doubted Tom could hear.

'We're safe now, Tom. Rest and be untroubled. Think of England; you could be home before winter. Tom...?'

As she looked up, Kit could see she was crying. He met her eye and shook his head.

'Let him sleep.'

'He is dead.'

She was right; he knew it before he checked for breath and pulse. He closed the lad's eyes.

'We'll give him a hero's burial here at sea.'

He beckoned to Jack and Lacy, and they wrapped Tom in an old sail and tipped him overboard, weighed down with bricks, to a salute from the guns. Those guns could serve for ballast later, if they ever got out beyond the banks.

Rob kept lookout while they said a few prayers, and the gunfire probably helped keep the savages at a distance. Not long afterwards canoes were spotted astern, but the sand banks before the ocean were already close to larboard, and the wind was helping them sail southeast without too much tacking. Their load was light and they could navigate the shallows and get to Port Ferdinando by the fastest route possible. They fired the guns to keep the savages back, and perhaps one was hit, though the pinnace was so far ahead by then it was difficult to be certain. They passed the islets before the channel, and then the foaming waters came into view that lay at the gateway between the sound and the sea.

There was a chance open before them to sail on and not stop, clear the passage and enter the ocean, leave Croatoan and head for England. Wasn't that where Emme should be – on her way to England, the 'home' she'd spoken of when she'd tried to give Tom hope? They'd never find the Planters now, not without a miracle. Chesapeake Bay was vast, and the Planters might settle inland without ever reaching the coast. If he led his company in pursuit they'd probably die in the attempt; they'd never survive alone. What would be gained?

He saw Lacy coming aft and held course for open water.

The Irishman gave him a wink. 'You'll get out to sea now, won't you?'

Kit looked across to the sand banks and back to the channel. It seemed as if Lacy had read his mind.

'Aye, Jim, we will.'

Lacy stripped off his armour, his jerkin and shoes, his breeches, shirt and hose until there was little left on him, and Kit knew what he meant to do when he stooped to offer an embrace.

'You won't mind if I stay with my Alawa?'

'No, Jim. You go, and God keep you both.'

Lacy jumped into the water as the pinnace slid by the dunes. Kit watched him wade ashore to Hatarask with only his pale skin to show he'd come from across the ocean. The Croatans would take care of him. This was the way it should be. Lacy would remain with his woman, and the Planters would send a message to Croatoan once they'd found a site for the new city. White would return to find them somehow, even if the pinnace never reached England.

Kit held course to race out with the flow, and his little crew made good work of getting the pinnace beyond the rollers where no canoe could follow. They headed northeast to cross the seas with the drift, and the sun was bright and the wind was light: a good day to begin a journey.

'For England!' he roared, and they all four took up the cry, none louder than Rob.

He'd wanted to find a new land for his boy, but perhaps he didn't need to. Rob had proved his resilience and now with Emme they were a family; together they could help one another no matter where they were. God willing, they'd get back. Emme came to sit beside him, his dear wife with whom he could now look forward to a future and children and living out his years.

She smiled, though tears still ran down her cheeks.

'Will we really get to England?'

'Yes, I think we will.'

She cried quietly and he held her.

'Poor Tom,' was all she could say.

'Yes. He was just a lad, a very brave one.'

'Poor Georgie.'

'Harvie will look after him.'

She pressed her cheek against his chest, with her arms around his waist, and drew a ragged breath.

'You are alive, and so is Rob, and we are together, here with Jack, and that is enough, more than enough, yet...'

'Yet,' he repeated softly, understanding what she meant.

'It seems we've left nothing behind, for the friends we have lost, for all we have done, all that hope, all those dreams. The Secotans will raze our city. They'll destroy everything we built.'

He stroked her hair and spoke of the conviction that burned in his core.

'The city will be built again.'

She raised her head, and there was certainty within her that he could hear swelling in her voice.

'Yes, it will. Dyonis and Ananias will found a new city with the Planters. They'll make it even better, and Jim will live with the Croatans so there'll always be a link with our Indian friends, both for us and for them.'

'And it may be that something will endure from the time we were at Roanoke.'

She wiped her eyes and slowly shook her head. 'Perhaps, though I can't think what.'

He squeezed her shoulders. 'You remember that acorn you gave me, the one from Richmond Park?'

'Yes.'

She looked at him in puzzlement, and her beautiful face made a question that he most yearned to answer with a kiss.

'I planted it in the garden of the Dares' house, the one I always thought of as yours. Maybe something will come of that.'

She smiled more broadly, caressing the thought in the way she spoke of it. 'An English oak in America . . . Could it grow there?'

'Yes,' he said, telling her the way he wanted to. 'I believe it will.'

# *Epilogue*

## Richmond Palace, England
### *November 1587*

'You may enter now.'

Lady Howard ushered Emme towards the upper gallery within the privy lodgings at Richmond Palace. The yeomen guards opened the creaking doors and Emme glimpsed the cold winter light streaming through a long succession of windows and a man stalking towards her dressed entirely in black: Sir Francis Walsingham, tall, sallow and stoop-shouldered with a skull cap over his balding head.

She looked away from his hooded eyes.

'Master Secretary,' she murmured and curtseyed low.

'Mistress Fifield, I am pleased to see you well. You have had an eventful journey, I hear.'

He drew close to her and stopped, gesturing for her to rise with a claw-like hand under the crook of her arm. His voice dropped.

'Perhaps you will tell me about it.'

The Queen's voice rang out behind him.

'I shall speak with her first, my Moor. Send her in alone and leave us.'

Walsingham inclined his head and beckoned for Emme to proceed through the open doors.

She took a few steps and looked over her shoulder before she passed beyond the threshold. Kit and Rob gazed back at her, standing to attention in the best clothes they'd been able to find during their brief sojourn at Plymouth, and she saw the concern in their faces. She carried their hope and faith; would she be able to repay it? Throughout the long voyage back from Virginia she had clung to the dream of starting a new life with them in England. But this was the reality: that she remained the handmaid of the Queen, and the Queen would determine her fate. Walsingham had heard of her journey, so had Master Ferdinando returned? Had Governor White already brought news of the colony's plight, in which case would the Queen receive her favourably? A sudden stab of fear transfixed her. Her Majesty might be furious when she heard that the City of Raleigh at Roanoke had failed. She might insist that Emme resume her duties as a maid of honour at court, and punish her for getting involved with an enterprise that had proved ill-founded.

Emme met Kit's eye, and her love was in her look. Too late for words, all she could do was hold his gaze for an instant; she hoped he understood.

She turned and advanced. The Queen stood some way along the long turning gallery: a glittering figure who walked away as the doors closed, a fleeting dash of rich burgundy and gold, high collar shimmering behind a pinned crescent of auburn curls; then she was gone around a bend in the corridor. Emme kept walking, quickening her steps. The Queen must have been taking her exercise when Lady Howard announced the arrival of the lady who had been known as Mistress Fifield, and the Queen liked nothing to interfere

with her morning activity. Emme felt the rhythm of the palace settling around her like a familiar cloak, heavy and constraining. She
could smell age seeping from the half-timbered walls, the damp
of the Thames on one side, and the frosted vegetation of the privy
orchard on the other. The air crept in through cracks around the
leaded windows, penetrating and cold. Her footsteps sounded loud
over the groaning boards, giving rise to small echoing thuds that
mingled with the Queen's tread ahead of her. Emme forced herself
to move faster. But her heart was still with Kit, and anxiety for her
future with him dragged at every step. At a word from the Queen
she could be confined for the rest of her life, and Kit could suffer
for marrying her without consent. Should she even confess to it?
Their union had not yet been blessed in church, or witnessed or
proclaimed. Would the Queen want to know now?

The country was on the brink of war; that had been apparent as
soon as they made landfall at Plymouth. The talk in the harbour had
all been of the mighty fleet gathering at Lisbon in preparation for
invasion. 'The invincible armada', as the wherryman had described
it on the passage upriver from London Bridge; '*la felicisima armada*',
as it had been named by the Spaniards, 'the most fortunate fleet'.
He'd spat in the river at that. 'May their fortune go to Hell.'

The fleet would be the greatest the world had ever seen, a force
with which King Philip and the Pope would be avenged for the
heresy of the Queen of England, and the execution of the scheming
Mary of Scots.

England might soon be destroyed.

Emme walked on, feeling a deepening sense of foreboding with
each step she took. The gallery angled round, and she had a sense
of completing a great circle, returning to the point where she had

started over a year before. This Palace of Richmond was where she had first met Kit and longed to escape. If she traversed all the outer galleries and re-entered the cantered tower, and climbed the little spiral staircase to the room above the royal bedchamber, then she would be back in the place where Lord Hertford had defiled her. She would have reached the point at which she had been impelled to flee. She had left Virginia full of joy that she and Kit had survived, but now she was returning to fulfil her promise and waiting for her was the role that she had relinquished when she departed. Each step took her closer to it. For the sake of the colonists, she would plead for their relief: for Eleanor Dare and her baby daughter, for Ananias and little Georgie Howe, and all the others she had left in Virginia. But would the Queen help them now? Would she be interested in a tale of hardship in the New World when the world around England was on the point of breaking apart?

A flash of low sunshine from across the river fields made her turn her head and blink. She glimpsed the top of a bare tree in the orchard bathed in golden light, like a crown of tangled thorns above a band of deep blue shadow. The steps ahead became louder. Emme looked forward and saw that the Queen had turned and was walking back in her direction. She almost hurried away but resolve held her rooted. She fell to the ground, prostrating herself over the boards.

The Queen paced sedately towards her.

'Arise, child. Let us walk together.'

Emme raised her eyes and saw that the Queen had extended her hand. She stood, curtseyed and kissed a jewelled ring on one of Her Majesty's slender fingers, noticing the veins that stood out on the back of her age-worn hand. The Queen's face was a mask, whitened and gaunt, but her presence was vibrant, charged with an aura of power and restless energy. Emme remembered how so often in the past she had felt diminished merely by being near her. She would have to be strong.

'Majesty, I return to you, as I undertook to do, to report to you before all others on your City of Raleigh in Virginia.'

The Queen made a small sound of acknowledgement and gestured for Emme to walk by her side.

'I have missed your singing. It was not the finest I have heard, but it had heart.'

With rapid, gliding steps the Queen proceeded along the gallery and Emme kept pace, feeling a sense of relief awakening in her because she had been received in a kindly way. She sensed the Queen eyeing her and kept her gaze fixed ahead, head bowed demurely.

'You have become a little thin,' the Queen said. 'But that is hardly surprising.'

What did she know? Emme chanced a glance at her and saw the Queen raise her hand.

'I have been informed of the colony's difficulties. Governor White arrived in London two days ago and has given a sorry account to Sir Walter at Durham Place. I have yet to receive the official report, but my Master Secretary is aware of the substance. Secretary Walsingham is also aware that the expedition's Pilot arrived in England some weeks before the Governor but in no better state. It would appear that both crews were so weakened by misfortune, death and disease that they could not get ashore without assistance.'

The Queen cast Emme another quizzical stare. 'You appear to have fared much better with fewer men and a less seaworthy craft.'

Emme looked down at the Queen's hooped skirts and the toes

409

of her dainty slippers as they appeared briefly with each step. She supposed it must seem barely credible that a small pinnace could cross the ocean crewed by two men and a boy together with a lady-in-waiting to the Queen, but they had done it, over great seas swept by icy winds, past Newfoundland and Terceira.

'I have been fortunate to return with one of Sir Francis Drake's men who is a skilled seafarer and navigator.'

The Queen raised her brows.

'The mariner who waits outside?'

'The same.' Emme nodded earnestly. 'Christopher Doonan, Master Boatswain: a most valiant and excellent mariner.'

The Queen made another wordless sound of acknowledgement. 'No one else knows of your return from Virginia?'

'We have told no one where we have come from. The news that I bear of your colony in the New World is for you to hear before all others.'

'Good. So tell me the nub of it as quickly as you will.'

Emme drew breath, aware of the pressure to distil everything she had been through into a few terse words. She must forget her own concerns, and concentrate on what mattered to the realm and the plight of those she had left behind.

'The City of Raleigh at Roanoke has been abandoned. It was attacked by the Secotans along with other hostile tribes. Most of the Planters left by boat or canoe travelling north towards the Bay of Chesapeake. They need help...'

'Were they under attack when they fled?'

The question stopped Emme short, though the Queen carried on walking.

'No,' Emme answered, hurrying on without the time to reason

what might lie behind the enquiry. She gave the facts as they seemed salient. 'A decoy of fireworks and gunfire was made at the fort on Roanoke to give the impression that they had not left.'

'The Planters escaped without pursuit?'

'Yes,' she said, realising too late that the Queen had drawn out answers which suggested the colonists were not at risk. She must correct any misapprehension. 'But they have new born infants with them, women and children. They will need food to see them through the lean months after winter, and help with building new houses. If they encounter aggression...'

'The savages around Chesapeake are reputed to be friendly, are they not?'

Emme gritted her teeth. The Queen forgot nothing and her mind was like quicksilver. Even now, with the dark clouds of war gathering, she was alert to everything. What could convince her of the settlers' plight?

'The Secotans around Roanoke were thought to be welcoming until they turned against us. We offered a truce and peace but our appeals were rejected.'

'There must have been some association with the savages for that to happen.'

Again Emme sensed her account was being undermined. She fell back to trying to explain, fearful that the Queen would dismiss her before she had even finished her appeal.

'Approach was made with the Governor's sanction through Manteo's people at first; then, after the Governor left for England to beg for help, Master Doonan ventured inland and sought a council with the Choanokes, our former allies. He found the old chief was dead and their new leader in battle was Wanchese, one of the

411

Indians once brought here who now sees us as enemies.' Her voice rose with a passion she could barely contain. 'He is intent on killing or enslaving every English man, woman and child. He hates us for the wrongs perpetrated against his kinsmen by Governor Lane…'

'Pah!'

The exclamation interrupted her, and Emme knew she had caused offence, but there was no time for delicacy. The Queen should know the truth.

'I am only conveying what I saw and heard…'

The Queen scoured her with a look.

'Did *you* hear this Wanchese?'

'Yes,' Emme said defiantly. 'I accompanied Master Doonan to the city of Choanoke. We believed that an alliance was the only chance for the City of Raleigh to survive.'

'You were taken to parley with the savages?'

The Queen's voice rose to an incredulous pitch. She must have thought her maid could not possibly have met the warriors face to face. Emme's blood raced.

'Nowhere was safe. The fort was under threat. I was at no greater risk at Choanoke than on the island which could have been attacked at any moment.'

They reached the doors leading to the Friars' Chapel tower and, seeing that she meant to advance, Emme opened them for the Queen, acknowledging the guards who then threw the doors wide on the other side. They entered another closed gallery overlooking the frozen symmetry of the Privy Garden. The long corridor had the hush of disuse, though Emme could remember when it had been thronging with visitors clamouring to watch the play in the tennis courts. She felt like an intruder.

The Queen resumed her brisk pace.

'What did you see in the Indian city: any evidence of wealth or advancement?'

Emme hesitated for an instant, aware that the Queen wanted to hear of riches but unable to stop thinking of the scenes she had witnessed. They flashed through her mind: the dark of the temple of the dead and the teeth of grinning corpses; the tattooed face of Wanchese contorted with rage, his hands gripping a loaded matchlock that he held to Kit's head. She grasped at memories that were more positive and saw rainbows from a magnifying glass dancing over high rush-screen walls, and fur-cloaked priests in procession through sunbeams beneath ancient trees. She thought of singing like a wave rising over a sea of river mist. Would the Queen want to know any of that?

Emme pressed on and half closed her eyes.

'The city is great but built without permanence. Some of the people wear pearls and large plaques of copper...'

'Copper,' the Queen murmured meditatively, a smile playing on her thin lips. 'That might be useful.' Then she turned to Emme and frowned. 'So you met with this Wanchese and he let you go?'

Didn't the Queen believe her? Emme could only tell her what had happened, and offer the conclusions she had arrived at since.

'Master Doonan told him that his villages near Roanoke would be attacked if he did not, though that was a ruse, and it was probably not the reason for our release. I think Wanchese believed that he could kill us whenever he chose and his pride as a warrior made him prefer to kill in battle. He said he would take me after Roanoke was destroyed. He told us to go back and advise everyone on Roanoke to prepare for death.'

She turned to the Queen. She should not look at Her Majesty, but the retelling had taken hold and the urgency to declare the truth.

'"Wait in fear," he said, "for in your agony we will savour our revenge." Those were his words.'

She saw the Queen's shock in her glowering eyes.

The Queen raised her fist and shook it.

'God's death,' she railed. 'I have had my fill of men who rule through force and threaten where they perceive weakness. Only a whipping will check them.'

They turned at the end of the gallery and Emme continued more softly.

'We came away from the council sure that everyone would die who did not flee straight away, and that escape would be impossible without some dissemblance to conceal it.'

'You chose to remain at the fort to try and help save the lives of the rest of the Planters?'

For the first time Emme heard a hint of wonder in the Queen's question.

'I did,' she answered. 'Kit . . . Master Doonan led the diversion.'

Emme cast her mind back to the terror and beauty of that night and the dreadful morning that followed: the horror of it that she could never have endured were it not for Kit's love. Everyone had been so brave. They should all be remembered before the Queen.

'There were four others with us. One of them was a youth from the Christ Church foundling hospital; his name was Thomas Humphrey and he died gallantly in the Indian attack. Another was an Irish soldier called James Lacy who left to join Manteo's people as we fled from the Secotans.'

'Who were the other two?'

'Master Doonan's page, Rob Little, who is waiting outside with him now, and Jack Tydway, a former debtor from New Gate gaol, without whom we would never have managed to sail back to England. A more trustworthy and courageous man there never was.'

'Is this Jack Tydway also here?'

'He is in Plymouth. We left him there at his request to join the fleet that Sir Francis Drake is assembling.'

'I see. No matter. Master Secretary will be able to find him.'

Apprehension seized Emme again. They passed back through the Friars' Chapel tower and her thoughts swirled in confusion. Why would the Queen wish for Secretary Walsingham to find Jack Tydway?

'Do you mean to honour him?'

The Queen moved purposefully around the bends in the passageway.

'I mean to ensure his silence.'

Emme rushed on behind, heart pounding. How did the Queen mean to silence him? Had she said too much and unwittingly sealed the good man's fate?

The Queen reached the doors and turned to Emme as she caught up.

'Let us speak with Master Doonan since he has played such a chief part in this story.'

Emme reached out her hand. Not Kit and Rob too. Let them be spared.

'No!' The word escaped from her lips just as the Queen gave a sharp knock.

The guards drew the doors open and the Queen spoke crisply to Lady Howard.

'Send in the mariner and his page.'

Emme stepped back as Kit and Rob entered, offering their reverence as the best custom of the court demanded, and she could hardly look. What if the Queen was about to condemn them?

But Her Majesty was gracious with them at first. She bade them get to their feet.

'Christopher Doonan, Master Boatswain, I have been pleased to hear of your bravery in England's cause in Virginia, and of yours, Robert Little.'

Kit spoke up before the Queen could say any more.

'His true name is Robert Doonan, Your Majesty. He is my son.'

Emme's heart gave a lurch. Surely Kit had spoken too soon and too boldly just when Her Majesty had been most generous in welcome. But at the same time she admired Kit's decency in acknowledging Rob even at risk to himself. The admission was just, but how would the Queen react? Emme stood petrified, looking from Kit to Rob to Her Majesty: from her fair and handsome husband, to the dusky youth she now considered her own child, to the regal splendour of the Queen, *Gloriana* to them all.

'Indeed?' The Queen raised her arched brows. 'A bastard by a blackamoor from the look of him.'

Kit stiffened and lifted his chin.

'A finer son I could not wish for, one who has served England well and manfully.'

The Queen's mouth curved towards a smile.

'So I gather, from the account Mistress Fifield has given me.'

Emme beamed at Kit and Rob, suffused with a warm glow of pride. Perhaps they would be spared the Queen's anger and receive some credit after all.

Kit caught her gaze then turned his blue eyes back to the Queen, bowing as he spoke.

'Mistress Fifield is…'

The Queen cut across him.

'Are you about to suggest that my maid of honour should also be known by another name?'

Kit looked taken aback, and Emme interjected quickly. Any petition for Her Majesty's approval had to be made in the right way. She had meant to broach the subject when she judged the time was right, but now there was no choice. She fell at the Queen's feet.

'With Your Majesty's permission, we most humbly request…'

'Enough!' The Queen stopped her mid-flow. She cast her gaze over Emme, then Kit and back again. Emme sensed her vision beginning to cloud, her fear for Kit on the point of overwhelming her.

The Queen placed her hand on Emme's head. 'Do you think I do not know when two people are in love? If you wish to ask for my consent to wed then you have it for the service you have already given me.'

Emme could barely believe what she had heard. Relief flooded over her. The Queen had offered what she most wanted. At Her Majesty's beckoning, she got to her feet and moved to stand with Kit and Rob. The Queen spoke commandingly to them all.

'If half of England is possessed of the courage you three have shown then we may spit at the feet of any prince who dares assail our shores, see off all the armies who fly a papist flag and sink any ships that venture to invade us. You have rekindled my faith in what my people can do, and for that I thank you.'

Kit placed one arm behind Emme and the other behind Rob and

stepped back as if they, and not he, were players in some drama worthy of acclaim.

'We will serve England loyally to that end,' he said, 'for the great love we hold for our Queen.'

'We'll serve loyally,' Rob chimed.

'Yes,' Emme breathed.

The response seemed to please Her Majesty because she nodded and smiled as much as she ever did when giving an audience.

'Very good, but I have more to ask of you.'

Kit stepped forwards again.

'What else would you have us do?'

The Queen moved to one of the window benches and leant against it, taking the weight from her feet while preserving the bell of her farthingale. She regarded them meditatively then turned to face the view outside. She spoke while looking towards the Thames.

'You must say nothing about Virginia, the whereabouts of the colony or its condition. The Spaniards must not know it has been put in jeopardy. Let them believe the colony thrives and keep them guessing as to where it is. I would have King Philip troubled to think our City of Raleigh is further south; may it remain a thorn to goad and distract him.'

Emme looked at Kit, remembering how he'd told her this could have been Ferdinando's secret objective. So Ferdinando *was* Walsingham's man, not an agent of Spain, and his bullying and apparent duplicity had been no more than a pretence. She'd never doubt Kit again.

The Queen turned round.

'You will swear your silence to this end?'

Kit clapped his hand to his chest.

'Upon my faith and all that I hold most dear, I so swear.'

'I swear this also,' Rob said.

'And I swear this too,' Emme added, 'as I will swear to anything you ask, though I fear for the Planters.'

Probably, she should say no more, but this would be her last chance to plead for the colony. Had she done enough? She beseeched the Queen with one last glance and dropped to her knees.

'Will you allow Sir Walter Raleigh to send relief?'

'Not when every vessel large and small may be needed to guard the coasts of this Isle.' There was a finality to the Queen's answer that brooked no argument. 'The safety of England must come before all else.'

Emme had expected no less, but she still felt the blow even in the midst of her happiness for the dispensation that she and Kit had been granted. She bent her head.

The Queen's tone became gentler.

'The colonists have as good a chance now as they did when they undertook the venture. You told me they were not pursued, and they were heading for the destination that was meant for them at first, one reputed to be hospitable, which is not to say that my answer may not change.' She waited for Emme to look up, and gestured for her to rise.

'I will consider this matter afresh when Sir Walter is ready to go to the aid of his City. I have no doubt he will do his best to assemble a fleet with provisions for the task. Once that is ready to embark, then we shall see whether the threat to the realm is any less.'

Kit inclined his head.

'Majesty; in your wisdom we trust.'

The Queen spread her hands.

'Now go with my blessing and say nothing of this to anyone. Go back to Plymouth. I release you from your service at court, Mistress Fifield, but you must keep the identity you assumed when you left. Wed this man, but do so discreetly. And I charge you, Master Doonan, to present yourself to Sir Francis Drake and offer to assist him in any way he thinks fit. Take your son with you. If the time comes for action then I expect you both to fight to your last breath.'

Kit looked at Rob then back at the Queen and his expression was grave.

'We will.'

Rob grinned.

'I'll fight with my father gladly.'

He would, Emme knew, and Kit would fight too, and perhaps war would tear them apart just as good fortune and the Queen's clemency had brought them together. She bit back tears as the reverences were made before leaving.

The Queen moved to the door.

'See the Lord Chamberlain before you leave. He will provide you with something in recognition of your loyalty.'

At a nod, the meeting was over. The Queen walked ahead of them and flung the doors wide, surprising the guards who sprang to attention, and startling Lady Howard, who stepped aside in a fluster, while an elderly courtier began hurrying away. Emme had no doubt that both of them had been listening, though the Queen had been careful to speak at a distance. Indeed the Queen seemed unconcerned and not a little amused by their embarrassment. She slammed one of the doors closed and watched the retreating gentleman jump and look back over his shoulder. At that instant Emme's blood ran cold. She knew who he was: Lady Howard's clandestine husband; the man who had shamed her and tried to claim her as his duchess.

'Lord Hertford!' the Queen called after him. 'Did I see you turn your back on me?'

Lord Hertford froze mid-step and gingerly retraced it. He turned his head.

'Ah, Your Majesty! I would never knowingly do such a thing. My delight is always to feast my eyes on your sight.'

He minced back towards her and proffered a perfunctory bow. The Queen moved on, reaching him almost halfway across the covered bridge that led to the Privy Lodgings. She beckoned for Emme, Kit and Rob to follow then swept her hand towards them.

'I give you Master Christopher Doonan and his son, Robert. I believe you already know the lady.'

Lord Hertford grimaced and shuffled back a step as if to avoid any proximity.

The Queen advanced until she was next to him, and waved the three of them closer.

'These good subjects have shown the greatest loyalty, courage and devotion to duty that any sovereign could wish for. I should not speak of their achievements publicly else I would favour them with titles. As it is, all I can give them is my gratitude. They deserve your respect, good sir.'

'Really?' Lord Hertford's face creased like a bladder ball deflated of air. 'Well, if you are sure and insist on it.' He tipped his head a little towards them and avoided Emme's glare.

The Queen narrowed her eyes.

'A bow would be appropriate.'

The Earl looked pained and placed a hand to the small of his back as if the action might cause grave discomfort; even so, he managed to bend a little.

'Lower!' the Queen ordered.

Lord Hertford bowed and Emme smiled back at the Queen. She could see Her Majesty's eyes were twinkling. The Queen turned and walked on, while Kit took hold of Emme's hand and the Queen's ladies gathered round behind them.

Emme could see the future opening before her, threading through the palace and out by the watergate, by wherry to London Bridge, and thence to the quays before the Tower, to reach the pinnace, freshly crewed, that would take them back to a new start in Plymouth. She saw a silver line over the sea stretching to a wide empty horizon, connecting the grandeur of Richmond with the bustle and dirt of London's streets and those of Plymouth, no less crowded, but folded together over cliffs and coombs, and there the thread ended because she could see no further. While England prepared for war would she and Kit keep course together?

Yes, yes – let the thread continue strong, her path and Kit's entwined as one. She took his hand again as they settled in the wherry, while Rob at the bow watched the ice at the water's edge.

In Kit's other hand was the packet that the Lord Chamberlain had given them.

'What is in it?' she asked.

He gave it a shake.

'Not gold, alas.'

He smiled, and she snuggled closer to him.

'That's no surprise, but you still haven't told me.'

He broke the seal and unfolded the paper then raised a brow as he held it out of her reach.

She tugged at his arm, and he hugged her with the other.

'It's a licence for us to wed without banns.'

'So no one will know,' she said, and smiled to herself. 'The Queen gives nothing away without reason.' She wrapped her arms around his waist and relished the feel of his warmth. 'There could be no better gift for us.'

'She was gracious, and with Rob too.'

Emme squeezed him again and kissed his chest.

'I still keep thinking of Lord Hertford's face when he was made to bow, and I cannot help laughing every time I picture it.'

He held her tight.

'That's good. Laugh at the fool; he deserved the requital. The wonder for me is that the Queen was content for him to see us.'

'He knew we were at Richmond anyway, and the Queen will have ways of ensuring he keeps quiet. He has enough secrets of his own to protect without stirring up trouble by revealing any more.'

Kit pulled a blanket over their shoulders and placed his arm around her again.

'I have something else for you.' He dug into his pocket and produced a large iron key. 'It's for a house in Plymouth. I haven't seen it yet but I know the place will have a garden and a view of the sea.'

He placed the key in her hand.

'I asked Will to make the purchase before I left for Virginia. When we got back to Plymouth, I went to his warehouse by Sutton Poole. The key was waiting for me with a letter.'

He kissed her cheek.

'Will has enlisted for Drake's *Revenge*. I shall have to do the same as soon as I can, and I will take Rob with me.'

So the time for parting would come soon; but it had to be, she could only accept it. She would at least have a house in which to wait for him. She folded the key into the palm of her hand and kissed him back.

'Let us wed first and share one night in this house before you go. I have something for you too.'

She took his hand and placed it on her stomach. This was the news she had for him, news she had only recently become sure about and had, for a month, hardly dared admit to herself. Through this, the thread might continue, while the strands she and Kit had begun faded and disappeared like a wake over waves.

'I am carrying your child.'

'O, dear Emme.'

He kissed her passionately, his mouth hard against hers, his smell and taste, his heat and strength, all around and so close that their senses flowed together, and she knew that, already, the person she had been was lost. With him she was born anew, as surely as the life within her would be new to the world.

# Author's Note

'What happened to the colony left at Roanoke?' This question has remained unanswered ever since John White returned to England in November 1587. He immediately began a series of ill-fated attempts to send assistance to the settlers but none was successful. A relief fleet assembled at Bideford under the command of Sir Richard Grenville was commandeered to assist Sir Francis Drake when the threat of invasion by the Spanish Armada became imminent the following year. White was left with two small pinnaces which embarked in May 1588, but they did not get very far before one was attacked by French pirates who decimated the crew and made off with most of the provisions meant for the colony. The Armada was famously defeated in August that year, and not until the spring of 1590 was White able to raise the resources to make another attempt to go to the aid of his 'Planters' with the backing of Sir Walter Raleigh and a consortium of London merchants. This time White managed to reach Roanoke, but he did so in the midst of a storm which overturned one of the landing boats and claimed the lives of seven men, including that of Edward Spicer who had sailed with the 1587 expedition. The disaster undermined the will to continue of many of the mariners, and led to a hurried search constrained by the need to leave quickly before their ship was blown out to sea.

When White finally arrived at Roanoke, he discovered the island deserted and parts of the forest burnt, with some trees smouldering as if from recent lightning strikes. The houses were in ruins, though a wall of tree trunks still enclosed them. Inside these defences, supplies of iron bars and heavy equipment had been left in disarray and were overgrown with weeds. Chests, plainly once buried, had been dug up and their contents scattered. White found many of his own books, maps and paintings torn and spoiled. Only one thing gave him heart. He had previously agreed a code for a message which would be left by the colonists if they departed – the name of their destination would be carved on a high tree, accompanied by a cross if their leaving was forced. So he was thankful to find the letters 'CRO' carved on a conspicuous tree on the way to the settlement, and then the letters 'CROATOAN' cut into a trunk at the entrance to the fort, without a cross or anything else to suggest that the colonists had been in distress. The fate of the colony has remained a mystery ever since.

White had no chance to search on Croatoan, the island belonging to Manteo's people; bad weather forced the expedition to leave. He returned to England, settled on one of Raleigh's plantations in Ireland, and died deeply disappointed, never knowing what had become of his daughter and granddaughter. 'My last voyage to Virginia … was no less unfortunately ended than forwardly begun,' he wrote to Richard Hakluyt in February 1593. 'I leave off from prosecuting that whereunto I would to God my wealth were answerable to my will.'

White's surviving watercolours provide some of the most sensitive, beautiful and faithful records of the southern Algonkian Indians and their culture before the influence of European colonisation. The originals are held in the British Museum. Two catalogues compiled by Kim Sloan produced as companions to exhibitions of these works have provided a wealth of material for the writing of this novel. They are: *A New World – England's first view of America* and *European Visions: American Voices*.

Raleigh continued to search for his lost colony up until the Queen's death in 1603 after which his fall from grace was catastrophic. He was charged with treason and imprisoned, briefly released after nearly thirteen years, and imprisoned again following a disastrous campaign to find gold in Guiana which brought him into conflict with the Spanish. He was executed as a traitor in 1618.

Subsequent expeditions to Virginia brought back stories of settlers who had moved to the Chesapeake Bay area and had then been massacred by the Powhatans, of pale-skinned people living with tribes far inland, of white captives who worked at copper-smelting in villages along the Chowan River, and of grey-eyed, brown-haired people living on the island of Croatoan. None was ever proved.

Efforts are continuing, using DNA testing, to try and find out whether Raleigh's colonists were indeed wiped out, or whether, through their descendants, they still live on. Many believe that they do.

The mystery was revived in the national media on both sides of the Atlantic in 2012 when a patch on John White's 'Virgenea Pars' map, over a position corresponding to the confluence of the

Chowan and Roanoke Rivers (known as the 'Moratico' or 'Moratuc' in Elizabethan times), was found to mask a fort-like symbol. Speculation then ran rife that this could mark the spot where the colony meant to relocate, but its significance remains the subject of conjecture. The fact is that no one knows for certain what happened to Raleigh's colony. Some of the settlers could well have travelled north, nearer to Chesapeake and the site of what would become the first enduring English colony at Jamestown; some could have become assimilated into the Croatan tribe; some could even have tried to return to England in the pinnace which was almost certainly left at Roanoke when White departed in 1587.

In *The Lost Duchess* I have suggested one possible answer to the mystery as the foundation for a story, but that's all it is: just a possibility, not a probability, and certainly not what actually did happen because now we can never know.

From my visits to Roanoke and the wider area my abiding impression is of a fragile region in the process of constant geological change. The sand banks around the Pamlico Sound are always shifting under the assault of hurricanes, tide and current. Some channels that led to the sea in Elizabethan times no longer exist; new islands have formed while others have disappeared. In over four hundred years, the pattern of what are now called the Outer Banks of North Carolina has altered considerably, and the north shores of Roanoke Island have become much eroded. It is quite possible that the site of the City of Raleigh, which has never been reliably pinpointed, now lies under the waters of the Pamlico Sound, having taken the secrets of the Lost Colony with it.

*The Lost Duchess* is a story that lies in the lacunae of historical knowledge, but its backbone is true insofar as the records provide evidence of the establishment and abandonment of an English colony at Roanoke. All the main characters are identifiable from the accounts, with the exception of Kit Doonan, who is purely a product of my imagination, and Alsoomse, Manteo's mother. We know that Manteo's mother was a leader of the Croatans, but her name was never recorded; I have made one up for her. There is even an 'Emme Merrymoth' listed amongst the 1587 colonists, about whom nothing is known apart from her name, along with a man or youth described as 'Robert Little'. There is a parish of Fifield-Merrymouth in Oxfordshire deriving, via 'Merymowthe', from the thirteenth century name of 'Murimuth', and I enjoyed building the character of Emme Fifield, who becomes Emme Murimuth, listed as 'Merrymoth', from these raw details. There is no evidence that a lady-in-waiting to Queen Elizabeth sailed with the Lost Colonists; I gave Emme the position of a Maid of Honour to the Queen to bring the Queen's involvement closer to the heart of the story. But there really was an Earl of Hertford, son of the usurped Duke of Somerset and first in line to that dukedom (though the title was then in abeyance), who was notorious for 'seducing a virgin of the blood royal' after secretly marrying the sister of Lady Jane Grey and getting her pregnant. He went on to marry twice more in secret, his second wife being Frances Howard, one of the senior ladies of the Privy Chamber.

I would just like to add a small point about names. I have tried to regularise these as much as possible and make the characters readily identifiable. So I refer to the *Lion's* Pilot as 'Simon Ferdinando', who gave his name to 'Port Ferdinando', though he appears in historical texts under various permutations of his name in Portuguese, Spanish and English, and frequently as 'Simon Fernandez'. I have kept to the names used most often in the first-hand accounts. Where there has been a possibility for confusion, I have made adjustments to try and avoid that, thus Manteo's kinsman Menatoan (whose wife was shot at by mistake in the raid on Dasemonkepeuc) becomes 'Enato' in the story so as not to confuse him with Menatonon, chief of the Choanoke tribe.

One problem for historians and novelists alike is that the Elizabethans did not care a jot about spelling; words were recorded phonetically and there was little consistency. Thus it was not unusual to have several permutations of a surname in a lifetime. Over forty versions of 'Raleigh' have been found, but 'Raleigh' has become the most familiar (though there's no evidence that Sir Walter actually signed his name with an 'i'!), and 'Raleigh' remains in common use, despite most English historians now referring to him as 'Ralegh'. So I've used 'Raleigh', and, for similar reasons, I've used 'Harriot' rather than 'Hariot'.

With variant spellings of other words, I have opted for the version that is most familiar or most memorable. 'Algonkian' is easier to remember than 'Algonquian' so I've adopted the former to refer to the North American Indians belonging to the language group spoken along the Atlantic seaboard. Many of the native words recorded by Harriot and White also now have several forms. I have come across at least five different versions of the word for 'chief'. The one that I have used is that recorded most usually in White's narrative: '*weroance*' for a male and '*weroanca*' for a female chief. The Algonkian words in the story come in the main from White's paintings: '*nahyápuw*' for the bald eagle, '*mamankanois*' for the tiger swallowtail butterfly, '*wisakon*' for milkweed, and so on.

Place names pose another problem since they were often very

different in the Elizabethan era from the names we know now. For example, 'Puerto Rico' was known as 'St John's' and 'St Croix' in the Virgin Islands was known as 'Santa Cruz'. I have tried to use names that would have been familiar to the Elizabethans and to make the locations clear in the narrative. I hope the map will help address any residual uncertainty. Often the names of tribes are the same or similar to the places they inhabited. So the Croatan tribe lived mainly on Croatoan, an island which now corresponds to part of Hatteras and Ocracoke combined. The nearest place to the Indian settlement of Croatoan is modern-day Buxton at Cape Hatteras.

I have suggested a secret brief for Simon Ferdinando, but that is only conjecture; his true role remains an enigma. On the voyage he made for Raleigh in 1585, Ferdinando grounded the flagship after attempting a risky passage in a storm through the sand banks off Virginia despite the fact that he knew a safer route lay further north. The action resulted in the loss of most of the ship's provisions with grave consequences for the survival of the garrison commanded by Ralph Lane. On the next voyage, Ferdinando made all the colonists disembark at Roanoke rather than sail to Chesapeake as had been planned. Again, this probably doomed the colony since the Roanoke Indians had become hostile (something that White's settlers plainly did not fully appreciate at the outset). There is no doubt that Ferdinando was unpopular; he was nicknamed 'the swine' by mariners, and White was at loggerheads with him throughout. He could have been a Spanish agent, or he could simply have been arrogant, careless and unlucky; another explanation is that he was under covert orders from Walsingham to establish the colony further south.

My most valuable resources in writing this story have been the first-hand accounts of John White, Ralph Lane and others contained in *The First Colonists – Documents on the Planting of the First Settlements in North America 1584–1590* edited by David B Quinn and Alison M Quinn. Other books always on my desk were *Roanoke – The Abandoned Colony* by Karen Ordahl Kupperman and *Big Chief Elizabeth* by Giles Milton.

For anyone wanting to find out more about life for the first English settlers and their contact with native American people, nothing can beat visiting the region of North Carolina that was once part of the English 'Virginia', looking at the excellent reconstructions and displays on Roanoke Island at the Fort Raleigh National Historic Site and the Roanoke Island Festival Park, then finding a remote spot facing the Atlantic on the islands of Hatteras or Ocracoke. Stand on those white sand shores where no one else and no building is visible, and gaze out to sea as Raleigh's Planters would have done over four hundred years ago. The view will be much the same as it was then; let your imagination do the rest.

Jenny Barden
Dorset, September 2013

# *Acknowledgements*

I would like to thank my steadfast agent, Jonathan Pegg, and the wonderful team at Ebury Press for all their help; my brilliant editor, Gillian Green, as well as Emily Yau and Ebury's Press Officer, Ellie Rankine; my copy editor, Charlotte Cole; my proofreader, Margaret Gilbey, and my colleagues in the Historical Novel Society, the Romantic Novelists' Association, and the Historical Writers' Association and Verulam Writers for their support and encouragement. As always my gratitude goes to my husband, Mark, for making it all possible.